PASSIONATE DESTINY

"I know all about your political ambitions," I declared to Sean Creighton, solicitor and personal secretary to my late father.

"You should use the past tense. There's little chance of me getting elected to anything now that Sir Lynhurst's backing died with him."

"Oh, I wouldn't be so sure . . . I suspect you always get pretty much what you want, one way or another."

He pulled me against him. "Do I?"

He lowered his mouth to mine. His kiss was like smoldering coals bursting into flames. His arms held me in a vise that barely allowed me to breathe. The thin cloth of my robe and gown were fragile barriers against the heat of his body.

I arched against him and my arms raised to slip around his neck. I felt a bewildering hunger that coiled deep within me and made me return his kisses with wanton desire. His hands splayed against my back, pressing me closer. His heartbeat was mine, his rising desire mine, and I lost all prudent thought to feeling. . . .

GOTHICS A LA MOOR—FROM ZEBRA

ISLAND OF LOST RUBIES
by Patricia Werner   (2603, $3.95)
Heartbroken by her father's death and the loss of her great love, Eileen returns to her island home to claim her inheritance. But eerie things begin happening the minute she steps off the boat, and it isn't long before Eileen realizes that there's no escape from *THE ISLAND OF LOST RUBIES.*

DARK CRIES OF GRAY OAKS
by Lee Karr   (2736, $3.95)
When orphaned Brianna Anderson was offered a job as companion to the mentally ill seventeen-year-old girl, Cassie, she was grateful for the non-troublesome employment. Soon she began to wonder why the girl's family insisted that Cassie be given hydro-electrical therapy and increased doses of laudanum. What was the shocking secret that Cassie held in her dark tormented mind? And was she herself in danger?

CRYSTAL SHADOWS
by Michele Y. Thomas   (2819, $3.95)
When Teresa Hawthorne accepted a post as tutor to the wealthy Curtis family, she didn't believe the scandal surrounding them would be any concern of hers. However, it soon began to seem as if someone was trying to ruin the Curtises and Theresa was becoming the unwitting target of a deadly conspiracy . . .

CASTLE OF CRUSHED SHAMROCKS
by Lee Carr   (2843, $3.95)
Penniless and alone, eighteen-year-old Aileen O'Conner traveled to the coast of Ireland to be recognized as daughter and heir to Lord Edwin Lynhurst. Upon her arrival, she was horrified to find her long lost father had been murdered. And slowly, the extent of the danger dawned upon her: her father's killer was still at large. And her name was next on the list.

BRIDE OF HATFIELD CASTLE
by Beverly G. Warren   (2517, $3.95)
Left a widow on her wedding night and the sole inheritor of Hatfield's fortune, Eden Lane was convinced that someone wanted her out of the castle, preferably dead. Her failing health, the whispering voices of death, and the phantoms who roamed the keep were driving her mad. And although she came to the castle as a bride, she needed to discover who was trying to kill her, or leave as a corpse!

Available wherever paperbacks are sold, or order direct from the Publisher. Send cover price plus 50¢ per copy for mailing and handling to Zebra Books, Dept. 2843, 475 Park Avenue South, New York, N.Y. 10016. Residents of New York, New Jersey and Pennsylvania must include sales tax. DO NOT SEND CASH.

CASTLE OF CRUSHED SHAMROCKS

LEE KARR

ZEBRA BOOKS
KENSINGTON PUBLISHING CORP.

ZEBRA BOOKS

are published by

Kensington Publishing Corp.
475 Park Avenue South
New York, NY 10016

First printing: December, 1989

Printed in the United States of America

My thanks to Elinor Gleesen, a librarian who has shown personal interest in each of my books from idea to completion. I am sincerely grateful for the Northglenn, Colorado Library and its staff for graciously and persistently honoring my requests for research material.

Chapter One

The Irish landscape was a strange and brooding one as I walked along the narrow dirt road between piled-high earth from ditches and stone walls crisscrossing the fields like a gray mesh laid upon the green and rocky hillsides. Mist rose from black bogs, scattered loughs, and stands of water left by recent rains, making the air thick with moisture. The mail coach on which I had bought passage had broken down, three miles back, and I had decided to walk to my destination, Danareel, on the western coast of Ireland. The driver had assured me that the village was only a short distance ahead. Impatient with this final delay and weary of sitting in a cramped, jolting coach, I started down the empty road carrying my portmanteau. The landscape was a far cry from the gentle English countryside outside London where I had been raised. Apprehension grew as every step brought me closer to a vague future which only recently had been thrust upon me. A disappearing June sun shed little warmth as it valiantly tried to peer through heavy layers of gray clouds settling on the horizon. The weather had been foul every mile of my journey, exposing me to days of intermittent rain, brief periods of clear skies which became overcast by nightfall, and mists blowing upon the tiny island which kept the landscape moist like the wet wash of an artist's brush.

I had been delayed in waiting for a packet boat to

take me across the Irish Sea to Dublin. I looked with trepidation upon the churning waters which crashed upon England's western shores. A leisurely canoe ride on the Thames had been the extent of my navigation experience and the heavily rolling sea offered a challenge I was not sure my stomach was ready to accept. This narrow channel was known to be fraught with danger and, in truth, the crossing turned out to be as rough and precarious as I had feared.

The boat rose and fell in deep troughs, pitching its bow nearly perpendicular while it careened from side to side like a piece of curd caught in a butter churn. I clamped my jaws shut, closed my ears to the din of crashing waters, and prayed the tiny craft would not fall apart from the sea's battering fists.

"Ye should try crossing in the wintertime," a stout-hearted passenger had advised me as he clamped down on his pipe and braced his legs on the floor to keep his seat, while I grabbed the board bench and prayed I wouldn't go sprawling out on the cabin floor every time the boat made one of its fierce lurches.

"I had no choice," I replied. A sickening despair sank to the pit of my stomach. I had never been farther than fifteen miles away from home. Every spring my mother and I had traveled to London and I had thought that the world was contained in those few miles between our village and the bustling city.

Weary and drained, I staggered off the boat and stepped on Irish soil like someone who had been wrestling a wild sea creature for life and limb. The muddy earth under my feet had never felt so wonderful and my spirits revived.

"A good journey to you," the captain said merrily, and I suspected he secretly enjoyed watching his passengers endure the trial-by-water on every crossing. "Be ye going far?"

"To Danareel."

"Ye have a journey cut out for yerself. Across the

8

isle, it be." He clicked his teeth in such a manner that I knew crossing the width of Ireland to the Atlantic side was not going to be a pleasant journey.

Dublin was a seething, crowded city that in different circumstances I might have enjoyed. While I waited for the departure of the next coach, I strolled down Dame Street. It was lined with noble shops and buildings. No butchers, fishmongers or poultry stalls fouled the air. Windows were filled with gowns of high style and Englishwomen chatted and bustled about as if they were shopping Bond Street in London. The familiar sights and sounds were reassuring. Maybe Ireland was not going to be so strange after all. Since Cromwell invaded and defeated the Irish in 1649, much of the land had been given over to English planters and settlers, and now, in 1837, I found Dublin living up to its name as one of the fairest cities in the world. A Parliament House of elegant stone and six noble Corinthian columns stood on one side of a green and Trinity College on another. The Queen's soldiers were everywhere and I felt as safe as any young woman could feel traveling alone under such circumstances.

There was much that was British here, I decided, but when it came to transportation, Ireland was not England. I had expected to continue my journey from one coast to the other with reasonable dispatch. Good roads had been laid from one end of England to the other, offering travelers swiftly drawn coaches and comfortable lodgings on their journeys. Not so in Ireland, I discovered to my dismay. The Irish system of transportation, if you could flatter it with such a term, was a patchwork of disjointed roads. I discovered this as I endeavored to master the puzzle which a traveler must put together in order to get from one place to another. Using as much information as I could find, I mapped my journey and took a mail coach out of Dublin, only to discover that it veered north a few miles out of the city.

"But I don't want to go north. I want to go west to Danareel," I protested when I realized I was already miles off my destination.

" 'Tis no fault of mine ye took the wrong coach," said the surly driver.

"But I told the ticket seller that I wanted to go west."

"And west we went . . . for nigh on ten miles." He shrugged as if that was distance enough to be going in one direction.

He set me off at the next crossroad. To my utter dismay, the coach disappeared over the next rolling green hill. I sat down on my trunk, clutching my carpetbag and wondering how long it would be before someone came along to give me a ride. About an hour later, when the first drops of a light drizzle sent bone-deep chills into my body, one of those peculiar Irish cars came along. It looked like a wedge moving on solid wooden wheels and was drawn by a horse with thick withers.

I stood up and waved my hands. An older man and his wife sat on the flatbed with a piglet and chickens. They stopped and listened to my sad tale and then looked at each other and shrugged. They spoke only Gaelic but my hand gestures finally communicated my need for a ride. He climbed on the horse's back and offered me his place with his wife, piglet and chickens.

I spent two days with this couple in their crowded cottage, sharing one room with a cow and two pigs. After two days of solid rain, they took me to the next village where I thankfully bought passage on a horse-drawn Bianchi car. I learned that this means of transportation was named after an enterprising salesman who developed a system which, thank heavens, made some effort to link up with mail coaches and canal services. I blessed his name as I traveled in fits and starts from one village to another in these open horse-drawn carriages. Sometimes harsh rains were so violent that we sought shelter in a cottage by the roadside or cowered under a peat-stack to keep from drowning in the downpour when there was no shelter to be had.

On the last day when I had almost reached Ireland's western coast and could smell the salt air of the Atlantic Ocean, the mail coach which was to carry me on the final leg of my journey split a wheel and spilled me and two other passengers out on the road.

"How far are we from Danareel?" I had asked the driver.

"Not fer," he spat.

"How far?" I insisted.

"Three miles, give or take a little."

I decided to walk the final leg of my trip and made arrangements with the disgruntled driver to leave my trunk in the village when the wheel was repaired. I started off at a brisk walk down the muddy road. I had covered at least four miles and still could see no sign of Danareel. The driver's "give or take a little" could mean ten miles, I thought wearily as I trudged on.

Light was fading from the western horizon. Still no sign of Danareel. Maybe I had missed the main road when several wagon tracks led off in different directions. Why on earth couldn't the Irish put up a signpost now and then, I fumed, biting my lip. My skirt was dragging in the cloying clay road, my shoes were coated with mud, and my feet grew heavier with every step. I realized then that I had been foolish to leave the protection of the coach and its driver.

A misty twilight settled upon the land. My uneasiness grew. I glanced behind me and on both sides of the road. A peculiar tingling between my shoulder blades made me swing around. I sensed another's presence but I couldn't see anyone. I turned my head

11

back around and screamed.

In the shadowy light, a weird creature jumped out in the road ahead of me. A tail stuck out in back, jagged wings flapped from its shoulders, its head was caught in a swirl of silver, and a thin, vibrating appendage waved in the air above it.

After my first startled scream, my cries caught in my throat. I stood paralyzed as it loped toward me. If I had been of an inclination to faint, I would have done so in that frightening moment.

"Many pardons," the creature said in an Irish lilt. "Was not meaning to be frightening ye."

I blinked my eyes, unable to stop the wild pounding in my throat.

"Would ye be liking a bit of company? 'Tis nary a time for a lass to be walking alone." He swept off a hat wreathed with fishing line. "Daddo McPherson, I be."

My legs nearly buckled with relief.

The funny little man cocked his head to one side. There was nothing frightening about the smile which cut across a weathered, freckled face, nor large human ears and shocks of black hair that stood up like a rooster's crown.

"You . . . you surprised me," I gave a strangled laugh, trying to get some moisture back in my mouth after the fright he had given me. His "tail" was a violin thrust under a rope belt at his back. A great double-caped greatcoat fell like wings from his shoulders and flapped in the air behind him. The thin appendage was a fishing pole.

With his other hand, he reached down and picked up my portmanteau that I had dropped in fright. "Let me be carrying this for ye."

I laughed nervously, a little ashamed. "Thank you. The case was getting heavy. The mail coach broke down and I thought I would walk ahead to Danareel."

"Yer almost there." He perked his head to one side as if my speech had given him a clue to my identity. " 'Tis an English lass, ye be."

His tone had changed. Gone was the open friendliness. He no longer smiled. The *Sassenachs* were not welcome on Irish soil. I had experienced the same cold resentment many times on my journey. Despite an outward pretense of servitude by people who sold tickets or provided lodgings, I had been aware of a smoldering hatred. Three times Ireland had been invaded and defeated by England and three times, the victors had remained to claim the land for themselves. When England defeated France in wars, most of the land was still left for Frenchmen. Not so, in victories in Ireland. Obviously every defeat had only transplanted more of England to the Emerald Isle, I had decided. My stay in Dublin had clearly demonstrated that.

"My mother was Irish," I said quickly.

The words were like a magic incantation. Daddo's smile returned. "A colleen, ye be! And pretty as a golden-haired fairy princess, if ye don't mind me saying so. Blue eyes as bonny as a water nymph's."

I could feel myself blushing. His poetic compliments embarrassed me and I didn't know how to respond to his easy chatter.

"Ye shouldn't be wandering about by yerself," he said in a chastising tone. "These are troubled times. The ghost of the Watcher is riding again." He sent quick glances along the ditch as if he expected an apparition to rise out of the mist. "He could be anywhere."

My mother had filled my ears with Irish ghost stories since babyhood. Banshees, leprechauns, and other magical creatures were the central characters in such stories. I tried to keep the amusement from my voice. "A ghost?"

Daddo nodded. In a hushed voice, he said, "The

13

Watcher's been seen on the moors."

"The Watcher?" I echoed, intrigued by the name.

"Killed a year ago, he was. Och, come back from the dead, he has. And now the Watcher stalks those who murdered him."

"Why do you call him the Watcher?"

" 'Tis the name the cottiers gave him 'cause he looked out after them when the tithe collectors came."

"How did he die?"

Daddo shook his head sadly. "The Royal Dragoons ran him off the cliff. Drowned, he was. 'Tis said the Dread Women of Moher, who take dead fishermen from the sea, carried the brave lad off. And now his spirit has come back." He shot another glance behind us. He whispered, "Three nights ago the Watcher murdered another informer, he did."

"How do you know it was he?"

"Because the Watcher always lays a wreath of black ivy on the traitor's chest after he slits his throat."

"Ghosts don't slit throats."

" 'Twas him, all right. Sure, he swore to get every one of the blackguards what caused six of the Irish patriots to be taken to Dublin and jailed."

The talk of ghosts and murder was not a comforting subject on this darkening, lonely road, I thought as my uneasiness grew.

Daddo hopped along at my side, filling my ears with talk about a peasant hero who had come back from the dead to help cottiers and farmers fight tithes imposed by English law. As a well-brought-up Englishwoman, I believed in the justice of English law. Of course, there were abuses, human nature being what it was, but I believed that common people were protected by the Crown and I felt defensive about my Queen Victoria and the English Parliament. I was well aware of Ireland's less than civilized history. Before Ireland came under British rule, Irish clans warred with each other, killing and ravishing each other in feuds that went on for generations. I wanted to set my companion straight about a few things, but I was too weary to engage in political discussion. My head reeled with talk of ghosts, murders, and black wreaths.

Suddenly Daddo froze.

"Listen!" he ordered in a cracked voice, looking back the way we had come.

A vibrating sound of horse hooves was unmistakable. "Hurry." He grabbed my arm and urged me over the banked ditch which ran along side the road.

"Maybe it's the coach?" I protested.

"Nay. Nay. Hurry!" His sense of urgency communicated itself to me and without reasoning the matter through, I hunched down with him behind a mound of dirt and rocks along the ditch and peered over to see what had frightened him off the road.

A regiment of soldiers galloped by. Green Horse Dragoon, they were called. I had seen them in Dublin with shiny helmets trimmed with horsetails, tailored uniforms and high black boots. The Queen's soldiers represented law and order and as a well-brought-up Englishwoman, I couldn't see why we were hiding in the ditch while they went by.

With a show of indignation, I stood up and brushed the dirt from my lavender blue pelisse, straightened my leghorn straw bonnet and retied the riband streamers. I was angry at myself and at this weird little man who had made me a part of his furtive actions. It was not soldiers that I feared, but a father whom I had never seen and who would most likely deny that he had ever given life to an illegitimate daughter.

"Why on earth did you do that? You're not wanted by the law, are you?" I demanded in indignation as we started back down the road.

"Every true Irishman is wanted by the law," he said

solemnly. "But it wasn't the fancy English soldiers I was a fearin'."

"Who then? The Watcher?" I asked in a derisive tone.

Daddo looked around in a furtive manner and then whispered hoarsely. "The Bog Boys."

His tone made my throat go dry. "Who are they? Bandits?"

"Auch! That's what they be, all right. Irish bandits who ride at night, kill stock, murder, set fires. Every landlord in these parts has been a victim of their terror."

"Why don't the constables stop them?"

"Who's to say the law don't ride with them?" He gave me a solemn wink. "The local constables are Irish."

I grew silent and only half-listened to Daddo's chatter. The country's political conflict was not of immediate interest to me and my thoughts centered on my own frightening problems. I had to come to terms with what lay ahead in Danareel.

Until my mother's death two months ago, I had thought my father had been a young soldier killed in India. My mother had perpetrated the misconception, telling me that our monthly subsistence came from a military fund. It was all a lie. When my mother had realized her death was near, she told me the truth. There had never been an Irish soldier — in reality it had been an English lord who'd come to Oxford from Ireland and fallen in love with her, a pretty Irish lass working as a housemaid. They were lovers while he was at the university. After graduation, Lord Edwin Lynhurst had gone back to his family holdings in Ireland, not knowing he had fathered a child until my mother wrote to him. Any expectations that he would return to claim her and the baby faded when news of his impending marriage to Lady Davina Waverly was announced.

Through the years, he had provided a monthly stipend and provisions for my education. On my mother's deathbed, she had told me the truth and made me promise that I would go to my father and ask that he acknowledge me and provide for my future.

If my mother had not ultimately made an unhappy marriage, I might have refused. She had been introduced to a nephew of our vicar two years earlier and in a short time the younger man had turned my mother's head despite warnings from the vicar, himself. After the marriage, my mother discovered that her new bridegroom was a wastrel, gambler, and lecherous man who cast his lascivious eyes at every woman—including me. More than once, I feared he would press his attentions upon me. I tried to keep my mother from knowing about his improper advances but I learned that she had been well aware of them. Fearful of leaving me in my stepfather's custody, she had made me promise to go to my father upon her death. I hated the idea of throwing myself upon a stranger, even if he was my real father, but I had few options open to me. So here I was, on a muddy road, hiding out in a ditch from a regiment of young Queen Victoria's dragoons, in the company of a jaunty little man who resembled a leprechaun.

"And where would ye be going?" he asked.

"To Lynhurst Castle."

Daddo whistled through his yellowed teeth. "Lynhurst Castle, is it?" He looked at my torn traveling pelisse and faded bonnet. "Is Sir Lynhurst expecting ye?"

"No."

Maybe, I should have sent a letter but I had decided against it, fearing that if Lord Lynhurst were warned of my arrival, he might make himself absent and I would have no chance to confront him with my parentage. He was married with grown children of his

17

own and might not even know that my mother was dead. I had taken the last monthly allowance to pay for my passage here.

"I'll be going in that direction myself," said Daddo. I was grateful for his company.

As thatched cottages grew closer together, I realized with relief that we had at last reached the outskirts of Danareel. The streets were roughly paved and broken with no signs of repairs in progress. Like most Irish villages that I had seen, it wore poverty in a make-do fashion. The splendor of Dublin did not extend to small Irish towns like this one.

We approached the main street and passed buildings occupying one side of the road along the sea front. Built closely together, small businesses faced the ocean and were like old men huddled against the wind and rain. Weathered by the ocean's spray, the lime-washed exteriors were cracked and peeling and a gray patina glistened on wet slate roofs. Decaying wood, soaked hemp, and dank earth blended with the usual seaport smells of fish and seaweed. Candles and lanterns shone through windows which were clouded with mist.

Women with cloaks thrown over their heads scurried along sidewalks made of irregularly shaped stones which did not meet. Children with tousled hair and muddy bare feet hopped along at their sides, leaping from crack to crack. Men stood close to the buildings and crunched down into their jacket collars, wearing slouched hats that were pulled low enough to hide their faces from view.

"How far is the castle?" I asked as we turned away from the village and followed a road skirting the edge of the cliffs.

"Not fer."

Night mist was beginning to envelop the landscape. I shivered as my thoughts raced ahead to what I should do and say. Now that I had reached my destination, I was sorry my journey was over and the time had come when I must face my father and ask for his protection. The roar of the ocean filled my ears as spumes of white-foamed water pounded against black rocks and tossed floating islands of black seaweed. A chilling mist rose over the cliffs and swirled wetly on the road.

Daddo's "not fer" meant about a mile. "There she be!"

I raised my eyes to a huge structure built of gray stone perched high above the Sea Wall Road. Against the quickly fading light, Lynhurst Castle appeared to be a mass of cold walls and blank windows, dark and formidable and well fortified. Nothing about its location or appearance welcomed intrusion by a stranger such as myself. My chest tightened and sweat beaded on my forehead.

A keeper's house stood beside a high iron gate which shut off passage to a twisting road leading up to the castle. Lighted torches moved in front of the gate and I saw that a crowd had gathered there. Voices, shouts, and loud wailing mingled with the clatter of horses' hooves. Mounted horsemen in uniforms like the ones that had passed us on the road were controlling the crowd.

"What's going on?" I fought back a lurch of fear.

"I'll be jiggered, if I know." Daddo quickened his step. "Come on, let's be finding out."

He hurried me to the edge of a crowd of men and women in peasant clothes. Because of the mounted soldiers, they were keeping their distance from the front gate and gawking like spectators waiting for a hanging to begin. My heart caught in my throat. Something was wrong. Terribly wrong. I couldn't understand the babble of voices.

"What is it?" I asked a motherly young woman wearing a large handkerchief over curly red hair.

Her blue eyes rounded in fright. "The saints pre-

19

serve us. 'Tis the Watcher."

"The Watcher!" echoed Daddo.

"Sure and he'd come back." She crossed herself.

"What's happened?" My breath was suddenly shallow as if I already knew the horror of her answer.

"Lord Lynhurst. Found on his doorstep . . . with his throat cut . . . and a black ivy wreath on his chest."

Chapter Two

"Ye knew His Lordship, then?" the woman asked, seeing my expression of stunned horror.

My mouth wouldn't work so I shook my head.

"There are slippery stones at the doors of the rich," she said prophetically in a dire tone.

"She's just come from England, Molly," explained Daddo. "Met her on the road. Was telling her the Watcher's come back to collect his due but I can't be believing this m'self. Sure and I never believed His Lordship would meet his end at the Watcher's hand."

"The devil's collecting his own . . . and about time, too," someone standing behind us growled.

"Ach! I heard Lord Lynhurst was going to sign a paper raising the church tithe. Another squeeze on Paddy, taking the very food from his mouth to send to the maggots in England."

"He won't be signing nothing now."

"Praise be, the cottiers will be spared another round of evictions."

"I was telling ye, the Watcher wouldn't let it happen," responded another man in a loud voice. "He came back and slit Lord Lynhurst's throat, that's for sure."

An agreeing rumble echoed through the crowd.

"The saints preserve us," breathed Molly, crossing herself again.

" 'Tis sorry I am meself to hear it," said Daddo. "His Lordship was better than some."

My father dead! *Murdered by a ghost*. I was caught in a vicious nightmare. Surely I would awaken at any moment and find myself back in the soft feather bed on Maple Lane. My mother would be calling me for breakfast and chiding me for the sleepyhead I was. But it was not her voice I heard in my ears but the loud keening of a woman who had crumpled to her knees near us, wailing and shrieking.

"Old Becky," said Molly, looking at the prostrate woman. "Poor soul. She'll be taking it hard. His Lordship sent her sons to school. Right prosperous they are now, working in Dublin. Ye can't fault him for looking after those who served him."

Daddo nodded. "There are plenty who'll say a good word for him—"

"And plenty who'll alert the devil that he's on his way," growled a man wearing a slouched cap and exuding the smell of brine and ale. His hatred seemed to reach out and touch me.

I took a step backwards. Swarthy men with caps pulled down on their foreheads glared at my fair hair and my attire as if they had found an enemy in their midst. The crowd closed in around me. My mouth went dry and my heart began to race.

"Are ye wanting to make your way to the gate?" asked Daddo, staying at my side. "Be there someone ye were wanting to see inside?"

I bit my cold lips. "No . . . no one."

His forehead wrinkled. "Ye did say ye was coming to the castle?"

My mind whirled like a devil's wind. The idea of introducing myself as an illegitimate daughter to Lord Lynhurst's wife and children was too appalling and humiliating even to contemplate. I couldn't do it. The promise I had made to my mother had been kept but any claim I had upon my father was gone now that he was dead. I would never know what his reaction would have been to an illegitimate daughter ap-

22

pearing on his doorstep. Would he have accepted or rejected me? If didn't matter now. I had come to Ireland only to find myself abandoned in a brooding strange country with less than a pound in my reticule.

"What do ye want to do, lass?" prodded Daddo.

I couldn't think.

Molly's questioning gaze went from my face to Daddo's.

"The mail coach broke down. I met her on the road," he explained. "Her ma was Irish," Daddo told her as if the latter excused me from my tainted English accent. "Hid out in the ditch, we did, not knowing why the dragoons were heading to Danareel." He shook his head. "Some poor Paddy will dance in the air for this."

I shivered, not so much from the cool evening air but from a deep-seated chill that came from within.

"Can't ye see the poor girl's beside herself?" chided Molly with a comforting pat on my shoulder. " 'Tis a warm cup a tea laced with a little poteen she be needin'."

"Yer special brew?" winked Daddo.

Molly laughed. "The same."

"Just what ye be needing. Go with Molly and she'll be putting you right as rain."

"She can sit awhile at me house and get some warm back into herself. Come along, girl. My man, Mike Ryan, has the Seaward Tavern at the bottom of the hill."

In my dazed state, I made no objections when she took my portmanteau from Daddo and slipped one plump arm under mine. I was grateful that someone was making decisions for me. Although I had always prided myself on being able to face a situation squarely, this one had come too fast and at the moment I had no idea how to handle it.

Daddo reacted to my bewildered expression by assuring me, "Molly will be takin' good care of ye.

There ain't a better welcome in Danareel than by Molly's hearth, right Molly?" He laughed as if enjoying a private joke.

"Get on with ye!" she grinned back.

Daddo tipped his funny hat, gave me his lopsided grin and with a quick step disappeared into the crowd.

Molly and I started back down the wet and slippery road. By now, night had cloaked the twisting road in darkness and a half-moon weakly lent a watery illumination to the landscape. The sea swept in and pounded against the rocks, echoing the thundering turmoil in my mind. My father murdered! The fact was a bludgeon pounding the horror into my head. My fantasies of rushing into his welcoming arms, safe and protected from the world, were as worthless as the clay clods crumbling beneath my feet.

Tears welled up in my eyes. What was I going to do? I was totally alone in the world. No father. No kin. No home. Nearly penniless in a strange country. I choked back sobs building up in my throat.

"Now, now," soothed Molly, feeling my body tremble as we walked. " 'Tis a rare trouble that won't take heels and flee with a hot drink in yer middle and a fire warming yer feet."

We reached the village and crossed an uneven street to a steep-roofed building on a corner. A weathered sign, SEAWARD TAVERN, creaked in the wind as it swung on rusted chains. Lantern light spilled through small glass squares in the front windows.

Molly led me to the side of the building and we walked along a muddy path to a door in the rear. We entered a shadowy, low-beamed kitchen that spanned the width of the building. Men's loud voices and mixed odors of ale and tobacco identified an adjoining taproom. A fiddle squawked above the din and I heard some lusty men's voices bellowing loudly to the tune.

Molly nestled me down in a cane chair in front of a glowing peat fire. " 'Tis fine ye'll be with something warming yer middle."

"Who's she, Ma?" asked a young girl, about ten years old, sitting on the floor near a reed cradle. Red, curly hair like her mother's lay in tousled strands around her face. She kept on filling candle molds with yellow tallow as she glanced up at us and back to her task.

"A friend of Daddo," Molly answered briskly, hanging her cloak on a peg in the wall.

"Daddo's coming?" the girl asked excitedly, her red curls bobbing. "Will he tell us some more stories?"

"No story tonight, Holly." Molly answered shortly. "Where be yer brothers . . . and Kerrie?"

An infant whimpered in a reed cradle placed near Holly's feet and she gave it a push with her toe before answering.

"The boys are in the byrne, Mama, and Kerrie's upstairs." The girl giggled. "She's putting papers in her hair." Her brown eyes sparkled. "She hates it because hers is so straight—and mine's so curly."

"It's that Shannon boy, again!" Molly went to the bottom of a crude staircase. "Kerrie! Hie yourself down here!"

My gaze traveled in a detached fashion over blackened walls, low-beamed ceiling, a scarred large worktable and crockery piled on a washstand. The floor was stone and splattered with mud and straw; small windows that were deep-set into thick walls were bare of curtains and the panes looked sooty. Two smoky lanterns at each end of the long room flickered uncertainly upon the walls and ceiling. Piles of stacked peat squares near the hearth gave off a rich, earthy smell that matched the odor of gray smoke going up the chimney. I warmed my hands on the turf fire which lent a ruddy reflection to the room, and tried to make my mind throw off the stupor that had engulfed it.

Strange noises brought my eyes to the corner of the room near the door and I saw a huge sow lying on a pile of hay with a litter of piglets routed at her swollen nipples. Their slobbering grunts blended with infant cries coming from the cradle. My travels across Ireland had introduced me to this companionable sharing of living space with livestock, but my prim upbringing recoiled every time I saw it.

I turned my gaze back to the fire. A feeling of homesickness washed over me. I longed for a dainty English cottage, bright and clean, smelling of beeswax and turpentine. Our home had golden maple floors covered with hooked rugs which my mother and I had hooked out of colorful woolen strips.

"Kerrie!" Molly called again. She removed a blackened kettle from the fire and poured the steaming liquid into a wooden mug.

This time, a barefooted girl about sixteen bounded down the steps, slim ankles and supple legs visible under the flying folds of a coarse brown skirt. Twisted papers wrapped around shocks of black hair stood out all over her head like curled tails. "Shannon said he's coming by tonight, Mama . . ." Her brown eyes coaxed her mother.

"Auch, he'll not be seein' ye, my fine miss!"

"Ma!" she wailed.

"Yer pa hasn't given his consent yet and 'til he does, ye'd best be forgetting about such foolishness as knotting yer hair up like that. Now, git that table laid for supper by the time I give this lady her tea."

Kerrie's eyes swung in my direction. Her pretty face scowled at me as if her mother's displeasure was my fault. I tried to smile but my lips were stiff and cold. Her bold eyes swept over my plain bonnet and traveling attire, which was modest enough by any standard, I thought, but my appearance brought a glint-like resentment into her eyes. She flounced away and began putting cutlery, crockery, and mugs on the table.

"If dear Shannon should see you now," teased Holly. "He'd run to the nearest ditch and hide."

"Yer just jealous." Kerrie tossed her head.

"I am not! Who'd want to marry an O'Brien, anyway? Pa ain't going to forget the time they busted up the place."

"Somebody else started it!"

Holly laughed. "Them O'Briens scaddled out of here when the fists started flying. Cowards, that's what they be."

"Enough, Holly!" scolded Molly, raising her eyebrows in an exasperated expression. She handed me a hot mug which warmed my hands as I held it. I sipped the steaming liquid which raced down my throat and into my stomach. I coughed, caught my breath, and took several swallows before the drink began to go down easily.

I had eaten very little at the last coach stop and I gratefully accepted an oaten cake and a hunk of cheese which Molly cut from a block wrapped in cloth.

Three boys scampered in from outside, tussling at each other. They continued some kind of a shoving game that must have started outside. In the scramble they nearly fell into the sow and her piglets. Laughing and pushing, they jostled each other in a game of tag around the kitchen.

"Ye better be saving that for chores, you hooligans!" Molly scolded the boys, who were all under eight years old.

"They're all done, Ma!" The biggest one, a slight boy with dark hair, grabbed Molly around the waist in a playful swing.

"Get on with ye, Patrick Ryan . . ." Molly pretended to box his ears, but she was smiling all the time she was scolding. Her eyes rested fondly on him.

27

"Did you see Father Rooney today?"

"Yes, Ma."

Molly smiled at me. "Patrick is going to be a priest." Pride shone in her eyes as she ruffled his hair.

The children's bright chatter filled the room and inquisitive eyes peered at me. There was such a sense of unreality about the situation that I felt I would blink any moment and they would all disappear.

Several times, a stout tavern maid came through the kitchen, disappeared into a back room and then reappeared with two pitchers filled with liquid. I had heard some of my fellow travelers talk about unbridled Irish traffic in poteen, a brew made in hidden stills and sold behind the tax collector's back. I suspected that Seaward Tavern was one of those *shibeens*, where people could get illegal whiskey. I half expected the Queen's Dragoons to burst in any moment and drag me off to the nearest jail.

Molly bustled about the kitchen, glancing my way now and again. It was obvious she was busting with curiosity to know why an English lady was sitting at her hearth, visibly shattered by the death of someone she had said she didn't know.

"And what be yer name?" she asked when she filled my cup the third time with the strong brew of tea and poteen.

"Aileen O'Connor," I answered, leaving off "Lynhurst," for the name was still new to me. My mother's maiden name, O'Connor, was the one I had been raised with and only when my mother had finally showed me my christening record had I learned that my full name was Aileen O'Connor Lynhurst.

"O'Connor? 'Tis a good Irish name," said Molly with a smile. She seemed reassured that all would be well. "Yer father moved the family to England?"

"My grandfather," I said. I explained that Davilin O'Connor had been like hundreds of other starving Irishmen who fled the country in the 1780s, seeking work on the English wharves.

Molly nodded and I grew silent with my thoughts, remembering the things my mother had told me. There had been little love of the Irish in England then, as now, and my mother had nearly starved with the rest of the family when disease and poverty slowly killed all of them but her. Starving and homeless, she was sent to a Protestant orphanage at the age of eight and when she was sixteen, she was sent with other girls to work as a housemaid near Oxford. Pretty and vibrant, she met Lord Lynhurst by chance and foolishly fell in love with him. Their passionate affair resulted in a love child that was me. My mother passed herself off as Widow O'Connor but it had all been a lie. All those happy, sunny years when I thought I knew who I was had been swept away at her death, leaving me with no sense of my real self. No wonder I had no idea where to go or what to do.

" 'Tis exhausted ye are," soothed Molly. She took the mug away. "Come, *avoureen*. There's a bed waiting for ye upstairs."

As if I were one of her children, Molly scooted me up the narrow back steps to a small room under the eaves.

"My trunk!" I said with sudden remembrance. "I left it on the mail coach."

"Don't ye be a worryin'. I'll send one of the boys to fetch it when the driver unloads. Can't ye make do with what's in your satchel?"

"Yes, of course."

She laid my portmanteau on a small bed, soft and sweet-smelling with sheaves of yellow gorse and bracken stuffed in the springy mattress.

After filling a pitcher with water and leaving it on the washstand, Molly bid me a pleasant good night. "Sure the morning will make everythin' look brighter," she promised. "Will ye be needin' help undressing?" she asked with her head cocked in amusement or maternal concern, I couldn't tell.

"Thank you. I'll manage nicely."

"Night to ye then." She smiled and shut the door.

I suspected that this attic room was one that they rented out and I despaired to think of the few coins remaining in my reticule. I couldn't afford lodging like this for more than a couple of nights. Where would I go? What would I do? My thoughts were like a bed of nettles, stabbing me everywhere my mind turned.

My hands fumbled clumsily with the fastenings on my dress. I realized suddenly that my head was swimming peculiarly. When I walked, I staggered about the room like a sailor with too much ale under his belt. No wonder Molly had been smiling. She knew what effect her tea was going to have. I realized with horror that I was probably drunk! My fingers were thick and clumsy. I couldn't find the front of my nightdress, nor the top nor bottom. I began to giggle. Laughter and tears blended together as I struggled to rid myself of pelisse, dress, petticoat, camisole, stays, stockings and muddy shoes.

Dropping them in a heap on the floor, I climbed into bed, leaving the front of my flannel gown unbuttoned and the ribbons hanging free. My usual fastidiousness was lost in a condition that allowed little concern about my slovenly behavior. My mind was so befuddled that I couldn't think and the floating euphoria was a blessing. In my inebriated state, I no longer struggled with questions that had no answers. The minute I closed my eyes, I promptly fell asleep, awakening only once because my mouth was hanging open and I was snoring loudly.

Sunlight lay upon the worn floorboards in bright patterns. For a moment, I couldn't remember where I was. During the weeks I had been traveling, I was always slightly disorientated when I first awakened in strange lodgings. Then memory would tell me how far I had come on my journey and how much farther it was to my destination.

This morning I was jolted wide awake with knowledge that my journey had ended. The truth was like the clanging of a harsh bell. The horror I had put aside came rushing back. My father was dead! Killed by the ghost. No, not a ghost. The superstitious tale of a peasant hero coming back from the dead might be accepted by simple souls like Daddo but I knew better. Someone of flesh and blood had slit Lord Lynhurst's throat and placed a black ivy wreath upon his chest. I shuddered as a cold prickling crept up my spine.

I threw back the covers and quickly dressed. An urgency I did not understand forced me to hurry down to the warmth of the kitchen and Molly's cheery smile.

"Well, there ye be!" she greeted me. Her hands were deep in bread dough and a streak of flour dusted her plump cheeks. The boys were running everywhere and the two girls were set at some task at a worktable. "Did ye sleep well?" she inquired, her eyes sparkling.

"Yes, very well." I hoped my returning grin wasn't too sheepish. She must have known my condition last night from her laced tea. "Thank you very much for . . . everything."

"A good cup of tea will do it every time," she said with a wink.

She set out a bowl of gruel which my growling stomach accepted enthusiastically. My healthy appetite had always been a joke between my mother and me and I was fortunate to have inherited a tall, slender build—from my father? The question lodged like a lump in my throat. Now I would never know. Once I had learned of his existence, Lord Lynhurst had never been far from my thoughts. I had imagined a

31

hundred scenarios about my reunion with him. Sometime the imaginings were like fairy tales filled with loving embraces as he welcomed me. At other times, perhaps in more realistic moments, my daydreams were dark and worrisome and filled with rejection. Now I would never know. My father was dead. Whether Lord Lynhurst would have welcomed me or denied my existence was a question that would be buried with him.

I looked up and saw a dark, swarthy man staring at me from the doorway into the ale room. His black eyes flashed with hatred so livid that his glare sent an arctic chill bone-deep in my body.

"Good morning," I managed in what I hoped was an even tone.

He spat on the floor. "So this is the English scum takin' up me bed and food."

"Mike!" gasped Molly. "Her grandpa left Ireland to find work. Her name's O'Connor." Fright edged her voice and I knew from the sudden silence in the kitchen that the children had frozen in an apprehensive waiting. It was as if none dared to breathe with their father in the room.

"Don't be daft, woman," he spat. "I don't care what her name is. She's English. I hear her talkin' just like one of them thieving, bloodletting bastards. Taking the food out of our mouths, she be. Sleeping under our roof—"

"I'll pay for the room and the food!" I countered quickly. The horrible man's ravings struck a flint on my ready temper.

"Bloodsucking *Sassenachs*. The English are all alike," he swore. "Taking food out of a man's mouth."

"Do not concern yourself that I would accept charity from your hand, sir." I kept my eyes leveled on his glowering face. "Yes, I was born and raised in England, and proud of it!"

32

"Then 'tis there ye should have stayed!" With his fists clenched, he stomped back into the ale room.

Molly let out a breath of relief. "Don't be minding 'im. 'Tis this Tithe War that's got Mike all stirred up."

I had not heard of any Irish-English war by that name. I knew that relations were strained because the English Parliament had passed an Act of Union which abolished the Irish Parliament but now offered seats in the British governing body to duly elected officials. "Tithe War?" I echoed.

"The tax that must be paid to support the Anglican church even though we be Catholics and hard put to meet the needs of our own church. 'Tis the tithe collectors fill their pockets first. Sure and the tithe always goes up and we have less and less."

"Have you protested officially?"

She looked at me as if I had suddenly started speaking in a foreign tongue. "And who would be listening to us?"

"The government. The English Parliament. The men you elected to represent you."

Her laugh was bitter. " 'Tis the English landlords who are elected. And they be the ones who strap on more taxes."

"Then you should protest."

"Aye, that we do. Men are hanged and killed and the ghost of the Watcher walks the land. This morning I saw a sign that more trouble is comin'." She crossed herself. Her eyes grew large. "I saw it with me own eyes. The windcock on the house was standing still even though the wind was a shiftin'. Trouble's a brewin'. Faith, 'twas a warning for sure."

Her ominous words settled on me like a weighted cloak. Suddenly I needed to get away from her superstitious chatter about harbingers of danger. "Thank you for breakfast. I . . . I believe I'll take a walk." I stood up from the table.

"Fresh air will do you good," She nodded, her

friendly smile was back. Her talk of dark, ominous signs seemed forgotten. The children scurried about, laughing and scuffling with each other. The tense atmosphere that their father had brought to the kitchen was gone. Molly was humming to herself as I let myself out the rear door.

A cow bawled at me from the attached byrne and an arrogant cock strutted in the midst of cackling hens in the yard. The day was overcast, with lowering clouds that softened the landscape like a moist watercolor. I made my way along the side of the building and paused in front of the tavern before crossing an iron-hard street which led to the sea wall.

As I walked along, I gazed out at the Atlantic Ocean. The coast was a rugged one. No quiet eddies and sandy beaches, just craggy rocks which rose straight from a white-foamed surf. Steep paths leading down to the sea's edge were precarious. Slippery, kelp-strewn rocks lay in wait at the bottom. Far out from the shore, small curraghs dotted the ocean waters as fishermen trolled nets behind their small boats.

I passed huge bundles of kelp that had been spread to dry upon the rocks and a pungent smell which I could not identify teased my nostrils. No one nodded nor spoke to me. I intercepted several glances among men who were working along the road or trudging up and down the rocky paths. Their expressions were neither friendly nor hostile but I sensed a guarded wariness that was almost as visible as a wall. The memory of Mike Ryan's malevolent glare caused me to shiver. Never in my life had I seen such hatred. Paying him for the room and food would take the little bit of money I had left but there was no question in my mind about settling my bill with him. I would not be beholden to him for a half-penny.

Pausing on the edge of the cliff, I watched men using huge rakes as their boats hugged the shoreline.

They pulled in green-black kelp and I suddenly identified the distinctive odor which mingled with the brine of fish and salt air. Iodine! My mother had told me that extracting iodine from seaweed by boiling it in huge pots was an industry that flourished in western Ireland.

I watched the men work for a few minutes and then moved on. I searched the faces of men passing along the road, hoping that I might run into Daddo again. The funny little man's friendship was something I could use at the moment. I had not intended to go as far as the castle but suddenly I was there, staring at its guarded gates and the drive which led up to a Palladian mansion that faced the sea. Made of white blocks of rock, it was lustrous in the morning light. The towers rose above four stories of windows, reflecting dark panes, shuttered alcoves and balconies.

On the level where I stood, hand-placed rocks rose in a high wall from the Sea Wall Road. Several doors had been placed into the rock wall at the level of the road and I wondered if they were storage rooms. Some of the heavy-planked doors were chained shut. A long staircase of more than a hundred stairs rose steeply from the road to the castle. The stones were worn and I knew the staircase had been used as a short cut from the castle to the sea road.

For a foolish moment I pictured myself at the front gate, knocking on the keeper's door to ask admission. And what would I say or do once inside? A black wreath hung on the wrought-iron entrance, indicating that the family was in mourning. No, I couldn't force myself upon them. They would treat my presence as the crude intrusion that it was. For a brief time, I had accepted "Lynhurst" as my name, but no more. I was Aileen O'Connor and must remain so. Somehow I must make my way back to England.

With leaden steps, I walked back to the Seaward Tavern with no more of an idea of how to provide for myself in this alien country than I'd had before. I had never been so alone in my life. Nor so frightened. Panic threatened to paralyze my thinking and a fullness in my eyes warned that tears were not far away.

I walked around to the back door but instead of going inside, I walked over to an overturned keg placed against the stone wall of a sweathouse. I had seen many of these windowless, beehive-shaped structures as I traveled across the island. I could understand why being hot enough to sweat was popular in this damp climate.

Sitting on the keg and leaning my back against the rough stone, I searched my mind for a way to get back to England, trying to think of someone who might send me passage money. There was no one but the vicar of our parish who even knew my situation, and he and his family of five children lived on a pittance. It was out of the question to ask him for money even if he had been willing to give it. He had warned my mother against marrying his nephew for he knew him to be a wastrel and a rake. When I told the vicar that my stepfather had made improper advances to me and that I feared he would force his attention upon me once my mother was dead, the vicar had been mortified and encouraged me to follow my mother's dying wishes. No, the vicar would not help me return to England.

I knew that if I spent one more night here, my money would be gone. Mike Ryan would never let me work for my keep. He would take great pleasure in tossing me and my belongings out in the street.

I stiffened. As if my thoughts had fashioned him out of thin air, I heard the back door slam and saw the tavern owner coming toward me. The malevolence in his black eyes was even more intense than it had been before. He growled, "There's someone here to see ye."

The coach driver, I thought. He's brought my

trunk. What will I tell him to do with it?

"Thank you," I said with as much composure as I could and swept by him into the house. The nape of my neck tingled as if his dagger stare were piercing my skin.

Molly showed me into a small parlor. "Ye can wait here."

There was a chill in the room and no peat fire was banked in the fireplace. Obviously this room was only used on special occasions, probably weddings or funerals, I thought. The furniture was sparse; white-washed walls held a few faded pictures and a wooden crucifix. A thinly silvered mirror reflected my taut face.

Looking into it, I tucked back a few wayward strands of hair that had slipped forward upon my cheek. For a moment, I thought I had taken leave of my senses. As I stood there looking into the mirror, another face was suddenly reflected beside mine!

For a moment, our eyes held. His were almost black and mine a startled blue. Thick dark brown hair drifted forward on a broad forehead and a slight smile curved the corners of a firm mouth. His gaze was like a grappling hook, holding me and drawing me closer. In that weighted moment, I knew that some strange fate had overtaken me. The ominous omens that Molly had predicted seemed to descend upon me.

I lowered my hand slowly from my hair and turned around.

Chapter Three

He stood some six feet tall. A forest-green silk dress coat fit smoothly over his muscular shoulders, narrowed at the waist with two rows of buttons decorating the front panels and a soft black cravat-accented white linen shirt, starched and pleated. Every inch the gentleman, he gave a polite bow. "Miss Aileen Lynhurst, I presume." I saw then that his smile was sardonic and hard and did not reach the dark depths of his eyes.

I felt myself stiffening. "Yes. But . . . but how did you know?"

He had something in his hand which he held out to me. I gasped when I saw it. Three Christmases ago, a struggling young artist had boarded with us. In return for our hospitality, he had painted a small miniature of me for my mother. It had not been among her things when I packed them away after her death and I didn't know what had happened to it. In the portrait, my fair hair drifted about my face and my blue eyes and mouth held a hint of a smile. The young man had entertained me with rollicking stories while I sat for the painting. The likeness was a good one, my mother said, although I thought the artist had flattered me a great deal to please both my mother and me. A flood of poignant memories rushed back as I stared at it. "Where did you get it?"

"Your mother sent it to Lord Lynhurst with a letter advising us of her ill health and your projected journey to meet him."

"But how did you know I had arrived?"

Again that quirk at the corner of his lips. "There is no news in Danareel which does not travel faster than summer lightning. The coach driver is the brother of one of our maids at the castle and we knew of your presence here before your trunk was lowered to the ground."

"I did not know that my mother had written and—" I hesitated, trying to find the right word.

"And warned us?" he finished with a sardonic rise of an eyebrow.

"Advised my father of my intent," I corrected evenly, silently bristling at his choice of words.

"No matter," he said curtly. "Your trunk is already loaded and if you will collect your other belongings, we'll be on our way."

"On our way? Where? And who are you?" I resented his attitude and even in my shattered state, I refused to be intimidated by his autocratic bearing. This handsome, dictatorial gentleman must be Lord Lynhurst's son—my half brother.

Again that mocking bow. "Forgive my bad manners, Miss Lynhurst. Sean Creighton, solicitor and personal secretary to Lord Lynhurst. At your service."

Blatant animosity coated his words. Why did he dislike me so intensely? He did not even know me! And his haughty bearing was not in rhyme with his position. His demeanor seemed above his employment. "How do you do," I said stiffly.

"I have been ordered by Lady Lynhurst to bring you to the castle," he continued crisply. "She very much wants to see you."

My hands closed tightly over the miniature I still held in my hand and the sharp edges of the frame bit

39

into my flesh. *Lady Lynhurst wanted to see me? Why?* I couldn't read any answer in Sean Creighton's arctic dark eyes. Could it be that she would be receptive to my plight? Maybe Lady Lynhurst was a caring, generous person who would understand my desperate situation.

"Are you certain?" I asked.

"Will you collect your things, please. I have a carriage waiting."

Hope sluiced through me like sun suddenly burning away a night mist. Perhaps all my fears were for naught, I thought. My arrival had been expected after all.

"I have only a small portmanteau. I will pack it and return in a moment."

"Very well."

I was aware of his eyes following me as I left the room.

I hurried into the kitchen and ran straight into Mike Ryan. He blocked my way so suddenly that I knew he had been eavesdropping at the open doorway.

"So 'tis Her High and Mighty, ye be. A Lynhurst, for all that? Lodging the devil under me own roof, I'll swear. Sure, I'd sooner burn the rafters down upon me head!" He spit tobacco juice that sprayed an ugly spot upon the hem of my dress. "That for all the Lynhursts and their bloodsucking kin."

Molly stood behind him, holding the baby. She stared at me with rounded, horrified eyes. "Lynhurst," she echoed.

I wanted to say something to her but she backed away and crossed herself, as if my presence were an evil omen she sought to dispel.

"A weevil worming its way into me house," snarled Mike. "Spoiling the air with its breathing. Ye'd better be taking yerself from me sight."

"I'm leaving—gladly." I hesitated, looking at

40

Molly, wanting to thank her for her kindness, but she looked so stricken I didn't dare say anything with her husband standing there with black daggers in his eyes.

"Then be gone with ye!" he growled. "And stay with 'em that sups with the devil with a long spoon."

There was nothing to do but go upstairs with as much bearing as I could manage and pack my few things. My mind raced ahead. I was going to meet my father's wife. What would she be like? Would she welcome me? The palms of my hands were moist under my gloves when I went downstairs.

I hoped to have a few words with Molly before I left but the kitchen was empty. Only the farrower and her piglets grunted in the corner. I took some coins from my purse and laid them on the kitchen table. With quickening steps I returned to the room where my escort waited.

He stood with one hand resting on the cold fireplace mantel, staring down into the empty grate.

"I'm ready," I said.

He turned around and once more I felt his scrutiny as his eyes traveled over my simple leghorn bonnet, a dark blue traveling dress and matching cape.

"Does my appearance displease you?" I asked boldly, rankled by his bold scrutiny.

A wash of color rushed into his face and I knew I had embarrassed him. Good, I thought. He needn't think that I was some poor relation who had come to grovel.

"I apologize. I confess that you are not quite what I was led to expect."

"The miniature flatters me, I agree."

"No, quite the contrary. The artist did not capture the boldness in your chin nor the blue fire snapping in your eyes. But then, the soft smile on your lips would suggest a different mood, perhaps?"

"Quite different. He was a gentleman whose manners were not boorish and offensive."

The verbal thrust seemed to surprise him. "I see you have a sharp wit with nettles to match."

"I can take care of myself, if that's what you mean."

His eyes held mine. "I certainly hope so," he said in an ominous tone.

We left the building and he helped me into a carriage waiting in front of the tavern. Men and women on the street sent black looks in our direction as they circled a wide path around it or stopped a respectable distance and glared. A coat of arms blazed on the sides, a blatant symbol of English nobility, and polished brass fittings gleamed against the carriage's black and red exterior.

When I had been installed inside, Sean took his place on the black leather seat beside me. A postilion dressed in uniform leaped back on the driver's seat and a sharp crack of his whip sent the pair of matched bay horses galloping up the Sea Wall Road.

I clasped my gloved hands in my lap, wondering if I should pinch myself to make certain I was awake. Had Molly's laced tea brought about this hallucination? Was I really in a carriage on my way to Lynhurst Castle to meet my father's wife? Nothing about the situation was real—except the man sitting at my side. He was very real. I wanted to ask him questions but my companion looked out the window at the rolling ocean as if oblivious to my presence.

I tried to gather my thoughts. This sudden summons to the castle had only created new anxieties. I was bewildered that Lord Lynhurst had been aware of my intent to seek his protection. My mother had paved the way for me as best she could by sending the miniature. Apparently Lord Lynhurst had told his wife about me. If only I had arrived a day earlier, I would have been in time to see my father alive. Now, it was his widow who had summoned me. For what reason? I could only pray that she felt no malevolence toward the illegitimate daughter her husband had fathered.

I shot a side glance at Sean Creighton. His profile was one of bold lines and taut muscles. What did he think about Lord Lynhurst's indiscreet past? His attitude toward me was one of forced politeness. I could see the sardonic derision in his eyes when he looked at me.

Some stubborn streak overtook my building apprehension and I asked boldly, "Had you been with Lord Lynhurst for some time? His death must be a great shock to you." *And what will you do now that he's dead?* I'm certain my silent question was evident in my tone for I saw his mouth and cheek muscles stiffen.

"His Lordship sent me to Trinity College in Dublin and I have been in his service for nearly five years." He turned back to the window as if the subject were dismissed.

"Creighton is a Scottish name, is it not?" I prodded, ignoring his reluctance to pursue any conversation with me.

"My grandfather came to Ireland from Scotland in 1785. He married the daughter of an Irish landowner, Kathleen O'Mallory. They accumulated land and handed down a family inheritance which my father gambled away. Lord Lynhurst rescued me from poverty, educated me, and made me his personal solicitor. Is there anything more you would like to know about me?"

"Yes. Why is your manner so hostile?"

"I have nothing personal against you, Miss Lynhurst. I dislike what you represent."

"And what is that?"

He made no effort to disguise the bitterness. "You are English, are you not?"

"You know I am."

43

"And will you be like the others? Taking what you will?" His jaw tightened. "The English take and never give back anything, not even the dignity of allowing Ireland to govern herself."

"I suppose you're referring to the Act of Union which dissolved the Irish Parliament."

"That among other things."

"My mother was Irish," I countered, "but she agreed that England would be in peril with an independent Ireland at her back. Especially one which has always hated the English. There is danger that in any war, Ireland may give aid to England's enemies. The Crown must protect itself and its colonies. Besides, English law allows elected Irish representatives in Parliament."

"Seats filled by Englishmen who live on its land, bleed its people, and continue to rape Ireland while they sit in Parliament and grow fat."

"But you worked for His Lordship. Did you not find him fair?"

"Lord Lynhurst was always most generous with his possessions."

"Possessions? What do you mean by that?"

"He liked to own people as well as things. As long as they were in his possession, he took very good care of them."

"But you disliked him, didn't you? Maybe enough to—" I halted, stricken with what I was about to say.

"To murder him?" He gave a short laugh. "You can lay the blame for that deed on the ghost of the Watcher."

"Don't patronize me," I flared. "The murderer of my father was flesh and blood."

I saw his hands tighten. "Yes."

I waited but he didn't say anything more.

"Someone must have hated him very much," I baited.

He gave a short laugh. "The Irish are very good at

44

hating. When they aren't killing the English, they're bashing in each other's heads. Feuds between clans have been going on for generations. The whole country is riddled with rival groups and secret societies."

"Like the Bog Boys?"

His eyes swung to mine, obviously startled by the question. "What do you know about them?"

"Nothing. I just heard the name."

"Where?"

"I don't think that's any of your concern." I didn't want to get Daddo in any trouble.

His eyes narrowed. "Perhaps not, Miss Lynhurst, but you'd best not mention the Bog Boys again. Not if you want that pretty neck of yours to remain in one piece."

With this dire threat, he turned away and stared out the window.

I was confused by his attitude but pride would not allow me to question him further. The whole country was permeated by hate and violence and I had no background for vicious undercurrents that surged around me. My mother had talked of Ireland in romantic terms but she had never experienced the Emerald Isle herself. She had been born in England and orphaned at an early age. Throughout her life she read of Ireland in British newspapers and books written by loyal Englishmen. When she talked to me about Ireland it was in a gentle and romantic tone. Nothing she had told me prepared me for the harsh, volatile situation in which I found myself. I was poignantly aware of emotion simmering just below Sean Creighton's outward composure. His hard, vigorous expression was like one sculpted in granite.

When we reached the castle's gates at the foot of the Sea Wall Road, the driver reined the horses and we waited for the iron gate to open.

My throat was suddenly dry. The stone castle on the rise above us was a formidable structure braced

45

against the relentless onslaught of Atlantic gales. "It looks like a fortress," I said in a hushed tone.

Sean glanced at me. Apparently, something in my expression made him break his silence. "At one time a Norman keep stood on the same knoll," he explained. "Ruins of the bailey, towers, and quarters for horses have been found. The Norman structure was replaced by a fortification that stood proud and foursquare when Cromwell sailed along the coast. When the English invader came to this spot, he ordered the Irish owners of the structure to surrender. And when they refused, his gunners found the range and reduced it to a pile of ruins. The land was then given to a Colonel Lynhurst who had served Cromwell faithfully as his English forces ransacked conquered territory. The Colonel built this castle which has passed down the line to the present Lynhurst family. You can be proud of your heritage," he said sarcastically as if I were somehow responsible for the blood that ran in my veins.

"Surely you don't hold me responsible for carnage that happened two hundred years ago?"

"Not at all." His smile was thin. "I only hold the English responsible for the carnage that is happening today."

Any crisp reply evaded me.

The gatekeeper nodded obsequiously to us as the carriage rolled past. I saw that the man's curiosity was undisguised as he turned his gray head to catch a glimpse inside the carriage. My lips were too stiff to smile at him and I realized later that he might have taken my fright for hauteur.

The road twisted upward around huge boulders and deep cuts in the side of the hill. I grabbed a strap to balance myself as the carriage was repeatedly pitched at a steep angle when maneuvering the sharp curves.

As we jostled together in the carriage, my escort

made no attempt to keep his body from brushing mine. In fact, I suspected that he deliberately let his long legs press against my skirts. A peculiar awareness of his muscular torso made me try to draw away from him in the narrow seat. Warmth swept up into my cheek and his smile told me he was aware of my discomfort. He was crude, impolite and arrogant, I fumed silently. As if amused by my reaction to his touch, he grinned and let his shoulder touch mine.

There was nothing I could do but try and maintain my composure until the road finally leveled out at the top of a high buttress. The walls of the castle towered over us and as I peered out, I gasped to see how large it was at close range. I had no idea how many rooms the building contained but surely as many as some of the Queen's royal residences, I thought in awe. The carriage made a circle and stopped in a wide clearing in front of the towering, rock-hewn castle.

I sank back in the seat.

"What's the matter?" Sean asked, raising an eyebrow.

"It's so big . . . so stark . . . . cold."

"The inside is better." I detected a softness in his voice that hadn't been there before.

The postilian opened the door. Sean stepped out and waited.

"Shall we go in, Miss Lynhurst?" He prodded when I didn't move.

His use of the unfamiliar name mocked my presence here. I was Aileen O'Connor. I had no legitimate claim to the Lynhurst name. What awaited me inside could be as cold and terrifying as the structure itself. Frightened and alone, my courage completely deserted me. I felt foolish tears threatening to spill from the corner of my eyes. A questioning smile seemed to linger on his lips. I stiffened my courage and stepped out.

"Careful," he said.

From his tone, I didn't know whether he was warning me of the step down or of what might await me inside. I couldn't read his expression. As he looked down at me, I saw nothing reassuring in his solemn dark eyes.

A wide terrace of blocked stone circled the ground floor and a long flight of wide steps led to the front door. Sean put a firm, guiding hand on my elbow and I did not object. Unlike my reaction to his touch in the carriage, I welcomed his support as we moved forward into the shadow of the vaulting walls. My gaze went upward to rounded towers, pointed spires and eaves decorated with grinning gargoyles. Small balconies softened the second and third floor windows but the exterior remained austere and cold.

We mounted the steps and were halfway up the staircase when a magnificent double door opened and a uniformed servant stood waiting stiffly. He averted his eyes as if watching our arrival and progress up the flight of steps was forbidden.

My feet halted. I was overcome by a weird sensation that once inside, there would be no escape from these rock walls. For a moment, I almost turned on my heels and fled. But this impulse was quickly followed by the shattering question: "Flee—to where?"

Sean tightened his hold on my elbow.

I reined in my apprehension and continued our climb.

When we reached the threshold in front of the door, he swore. "Why are these stones still here, Dolan? I ordered them replaced immediately!"

My stomach turned over as I looked down at huge marble stones in front of the door. Deep stains were unmistakable where blood had made a dark pool on the stones and had seeped into the cracks and crevices.

"Yes, sir, Mr. Creighton," said the butler. "A wagon was sent out early this morning to bring back the hewed marble. The quarry is a half-day away, sir."

"Well, for God's sake, tear these out now. Have visitors use the side entrance until this spot is repaired."

"Very good, sir," said Dolan, his Irish countenance both obsequious and arrogant. His eyes darted quickly in my direction and I knew they took in everything about me in that one surreptitious glance.

I swallowed to settle my queasy stomach. My father's throat had been slit while he stood on this very threshold. He must have opened the door to someone—but not a ghost, I was certain of that. Ghosts had no need of doors or windows and no wraith-like creature had wielded the knife that cut his throat nor placed the ivy wreath upon his chest.

"I'm sorry about that," apologized Sean as we entered a large hall.

I jumped slightly as the butler firmly shut the door behind us. My nerves were like the taut strings of a violin.

Sean hesitated. "Your father is laid out in the main parlor. Would you like to see him before you go upstairs?"

I nodded. I could not tell from his expression if he were surprised or annoyed by my response.

"This way."

Our footsteps echoed upon a stone floor as we crossed an entrance hall nearly forty feet wide and twenty feet high. A dank chill was caught inside the thick walls and patches of sunlight coming through high windows did not reach the floor below. Huge tapestries on the walls failed to add warmth to the long corridor which led to an arched doorway.

In a large room dominated by two huge fireplaces and numerous clusters of dark furniture, my father's body had been laid out on a bier flanked by candles. The sickening, sweet odor of flowers mingling with that of burning wax was a cue for remembering my mother's recent funeral.

I moved slowly toward the bier. My heartbeat quickened and moisture fled from my mouth. I was not afraid of the dead man who lay there. Such squeamishness was not a part of my make-up. The rigid body was not the cause of my emotional up-heaval. The reason my head reeled and my body swayed was that I was, at last, looking down into the face of my father!

"Steady." Sean put a firm arm at my waist and held me as I looked down upon Lord Edwin Lynhurst.

This was the man my mother had loved passion-ately. I tried to reconcile his face with the one I had formed in my mind. He was not the romantic figure that my mother's words had drawn of him, but then, I reasoned, he was twenty years older than when she had seen him last. As a man in his forties, his hair had grayed at the temples and lines in his face had erased any sense of youth. His lifeless form only touched me with a grief I would have felt for anyone who had lost his life. I had nothing to draw upon for any personal mourning.

As I looked down upon his body lying in state in this huge castle, I felt a rising surge of resentment. *Why did you desert my mother and me!* I silently flung the question at his placid face. As far as I knew, he had never made any attempt to return to England to see me or my mother. Funds paid through someone like Sean Creighton were the only admission that we existed. His death had cheated me. I had wanted to accuse him of indifference, of betrayal, and express other emotions I had felt when I learned that he had only contributed money to my upbringing and noth-ing more. I had been a love child, conceived in youth-ful passion, and I had come to Ireland as I had promised my mother to find my identity as his daughter. But it was too late. He could not even give me that.

"What is *she* doing here?" A young woman, sixteen or seventeen, sailed into the room, her black gown whipping like an overblown dahlia around her slender form. Violet shadows lay under her eyes and the deeply lashed rims were red from crying. "How dare you!"

I stepped back, fearful that she was about to attack me with clawed hands. Sean grabbed her arm.

"Lorrie! Get hold of yourself," he ordered.

"She has no business here. How dare she parade herself in front of us like this! I won't have it. I won't have it!"

"Your mother wants to see her, Lorrie," he said gently but firmly. "Now behave yourself. I know you're distressed but there's nothing to be done."

She turned and buried her face in his shoulder, sobbing and trembling. Sean stroked her dark brown head and for the first time I saw a loving gentleness steal into his eyes. The rigid sweep of his cheek and jaw softened.

Could they be lovers? The possibility shocked me.

"Sean," she sobbed. "Make her go away."

"Your father would be disappointed, Lorrie. He expected you to behave better than this," he scolded her gently.

"I told him I wouldn't! It's all too horrible. Her coming here! Humiliating us all."

I didn't know what to say.

The young woman sobbed in his arms and Sean shot me a look which I interpreted as a warning to keep silent. He kept his arm around her and led her out of the room. "Take Miss Loretta up to her room, Rosa," I heard him order. "And give her a sleeping draught. She is overwrought."

He came back and apologized. "I'm sorry that happened. Loretta is very emotional—and was devoted to her father. She did not take the news of your existence as well as His Lordship expected. The secret of his

51

youthful dalliance came as a shock to everyone . . . except me, of course. As his solicitor, I had arranged for the monthly sum to be sent to you and your mother. Up until the time he heard that you were coming, there had been no need for anyone else to know. However, when he received the miniature and your mother's letter, he was forced to admit to the family the existence of an illegitimate daughter."

I flinched. Illegitimacy was a term I had not been able to accept unemotionally. My mother had lied to me for so many years that her deathbed confession still lacked a creditable acceptance on my part. I suddenly wished she had taken the secret to her grave.

"His Lordship had made preparations for your arrival," said Sean. "I think he was looking forward to seeing you."

Maybe the happy reunion I had fantasized would have occurred if only I had arrived before his death. A peculiar spurt of joy went through me. "He told the family about me?"

Sean nodded.

"He could have lied about his responsibility and denied my claim when I arrived."

"Yes, he could have, but he had decided to acknowledge you as his daughter. You see, he loved your mother. Deeply. Passionately." Sean said it so matter-of-factly that at first I thought I had misunderstood him.

"He told you?"

"His Lordship talked about his first love many, many times."

"Then why did he desert her—and me?"

"A true Englishman patterns his life as society dictates." Sean's smile was brittle. "Your mother was a penniless orphan. Marrying her would have denied the traditions of his class and culture. Surely, your mother did not expect that."

"She accepted the situation as it was and dealt with

it," I said with pride. "To the end, she never reproached him."

I looked down once more upon His Lordship's face and my tears were not for him but for the young Irish girl who had loved him so much.

"Are you ready now to go upstairs and meet Lady Davina?"

"Yes," I said, dabbing my eyes.

He took my arm and guided me out of the room. We mounted a long staircase which possessed a wide landing with windows looking out upon the ocean. The view was as astonishing as the lofty site of the castle had promised. The Sea Wall Road looked like a narrow silver ribbon far below. I would have lingered to drink in the panorama of sea and sky if Sean's pressure on my arm had not urged me upward.

At the top of the long flight, we turned right and moved down a long, shadowy corridor. New fears raced through me. After experiencing Lorrie's open hatred, I knew better than to expect any acceptance from my father's titled wife. If my father had been here to protect me, my reception would have been different. Now, I could only defend myself as best I could against hatred such as I had experienced downstairs.

We stopped at a pair of carved double doors. "This is Lady Davina's apartment."

I swallowed a hard lump in my throat. I looked up at him. Deep in his eyes there was a flicker of warmth that seemed to offer encouragement. Here was someone who had known about my existence for years. Undoubtedly, the prospect of my arrival had distressed him because of the unhappiness it would bring to the family he served. He cared for Loretta. That was plain to see.

"I'm sorry," I said. "I shouldn't have come."

"It's a little late for that." His eyes shuttered again and the warmth was gone.

Briskly, he knocked upon a gold-embossed door. At a muffled order to enter, he turned the knob, stepped back, and waited for me to precede him through the doorway.

Chapter Four

We entered a sitting room which was more like a long, wide audience hall. It was large enough to have engulfed three rooms of the cottage I had left in England. I could visualize petitioners lined up against the walls, waiting for permission to make royal presentation.

Gigantic Flemish tapestries and scores of portraits hung by long gold cords and were mounted on the wall in a dramatic display like that of a gallery. A wide, thick carpet ran from the doorway to a white marble fireplace at the far end of the room.

Sean put a guiding hand at my elbow and we moved forward like two subjects about to be presented at court. Dark walnut Renaissance-style furniture edged the walls, and less heavy French-style chairs and brocade settees were grouped in islands down the center of the room.

My nervous glance traveled up to a high embossed ceiling where painted French pastoral scenes looked down upon our heads as we passed under them. Muted light came through mullioned windows heavily swathed in velvet lambrequins thrown over gilded wooden poles. Lace curtains drawn back very low were gathered at the level of dark baseboards. A myriad of candle sconces on the walls did not dispel shadows lurking in the corners. Despite the elaborate furnishings, there was an echoing emptiness in the large chamber.

We passed open double doors about midway and I glimpsed an adjoining bedroom with a regal canopy bed that would have been appropriate for young Queen Victoria. My heartbeat quickened, my mouth was void of moisture, and once more I stilled an impulse to turn and flee. The surroundings would have been overwhelming under any circumstances; in my present situation, the grandeur was paralyzing.

Sean must have felt my trembling, for his guiding touch on my arm tightened in what I chose to interpret as a reassuring squeeze.

I gave him a grateful smile. I was an emotional beggar, willing to accept support however tenuous.

We approached a deep marble fireplace rising to the ceiling, framed by inlays of hunting figures carved in wide panels of dark wood. In contrast to the mammoth room and its furnishings, a short, squatty woman dressed in black sat in a high-backed chair in front of a glowing fire.

A large gray dog with pointed ears lay at her feet. He raised his head and growled at our approach but she touched his arched head and he quieted. Her measuring glance swept over me.

Sean stepped forward. "Lady Davina, may I present Aileen O'Connor Lynhurst," he said in a measured tone and with a polite bow.

I made a modest curtsey. "My pleasure, Your Ladyship."

Without a change in her stiff position, Lady Davina said evenly, "It is not *my* pleasure, I assure you." Her voice was deep and cutting. "My husband's past unfortunate indiscretion is of no interest to me. Nor do I intend to press a leech to the bosom of our family because of it."

My breath was swept away by her vindictive attack. I saw that she was a plain woman, thickly built, with mousey-brown hair styled in an elaborate coiffure with false hairpieces on the top of her head to give

56

her height. Her high-necked, black silk gown gave her shallow complexion a yellowing tinge and unlike her daughter's red-rimmed eyes, Lady Davina's face showed no outward sign of mourning. Her piercing black eyes were unsmiling and cold, and I knew that any hope I had for an understanding with Her Ladyship was misguided.

Common courtesy demanded a more civilized greeting even under these strained circumstances. Anger sluiced through me and dispelled the shock her vitriolic greeting had given me.

"My purpose in coming was to meet my father," I said crisply. "Now that he is dead, I will be returning to England. I assure you that I want nothing from his family that is not freely given."

"And I can assure you," she said with deliberate emphasis on the last word, "That you will not profit a farthing from this household. How dare you presume to intrude upon us? Especially at a time like this?"

"The unfortunate timing was not of my making. I experienced many delays in my journey or I would have been here in time to see my father alive."

"Then God is merciful, even in this tragedy. We are spared the humiliation of having His Lordship thrust his bastard child upon us. I will not suffer your presence in our household as a reminder of the humiliation he inflicted upon us. I was not even aware of your existence all these years."

I thought I saw her lip quiver. *She is hurt, terribly hurt.* A little of my anger subsided. "I can understand your position, Lady Davina, and I do not wish to embarrass you in any way. I cannot but wonder why you summoned me to the castle at all."

"Because I wanted to see you. Do you resemble your mother?" she asked abruptly. *Could raw jealousy lie under her attitude?* She was not an attractive woman, far from it. Her short, thick build matched a broad nose and wide jaw. Nothing about her was soft

57

and petite, as my mother had been. I scarcely knew what to say.

"May I sit down?" I asked boldly, for she had kept me standing like a truant in front of her.

She had the grace to blush as she nodded toward another high-backed chair placed nearby.

"Was your mother fair?" she demanded, her gaze glancing off the pale yellow coils of my hair protruding under my bonnet.

"No, my mother's hair was dark as raven wings, but I'm told her features are mine. My tall, slender build must come from Father," I said boldly.

Sean had remained at my side during this exchange and now he leaned against the mantel of the fireplace as he surveyed the two of us facing each other like adversaries. His expression was bland and I wondered what he was thinking about this confrontation. I wished Lady Davina would ask him to leave. I saw no reason for him to be privy to the conversation between me and my father's widow. I sent him a look that said as much, but his mouth curved slightly in response and he stayed where he was.

Lady Davina seemed unaware of his presence as she continued to ask me questions about my mother. Her earlier statement that she had no interest in her husband's unfortunate indiscretion seemed untrue. She would not let the subject of my mother go. I could see that she was comparing herself to the young Irish girl who had captured her husband's heart before they were married. I didn't want to hurt her by comparing her plain, unattractive features and figure with the natural beauty that had been my mother's. This stiff, drab woman had none of my mother's sparkle and spontaneous joy. I wondered how my father could have married her and then I remembered what Sean had said in the carriage: titled Englishmen married to carry out traditions.

"My husband kept this romantic alliance from me

58

all these years," she said in a caustic tone as if I were somehow responsible for this outrage.

"And my mother from me," I countered. "I knew nothing about my true parentage until a few months ago. I didn't know that she had written to Lord Lynhurst, nor sent him a miniature of me. On my mother's deathbed, I promised that I would do as she wished and come to Ireland."

"Better that you had stayed in England. Why anyone would want to come to this godforsaken country, I don't know," she said abruptly. "I've hated it since the moment I came here as a bride and stepped upon its muddy soil. His Lordship would never allow me to go back home." I was startled to see her expression tinged with something akin to homesickness.

"Surely, for a visit?" I asked.

"Never. His Lordship went over many times but I was never included in the visit." She glared at me as if my mother or I had been at fault for this omission. "Now, I see why. He did not want me to know of his continued dalliance."

I drew myself up. "You are mistaken. My mother *never* saw His Lordship after he was married to you. It's true that he supported us with a monthly stipend all these years—but nothing more. I never knew until a few months ago that my father was not dead, as she had always told me."

"And we never knew of your existence. How much better it would have been for everyone if your mother's secret had died with her."

"I heartily agree!"

She seemed taken back by my vehement reply.

Sean straightened up and cleared his throat. "I'm afraid such wishful thinking is folly, ladies. As His Lordship's solicitor, I was privy to his secret and I have been responsible for maintaining the financial support of his daughter and arranging for her education."

My eyes widened. *This man knew all about me!* My enrollment in a private young ladies' school had been his doing! Undoubtedly, he received reports of my grades and progress the two years I attended. If I had done badly, he would have known it. Thank God, I had distinguished myself with excellent evaluations from the schoolmistress upon my graduation. I was appalled that the bills for my daily living had passed through his hands. He had an intimate knowledge of my life and I hadn't even known of his existence.

"I am disappointed in you, Sean," Lady Davina chided him but her tone lacked the caustic edge that she had used on me. "How could you be a party to bringing her to Ireland?"

"I assure you, Your Ladyship, the news of her impending arrival was a shock to me as well. However, the true circumstances of her existence would have all come out at Lord Lynhurst's death, in any case."

"What do you mean?" asked Lady Davina. Her pudgy lips trembled. The heavily ringed hands she clasped in her lap tightened so fiercely that her knuckles whitened.

"Your husband's last will and testament will not be read until after the funeral, but I can tell you now that His Lordship made provision for his illegitimate daughter, Aileen O'Connor Lynhurst."

I gasped and Sean shot me a warning. He obviously wanted to control the conversation. My thoughts were so confused by this new revelation that I doubted I could put them in any sensible order. *I was mentioned in my father's will.* Surely that meant I would have the means to return home. A heavy weight rolled off me. If His Lordship had continued the monthly stipend, I could find a modest dwelling away from the reaches of my stepfather and live quite comfortably. Gratitude swelled up in me. I should have never doubted his love for my mother—and for me.

"I don't believe it!" protested Lady Davina. "After all these years of keeping me financially destitute and completely dependent upon his parsimonious greed, he made a bequest to *her?*"

"Yes, my lady."

Lady Davina's mouth curved in an ugly smile. "So even in death, he imposes his will upon us. In life, he controlled every breath we drew. I should have expected as much. My domineering husband was a devil to the end." As she condemned her late husband, I saw a bitter woman who had been forced to spend her life in a country which she hated, among people she neither understood nor liked. "And what about me? Did he remember his faithful wife generously?" Lady Davina's tone was edged in sarcasm.

"He left his estate to Lawrence. Your son inherits everything."

"Which leaves me without income."

Sean nodded. "There is no provision for you unless you remain at Lynhurst Castle." He turned to me. "The same stipulation is made concerning your bequest, Miss Lynhurst."

"What do you mean?" There must be some mistake. I must have misunderstood Sean. My father's bequest would surely see me home safely again and provide substance while I found a way to sustain myself. The leaden weight in my stomach lurched back.

"Your needs will be provided for, as long as you remain under this roof."

"Remain under this roof?" I echoed.

"Yes."

"But that's impossible! I want to return to England." A magistrate's sentence could not have been more repugnant to me. Stay here? In this horrible castle filled with insidious hate? The very walls reeked of dark broodings and murder. "No, I can't."

He shrugged. "That's your choice, of course."

61

I hated him then. He knew I had no choice. Without money I was trapped.

Lady Davina gave a bitter, hysterical laugh. "My husband is dead and yet none of us is free of him. Not even you, Sean. He bought you when you were just a lad. He's always controlled your life and you'll never get free. Not now. Not ever."

"We'll see," he said coldly.

From his expression, I knew that Sean Creighton's future had also been tied to Lynhurst Castle. What had my father done to all of us? What was it Sean had said in the carriage about my father's possessions? Did he really own people? In life—and in death? It was as if his presence were here in the room with us. He had set in place an arrangement of hate and rancor which was like an ugly miasma surrounding all of us.

"His Lordship intended that Miss Lynhurst remain here," Sean said in a firm tone. I judged from his expression that he found the dictate as abhorrent as his mistress did.

Lady Davina glared at me. "I don't care what my late husband intended. I will *not* suffer your presence in my home."

"And I have no intention of remaining . . . any longer than necessary." I didn't know what else to say. Pride kept me from confessing my impoverished state. For the moment I had no choice but to suffer the degradation of forcing her hospitality.

"An hour is a moment too long," she countered.

Sean cleared his voice. "His Lordship has acknowledged Aileen as his daughter and she is within her legal right to stay here as long as she wishes, Lady Davina. As trustee of the will, I must see that his wishes are carried out."

"Then, I demand that she stay out of my sight! I won't take any more, I won't."

Her eyes glowed with red heat and I suddenly wondered if she could have been the one to slice her husband's throat. Maybe she had thought his will would provide a means of escape for her, I speculated. The malevolence in her glare was wild and I was suddenly frightened. It was plain she hated and resented me and my mother. Undoubtedly Lady Davina blamed us for her unhappy marriage and the fact that my father had kept her at Lynhurst even though she despised the country. Just looking at me fueled her rancor and I was a target for her hatred.

I rose to my feet. "I will not impose upon your privacy."

"And you are not to show yourself at the funeral."

"Your Ladyship—" began Sean but she cut him off with a wave of her hand. "I will not have her parading herself in front of everyone. Bringing shame and embarrassment upon us."

"Whatever you wish, Lady Davina," I said quickly. I could understand her feelings. "I will not attend the services."

Her mouth tightened in an ugly line. "Nor be seen by guests who will be staying here."

"You can't impose such restrictions upon her," protested Sean.

"I can . . . and I do! This is my home. She may well wish she'd never set foot inside of it." Lady Davina lurched to her feet and the dog growled. "Now go!" She thrust out her arm and pointed a finger which trembled with rage.

"Good day." With my head held high, I swept across the long room toward the door, filled with a desperate urgency to escape the woman's venomous presence. Sean said something quietly to her and then followed me into the hall.

Once out in the hall, my eyes filled with tears and my whole body started shaking.

"Here, now." Sean put a steady hand on my shoulder. "The worst is over. Lady Davina isn't as fierce as she sounds."

"Thank heavens . . . or I'd be drawn and quartered by now," I said. I straightened up and he dropped his hand. I said as firmly as I could, "I have nowhere to go at the moment . . . and no money."

"I know," he said with infuriating bluntness.

"How—" I began and then stopped. Of course, he would know. He was privy to every pound that had passed through my hands.

"I can probably guess how much money you have left after your journey."

"Then you know that I cannot afford to lodge at the Seaward." I wasn't going to give him the satisfaction of knowing how his insight into my affairs rankled me.

"I wouldn't let you go back to that place, in any case," he pronounced in an authoritative tone that irritated me.

"I appreciate your concern," I said sarcastically, "but I'm perfectly capable of taking care of myself."

"I doubt it," he said flatly. "That Mike Ryan is a mean one. Too bad Molly is stuck with such a scoundrel."

I remembered the hatred in Mike Ryan's eyes and I knew I couldn't go back there.

He pulled on a bell cord hanging on the wall. "You'll be needing a good rest from your journey."

Almost immediately a female servant appeared from the end of the hall. A large Irishwoman with gray hair tucked under a white cap walked toward us with a firm gait. A large bosom and wide hips strained at the seams of her bombazine black dress.

"Rosa, will you kindly take Miss Lynhurst to one of the guest rooms."

"There's only the third floor rooms left, sir. Her Ladyship has ordered the others laid out for people coming for the funeral."

"I don't care what Her Ladyship ordered," flashed

64

Sean. "See to it Miss Lynhurst has one of the large guest rooms."

"No," I protested. "I'd rather not be in the midst of things. The third floor will be fine." I smiled at the servant.

I couldn't read her expression. Friendly? Or hostile? Suddenly I was too tired to fight against the loneliness, bewilderment, and fright that engulfed me. "I just want to retire."

"All right." Sean nodded. "We'll work out different accommodations after the funeral tomorrow."

I started to follow Rosa down the hall.

"Aileen?"

I turned around, surprised at the intimate use of my first name.

"Welcome to Lynhurst Castle."

I couldn't tell if he was being facetious or sincere. "Thank you," I said in a neutral tone. My gaze lingered on his face for a moment, and I was disappointed that no smile appeared there. He didn't want me here any more than anyone else did.

Straightening my shoulders, I followed Rosa down the long corridor. Despite her bulk, she was light on her feet and moved noiselessly on the tiled floors. I wondered how long she had been a personal maid to the ladies of Castle Lynhurst and if she also hated the English.

After climbing the stairs to an upper floor and making many twists and turns along several corridors, the servant stopped at a door and turned the brass knob. The door swung open silently on its hinges and Rosa waited for me to precede her.

I hesitated to enter the room. Some inner voice warned me that I was making a great mistake in staying even one night under this roof. No sounds except the impatient rustle of the servant's skirt reached my ears. The room was an isolated one, away from everything and everyone as far as I could tell.

Would Rosa turn the key in the lock once I was inside? The Irishwoman's unsmiling face held no hint of her thoughts.

At that moment, I heard a heavy tread on a back staircase. A manservant lumbered into view carrying my trunk. The sight of this familiar, scarred luggage strangely reassured me. It was like an old friend. In my state of impoverished courage, I foolishly chose to accept its presence as a sign that I was a welcome guest, after all.

I entered the chamber. The air was stale but the room was tidy and clean. The man deposited my trunk and left. Rosa quickly lighted a peat fire that had been laid in the fireplace. Whorls of smoke drifted up the blackened chimney and out into the room.

The room was a pleasant size, overlooking the steep drop-off to the Sea Wall Road and the cliffs below. A somber tapestry covered one wall depicting a hunting scene with a slain deer and a hunter on a prancing horse. The subject was not one to soothe the nerves. I wished the huge, dark walnut bed had been placed in a different position so I wouldn't have to lie there and look at the slain animal morning and night.

Two high mullioned windows and a door which opened onto a small balcony allowed soft, misty light into the room. Forest-green damask draperies framed the windows. Bed hangings of the same deep shade draped the bed. The dark color and stiffness of fabric added to the heavy, somber atmosphere in the room.

Rosa opened the door to a small water closet and laid out towels on a marble washstand. "Would ye be wanting me to unpack, Miss?"

She had waited silently as my gaze swept the room, watching me with shuttered dark eyes that revealed nothing.

"No, thank you." The idea of someone else handling my well-worn dresses, undergarments, and personal effects was too embarrassing to contemplate. Besides, I hoped I wouldn't be here long enough to put anything away. A building urgency to leave as quickly as possible sluiced through me, and although I had no idea how to accomplish it, the need to free myself from this impossible situation was uppermost in my mind.

"A cup of tea, perhaps and some refreshment?"

"Yes, thank you," I said quickly, more to please her than to appease my appetite; though I had not yet had a noonday meal and the bowl of gruel Molly had given me that morning was long gone.

I sat down in a chair near the fire and coaxed it along with a blackened poker as something to do with my hands while my thoughts whirled. From the moment I had looked into the mirror and had seen Sean Creighton's face reflected with mine, the world had gyrated like a lopsided top. He had filled my senses in some indefinable way that diminished rational thought. I had never been so peculiarly taken with a man before. How could I possibly be attracted to one whose smile mocked me and who coldly performed his duties in a detached, almost abrasive manner?

And yet, the memory of his tingling touch upon my arm as he led me upstairs mocked an upheaval in my mental and emotional equilibrium. I didn't want to think about the way he had stroked the sobbing Lorrie and held her close. The tenderness in his eyes as he comforted the young woman was a sharp contrast to the distant, narrowed looks he had given me. His behavior seemed to point up the disdain that had bubbled under the surface as he carried out his duties. Sean Creighton had disliked me before he met me. It was obvious he had not agreed with Lord Lynhurst about acknowledging me to the family. Like the others, he did not want me here. I sat there in the chair and hugged myself, blinking rapidly against a fullness in my eyes.

Rosa returned with the tea and I continued to sit in the chair while I ate. The aromatic, robust tea eased warmth into my leaden limbs. I was glad she had brought me a pot kept warm by a crocheted cozy. Freshly baked scones, cuts of cured ham, and a bowl of sugared berries were too tempting to be ignored. I ate heartily and felt much better. Food always had a recuperative power for me and the tension began to ease from my body.

I realized that I had not yet taken off my bonnet nor my cape. I walked over to a huge wardrobe that could have held twenty times over the dresses I owned. My cape looked pathetic hanging alone in it.

I walked around the room, touching the rest of the furnishings and emptying the contents of my trunk. A lady's dressing table had been cleverly divided into compartments for articles of the toilette. I placed my beaded reticule in one and wondered how many fashionable women had sat on this cabriole-legged stool and applied rice powder to their noses. My tortoise-shell brush and comb looked out of place laid out below the beveled mirror.

A pitcher of warm water stood on a washstand and I poured some into a porcelain basin and bathed my face. An oyster-white towel smelled of fresh air and a hint of tansy and I lightly dabbed my face with it. Refreshed, I pushed open the arched door leading out onto the balcony.

The sea was an ever-moving cauldron of white combs beating against saw-toothed rocks rimming the coastline. A smell of salt and kelp tingled my nostrils as I leaned against the wrought-iron railing. I watched a sea gull as it rose and fell in the wind and listened to its melancholy cry. My hearing quickened as a rising breeze brought the sound of horse hooves up from below.

Two riders came into view and I saw Lorrie on a sorrel horse beside Sean's gray steed as they rode away from the castle. My half-sister wore a black habit and a small feathered hat with a black veil thrown back from her face. Her face was animated and she laughed at Sean as she kicked her sleek sorrel mare into a gallop. He called something after and urged his horse into a run. In the next moment they were gone.

I returned to my bedroom, leaning up against the balcony door as I shut it. More than ever the somber bedroom weighted down my spirits. Firmly I took hold of my thoughts. For the moment, I must accept my situation. I had no money to go elsewhere, and until I could figure out some means of getting funds, I had to remain here. Maybe Sean would make me a loan just to get me out of the way. Or Lorrie? Or maybe even my half-brother who had inherited the estate. I wondered if he felt the same ill will toward me.

I stretched across the bed and closed my eyes against the heavy green hangings and the tapestry of the dying deer felled by the dark-haired hunter. Fatigue mingled with despondency until my thoughts finally found surcease and I slept.

When I awoke, twilight had mingled with the shadows of the room and I quickly lit a three-candle candelabra which stood on a small table beside the bed. I was trying to decide if I should pull the bell for my evening meal when there was a knock at the door.

A young kitchen maid came in carrying a dinner tray. She placed it on a round table flanked by two high-backed chairs. "Will that be all, Miss?"

The girl was a pretty Irish lass, probably no more than thirteen. The isolation Lady Davina had imposed upon me was as real as a locked door. I wanted to ask the girl to stay and talk with me for a while but I nodded and said, "Yes, thank you."

She turned and fled as if I were ready to cast some kind of spell on her.

I had little appetite for the slices of roasted lamb,

boiled potatoes, and pickled greens and only drank the strong tea and ate a slice of bread. I thought about Molly's warm kitchen and her children scooting about, laughing and chattering. She had been my friend until Sean came. Now she thought I belonged at Lynhurst castle. *Belonged!* I laughed bitterly at that.

The dreary evening dragged on. I sat slumped in front of the fire, listless and dejected. Finally I made ready for bed and climbed under the goose-down covers. Tomorrow, I would make some plans, I told myself. I would take control. This mental declaration seemed to help. I blew out the candles and gave myself up to sleep.

It must have been nearly two in the morning when I awoke in a cold sweat. At first I didn't know whether it had been a dream or something else that had brought me sitting straight up in bed. Then I heard the sounds again, like creatures wailing in pain. The cries seemed to come from the very walls of my room. Horrible strangling noises. Macabre whispers. Rising and falling, chilling my blood.

My fingers fumbled with a match to light my candles but I tipped over the candelabra before I could light it. A spine-chilling wail echoed from ceiling to wall. The creature was in the room with me!

I screamed and bolted out the balcony door which was the closest exit, slamming it behind me. The wind whipped my loosened hair and molded my nightdress against me, but I could no longer hear the weird sounds. The ocean's surf rolled in high combers and the night sky was low with darkening clouds. I tried to scream but my breath was driven back down my throat. In the cacophony of wind, ocean, and rain, my feeble cries were lost.

Suddenly, the rain came down like an open spigot. I jerked open the balcony door, intending to run through my room as fast as I could to the corridor door. Once I stepped inside my room, I realized that the macabre noise was gone. Raindrops beating against the castle walls and windows were the only sounds.

Had I really heard those strangling cries? Had I been engulfed in a nightmare that had extended beyond the sleeping stage? Shivering and drenched, I dried myself and changed to another of my linsey-woolsey nightgowns. I climbed back into bed and held the covers tightly around my neck. My eyes were wide open, and every muscle tensed as I waited for the night whispers to begin again.

Chapter Five

I fell asleep at dawn, only to awaken about mid-morning to the sound of a mournful drumbeat. For a moment I was disoriented. I sat up and stared at the hunting tapestry and then threw back the covers. Barefooted, I hurried to a window.

Below, in the front courtyard, Lord Lynhurst's funeral procession was just leaving the castle. Six dark horses with black plumes on their heads tossed their harness as they drew a hearse down the twisting road. The sky was dark and overcast, the weather misty and dreary. Truly, a day in harmony with funereal drapings, I thought as I watched carriages, horseback riders, and lines of plodding servants and villagers follow a long, black wagon taking Lord Edwin Lynhurst to his final resting place.

In one of the black-draped carriages, I glimpsed Lady Davina's profile and that of Sean, Loretta and a young man I assumed must be my half-brother, Lawrence. They were going to bury a man I'd never known but whose blood ran in my veins. My religious training had been Anglican, so I said a familiar English prayer for the soul of my father as I watched the procession pass out of sight.

Even though I had never known him, Lord Lynhurst had acknowledged me in the end and in some sense I felt that I had betrayed him by not insisting that I be included in the funeral services. Had I betrayed my mother, also? Should I have insisted on representing her at the burial? No, I didn't think so. My mother had not intruded upon his family when she was alive; and now she had gone to her rest and so had the man she had loved. They were beyond any declaration I might make by being present on this solemn occasion.

I could sympathize with Lady Davina's position. Not wanting to acknowledge an illegitimate child of her husband's under these circumstances was understandable. No doubt Loretta would have made another scene, adding to the embarrassment of all. It was better that I remain in my room while my father was taken to the churchyard for burial.

What if I had arrived a day earlier? I shoved the speculation aside. Wishful thinking was a coward's way out. The real situation was the one with which I must deal.

I turned away from the window and performed my morning ablutions and finished unpacking the few things left in my trunk. My wardrobe was simple, three modest day dresses and two Sunday gowns. My mother had edged my undergarments and the sight of her handiwork on a camisole and petticoat brought a fullness to my eyes as I slipped the garments over my head. In deference to my father's death, I chose a dark black and gray wool dress I had worn to my mother's funeral.

After placing a few favorite books on the bedside table and my basket of handwork by the fireplace chair, I was soon finished unpacking. My limited possessions mocked my determination to make a temporary place for myself at Lynhurst Castle. These opulent surroundings only highlighted my impoverished state. It would have been better if I had been given accommodations in the servants' quarters, I thought, and then remembered the austere butler, Dolan, and Rosa's guarded hostility and changed my mind. No, my dubious family position put me in isolation between the two social groups. I firmed my chin. I had no choice but to make the best of it. For the present I had found shelter and a means of survival. Nothing, not even weird creatures who wailed in the night, was going to drive me away until I had found a means to return to England.

I had just finished dressing when the same young maid who had brought my dinner the night before timidly knocked and asked if I would like a breakfast tray.

"Yes, thank you." Then I asked with a smile. "What's your name?"

"Callie, mum," she answered with an Irish lilt. She was about the age of Kerrie, I guessed. Not as pretty as Molly's daughter, but there wasn't any hostility in her young gaze, only nervous fright. The class barrier between the Lynhurst family and their Irish servants was obvious. Only Sean seemed to have bridged the gap. I found I did not want to think about him.

"I just saw the procession leave," I said in way of conversation, desperately needing human contact.

"Yes, mum." She crossed herself. " 'Tis early I went to church and said a Pater and Ave for the master. Sure, and the Lord won't be minding a few Paddy prayers to go along with the English ones."

"I know His Lordship would appreciate your praying for him, Callie." Secretly, I wondered how Lord Lynhurst had felt about Irish Catholicism. The English had been trying to convert the heathen to the Church of England since the first Protestant stepped upon the land. Maybe my father had been no exception.

"His Lordship was always one for letting us celebrate our saint days."

"He was a good master then?" I asked, shamelessly grasping for an understanding of the man who had fathered me.

For a moment, Callie's brown eyes flickered over

74

my face, and then instantly shuttered. "Yes, ma'am," she murmured but there was no conviction in her tone.

"Lord Lynhurst was my father—but I never knew him."

No expression of surprise shown on Callie's face. I realized then that my identity was already known to the servants and probably everything else that had happened. The servant, Rosa, had appeared so quickly after I left Lady Davina's room that I suspected she had been nearby, gleaning every word we spoke. There had been a door in the lavish bedroom which probably opened into the hall near the spot where she had appeared.

Impulsively, I decided I might as well provide the gossipers with some accurate information. I didn't want Lady Davina's vile accusations to go unchallenged. "My mother was Irish and her parents went to England before she was born. My name is O'Connor, a good Irish name, is it not?"

Callie gave me a hesitant nod and I thought there was less tension in her slim shoulders. Her gaze flickered over my blond hair and blue eyes and I knew she was noting my fair coloring, a clear stamp of my English blood.

"My mother died two months ago. On her deathbed, she made me promise that I would come to Ireland. Only I arrived too late . . ." My voice caught in spite of myself.

"I'm sorry, mum. 'Twas a terrible thing . . . him dying in his own doorway."

"I don't understand, Callie. Why did someone want my father dead?" My eyes were suddenly tearful and I reached for the handkerchief in my pocket.

" 'Tis said His Lordship had agreed to send armed men to collect the Tithe Tax," the girl said in a hushed voice. "That's why the Watcher's spirit rested uneasy in his watery grave and he came back." Her rounded eyes held a warning. "Sure, I hope no harm comes to ye."

"Why should I be in danger?"

"Because the Watcher's here . . . amongst us!"

I did not want to challenge her belief in ghosts. "I heard strange noises last night and—" I broke off as I saw pure horror on her face. "I'm sure it was nothing but the ocean and the wind," I lied. Frightening this young girl would not help anything.

Her rounded eyes fled around the room. "Will that be all, mum?" she asked nervously.

I nodded and she darted out of the door as if a ghost were about to grab her by the apron strings.

I ate my breakfast mechanically. No, I did not believe in ghosts. The eerie sounds that had sent me out into the rain had been real. Was someone bent on frightening me away? If so, they would find me of stronger heart than they had hoped. I was not running away, not because I wanted to prove how brave I was, but because I had no place to run.

By the time I had finished eating, the sun had broken through the night's rain clouds and the sight of sunshine brightened my spirits—and my courage. I knew that the family and guests would be away for a couple of hours at church and burial services. It was my chance to escape from my room without breaking my promise to Lady Davina that I would stay out of sight. I had given in to her insistence that I not show myself at the funeral services, but by allowing myself to be intimidated and ostracized, I had somehow disgraced the memory of both my father and mother.

I threw a shawl over my head and shoulders and peered out into the hall. I had not paid any attention where I was going when I traversed the halls with Sean nor when Rosa had shown me to my room. Retracing my steps would be impossible but I felt confident that I would eventually find my way down to the lower floors. When I came to a narrow staircase plunging downward, I realized it was not the wide curving staircase I remembered, but I let my hand trail upon the banister as I descended.

I had just reached a ground floor landing when a hand reached out and stopped me. I screamed as I jerked away.

The butler who had let us in yesterday filled up a doorway that I had not noticed in passing. Surprise flickered on his face and then hardened into disapproval.

"My apologies, Miss. I thought you were one of the servant girls. The family does not use this staircase." His hairy hand dropped to his side. An expression of servitude coated his face. "May I be of help?" The formal English speech seemed incongruous with his Irish countenance and name.

My reaction was mixed. Dolan had frightened me, but in a way I was pleased that he thought of me as one of the family. I would have hated to be a servant girl under his cutting gaze.

"I was looking for an exit to the garden," I said evenly. "I wanted some air before the mourners returned."

"Yes, ma'am. This way, please." Dolan turned a brawny back on me and led me though a labyrinth of halls to an outside door. As we walked I wondered why he wasn't at the funeral services. Surely, he was the servant at the top of the hierarchy.

"Thank you, Dolan. It's a sad day, isn't it?" I commented, watching his face.

"Yes, ma'am."

"You have been with the family a long time?" I made the statement a question.

"Since Lord Lynhurst and Her Ladyship married . . . nearly nineteen years ago." His formal speech had only a hint of an Irish brogue but his heritage could not be denied. It seemed to me that all of Ireland must have those brooding dark eyes and dogged chins.

"I wish I could have known him," I said impulsively.

"Always fair to those who deserved it."

The clipped response seemed sincere. *And to those who didn't?* The unspoken thought came unbidden, like the dart of jagged shadow. "But someone hated him. Do you think it was the Watcher ghost, Dolan?"

His jaw worked. "No, Miss."

"Then who?" I knew I was pushing him but I couldn't help it. I had to know who had wanted my father dead.

"I don't know." I thought that was the only answer I was going to get but suddenly he stopped and looked me straight in the eye. "No one knocked at the door that night. I would have heard the summons. Besides, His Lordship would never answer the door."

"Maybe he was going out and the murderer waited outside for him?"

Once more, the butler shook his head. "My lord was not going out."

"How can you be sure?"

"He never asked for his wraps that night. They were still in the hall." Dolan's eyes narrowed. "And the way his body was sprawled, he was attacked from behind."

"Someone in the house?"

Dolan's eyes were suddenly pinpoints of steel. "No outsider did the foul deed."

The skin on the back of my neck prickled. Callie had said, *The Watcher is here—amongst us*. But Dolan did not believe it was a ghost. "But who could it be? And why?"

"His Lordship was murdered by someone in the castle who masks himself. I would take care if I were you. There are unfriendly forces at work here. Maybe you've felt them, Miss Lynhurst?" His eyes narrowed.

For a moment I wondered if Dolan could have been

responsible for the night whispers that had frightened me. Was he also trying to drive me away?

"My name is O'Connor," I corrected him.

"No matter. You are a member of the family." His jaw was firm as he held the door open for me.

His ominous tone stayed with me as I left the house and descended wide steps leading to a stone walk flanked by grass and shrubbery.

The front of Lynhurst Castle had been built close to the descending ocean cliff. In contrast, cultivated grounds in the back and at the side of the castle spread away in wide expanses of trees and lush grass. A formal English garden had been transplanted to Irish soil, complete with precisely clipped hedges forming geometric patterns.

Pulling my cape hood over my head, I strolled along smooth, well-defined paths, passing Greek statuary and marble benches placed near flowerbeds and sparkling fountains. Ireland's moist climate encouraged rampant greenery which had been carefully controlled and artfully adapted to the precise patterns of English landscaping. Wide expanses of green lawn sloped to a small lake. A delightful spot for a summer picnic, I thought, if the heavy clouds pregnant with rain ever cleared and allowed the sun to shine. Was there warmth anywhere in this country? Certainly not inside the castle. This musing brought my thoughts back to Dolan's conviction that my father's murderer had been inside the castle, and not outside, when he wielded a throat-slashing knife.

Dolan's dire speculations made me consider the people I had already met at the castle: Sean Creighton, Lady Davina, my half-sister, Rosa, Callie, and Dolan. My half-brother who had inherited the estate was still unknown to me. I hoped that he would not be a part of the rancor and hatred which seemed imbedded in Lynhurst Castle. Any one of the family could have wished my father dead for personal reasons. The Irish servants could have as well, if their master was about to enforce the hated Tithe Tax, which demanded that they support the Anglican Church when they were Catholic through and through.

The animosity I had experienced was not confined to Lynhurst Castle. Despite Dolan's conviction that it was someone inside the house, I had seen the malevolence in Mike Ryan's eyes and Daddo's hushed talk of the Bog Boys. I couldn't dismiss the real possibility that factions outside the family could have plotted and carried out my father's death.

Speculation filled my head as I walked a short distance around the lake and then back to the castle again. The gardens and grounds were like the inside of the castle—too large, too open to provide any feeling of private contentment. I felt as lost outside as in. When a bricked-in garden caught my eye, I impulsively lifted the latch on the gate and let myself through it into a well-kept kitchen garden. My heart lightened at the sight of neat rows of vegetables, pruned vines, and fruit trees. My mother and I had kept such a garden for years. A familiar fragrance of mixed herbs teased my nostrils with a welcome.

A garden maid was hoeing a stand of corn with sharp, quick motions. She glanced in my direction as I walked down the path toward her.

"Good morning."

"Mornin'," she responded without interrupting the rhythmic swing of her hoe. Her muscular shoulders and arms were evidence of the hard work she had put into the garden.

I asked her a few questions and found out that her name was Willa and that she was Rosa's younger sister. Dull dark hair was covered by a kerchief, and a coarse brown dress and full apron draped her solid figure. Her high-top, thick shoes were caked with mud and the gloves she wore were black with grime.

"Nice garden," I declared with a smile. I looked about and made complimentary remarks about the state of the climbing peas and feathery carrots.

She nodded her head as if I had only given her her due. She only responded to my remarks or questions with a nod or shake of her head.

Not wanting to disturb her, I continued my stroll and delighted in the wonderful variety of vegetables and berry fruits.

Willa glanced in my direction from time to time and when I reached down and pinched a few leaves of peppermint, she frowned.

I held the leaves to my nostrils, and the familiar sharp smell brought back memories of the iced tea and sugar cakes my mother and I frequently enjoyed in our garden. A spur of grief that I feared would never fade brought tears into my eyes. I gave them a brush with my gloved hand and I noticed that Willa was watching me.

I walked toward her, holding the twig in my hand. "We had a patch of peppermint at home," I explained quickly, embarrassed to be caught with my emotions on my sleeve. "Forgive me for picking some."

"No matter," she said with a shrug of her shoulders. She was not as coldly reserved as her sister but not a fountain of friendliness either.

I bade her "Good day" and left the garden, taking the sprig of peppermint with me.

Once inside the castle again, I found myself completely lost in the never-ending corridors and staircases. I had always prided myself on an acute sense of direction and could usually form correct bearings in my mind, but once I became disoriented, my stubborn mind refused to make any corrections. Because I had been so distraught when Sean took me upstairs to Lady Davina's room, I had not paid any attention to the direction we had taken. When I finally met Callie in one of the halls with her arms loaded with bedding, I could have hugged her.

"I'm lost," I readily admitted.

With a chuckle, she showed me back to my room on the third floor.

My outing had improved my spirits, but when I heard the return of carriages and the bustle of mourners entering the castle, despondency descended on me again. Didn't anyone care that I was alone in this huge structure of rock and marble? Sean, perhaps?

I knew that it was foolishness to think that my father's solicitor would take any notice of me. He had only been carrying out orders when he came to the tavern to fetch me. I suspected that any further contact with me would only be the result of Sean's duties, nothing more. My father's will was the only reason he had intervened between me and Lady Davina.

I determined I wouldn't think of him any more, but like an annoying melody one would like to forget, he kept returning to my thoughts. He was an enigma. A Scotsman with an Irish grandmother, educated and employed by an English Lord. The way he had soothed Loretta and ridden off with her indicated a relationship that went beyond the boundaries of paid family solicitor. Once more I wondered if there was a romantic involvement between them.

Trying to pull my thoughts away from the quagmire of my present situation, I took out a half-finished piece of embroidery and tried to concentrate on the tiny feathered stitches. "Busy hands are happy hands" was a favorite homily of my mother's, but the thread knotted hopelessly and I tossed the stitchery away in exasperation. Usually reading my favorite book of Shelley poems had the power to soothe me, but I continually found my eyes focused blankly on the pages.

For the next hour, I paced the room, watched the ocean through the balcony windows, and then sat down in front of the dressing table. I brushed my hair until the long, fair strands snapped and gleamed. Idly fooling with it, I pinned a twist on top of my head like a coronet with only soft ringlets framing my face. The coiffure was quite a change from my usual style of parted hair pulled into a modest coil at the nape of my neck. Impulsively I pinched my cheeks and lightly bit my lips to bring a rose hue to them. Then I lightly dusted my nose with rice powder. The result made me a little self-conscious. Play-acting with my reflection in the mirror, I gave my chin a haughty tilt in the air and curled one finger in an exaggerated hand gesture. "Charmed, I'm sure, Mr. Creighton," I said in a falsetto voice.

A knock at the door brought an abrupt end to my playfulness. "Come in."

"Yer wanted in the library, mum," said Callie.

"Now?" My hands were suddenly sweaty.

"Yes, mum. I'll show ye the way. Ye'll just be gettin' yerself lost again," she chided.

I touched a nervous hand to my hair. Dare I venture out of my room with my hair in such an elaborate state?

Callie grinned, seeing my hesitation. "Ye'd best come quickly. They don't like to be kept waiting."

I couldn't tell if she was laughing at my regal coiffure or smiling in approval. "All right. Just a minute. Who wants to see me?"

"Don't know, mum. I was just told to fetch ye."

Quickly I slipped in my best pair of earrings, tiny pearl droplets that had been a gift from my father to my mother in their halcyon days. I smoothed the modest collar of my dark dress, stood up, and took a deep breath. "I'm ready."

My mind whirled with unanswered questions as I followed Callie down a twisting staircase to the main floor. Who had summoned me? Sean! My heartbeat lurched crazily and I chided myself for being such a ninny. No, not Sean. More likely Lady Davina. Was my presence under this roof such a thorn that she couldn't refrain from attacking me the day her husband had been buried? I had kept away from the funeral services as she had requested. Why would she summon me now, if not to humiliate me in some fashion?

"Comin', mum?" questioned Callie.

I had stopped on the stairs and was tempted to turn and run back to the safety of my room. Then my resolve stiffened. No, I wasn't going to let anyone know how terrified I was. I gave Callie a firm nod. "Yes, I'm coming."

When we stopped in front of a pair of closed doors, I feared my legs were too weak to carry me across the threshold. Callie knocked, opened the door and stood back, allowing me to enter.

Unconsciously, I geared myself for battle and I sailed into the large, book-lined room with my hands slightly clenched and my head elevated. My mouth was dry and a trembling made my stomach muscles jump in rigid spasms.

For a moment I paused inside the room, completely disconcerted. No Lady Davina. No Sean. An elderly, portly man rose from a black leather chair at my entrance. He smiled and nodded his nearly bald head appreciatively as he held out a plump hand in greeting.

"How do you do, my dear." A bushy gray mustache spread above his full smile. "I'm Sir Alfred Wainwright, a dear friend of your father. I insisted upon meeting you before leaving for my nearby estate. You see, I was with Lord Lynhurst at Oxford when he met your mother and very much wanted to meet their daughter."

Joy rushed through me and this unexpected emotion brought its own kind of weakness. "I'm happy to make your acquaintance." My voice trembled.

"Please sit down." He motioned to a chair facing his. "May I call you Aileen?"

"Yes, of course," I said excitedly. My dire fears of a moment ago completely disappeared. A warmth like bright sunlight bathed me as he beamed at me. "I can't believe you knew my mother."

"Not well, but I saw her with Edwin many times while we were at university." His clear blue eyes studied me. "You have your mother's features but your stature and coloring are Edwin's. I must confess that I was astounded to learn that they had had a child. In all these years, he never said a word to me. And now, here you are. A beautiful young lady. How proud Edwin would have been. And how welcome he would have made you."

"Do you think so?" I realized then how desperately I wanted this friendly gentleman to validate my presence here.

"But of course. Edwin was very much in love with your mother. If things had been different, he would have married her, you know."

"If she hadn't been Irish, you mean?" I responded testily.

"Partly that," he nodded, "but there were other considerations, too. My dear, only the peasantry are able to marry as they please. Unfortunately, responsibilities come with status. The upper classes must endure shackles which are put on at birth and last a lifetime." He sighed and then his frown eased into a smile. "And now that you are here under these sad circumstances, I must do my best to welcome you as Edwin would have done."

"And I will help you, Father." A young man with a ready smile that deepened his blue eyes came through the doorway. Fair-haired, tall, exuding a confident air, he crossed the room and smiled down at me.

"My son," said Sir Wainwright, affectionately. "Never far when there's a pretty lady about. Bryant,

85

may I present Aileen Lynhurst."

With feminine vanity, I was glad that I had swept my hair up and taken the time to put in the pearl earrings. "I'm happy to meet you," I said politely, flushing under his direct gaze.

"My pleasure, I assure you." He bowed. "And how may we make your arrival more pleasant in these dour circumstances, Miss Lynhurst?"

"Your expressions of welcome have already lifted my spirits considerably," I admitted with a smile. "It's been a long day."

"You were not at services?" questioned Sir Wainwright.

"No. Lady Davina requested that I not embarrass her with my presence." I saw no need to lie about the situation.

Sir Wainwright nodded in understanding. "I'm sure the family was as surprised as I was to hear of your existence. It will take them time to adjust, of course."

"Aileen must come to Windbriar," announced Bryant. "Our estate is only a two-hour ride from here," he informed me. "My sister, Dorthea, would be delighted for the company. And I would be only too happy to do my part to show you the countryside." His smile was openly flirtatious.

"Thank you, I . . . I really don't know what my plans are at the moment."

"Of course you don't," nodded Sir Wainwright.

Bryant sat down in a nearby chair. "Tell us about yourself." He bent his head in my direction as if nothing in the world was more important than hearing about my dull life in an English village.

I laughed, flustered by the attention of this handsome young man.

Sir Wainwright asked me for news of England. For nearly a half hour, the three of us chatted in a companionable discussion of the young queen and speculated as to how Her Highness was going to respond to

Louis Napoleon Bonaparte's latest conspiracy. They asked me about the new House of Parliament that would reportedly take ten years to complete and in a lively discussion we shared the pleasure that the City of London offered.

When Sean entered the library the mood was broken. He was obviously displeased to find me laughing and talking with these two English gentlemen. The dour atmosphere of hate and resentment came into the room with him. With childish revenge, I deliberately ignored him and smiled at Bryant, asking him about Windbriar and showing interest in accepting the invitation that had been extended me.

Sean informed Sir Wainwright that his carriage was waiting.

"We must go, then, if we are to arrive home at a decent hour," said Sir Wainwright in a regretful tone. "Lawless bandits, organized as secret societies, rove the night roads," he told me. "Our lives are in peril even on our own lands."

"Irish discontents are like locusts," said Bryant looking straight into Sean's darkening face. "They cover the land and breed."

"Maybe because they are foolish enough to think of the land as Irish soil," Sean countered.

"No matter," said Sir Wainwright, waving his hand and stilling a brewing confrontation. "Such deep problems are not going to be settled by verbal arguments."

"Nor by outlaws who have no respect for life and property," added Bryant. Then he bent his handsome head in my direction. "We shall look forward to your company at Windbriar, Aileen. Please make it soon."

Sir Wainwright added his invitation to his son's and then they took their leave.

The silence in the library after their departure was leaden. Sean stared at me and I could see his gaze traveling over my piled-high hair and dangling earrings. Unlike Bryant's flirtatious blue eyes, there was no warmth in Sean's dark ones. "You are *not* going to Windbriar," he said flatly.

Instant indignation made my tone sharp. "Is there anything in my father's will that says I can't pay a visit to neighbors?"

"It is too dangerous."

"To go . . . or to stay?" I taunted.

"You're protected here."

"Of course, I am," I retorted sarcastically. "Just as my father was protected. Dolan is convinced that someone within these walls slit his throat."

"Don't pay attention to servants' tattle. And don't let that English fop, Bryant Wainwright, turn your head."

"How dare you!" I bristled. "Who are you to criticize him in such a fashion?"

"I know what I'm talking about."

"You know everything about everything, don't you?" I replied. Why did Sean always show his brittle side to me? Why couldn't he be soft and gentle the way I had seen him with Loretta?

"I know the Wainwrights," he answered curtly. "Playing the fool with Bryant is dangerous. Don't go to Windbriar."

"The Wainwrights are the only people I have met who have offered me a warm welcome. Why should I turn my back on their offer of friendship?"

"You'll have to trust my judgment."

"And why should I? You have no authority over me. You are, after all, just an employee of my father's." The moment I said it, I wanted to drag the words back.

His glower was frightening. He moved so close to me I could feel his warm breath upon my face. "And you, my dear Aileen, had better pay some heed to this lowly servant."

"I'm sorry," I stammered. "I didn't mean that. It's

just that I'm so lonely, so scared—and you just act as if you hate me." My eyes unabashedly searched his face.

"I don't hate you." His eyes softened for a moment and his hands rested on my shoulders. I was certain he was going to lower his angry mouth upon mine. My emotions sped out of control like leaves whipped in a devil's whirlwind. I found myself leaning into him. Suddenly he dropped his hands and moved back.

Without a word, he left the room, leaving me standing there, shaken and trembling with a rush of bewildering emotions.

Chapter Six

The next few days and nights passed without incident. I did not hear the night whispers again. I kept to my room except for a brief outing each day in the kitchen garden, watching Willa work. My hope that Lady Davina would relent or that my half-brother would make a point of meeting me was only wishful thinking; no one came to my room but Callie and a cleaning maid who spoke with a heavy Gaelic accent.

My thoughts very foolishly centered on Sean. I wished that I had conducted myself differently in the library. Instead of viewing him as an adversary, I should have been grateful for any advice he offered. I knew nothing about the country nor the people who lived according to well-established rules and customs. At the very least, I could have controlled my temper and inquired in a reasonable manner why he objected to my visiting the Wainwrights.

I was nervous about seeing him again, wondering if the same bewildering attraction would be there. As the days passed and he made no effort to see me again, I decided that he was probably used to having women swoon under his touch. In my impoverished emotional state, I had given too much importance to that brief moment when his hands tightened on my shoulders. For those few suspended moments, the air had been charged like summer lightning.

I blushed to remember how I had leaned into him. How could I have been so wanton as to be disappointed when he didn't kiss me? What was the matter with me? The answer to that question was not one that I was willing to accept. But it was true. I had become an emotional beggar where Sean Creighton was concerned and I was appalled at how many times he entered my thoughts during the night and day.

Every time I traversed the halls, coming and going from my walk, I wondered if I might meet him. The possibility sent a peculiar tremor through me. Was he still angry with me for my insensitive remark? I couldn't blame him if he was. Even though I was still angry at the way he presumed to order me about, I regretted the taunt I had flung at him. I regretted behaving in such a rude manner. No wonder he was deliberately avoiding my company.

Then unexpectedly, one afternoon when I let myself out the garden gate, I turned and saw him standing only a few feet away, watching me. Warmth flushed into my cheeks and my heart began racing like a lopsided top. "Good morning," I managed in what I hoped was a neutral tone.

"Is that where you've been hiding out? In the kitchen garden?"

"I haven't been 'hiding out,' as you put it. I was told to keep myself scarce and that's what I've been doing."

"All the guests are gone now and Lady Davina is going to have to come to terms with your presence here whether she likes it or not. Join the family for dinner tonight."

"I have not been invited."

"If you wait for an invitation, you may languish in your room indefinitely. Surely, you don't intend to spend your life in the kitchen garden?" A teasing glint in his eyes brought a smile to my lips.

"I find Willa very good company. Not like some of the members of this household."

"And that includes me, of course."

The conversation was getting on dangerous ground. I didn't want to quarrel with him again. "Where is my half-brother? Why hasn't he made any effort to meet me?"

"I think you will find Lawrence Lynhurst more interested in hunting, gambling, and sporting than in making difficult decisions. He gladly leaves all unpleasantness to others."

"But surely, he doesn't intend to completely ignore me. Doesn't he know that my father intended me to remain here with the family?"

"Of course, he knows," answered Sean shortly. "But if you're waiting for Larry to offer a gracious hand of hospitality, you had best forget it. If you are to live here, you will have to make a place for yourself."

"There is nothing here for me. No family, no purpose, nothing but a means of survival. I know my father intended much more for me. Can't you bend the letter of the law and give me enough money for my return passage to England?"

"And what would you do when you arrived there?" he asked in a businesslike manner. "You have relatives, perhaps, to offer you a home?"

I blanched, thinking of my stepfather. "I could find lodgings. There are many respectable boarding-houses. I would rent a room in one of them while I looked for employment."

"And what kind of employment would that be? Household service, perhaps?"

His tone rankled me. "I would gladly go into service and fill my life with honest work, rather than remain here as an unwelcome intruder."

His smile mocked me. "I didn't think you would give up so easily. And I'm sure Lord Lynhurst didn't expect his daughter to turn tail and run away."

"He didn't expect everyone in his household to treat me like a leper, either. Will you please advance me some money?"

"No. Now, if you will excuse me, I must ride to the next county and take care of some of those unpleasant decisions I was talking about." He paused and gentled his tone. "I'm sorry, Aileen. It's not possible to break your father's will. I wrote it myself. As long as you remain here, you will have a home and all the necessities."

"What about a monthly allowance?"

"No allowance."

"In other words, I am to be kept penniless."

"Lord Lynhurst did not trust the female members of his family with any negotiable assets. I warned you about the way your father controlled his possessions."

Now I understood what Sean had meant. Lady Davina had expressed her frustration at being kept totally dependent upon her husband's good will. Now I was trapped by the same shackles.

We had been walking toward a cluster of buildings which included a stable, a huge barn, and some other smaller outbuildings clustered together. "Do you ride, Miss Lynhurst?" he asked abruptly.

"Please don't call me by that name. O'Connor is the name I have carried all my life and I much prefer you call me by it. Unless you feel comfortable with Aileen."

"All right, Aileen. Do you ride?"

"No, I don't consider myself a horsewoman."

"That situation will have to be remedied. No one can remain on Irish soil very long without learning to ride. It is almost a necessity. The muddy roads and sinking bogs make it nearly impossible to get places by coach."

I laughed in agreement. When he looked at me quizzically, I told him about some of my adventures on the road. He chuckled at the picture of me sitting under a peat-stack with buckets of rain pouring over me.

When we reached the stables, a prancing gray stallion was brought out to Sean. He took the reins from the ostler, and swung gracefully up into the saddle. His breeches fitted snugly over his firm legs and I was deeply aware of his virile masculinity as he smiled down at me. "See you at dinner?" The question was a challenge.

"Will you be back in time?"

"I'll try."

"Then I'll be there," I promised recklessly.

"Good girl." With that he kicked his mount and galloped out of the stable yard.

I heard a familiar voice. "And top of the mornin' to ye."

"Daddo!"

" 'Tis a pretty sight, ye be," cackled the little man. He was sitting on a stool with a horse's hoof in his lap, trimming away the excess.

"I didn't know you worked here."

"Here, there, and yonder. A man of many parts, I be, but when there's pretty little fishes flipping their tails at me, I can't be found at any job." He made the confession with a grin.

"I'd say that you're a wise man, Daddo." I sat down on a bale of hay. "How about telling me one of your famous stories?"

"Famous, is it now?" He peered at me. "And who be telling you that?"

"Molly's girl, Holly. She was hoping you'd come by and spin a yarn or two."

"Nice girl, Holly. And Kerrie, too, eh, Shannon?" He addressed a young boy currying a horse a few feet away.

I looked at Shannon with interest. So this was the young man causing Kerrie to put papers in her hair. He was a husky lad, with broad back, thick arms and a pleasant face that blushed at Daddo's teasing.

"Them two will get buckled one of these days,"

Daddo said, chuckling and snipping away at the horse's hoof. "Ever been to an Irish wedding?" he asked me.

"No."

"Then ye've a treat in store. Such dancin' and drinkin' and sportin' never be seen as the likes of a wedding. We'll be sending ye off in fine style, Shannon, me boy!"

Soaking up the sunshine, I sat on the bale of hay and listened to Daddo's cheery chatter. His company was the tonic I needed to dispel my earlier loneliness.

"I'll be back," I promised when I finally took my leave and returned to my room.

The pleasant time I had spent with Daddo renewed my spirits but my promise to Sean to invade the family at dinner resulted in a nervousness that settled in my stomach like a twisted rope, knotting up and keeping my muscles tense. As the dinner hour drew near, I wondered how I could possibly eat anything. I waited until the last minute to tell Callie that I would not be needing a tray.

"Are ye not feeling well?" she queried, no doubt seeing my high color.

"I feel fine. Would you advise the cook . . . or whoever should know . . . to set a place for me at dinner tonight. I'll be eating with the family."

"Yes, mum." An eyebrow flickered, and nothing more.

"Do you know if Mr. Creighton has returned from his business?"

"No, mum."

"No, he hasn't returned, or no, you don't know?" Nervousness made my tone more strident than I had intended. I saw Callie swallow quickly in fright.

"No, mum, I don't know."

"It's all right, Callie. I'm just a little nervous, that's all. What time is dinner?"

"Eight, mum. Would ye be needing help dressing?"

"No, thank you, Callie. I'll manage fine."

She bobbed and scurried away.

I knew from the girl's question that I'd best wear my Sunday gown, a dark blue moire with touches of lace softening the sleeves and modest neckline. I drew my hair back in its usual coil upon my neck. I had seen the way Sean had looked at my regal coiffure that day in the library and I suspected he found the style pretentious. Even as I scolded myself for letting him dictate something as personal as the way I wore my hair, I admitted the truth that what he thought of me was very important. Tonight I would need him as an ally.

I put on the pearl earrings and the sight of them dangling beside my cheeks somehow strengthened me. My father had given them to my mother and in some mystical way, the gift brought my parents closer to me in spirit. I knew that in some undefinable way I would be representing them at the table tonight. No matter how I was treated, I must remember to hold on to my dignity. With this admonition clear in my mind, I made my way downstairs.

In the last few days, I had oriented myself enough to find my way down to the gardens but the main floor of the castle was as foreign to me as it had been the first day I entered with Sean.

The main staircase eluded me so I took the backstairs to the second floor and wandered along a myriad of corridors. Gold embossed doors like the ones that had opened into Lady Davina's room greeted me on every side and I feared that any moment one might fly open and bring me face to face with the vindictive woman. I wished that I had asked Callie to guide me to the dining room. Minutes later, when I reached the round tower rooms, I knew I had walked the length of the castle. Time was going by quickly and I was going to be late!

Picking up my skirts, I retreated hastily down the

corridors the way I had come. My breath was coming in short gasps when I turned a corner and came face to face with Rosa. The servant glared at me as if I were an intruder who had invaded sacred premises.

"Oh, Rosa. I . . . I'm lost," I stammered. "Would you show me the way to the dining room?"

"The dining room?" she echoed, a flash of surprise on her round face.

"Yes." I took a deep breath. "I'm dining with the family tonight."

She continued to glare at me.

"Please. I fear I'm already late."

"My sister, Willa, tells me you have been in the kitchen garden every day." Her eyes were accusing.

I nodded, wondering why she felt it necessary to comment on my behavior.

Rosa drew herself up. "We have been in service to the Lynhursts for a long time. You will not be able to get us discharged."

"Discharged? Don't be foolish. I don't go to the garden to spy on Willa. I just like being there. It's the only pleasant refuge I've found in this cold, unfriendly house. Now, please, take me downstairs."

I put as much command in the words as I could, fearing that she might turn her back on me and leave me lost in the upper corridors.

I let out a slow breath of relief as she turned and led me through several passages to the main staircase which circled upon itself. Cursing myself for wandering around from one end of the castle to the other, I followed her down the curved stairs which ended in the large hall I had seen upon my arrival. Rosa turned in the opposite direction from the stately parlor where my father's body had lain, and I knew that I never would have found the dining room even if I'd made my way to the main floor by myself.

The closer we came to the moment of confrontation, the weaker became my resolve. My stomach was squeamish, my forehead was moist with nervous perspiration. Better to go back upstairs unseen and try another time, I decided, just as we reached arched doors opening into a formal dining room. A rumble of voices greeted my ears. Lady Davina's was loud and clear above the rest.

"Why is there an extra place set?" she was demanding. "I was not told of any guest."

Rosa watched my face. A slight smile hovering at the edges of her mouth and a glint of derision in her expression fueled my courage. I knew that she would relish telling everyone about my cowardly retreat. Smoothing my dress, lifting my chin, and taking a deep breath, I sailed into the room.

Three people were already seated at the table: Lady Davina at one end, a young man who looked very much like her at the other, and Lorrie in the middle, facing the door. My heart sank. There was no sign of Sean.

"Good evening," I said, sending a smile around the table as a servant moved forward and drew out a chair opposite my half-sister. "I'm sorry I'm late. I was afraid you might have started without me."

"I was not aware that you had been invited," snapped Lady Davina.

"Nor I!" spat Loretta, tossing her dark curls.

I sat down, knowing that my legs would not have held me up two seconds longer.

"Now, ladies, an entertaining diversion at these boring family affairs is most welcome," chuckled the young man at head of the table.

I turned grateful eyes in his direction, hoping I had found an ally in my half-brother. Lawrence had inherited his mother's short, stocky frame and bland features. I judged him to be no more than seventeen and yet his youthful face was already bloated and ruddy, evidence of too much eating and drinking. Tailored, expensive clothes did not hide flabby muscles and flaccid skin. I remembered what Sean had said about his lack of industry but maybe Sean had been trying to prejudice me against him, I thought hopefully.

"I'm weary of eating alone," I said. "And I've been most anxious to meet you." I directed my remark to Lawrence in a conversational tone.

"And I have been curious about you." His lips were wet with claret as he put down a half-emptied goblet.

"Do we have to suffer her presence, Mother?" wailed Lorrie.

"For the moment, it would seem we have no choice," Lady Davina said coldly.

"How could Father do this to us!"

I spread a damask napkin in my lap, grateful that my education had included proper dining etiquette. The array of silverware and cut glass was almost blinding. Two large candelabras bathed the table in mellow light.

Lawrence emptied his glass and gave a curt gesture to the servant standing behind him. Silently and speedily, the table was laden with food and steaming dishes were offered by maids moving around the table. Out of nervousness, I took more food than I could possibly eat.

As the meal progressed, I wondered why I was there. What had I accomplished? Lady Davina and Lorrie pointedly ignored me. If their glances had been pointed rapiers I would have been pinned to my chair. Silently I cursed Sean for goading me into coming. Where was he?

I felt Lawrence's eyes upon me as he stuffed food into his mouth. When he had gorged himself and wiped away grease splattered around his mouth, he leaned back in his chair and emitted a rude belch. His ruddy lips smiled at me. "Your mother was Irish, I understand."

"Yes."

"A hot-blooded wench, no doubt."

I suddenly felt sick.

"Larry, don't be vulgar," chided his mother.

"I speak only the truth, Mama. Only the truth. Irish peasant girls know how to pleasure a man as dear Papa must have found out." He chuckled lewdly. "Who would have thought that one of his indiscretions would come across the Irish sea to sit at our table?' He leaned forward. "Tell me, are you cut from the same pattern as your mother, Aileen?"

Lorrie giggled at the pointed insult.

I was so floored by his crudity that for a moment I was stunned. It took great effort for me to find my voice. "My mother reared me in good manners, respect for others, and integrity. I would like to think that I am, indeed, like my mother. May I inquire if your behavior is representative of the training you received?"

Lady Davina gasped.

"Touché!" Lawrence laughed loudly. "Mama, how neatly she put the feathered cock in your court! How do you explain your wastrel son and your promiscuous daughter?"

Lady Davina lowered her eyes and I was suddenly embarrassed for her. My remark must have hit her like a blow to the stomach for there was no fire in her eyes nor starch in her bearing. Her son's booming chuckles taunted her silence.

"I'm sorry, Your Ladyship," I said hastily. "I meant no offense."

She raised glazed eyes to mine. "In answer to your question, I have no explanation. I apologize for my son's behavior. If my husband were alive, we would have been forced to suffer your presence in our family circle. He would have delighted in this deplorable situation and used it as another cudgel to force obedience from me and my children. But he is dead!" Her mouth trembled. "I will not be humiliated in my own home. You are not welcome in this house and there can be nothing but unpleasantness for you here if you remain."

"If I had the means, Lady Davina, I would leave immediately," I assured her.

Loretta turned to her brother. "Give her passage back to where she came from, Larry. You're the head of the house now. Tell Sean to pay her off."

"I think not." Her brother took a sip of wine and his eyes laughed at me over the rim. I knew then that cruelty was a part of his make-up. He was a young, spoiled brute and I trembled to think of those who must have already suffered under his callous behavior. Now, he had the authority and resources to extend his debauchery as he wished. "Papa wanted her to live here, so stay she must."

His gleeful smirk left no doubt that he would delight in making my life as miserable as possible. Cruelty was in the twist of his smile. *Could he have killed his father?* The thought came full-blown in my mind. If Dolan was right and the murderer lived under this roof, the evil deed could have been done by Lawrence. Maybe Lord Lynhurst had been pressuring his son for a change of behavior. Sean had said that Lawrence gambled. Such debts could make it imperative that he get his hands on more money. Slitting his father's throat might be the only way to continue his debauchery. My eyes fixed on the knife he held in his hand and horror crept up my spine.

He leaned forward, a smirk on his wet lips. "We are going to enjoy hearing all about your colorful mother. Too bad Papa isn't here to enjoy all the juicy details."

"Give me the money to leave. Just enough to see me to England and a few months' subsistence until I can find a way to support myself."

He only laughed and downed his fourth glass of wine.

101

"If I had any money, I'd give it to her," said Loretta in a petulant voice.

"But you don't have any money, Lorrie . . . and neither does Mama," he mocked. "Dear Father kept all of us on a tight leash. He threatened to disown me but now everything is mine . . . mine . . . mine!"

"Including the responsibility of running the estate," reminded his mother. "It is time for you to fill your father's boots, Lawrence, and learn how to manage the tenants."

"Our devoted Sean will take care of all the boorish details. Father has him tied to our service. He would lose too much by leaving and he has too much to gain by staying. Father's will made that plain. He was determined to reap the rewards of the education he provided Sean. It was no surprise that he favored a match between him and my dear sister. Marriage would keep him looking after the Lynhurst holdings for the rest of his life."

"There will be no match!" Lady Davina's fist came down on the table. "Your father's acceptance of Sean's Irish background was too much! I will not have grandchildren who are not English bred."

Larry laughed. "I don't know, Mama. My dear sister looks at Sean with adoring eyes. I think a marriage could be arranged, right, Lorrie?"

"Larry! Remember yourself! Sixteen is too young for Loretta to be settling her attentions on anyone," snapped Lady Davina. "And your sister will marry someone from a proper family at the proper time, not just someone who will make your work lighter."

"Where is Sean?" asked Lorrie. She touched her hair and straightened the neckline of a dark green watersilk dress. Apparently she was not going to observe any period of mourning even though Lady Davina still wore black, I noted.

Lawrence shrugged.

Where was Sean? I silently echoed Loretta's question. I was in this horrid situation because of him. Now, I doubted that he had ever intended to be back in time for dinner. He probably knew all along that his business would keep him away past the dinner hour and for some macabre reason had encouraged me to expose myself to the kind of insults that had come my way.

"If you will excuse me," I said formally, preparing to rise from the table. "I will return to my room."

"No, stay," ordered Lawrence. "I find your company entertaining. I'm eager to hear all about my father's clandestine affair. I bet your mother was a luscious beauty. Father appreciated beautiful women. And I bet you look just like her. Beautiful eyes, soft lips, sensuous body . . . just the kind of woman who would please Father, wouldn't you say, Mama?"

Lady Davina gave a choked gasp and before I could say anything, the woman pushed back her chair. "I will not stay and be made sport of by my own son."

She swept out of the room with as much dignity as her short, squat figure would allow. I was horrified that Lawrence had insulted his mother in such a manner.

He laughed gleefully at her exit and Lorrie chided him playfully. "You shouldn't have said that, Larry. You know how sensitive Mother is about her looks."

"And well she should be. She's as homely as a hedgehog."

I had had enough of his boorish crudity. Pushing back my chair I stood up. "I'm surprised to hear you say that, Lawrence," I said sweetly. "I was just observing to myself what a remarkable resemblance there is between son and mother. You look exactly like her."

Lorrie's giggle followed me out of the room and I could feel my half-brother's barbed glare biting into my back.

I did not sleep well that night. My dreams were punctuated with nightmarish visions of Lawrence's pudgy, greasy face leering into mine. He struck out at me with a loaded whip and I ran into deep woods; briars scratched me and quicksand sank under my feet. In the darkness, I fell into a dark bog. Sinking in the mire, I felt mud trapping my arms. I awoke screaming, thrashing about, trying to untangle my arms from the bedcovers.

My cries mingled with horrible wails coming from the walls of my room. The castle's night whispers had come back again. I covered up my head with my pillow and pressed my tear-stained cheeks into the sheet. Almost smothered in the cloth, I could still hear the horrible straggling gasps and moans, like specters writhing in pain. The creatures were all around me and mocked my own helplessness.

Chapter Seven

I gratefully accepted a tray the next morning when Callie asked if I wanted to eat in my room or go downstairs. Still shaken from a night of bad dreams and loud wailing that didn't fade away until nearly dawn, I spent the morning listlessly moving about my room, mending a few seams in a dress and replacing a bone button on a ribbed glove.

I knew it was time to put away my Sunday clothes and quit pretending I was one of the family. I would never be accepted as one of them. Last night's dinner had verified that. My cheeks still stung from the insults Lawrence had given me and my mother. His lewd smiles made me furious and I knew that I would never seek his presence again. I was horrified at his treatment of his mother. How could my father have allowed it? Smug, spoiled, rude, and coarse, Lawrence's behavior had undoubtedly been of long standing. Lady Davina must have long since given up control of her son—and her daughter, too.

Lawrence had called Loretta promiscuous. Could it be true? The memory of her and Sean riding off into the woods together brought a bitter taste to my mouth. I could not forget the softness in his eyes as he tenderly stroked her hair. Their affection bespoke a loving intimacy. Lawrence had said last night that his father had been encouraging a marriage between them to keep Sean tied to Lynhurst. From her hysterical protest last night, it was obvious that Lady Davina was appalled at the possibility of her grandchildren having Irish blood in their veins. She wanted her daughter to marry an Englishman of good family but it was clear from my half-sister's behavior that it was Sean whom she wanted.

I sighed and hung up my mended dress in the wardrobe. I wouldn't be wearing my Sunday best any more. The hope I'd had of putting my best foot forward was futile. If only I could find a job here and earn wages like the rest of the help. I knew such a thing was not possible. The Irish servants would resent me if I tried to take one of their jobs. I was neither fish nor fowl — family and yet not family. Caught between two classes and belonging to neither.

This train of thought reminded me of the kitchen maid, Willa. Apparently my presence in the garden had distressed her enough to speak of it to her sister, Rosa. She must have thought I was supervising her work. Wanting to reassure her of my innocent intent, I dressed in a navy blue walking skirt and a simple white blouse with bishop sleeves and high collar. My walking shoes had been cleaned by someone and brought back to my room; my mended gloves and simple bonnet completed my attire. As I tied the worn streamers under my neck, I knew that Loretta and her brother would have a good laugh at my provincial dress, but I didn't care. I had tried to present myself in the best possible way and all I had gained were insults and embarrassments.

Willa was already in the garden when I slipped through the gate and shut it behind me. As always, I loved the protected feeling of the walled garden and the wonderful smells of green leaves and overturned earth. Droplets of dew glistened on stalks, beaded on summer-green foliage, and caught the morning sun in rainbow prisms. Floating whorls like the folds of a wedding veil hung upon the tops of fruit trees. Here and there in several of the larger trees, disgruntled

106

house finches flapped in wet branches like house-maids shaking out dusters.

As always my spirits rose once I left the cold chambers of the castle. Wet earth brought its own perfume and the essence of continuous life and rebirth. All worship services should be held outside, I thought, as my heart expanded to drink in the natural loveliness.

Willa was hammering stakes to hold up vines. The brawny servant glanced at me as I came down a row of vegetables toward her but she did not stop the rhythmic movement of her strong arm.

"Good morning," I greeted her above the pounding blows.

She nodded but her bland expression didn't change. She had pretty brown eyes but heavy eyebrows, a prominent nose, and strong facial bones that destroyed any aura of femininity. She obviously was at home in her garden and intruders were not welcome.

I waited until she had finished her task before I took a deep breath and apologized. "I'm sorry, Willa, if my daily visits to your garden have caused you any discomfort. Please believe me, I wasn't trying to intrude in any way. I just felt at home here because my mother and I always enjoyed our gardens so much."

Without answering me, she picked up extra stakes from the ground and piled them against a shed at the side of the garden.

I followed her shamelessly. "I would like to work in the garden, if you'd let me."

"You forget your place, mum," she said gruffly.

"And what place is that?" I demanded angrily. "The family won't have anything to do with me. The only friend I have is Daddo." I arched my head defiantly. "I have to find a place for myself. At the moment, it's here in your garden! Please, let me stay, Willa."

" 'Tain't my place to say 'stay' or 'go,' " she responded flatly.

"Yes, it is. If you are uncomfortable with me here, I'll leave."

Her steady gaze swept my face. Then she shrugged. "It pays me no mind if you want to stay."

"Oh, thank you, Willa. Can I just do a little weeding . . . over there in the herb garden? Just to feel my hands in dirt again will help my peace of mind. Whenever I was upset at home, I'd go out to the garden and pull anything in sight." I laughed. "Sometimes I got a little carried away . . ."

"Don't ye be pulling up any of my plants," she warned in her hoarse voice.

"Oh, I won't. I promise."

She shrugged again and went inside the shed.

Well, not exactly the friendly type, I thought as I got down on my knees and began pulling wild grass away from the tiny shoots of chives. But she hadn't made it impossible for me to enjoy her garden. I made myself a promise to stay out of her way. If I didn't, she'd complain to someone and I'd be asked to quit interfering with the help. I liked her better than her older sister, that was for sure. Rosa made shivers go up and down my back. The stables were filled with men workers and I couldn't very well hang around there even if Daddo made me welcome.

My hands went out and in the tufts of slender shoots, removing grass and weeds. The activity lulled the warring factions of my mind and nearly an hour went by before I leaned back on my haunches, then wiped my sweaty cheek with my dirty gloves.

"So here you are?"

I peered up and shaded my eyes against the sun. My gaze traveled up Sean's high boots, and fitted dove trousers to his waist and then to the hand he had stretched out to me. For a moment I almost refused it, angry about his not keeping his promise about last night's dinner, but I stripped off my glove and put my hand in his and allowed him to pull me to my feet.

"You've dirt on your nose," he said with infuriating frankness.

I flung my head back in indignation and my bonnet fell off my head and dangled around my neck by the ribbons. To make matters worse, the pins loosened the coil at my neck and I feared the heavy mass of hair was going to go plunging down my back. Quickly I raised my hands to retrieve the pins and shove them back.

"Why don't you leave it down?" He held his head a little to one side, watching my fumbling fingers. "Better style than that old woman's twist or that uppity coronet on the top of your head."

"When an English girl reaches a certain age, she puts her hair up," I informed him haughtily.

"Too bad. But you're not in England now. Why not enjoy the local customs? Irish blood runs in your veins and a pretty colleen would flaunt that mass of golden hair." He glanced down at my muddy shoes. "And let her lovely feet run barefoot in the earth. No young girl wears shoes, except on Sunday, and then she carries them around her neck until she reaches the church."

"How uncivilized," I snapped.

"No, very practical. I think you'll find Irish customs are very pragmatic."

"Like liars who say one thing and do another?" I gave my bonnet strings a vicious tug as I tied them and glared up at him.

He frowned. "I'm sorry I missed dinner last night. I didn't get back until this morning. I really meant to, Aileen, but there was trouble. The cottiers are uneasy." His jaw muscles flickered. "The Bog Boys will be causing trouble around here very shortly, I'm sure of it. Rumors are that a meeting has been called. I wish I knew where and when so I could head them off."

"Wouldn't that be dangerous?" I asked, forgetting my irritation with him. Suddenly my displeasure seemed childish. "Going to a secret meeting like that?"

He nodded and his thoughts seemed suddenly weighted. "There's always danger when you're trying to deal with a bunch of overwrought patriots."

"Why do you call them 'patriots' instead of bandits and murderers? Men who rustle cattle, set fires, and do all the other horrible things I've heard about are nothing but outlaws."

"Spoken like the English who never see themselves as robbers and thieves. Under English law, only the people whose land they stole are bandits and any Irishmen who refuse to pay taxes are law-breakers, rightfully strung up from the nearest hanging tree."

"But why have you stayed in an Englishman's employment if you feel that way?"

"Because the only chance for change is working within the system. For years, Irishmen have lost their lives trying to oust the intruder from the land by every violent means there is — and failed. The bog Irish who struggle to survive have only been persecuted, exiled, and placed in servitude. Now the numbers of loyal English subjects are against them. The time is past when the mighty British Empire can be physically challenged. If the lot of the Irish is to be improved, the change must come through lawful channels. I have been hoping that I might be allowed to represent this district in Parliament. Only —"

"Only what?"

He clamped his jaw in such a way that I knew he wasn't going to tell me anything more. I sensed that it had to do with Lord Lynhurst and his will. Lawrence had hinted last night at the table that Sean wasn't free to leave. Whatever plans Sean had for the future seemed to be conditional upon my father's wishes. Was Sean as penniless as the women in the family?

Did his prosperity depend upon marriage to Loretta?

"How did dinner go last night?" he asked as if reading my thoughts.

"Probably in the same vein as you expected. Lady Davina ordered me from the table. When I refused to go, she advised me that only unpleasantness would result in my intrusion into the family. She was right. Loretta openly showed her displeasure and my half-brother laughed and made crude remarks about my mother and my tainted heritage. He insulted his mother, as well, and we both abruptly left the table."

"I might have expected as much. I've seen Larry when he's in one of those moods. I'm sorry you were exposed to his vulgarity. If you'll permit, I'd like to try to make up for the family's rudeness. Will you take a walk with me?"

"I'm sorry but my skirt is soiled." I gave him a rueful smile. "And I have dirt on my nose."

"And your chin," he added frankly. "No matter. I want to show you a more pleasant place to spend your idle time." He slipped his arm through mine as if consent was assumed.

Willa watched us leave the garden and I thought I saw an expression of relief flit across her homely face. Maybe I shouldn't have intruded so much in her garden, I thought guiltily. She was obviously glad Sean was taking me away. And so was I! I accepted his explanation for not being at dinner as he had promised. He seemed sincerely worried about the unrest that was brewing. Concern for his safety told me how strong my feelings for him had become. Even though I knew it was foolish, I felt very special as he guided me along the terrace spanning the back of the castle.

I had never walked in this direction. A rounded turret had been built nearly on the edge of the cliff overlooking the ocean and as we rounded a side of the castle, I saw the stone steps that had been cut into the side of the hill. Nearly a hundred steep steps led downward to the Sea Wall Road. I remembered noticing them on my walk that first day.

"Where are we going?" I asked, grateful that he steadied my progress down the steps by keeping a hand firmly on my arm.

"You'll see." There was almost a boyish glint in his eyes that I had never seen before. I knew then the place he was going to show me must be something very special. I was delighted that he was going to share it with me.

As he unlocked and shut the gate at the road level, I asked him about the heavy padlocked doors in the rock retaining wall.

"There's a warren of passages and chambers under the castle. Been there since the Norman keep I told you about stood where the castle is now. At one time guns, food, and weapons were stored there. Whenever the people of this area were in danger of being attacked, they hid in the underground passages. During the Cromwell scourge, British soldiers slaughtered hundreds of women and children who were hiding there. Legend has it that blood ran like a river on this road when the massacre was over and some people say you can still hear the women and children at night, weeping and begging for their lives."

"I've heard them," I said with my throat dry. "Twice. Horrible whispering sounds, melancholy, pitiful, and pleading."

He startled me by laughing. "Surely, Aileen, your inbred English skepticism does not hold with such superstitions of wandering and wailing ghosts?"

"I know what I heard. The wailing comes right through the walls. Haven't you heard it?"

"No, but I'm in a different wing of the castle. The noises are probably caused by the wind surging through the underground passages. Some of them lead from the castle down to these locked doors. Only fishing and boating equipment is kept there now."

I was relieved to discover that the horrible night whispers had a logical explanation. "Apparently wind invades the caverns when certain weather conditions exist," I speculated. "Since, I've only heard them twice. The first night I came and last night."

"I'm sorry you were frightened."

I confessed to nearly drowning myself on the balcony before I fled back into my room out of the rain. Walking beside him in the bright sunlight, it was easy to forget and make light of my terror. At that moment, laughing and talking at his side, I felt so confident that I doubted that I would ever be afraid again.

We walked a short distance along the Sea Wall Road in the opposite direction from the village. The coast was as rugged as I had ever seen. Not even a tiny strip of sand formed a beach. Large rocks, shaped by wind and sea's constant grinding, stood darkly in the water like misshapen creatures from the deep. Spumes of white-foamed waters spilled over them and surging maelstroms ran in swift channels around rock islands that defied passage through them. I shivered thinking about what that ruthless pounding would do to a boat or body. My ears filled with an ever-rising crescendo and retreat of the surf. High-pitched calls of wild birds darting along the steep cliff in search of food or nest provided a musical counterpoint to the ocean's orchestration.

When Sean stopped at a small path, barely wider than two feet, I gasped. "We're not going down there, surely?"

"Only a short distance. The path's safe enough."

"It doesn't look it."

Constantly bathed by the sea's mist, the ground was wet and shining. Just looking at it, I could feel it slipping under my feet. My gaze fled to the crashing surf below. Treacherous rocks seemed to await like vicious teeth.

"Don't look down," he warned. "It's safe enough."

113

He took my hand and pulled me after him.

His tight grip on me was suddenly a cue for fright. He was a stranger . . . perhaps a dangerous one. What was I doing here? My father had been murdered and his family was filled with hate for me. Sean was a part of the family. Had he deliberately brought me here for some diabolical purpose?

I stopped in the middle of the narrow path and pulled back. "Let me go," I yelled above the surf in sudden panic. I tried to pull free but he held my hand in an iron grip. With the other one, I flayed out at him, trying to get free. In my lunge, one of my feet stepped off into open air. Screaming, I lost my balance.

Unable to catch myself, I dangled over the edge of the slippery bank, trying to find purchase for my feet and my other hand. If Sean hadn't maintained such a deathly grip on my arm, I would have fallen to my death below. For a terrifying eternity it seemed that my swinging weight was going to pull him over also. He braced himself on the muddy path and slowly pulled me back up beside him.

Hysterical tears blinded me, and I made no protest as he put his hands firmly on my shoulders and forced me to move ahead of him along the path which reached a wide ledge above the tormented lashing waters.

I saw then that the ledge extended into a small chamber hollowed into the side of the cliff. We took a few steps inside and he eased me down upon a pile of rushes that had been gathered into a crude pallet on the ground. I bit my lip and tried to recover my composure.

He sat down on a pile of turf which had been stacked near a blackened fire hole. Obviously he built a fire sometimes while he sat here and watched the sea. I realized he had wanted to show me his own private place.

114

"I'm sorry . . . I usually don't panic like that," I apologized.

"I usually don't give in to impulses," he answered coldly. "This was obviously a bad one. You can rest a minute and then I'll take you back."

"No, I don't want to go back."

He gave a curt laugh. "You're scared to death of me, Aileen. Your eyes give you away. On the path back there, you looked as if I were the devil himself. Well, maybe you're right. No proper young English lady would go off with such a renegade as myself. I should have taken you into the rose garden where we could sit in proper chairs, curving our little fingers over tea."

I laughed. "I can't see you curving your little finger over a teacup."

"You'd expect me to stir it with my little finger, wouldn't you?"

His tone made me angry. "No, I wouldn't. And don't try to depreciate yourself with me. I'm not Lady Davina."

He raised an eyebrow. "She must have said something about me at dinner last night."

I wished then that I'd kept my mouth shut. "I'm sure you know what it might have been."

"About Lorrie and me, of course," he answered flatly. "She has . . . reservations . . . about accepting me as a son-in-law. Not that I can fault her for that. Given her hatred of everything Irish, she couldn't be expected to give her blessing to such a bitter disappointment."

"Lawrence seemed to approve," I said with my voice held as much as possible in a neutral state.

Sean's laugh was short. "And why not? I enjoy a unique position with the English gentry and the Irish peasantry. My grandmother came from an important and respected Irish family who owned land for many years in this area. Even though she was criticized for marrying an Anglican Scotsman, they never stopped loving her. When her other children were killed, they grieved with her and when my father went to England and gambled everything away, the Irish peasants who had been through good and bad with her family retained a deep affection for her grandson, me. Lord Lynhurst capitalized on my unique ties to this land and its people and educated me for his own purposes. I've served him well."

"And now you are serving his son." *And you are going to marry his daughter.* I did not say the last aloud. My pride had not completely deserted me.

"Yes," he said curtly. "For the moment." He grew silent and I watched his forehead knit as if his thoughts were weighted. Then he raised his eyes and smiled at me. "But enough of that. How do you like my hideaway? Better than a kitchen garden, don't you think?"

"No, but I'm glad you showed it to me." I untied my bonnet and placed it beside me. I was relaxed now, content to stare out at the sea and fill my lungs with salt air.

"I do apologize for frightening you. I'm so used to going up and down that path that I never realized how it must seem to someone else."

"Usually it would have been no problem. I'm very fleet of foot. Too much so, my mother used to say when she'd catch me walking narrow boards in a picket fence. It was all the talk about night whispers and murders that made me behave so foolishly."

He seemed to accept my explanation and leaned back against the cave's wall, stretching his legs out comfortably in front of him. He sighed contentedly and his expression eased.

"Thank you for sharing this place with me. Do you come here often?"

He nodded. "It's a good place to shed problems . . . or at least see them with a detachment which isn't possible when people are around. I've come here often since Lord Lynhurst's death."

"Who do you think killed my father?" I asked boldly.

"It could have been anybody. The Bog Boys have been on the rampage for months now, ever since some of their members were hanged. I'm pretty sure that Mike Ryan is one of their leaders. He or someone else could have been taking revenge."

"How long ago were the hangings?"

"Last winter."

"Why would they wait until now? It seems to me the cause might be something more current."

Sean nodded. "Sir Wainwright and Bryant were in the castle that night, trying to persuade His Lordship to sign a request that the Queen's Dragoons enforce the next collection of tithe taxes."

"The Wainrights were in the castle the night my father's throat was slit?" My eyes widened. "I thought they had just come for funeral services."

"No, they had come early that afternoon and were holding an informal landlords' meeting with your father. I stayed for part of the meeting, protesting as forcibly as I could against the measure which would only enflame the cottiers. Bryant and I almost came to blows. Sir Lynhurst asked me to leave."

"And did you?"

He nodded and took a deep breath as if anger were rising up in him again. "You see, once a cottier refuses to pay the tax, he can be evicted even though he has a signed lease on his property. Forcing the collection of the Tithe Tax gives the Wainwrights the excuse they need to start throwing cottiers off land they wish to use for something else. They needed your father's cooperation."

"And he gave it?"

"No. That's the ironic thing. I learned later that your father wouldn't agree. The Wainrights were furi-

117

ous. They swore that they'd get what they wanted, with or without his cooperation. I've wondered if one of them could have killed your father, knowing that Lawrence will do anything to bring in a few more pounds for drinking and gambling."

"The Wainrights are too civilized for such brutal treachery," I protested. "They would have found more subtle means to make my father do what they wanted."

"I'm inclined to agree with you," he said. "But one can never be sure."

"What about the family? Loretta is the only one that showed any sincere grief. Lady Davina has only shown bitterness and resentment."

"It was a loveless marriage. I told you that His Lordship loved your mother. Although he had other women in his life besides his wife, I don't think he entertained any deep feelings about any of them."

"Why did he keep such a short rein on Lady Davina?"

"He feared she would desert him if he allowed her to return to England. Your father was a proud man, perhaps too proud." He looked at me in a peculiar way, as if assessing my own character. "A downfall of the English, I believe."

"Being proud of England and her accomplishments is not false sentiment."

"In Ireland, it is," he said flatly.

I wasn't going to get into a political argument with him. My personal situation overshadowed any broad disagreements about English law. "What about Lawrence? Could he have killed his father?"

"His Lordship was always threatening to disown Lawrence. Motive enough, I guess."

"But you don't think so?"

He pulled up his legs and circled them with his arms. Deep in thought, he looked out at the ocean. "I don't know what to think."

118

"What about the ghost of the Watcher?" I challenged.

His smile was wan. "No ghost wields a knife so purposefully."

"Who was the Watcher anyway? Daddo made him sound like a local hero whose spirit continues to lead the patriots' causes."

"He was a young cottier killed by the Queen's soldiers last year. When collectors came to Danareel to make the Irish peasants support the Church of England, he led an attack against them. The collectors took livestock, killed chickens, confiscated grain and potatoes, burned houses and left starvation and empty cupboards."

"Why didn't the people protest?"

He looked at me as if I came from an alien planet. "They did. The only way they know how. The Watcher led a raid and recovered the confiscated goods but left in his wake six collectors with their throats cut. All were found with a black ivy wreath laid on their chests. The Royal Dragoons hunted the young man down as he fled along the Sea Wall Road. When they trapped him on the road from both directions he threw himself into the sea rather than be taken alive. He was battered to death on the rocks and his body carried out to sea. Legend has it that the Dread Women of Moher claimed his body and spirited it away."

Looking below at the savage pounding of the relentless surf, I visualized the limp body of a man being beaten to death against those rocks. A cold chill eased up my spine. "Please take me back."

"Why?"

"I'm frightened."

"Of what? The Watcher? He's dead."

"But someone is responsible for the slit throats and black wreaths," I protested.

"Yes, but there's no place to run, no place to hide,

Aileen. The Irish believe that Death is always riding your coattails."

"It's a horrible country. Uncivilized. Dirt and filth, everywhere. I wish I'd never set foot in it. Thank God, my mother's family had the sense to leave when they did."

If I had slapped him, his reaction wouldn't have been any more intense. His mouth thinned in an angry line. He stood up, glaring down at me.

Suddenly, I was frightened of him again. "I'm sorry, I didn't mean that."

"Yes, you did." His dark eyes were blazing with glints of fire. "Forgive my mistake, Miss Lynhurst." He rose to his feet.

The use of the formal name was like a dagger. "Mistake?"

"I mistook you for someone who cared about her Irish heritage."

"I do, but—"

"No. Only thick English blood runs in your veins."

"Please, try to understand. You owe me that much." I stood up and faced him. "My upbringing has been English. My values are those that have been taught to me. They're all I have to draw upon. You cannot expect me to embrace a culture that is completely alien to me." I knew my lower lip was trembling and I hated myself for it.

"Aileen," he said softly. He reached out with his long fingers and traced my cheek. "I'm sorry. You're right. Forgive my stupid ravings."

"I am not your enemy," I said with a catch in my throat as a trail of warmth followed his touch.

"You would be a formidable one." His hand cupped my chin and he stared into my eyes as if he could read the deep longing that suddenly spurted within me. He bent his face near mine and his gaze was a caress as it touched my eyes and mouth.

I offered my lips with a boldness that defied my

120

innocence. His kiss was light at first, only a light brushing of his mouth, leaving a tingling upon my skin. My hand slipped around his neck to hold him closer. His kisses deepened and when he drew away, my breathing was rapid and a bewildering desire stirred within me. I didn't know where to look. In his face? At his chest? Or should I close my eyes against the trembling rising within me?

"I think we'd best leave now," he said huskily.

I nodded. My face was hot with embarrassment and I was glad for the excuse to reach down and pick up my bonnet. I tied the streamers with shaky fingers.

As we made our way back up to the Sea Wall Road, I wondered if he had ever brought Loretta to his special hideaway.

Chapter Eight

The next morning, a written invitation arrived from Sir Wainwright to spend a few days at Windbriar. With the memory of Sean's kisses still stirring my emotions, I had lost my former urgency to escape from Lynhurst Castle. I no longer felt lonely, cut off. The time we had spent together had changed everything. Even the harsh words we had exchanged softened as I relived every moment over and over again, hearing my name on his lips and feeling that incredulous tingling buoyancy.

When Callie brought in my breakfast tray, I was smiling, rather foolishly, I expect. "It's a beautiful mornin', Callie," I greeted her warmly.

My high spirits obviously puzzled her but she smiled back and lingered a moment longer than usual. "Yes, mum, 'tis that. Summer's me favorite time of year."

"Do you have a family, Callie?" I asked, suddenly interested in everyone around me. The joy I felt inside turned my eyes outward. I saw Callie as a young girl with hopes and dreams of her own and not just a servant performing chores.

She laughed. "Sure and there's eight of us at home and three married. I be the only one in service," she said proudly. " 'Tis a fact, for sure, that there'd be no meat on the table 'tweren't for me wages."

"What does your father do?"

"Cuts turf mostly, he and me brothers. Ain't much else to be doing with the bog land, hereabouts. 'Twas a lucky day when I turned twelve and came to the castle. Started in the washhouse but here I am now—" Her eyes widened. "Sure and I'll be in hot grease with Dolan if I don't get meself back to the kitchen."

"Thank you, Callie . . . for talking to me."

"Yes, mum." She gave me a puzzled look and fled.

After breakfast, I walked out on the balcony and gazed down upon the Sea Wall Road where we had walked yesterday. I couldn't see the place where we had taken the path down to the small ledge and cave, Sean's private place. I wondered how often he escaped the heavy burden of his responsibilities and restored himself in that quiet place. Now that I understood his background, I could appreciate the taut rope he walked in his position with the Lynhurst family and his own family history. Even though I bristled at his flat condemnation of everything English, I could understand his frustration and I admired his stand that violence would not solve the problems.

Suddenly I had to see him again. Quickly I drew on my gloves and bonnet and made my way downstairs. Maybe he would stop his work and take me for a morning's walk. Now that I had experienced the joy of being with him, I was greedy.

The library doors stood open. I peered inside, hoping to see him behind the large desk that stood near the terrace doors. The room was empty. No fire had been lit and the room was still chilled from the night air. Disappointed, I felt my optimistic outlook begin to wear a little at the edges. Maybe he had gone someplace for the day? I knew he spent a great deal of time looking after the estate. He must have overseers and other employees who were under his supervision. And then there was Loretta? I knew she maneuvered as much time with him as she could. Maybe they were eating breakfast together.

Summoning my courage, I walked down the marble corridor in the direction of the dining room. The urgency to see Sean was so great that I pushed aside any apprehension that I might be letting myself in for another unpleasant scene. I didn't know what I would say or do if he was there having breakfast with the family but the need to see him again, hear his voice, and watch his lips spread in a smile was greater than my reluctance to face Lady Davina, Lorrie, or my half-brother. I would gladly suffer their presence if I could be with Sean.

The dining room was empty except for Lady Davina, who sat alone at the long table. Even with her hair piled high, she could not achieve an imposing stature as she sat in the heavily carved chair. Her short, square frame made her look dwarfed and insignificant, more like a peasant woman from the kitchen who was playing lady of the house.

As I entered, the imperious lift of her blunt chin and her biting gaze, honed-sharp, dispelled any physical inadequacies and made me fully aware of her rank and position.

"Good morning, Lady Davina," I said pleasantly, even though my mouth was suddenly parched.

"It was—until now." Her glare condemned my greeting.

"Forgive my intrusion. I was looking for Mr. Creighton. Do you know where I may find him? I already checked the library and he wasn't there. I thought, perhaps, he was still at breakfast." I knew I was babbling, a weakness of mine when I was nervous. "It's not important, I just thought—"

"Try the stables." She cut me off with a wave of her hand.

I murmured a quick "thank you" and fled the room. I was furious with myself for allowing the woman's glare to make me feel she was six feet tall while reducing me to an insignificant weevil that should be squashed underfoot. Lady Davina was able to arouse in me feelings of pity, empathy, and pure rage, all at the same time.

Once outside, I lifted my skirts and hurried in the direction of the stables. Before I had crossed the clearing which led to the outbuildings, I heard Loretta's loud laughter. I took a few steps closer and then froze, keeping in the shadows of a feed shed jutting out from the main barn.

The stableboy, Shannon, was leading Sean's gray stallion and a sorrel mare to where Sean and Lorrie waited to mount. Loretta's arm was slipped through Sean's in a possessive way and they were both laughing. The bright sunlight bathed his handsome face and I saw reddish highlights in his warm, dark hair. The sun's warmth was lost in a chill that invaded my body as I looked upon the intimate scene.

Sean put his hand on Lorrie's waist and lifted her into the saddle. For a moment he stayed there looking up at her and she leaned over and affectionately ruffled his hair.

Feelings that I had never entertained before warred within me and pain stabbed me like a knife. Jealousy was a stranger to me, setting me adrift in a wash of bewilderment that I didn't know how to handle. I only knew that I would not willingly expose myself to that kind of shattering upheaval again.

That evening when Sean sent word he would like to see me in the library, I sent back word that I was indisposed. I wrote to Sir Wainwright, accepting his invitation and told him to send a carriage for me.

No one but Callie seemed to be aware of my departure. She helped me pack and carried my things down to the carriage.

When Sean did not appear, I asked Callie at the last minute to inform Mr. Creighton that I had left for Windbriar for an indefinite visit.

"Yes, mum. 'Tis a pretty ride you'll be having." She

125

gave me one of her wide smiles. "Have yerself a nice time, mum."

"I will. Thank you, Callie."

She gave me a wave of her hand and then hurried off toward the kitchen entrance.

The carriage pulled away from the castle and I looked up at the mullioned windows. Was anyone watching me go? Lady Davina, perhaps, with a sigh of relief in her broad chest? Good riddance, she would think and hope that my visit would extend indefinitely. The only one who would notice I wasn't there was Callie, and not because of any personal interest but only because my absence would make her work lighter.

Of course, Sean would be furious when he received my message because I had ignored his instructions not to go. I didn't care. His feelings about Bryant, Sir Wainwright, and Irish politics had nothing to do with me. I would choose my own friends, on my own terms. No one wanted me at Lynhurst Castle and I was glad to be free of the oppressive atmosphere.

With the air of a trapped pigeon given unexpected freedom from a cage, I settled back in a tufted leather seat and enjoyed the passing landscape as the small carriage rumbled down a country road away from the sea—and Lynhurst Castle.

Callie was right. The two-hour journey was a pretty ride through woods thick with sloping groves of ash and evergreens. Patches of emerald moss appeared like splatters of paint upon rocks and tree trunks; a smell of dank earth mingled with the scent of wild flowers that lined the byways and banks of small ponds.

I was delighted to see birds everywhere. Hidden larks sent bird songs trilling above the warble of thrushes and I heard the harsh call of a blackbird to his mate from the top of a white-thorn bush. When we passed a lake that was fed by a lyrical waterfall, I caught my breath. The loveliness of the scene was almost a weight on my heart. This was an Ireland I had never seen before. Foolish tears came to my eyes. The land was the birthplace of my grand-parents and for the first time I felt a thrill that my ancestral roots were here.

When we left the woods, a rolling green landscape stretched out on both sides of the narrow road. Fields of wheat and corn wore summer green and thatched cottages and byrnes were covered by trailing ivy that softened their stone exteriors. Workmen in the fields stopped their tasks in a pose of humble reverence as the carriage rolled by. I was too far away to see their faces and I wondered if they held the same dark, brooding expression I had seen on so many Irishmen since my arrival.

For nearly an hour, the carriage road wound through a well-kept park studded with various kinds of trees. All undergrowth had been cleared from under hazel, rowan and hanging willow as if a giant sweeper had brushed the ground under their arched branches. Grassy knolls sloped downward toward small lakes which were dotted with white ducks and speckled drakes.

I knew when we had entered the Wainwright estate. An avenue of lime trees stood in royal procession, flanking the approach to an imposing house built on a grassy knoll at higher elevation than the rest of the surrounding land. Tall chimneys balanced a hipped roof that extended over the three-storied, rectangular-shaped building. Unlike Lynhurst Castle, a warmth radiated from the mansion's pleasant lines and deco-rated eaves. A cream-colored exterior was softened by vines climbing upon the walls and trailing around mullioned windows.

I had seen many similar English homes of the same architectural style and for a bewildering moment, I felt as if I were stepping out on English soil when I alighted from the carriage.

The front door of the house opened almost immediately. A sandy-haired girl about my own age gathered the folds of a cherry-colored morning dress and hurried down the front steps to the carriage.

"I'm so glad you could come." She startled me with an affectionate hug as if we were the best of friends. "I'm Dorthea."

"Thank you for inviting me," I managed, stunned by the display of spontaneous friendship.

Sir Wainwright's daughter! Dorthea's resemblance to her brother, Bryant, was obvious but, unfortunately, the family features sat better on a masculine visage than on hers, I thought as I returned her smile. Only expressive blue-gray eyes lent a feminine grace to features dominated by a strong chin and broad forehead.

"I couldn't believe it when father told me he had invited you for a visit." Dorthea slipped her arm through mine and laughed merrily as we mounted the front steps. "Since my return from my trip abroad, there has been nobody . . . and I truly mean nobody . . . to help me survive these long, tedious days. I just hate it . . . summer, I mean . . . don't you? I pleaded with Father to let me stay over, but no, he said I had to come home. Tell me, what part of England are you from?"

Before I could answer, we were inside the house. I soon learned that Dorthea did not require answers to her questions because she never really listened to the reply. Her bubbling effervescence was contagious and I found myself smiling for no reason at all as I listened to her chatter.

"You will have a room near mine," she informed me. "It's a nice room, used to be my aunt's but she went off to France on a holiday and never came back." She lowered her voice. "She fooled Father into letting her go. I found one of her old diaries.

She had it all planned. 'Escaping from Hell,' she called it." Dorthea rolled her pretty eyes. "Aunt Marta described Ireland in the vilest terms. I don't really believe in hell, do you?"

We crossed the foyer which was pleasantly furnished in soft colors and furniture which looked functional as well as stylish. We mounted a lovely curved staircase and I had only a moment to glance over the banister and see a two-storied chimney-piece and high windows rising from the entrance hall. A pouring of light into the stairwell make it as bright as any room.

The second floor landing was wide and carpeted. We had traversed a short distance down a corridor when Dorthea flung open a door of a bedroom.

"It's just like Aunt Marta left it. Father was furious when she wrote that she was going to stay in France and teach English in a school for young girls. You should have been here! The roof went up two feet, at least." She laughed. "I hope you don't mind using this room. It's better than one of the guest chambers. Anyway, I wanted you close to me . . . my room is just across the hall. Will this be all right?"

"It's lovely. Very comfortable." Once again I felt as if I had entered an English manor. Cherrywood furniture was placed against a nicely papered wall and I was relieved to see a grouping of watercolor scenes opposite the bed instead of the horrid hunting tapestry I had been seeing every morning when I opened my eyes. Thank heavens, there would be no night whispers to haunt me.

"Why are you frowning?" she asked.

I knew then that for all her outward flutter, Dorthea was very perceptive. She had caught the flicker of apprehension that went through me.

I gave an embarrassed laugh. "My room at the castle has ghosts."

"Really?" Her eyes were wide. "What kind of ghosts?"

We sat down on the bed and I told her about the horrible sounds that came through the walls when the wind blew through the underground chambers. I repeated the legend about the spirits of murdered women and children wailing and weeping. "The whispers sound just like that."

"I don't like Lynhurst," Dorthea stated flatly. "It's awful what happened to Lord Lynhurst. I'm glad I wasn't there that night. Father and Bryant wanted me to go with them but I don't enjoy Lorrie's company and Larry's a bully so I wouldn't go. When I heard that you were so charming and pleasant, I jumped up and down with joy. My brother seemed really taken with you. Wouldn't it be something if we ended up sisters?"

Her astounding leap in thought patterns left me reeling so far behind that I wouldn't have had a response to this question even if she had waited for one.

"My stepmother, Claudia, told me to make you welcome. She's out hunting . . . no one rides a horse better than she does. I hate the smelly creatures. Are you a horse-lover? Good," Dorthea said with satisfaction in response to the tentative shake of my head. "At least, I'll have some support when Claudia tries to organize some horrible fox hunt for you. That's her first love! Sometimes I wonder why she bothered to marry Father when she prefers the stable to the house." There was a thread of bitterness in the remark.

"Your mother died?"

She nodded. "When I was five. Consumption. This foul Irish weather, you know. The air's so thick you can drink it. Anyway, Father married Claudia on one of his trips to London, brought her to Windbriar. Hounds and horses are her passion and she couldn't be happier. She never took to two little children. Aunt Marta was the one who raised us. I hated to see her leave. The house has been empty without her."

"What about Bryant?"

"Oh, he's busy." She cocked her head. "He seems happy enough but I really don't know what Bryant thinks about life. Most of the time he's so agreeable, you don't realize there are hidden depths to him. Whenever I have a problem I go to Bryant. He's my Rock of Gibraltar." She gave a merry laugh. "And whatever I want, he'll see that I get it. Now tell me about your mother and Lord Lynhurst." She clasped her hands excitedly. "It's so romantic. *La grande passion*. Where did they meet?"

I knew that I might as well give her a full account of their love affair. Dorthea was not going to be satisfied with anything less.

"That's the kind of love I want." She threw herself back on the bed and raised her eyes to the ceiling. "Wild, tempestuous. Totally engulfing." She shivered in anticipation. "I want a man who makes me tremble at his touch. One glance and I melt into his arms." A deep sigh came from her chest. "Oh, Aileen, I can hardly wait."

I thought of Sean's passionate embrace that made me forget everything but the explosive rapture of his kisses. Dorthea could talk of fairy book romances with a sparkle in her eyes but I had lived with my mother's loneliness. I knew full well that heartbreak was the bittersweet end to such tempestuous love affairs. I determined that I would not be caught in such a fool's love-net despite my strong attraction to Sean.

Dorthea sat up. "Your mother loved with mad desire, didn't she? And bore his child. And now you're here." She gave me another impulsive hug. "You don't know how desperately I need a friend, a confidant. Are you good with secrets?"

Her expression warned me that I might be inviting confidences that were not just girlish fancies. Fortunately, I was saved from answering by the sound of barking hounds and galloping horses that rose from the courtyard.

"They're back." Dorthea jumped from the bed. "I'll give you a few minutes to freshen up and then we'll join them downstairs. Here's Winston with your baggage now. Is that all you brought?" she asked as a servant entered with my things. "Well, no matter, I have scads of clothes that will just fit you. We're almost exactly the same size. Just like sisters. You do like me, don't you, Aileen?"

I laughed at her solemn question. "Of course I do."

"But I talk too much."

"A little."

"And I'm too impulsive."

"Probably."

"But I'm loyal to my friends."

"Then I'd be honored to be your friend." We both laughed and this time I hugged her first.

"We're going to have a wonderful time together," she promised.

After she flitted out of the room, I sat on the bed and took a deep breath. Dorthea's whirlwind reception had left me slightly dizzy. The sudden change from the unfriendly atmosphere at Lynhurst Castle to Dorthea's overflowing affection had left me a little in shock.

A continuing cacophony of noises drew me to the window and sitting on a cushioned seat, I peered below. A dozen or more people on horseback were in the process of handing hunting rifles and horses' reins to waiting servants. Laughter and voices rose above the snorts of horses and the scramble of hunting dogs bounding about, yapping and wagging their tails, almost dancing in circles with excitement.

I saw only one woman wearing a riding habit and plumed hat. Claudia Wainwright, no doubt. There were strings of fowl being carried into the kitchen by women who took them from menservants who had accompanied the hunt. The shoot must have been a good one, I thought, as I left the window.

Dorthea's aunt had her presence in the room and I felt like an interloper as I took off my bonnet, and hung up my pelisse in a cherrywood cupboard. An adjoining vanity room was complete with brass tub and waterstand. Gratefully, I splattered water on my face and dried myself with a sweet-smelling towel. As I patted my face, I stared for a moment at my reflection.

Surely there must be some outward sign that I had been kissed by a man for the first time. I felt so different. Ever since that moment when Sean had held me so passionately, latent desires in my awakening body had stirred with disturbing frequency. The memory of his mouth upon mine and his hands pressing me against the length of his virile body continued to bring unbidden warmth spilling through my veins. I feared that Sean had lighted a fire that would continue to smolder like banked coals. Yes, there was new color in my cheeks. A new intensity of blue in my eyes. I was not the same. I would never be the same again. And that frightened me.

I changed into my best summer frock, a plaid foulard in shades of oyster white and yellow. Two ruffles trimmed the puffed sleeves and a small satin collar dipped slightly in front where a small bow with streamers decorated the tight bodice. Although I had worn the dress for several seasons, it still was crisp and I thought it flattered my slender figure and fair hair.

Dorthea nodded with approval when she came to fetch me. She had also changed from her morning dress to a saffron-colored gown of sheer lawn, embroidered with tiny yellow flowers. I didn't think the color was quite the best choice for her sandy hair and slightly ruddy complexion. She needed to wear soft greens and blues, I thought, colors which would enhance her pretty blue-gray eyes.

Dorthea chatted about her recent stay in France and I suddenly felt out-of-place. What would I say to these people? My provincial upbringing would stand out clearly. I couldn't talk about trips abroad, fox hunting, or current fashion trends. After a few dull comments, I would be an embarrassment to myself and everyone else.

Once again, Dorthea surprised me with her sensitivity. "What's the matter, Aileen?" she asked as we descended the curved staircase to the main floor again.

"I'm not sure I should be here." My throat was suddenly dry.

She squeezed my hand. "Bryant will be delighted to see you again. He said you were most charming. And Father was quite taken with you, too. Lord Lynhurst was his best friend, you know. What could be more proper than his welcoming his friend's daughter to our house?"

I couldn't tell her that my experience at Lynhust had taught me not to expect anything but cold antagonism and derisive remarks about my parentage. I was wary of being humiliated and embarrassed by people I didn't know. Dorthea's warmth and friendliness might prove to be the exception in this visit. Everyone would know I was Lord Lynhurst's bastard child. What had ever possessed me to come here?

Dorthea took my hand firmly in hers. She must have felt it trembling for she said firmly. "You are my friend. And if any persons are rude to you, I'll scratch their eyes out."

She said it with such conviction that I had to smile. "I hope that won't be necessary."

Laughter and voices from the terrace led us down a marble corridor and through open French doors. A group of gentlemen were taking drinks and food from servants who were passing trays. These middle-aged men with red jackets and black pants stretching over

134

ample stomachs and thick legs spoke loudly as they carried on lively discussions in the Queen's English. The scene could have been taking place in any British colony.

"The new building for the House of Commons will take at least ten years." "It's about time they jolly well got started." "Since Beau Brummel has got himself in trouble and left England, who will set the fashions these days, I ask you?"

Dorthea led me through the gathering to Sir Wainwright, who was sitting at a table with two older men about his own age.

"Here she is, Father," said Dorthea.

All three gentlemen rose to their feet and Sir Wainwright extended his hand. "Welcome, my dear. May I present Colonel Bainbridge and Sir Alexander from neighboring estates. Aileen Lynhurst, Edwin's daughter. She's just arrived from England."

"So sorry to hear of your loss."

"Welcome to Ireland, Miss Lynhurst."

"We hope your stay will be a pleasant one."

I smiled. "I'm sure it will be." I could not see anything but polite interest in their manner. I began to relax. "I appreciate Sir Wainwright's invitation."

"I hope that my daughter has made you welcome. She's a scatterbrain, I fear. Never quite got her feet on the ground."

I could see that her father's remarks had brought a pained furrow to her forehead. Her manner was instantly subdued.

"Dorthea has been a perfect hostess," I quickly assured him. "She was waiting to greet me when I arrived and my room is lovely."

"I put her in Aunt Marta's room . . . so she would be close to mine."

Her father nodded. "That scalawag of a sister won't be needing it. I doubt that she ever steps foot on Irish soil again. Never could acclimate herself, Marta

135

couldn't. Not like Claudia. Dorthea, why don't you take Aileen out to the stable. Your stepmother is there." He chuckled tolerantly. "Claudia has a filly about to foal and must play midwife."

"Where's Bryant?" asked Dorthea.

Sir Wainwright frowned. "Your brother didn't go with us on the hunt. Don't rightly know where he took himself off to. No doubt, he'll be back by dinner time. Now you girls enjoy yourselves." He gave us a nod of dismissal and I knew that my welcome would wear thin if I intruded upon his presence too long or too often. I had the feeling he felt that way about his two children, also; especially his daughter.

"Wouldn't you rather take a walk around the grounds?" asked Dorthea when we had left the crowded terrace down a flight of wide garden steps. "I don't think Claudia would want to be bothered if she's waiting for a foal. You have to be a four-footed creature to get her attention."

There was a wistful edge to her voice and I knew that Dorthea had not gained a loving surrogate mother when her father married Claudia. It was apparent that an indifferent stepmother and a father who readily dismissed her from his presence had made Dorthea a very lonely girl.

"I would love a walk," I assured her. "I've never seen grounds as lovely as these."

We strolled through an English rose garden bordered by trimmed hedges and laid out in a geometrical color pattern.

Several gardeners said, "Good day" in clear, British accents.

"Is all the help English?"

"All the house servants are. Father hired them in England and brought them over. He wouldn't have a Paddy inside the house. Even in the fields, they cause owners all kinds of trouble. Your father should never have let them inside Lynhurst." She shivered. "I know

why Aunt Marta left. All the robbing and killing."
Then she brightened. "Let's walk to the chapel. I go
there lots of times. I like to take flowers to my mother's grave. Reverend Whitestead will be glad to see
us."

She picked an armful of daisies and delphiniums
and we followed a carriage road to a small chapel
about a half-mile's distance. A small manse was connected to the rear of the church. A graveyard was
encased by a small, white fence.

"It's a pretty little church, don't you think? We'll
have to go to services on Sunday." Dorthea laid the
bouquet in front of a marble marker bearing her
mother's name.

A man in cleric garb came out of the back door of
the manse. "Dorthea, my dear," he greeted her but his
eyes traveled over me. He had a pinched face set on a
long neck.

He did not return my smile. Not at all like the
round-faced, friendly vicar who had helped me
through my mother's death and the improper advances of my stepfather, this man's posture was stiff
and rather distant.

"This is my friend, Aileen Lynhurst, from England," said Dorthea. "Edwin Lynhurst was her father."

A questioning frown creased the vicar's forehead.
"I did not know there was a second daughter."

"Yes," said Dorthea simply. "She's paying us a
visit."

His eyes narrowed. "Lord Lynhurst was well known
in these parts and a true opponent of the decadent
Popery that defiles this land," he said in a pompous
tone. "Through his endeavors, more stringent efforts
were planned to collect the Tithe Tax from the unbelievers. You are, of course, my dear, a member of the
Anglican Church?" he probed with his nostrils twitching as if a negative reply would thrust the Devil into

our midst.

"I was christened in the Church of England according to the dictates of my father."

"But why were you raised in England? I would have thought that Lady Davina . . ."

"She's not my mother."

The moment of silence was damning.

"I see," he said coldly, stripping away every ounce of my respectability with that short response. My illegitimacy was like an invisible brand which his judgmental eyes instantly burned onto me.

His attitude condemned me and my mother in one fell swoop. I met his gaze fully, without flinching. "My Irish mother was raised in a Protestant orphanage and she raised me according to that faith." I smiled. "But on her deathbed, she asked to see a priest."

He choked and turned a peculiar shade of puce.

"Good day, Reverend," said Dorthea quickly and hurried me out of the churchyard. "I'm so sorry, Aileen. Please forgive me. I didn't think." She caught her lower lip and tears flooded her eyes. "Now, you'll hate me. I've ruined everything . . . everything."

"No, you haven't," I said rather crossly. Then I took a deep breath and reined in my anger. It wasn't Dorthea's fault. My humiliation wasn't anybody's fault except that of my parents who had defied social mores and brought me into this world.

"Just remember, Dorthea, when you are thinking about *la grande passion,* that somebody pays . . . and pays dearly."

The warning echoed in my own ears and I knew with a sickening certainty that I was capable of the same heedless passion that had engulfed my father and mother.

Chapter Nine

I saw both Bryant and Claudia for the first time that night. Dorthea had indicated that I was expected to change for dinner. My good Sunday dress was the only one I had left since I had worn my best traveling dress for the journey and had changed to my summer foulard upon my arrival. Two dresses in one day, and now I was obliged to change for a third time. I sighed, wondering how my hosts would react to a repeat performance of my wardrobe every day. I could see why Dorthea was surprised I hadn't brought more baggage with me.

The fact was, of course, I didn't have any more suitable gowns to bring. At school I had worn simple white bodices and walking skirts and they still composed most of my wardrobe. Through the years, my mother had fashioned most of my dresses for me. Although they were neatly sewn, the styles were modest and I had left most of the dresses behind because they were worn and faded. Maybe I would have to cut my visit shorter than I had intended. My appearance might be an embarrassment to my hosts.

Dorthea came in while I was still styling my hair. "What a lovely shade of yellow gold," she said with obvious envy. "And such a petal white complexion!"

She plopped down on the bed, looking a little like a wild purple aster in a gown with many flounces edged in black ribbon. I didn't know why she chose colors of such poor contrast to her hair and complexion. Apparently she didn't favor soft colors and simply wore what she liked. Her present gown of black and purple, or the saffron yellow gown she had wore that afternoon, would be flattering on someone like Loretta whose dark brown hair and brown-black eyes could complete the vibrant colors. That thought led me to a mental picture of Loretta in her deep wine riding habit and I shoved the haunting memory away. I did not want to think about her riding off with Sean with laughter on her lips and a tender look in his eyes.

"You're frowning again," said Dorthea, watching my expression in the mirror. "You're not thinking about this afternoon, are you? Reverend Whitestead's too dour for words. Truly, I believe a smile on his face would crack it beyond recognition. Don't pay him any mind. He's always ranting and raving about the heathen papists. When he first came he bragged that he would convert all our tenants to the true faith but he's had little success with them and not much luck collecting any church tithes. He's been pushing Father to take some action against cottiers who won't pay."

I was glad that Dorthea had misread my thoughts. If I hinted that there was something personal bothering me, she'd be at me to find out what it was like a puppy wearying a bone. "It doesn't seem fair that Catholics should be required to support their own church and the Anglican Church, too," I volunteered.

"The Church of England is the official religion of the country," she said flatly. "All citizens are required by law to support it and there's no Christian tolerance for those who don't. It's all so dreary. No wonder Aunt Marta left and didn't come back. I wish my hair were that lovely golden color," said Dorthea, wistfully in her usual abrupt switch of subject.

I had decided to put my hair into a twisted coronet as a means of bolstering my confidence. Dorthea sat on the bed watching me maneuvering the thick coils and long pins. Her own hair was in a Psyche knot at the back of her head, not too smooth nor neat but her bubbling, vivacious personality made her appearance seem unimportant.

"I can't bother fiddling with my hair," she said as if echoing my thoughts. "And I can't stand sitting still while some maid brushes and coaxes and twists each strand for an hour on end. And when she gets through, we still have the same old me. You're so pretty," she sighed. "I bet you've had dozens of suitors for your hand."

"Nary a one."

"I don't believe you. Don't tell me you've never been kissed."

Unbidden color rose in my cheeks.

"I thought so!" She pounced upon my betraying blush. "Oh, Aileen, do tell me. How was it? How did you feel? Was it wonderful?"

I laid down my brush. Wonderful? How could that bewildering burst of desire, longing, yielding, and terrifying emotion be defined in one word? Even the memory of Sean's mouth on mine was enough to send hot blood sluicing through my veins. His kisses had left within me a confusion that was not wonderful but bewildering.

"Oh, I know I would soar to the heavens if that happened to me. Who is he? Are you going to marry him? Is he waiting for you to come back to England? Oh, Aileen, I'm so envious. The man I'm going to marry hasn't even kissed me yet."

I smiled at her pout. "Does he know he's going to be your husband?"

"Not yet, but my father and Bryant are going to arrange everything."

141

I patted the last hairpin into place. "And who is the honored bridegroom?"

"Sean Creighton."

My hand froze in the air. My breath came in shallow jerks. I quickly lowered my hand to my lap. Any warmth that had been in my cheeks a moment ago gave way before a draining of color from my face.

Dorthea didn't seem to notice. For once her acute perception was clouded by her own enthusiasm.

"Sean Creighton?" I echoed.

"Yes, you know. Lord Lynhurst's solicitor. You've met him, haven't you?"

I avoided any contact with her sharp eyes. "Yes, of course."

Eagerly she confessed that she had been in love with Sean from the first moment they met. "I used to make excuses to go to Lynhurst so I could see him. Pretended that it was Loretta I wanted to visit. She loves him, too, you know . . . and Lord Lynhurst was in favor of the match because he didn't want to lose Sean. His Lordship spent a lot of years and money training him to manage all his affairs — as insurance against losing his holdings when he died. He knew his son would never be able to handle his inheritance. Larry is such a nincompoop! Sorry, I forgot I was talking about your half-brother, but it's true."

I nodded because I couldn't find my voice.

"Father said that Sir Lynhurst had promised Sean that he would back his political ambitions."

"Political ambitions?" I echoed.

"Yes, Sean wants more than anything to run for Parliament. He has the confidence of the Irish peasantry and he could probably win if someone like Sir Lynhurst endorsed him. He's been kept dangling for years and I don't think His Lordship ever intended to carry out his promise. Now that Lord

Lynhurst is dead, the chance Sean wanted is gone. Larry would never back Sean for local constable, much less Parliament." She laughed joyfully. "That's what's so wonderful. My father will finance Sean and see that he's elected to the House of Commons . . . on one condition. That he marry me. Isn't it wonderful? Being a member of Parliament, Sean will need an active wife, someone of good background. That's me! What could be more perfect?"

"What, indeed?" I hoped she couldn't see the devastation that lay behind my curved lips.

"It's going to happen next weekend."

"What is?"

"Father is asking some people in for Claudia's birthday. And Sean's coming! Oh, Aileen, I'm so happy. I don't think I can stand it. You'll have to help me. Tell me what I should say when he proposes. I don't want a long engagement. He'll need me to travel with him when he's campaigning." She bounded up from the bed and gave a twirl in the middle of the floor. "No more boring, tedious days. My life is going to be wonderful!" She pulled me up from the vanity bench. "Come on, let's go to dinner. Suddenly I feel ravenous!"

My own stomach was tightly coiled in dismay. Dorthea and Sean? Was it true that Sean had political ambitions? Looking back on our conversation, I realized now that he had hinted as much when he talked about bringing about change in other ways than violence. Apparently this ambition of Sean's was of long standing. From what Dorthea had said, my father had dangled his support for Sean like a carrot for a long time but His Lordship's death had ended any chance that he would provide the financial means for him to run for office. His will must have omitted any bequests in that direction, I thought, remembering Sean's glower when the will was mentioned. What a disappointment for Sean. He wanted to represent Ireland on a level that might bring about changes in the laws governing the country. And Dorthea would be a good wife for him . . . much better than my spoiled half-sister.

Dorthea chatted all the way downstairs to a long drawing room that stretched from the center corridor to windows and doors stretching along one side of the house overlooking the terrace.

"Bryant, she's here!" Dorthea's greeting brought a swirl of heads in our direction as we came out on the stone terrace.

I only had time to nod at Sir Wainwright and his friends before Bryant came toward me with a welcoming smile and an outstretched hand. Impeccably dressed, he was the epitome of a young Englishman of means and prosperous upbringing. Longish golden hair curled upon his neck and drifted over his forehead in a slight wave. His ready smile put attractive curves in his cheeks.

"Aileen! How wonderful to see you. Please, accept my apologies for not being here upon your arrival." He bent his head slightly toward mine. "You're as lovely as I remembered."

Dorthea sent me a knowing look and a wink.

"Will you allow me to make amends?" Bryant asked smoothly.

"No apologies are necessary." I assured him. Sean's warnings faded away. His attentive manners were like water to a parched soil and I drank greedily of his flattering attentions. "Thank you for the invitation."

"Ever since our brief encounter, I have been looking forward to seeing you again."

"You're not going to monopolize her, brother dear," warned Dorthea. "She's my friend, too. We have lots of things planned. Haven't we, Aileen?"

I stood between them, not knowing quite how to

144

respond.

"Don't think you are going to spirit her away from me," argued Bryant. "I saw her first, remember? She came to see me, didn't you, Aileen?"

I only laughed, suddenly feeling less empty. For the moment I would thoroughly enjoy having two vie for my attention.

"Father is planning a birthday fete for Claudia next weekend," Bryant told me. "I would be honored to be your escort at the affair."

My stomach sank. *Sean would be here.* How would I endure his presence in these very rooms? I desperately needed to fill that empty void that Dorthea's secret had left in me. If Sean and Dorthea's engagement was going to be announced, I needed all the support Bryant could give me. This was the excuse I gave myself when I deliberately gave him a flirtatious smile. "I would be delighted. Thank you, for making me feel so welcome."

He grinned. "What a delight to have you here."

Dorthea looked at us with a knowing grin. "Isn't life just wonderful?" she bubbled.

We joined Sir Wainwright and his guests and chatted a few minutes before his wife, Claudia, breezed into the room, dominating the scene with her robust carriage and resonant voice.

"I'm delighted to meet you, my dear," she told me when Bryant introduced us. "So sorry I've been busy in the stables all day. A prize filly was foaling. Difficult dropping but all is well. Tell me, did Lord Lynhurst buy that stud I recommended?"

"I don't know, I . . ."

"She's only just arrived," Bryant interposed quickly. "From England."

"Oh, such a tedious journey. I absolutely refuse to ride in a public coach. I guess I'm going to miss the Grand National this year. Did you see last year's run?"

145

Sir Wainwright took her arm. "Dear, I believe dinner is waiting. Shall we . . . ?"

He offered his arm to her and they led the way through a huge archway. Bryant put a guiding hand on my elbow and one of the older gentlemen escorted Dorthea.

The dining room was as cozy and comfortable as the one in Lynhurst Castle was cold and lofty. Bryant conducted me to a center place at the table facing Dorthea and the two men guests who sat beside her. Sir Wainwright seated his wife and then took his place at the head of the table. Bryant sat down beside me.

A procession of servants from a butler's pantry began serving a seven-course meal which included consommé, roast duckling basted with wine sauce and served with sausage dressing, a bacon with kidney dish, fresh vegetables in rich cream sauce and seasoned lightly with tangy herbs. Several greens which I could not identify had been tossed with nuts, berries, and bits of hard-boiled eggs.

Three enormous candelabras were placed strategically along the table and the fountain of candles sent prisms of reflected light into polished silver trays, exquisite china, and delicate glassware. Bryant's easy manner put me at ease and I found myself enjoying every dish in the same way that an adventurer experiences new territory. He watched me as I tasted each offering and then gave a sigh and smile of approval.

The men kept up a volley of talk. Subjects were batted from one to the other like opponents in a badminton game. Claudia seemed at ease with the masculine topics of conversation but Dorthea's usual exuberance was missing and I wondered how many meals she sat through without uttering a word. There seemed to be no attempt to keep the conversation general or to include her in any way.

Her quiet withdrawal was at odds with her usual bubbling, outgoing manner and I wondered if she had been chastised severely for talking at the table. Sir Wainwright's wife and guests ignored her. Their attention was devoted to the topics of conversation which their host introduced.

"I tell you it's absentee landlords who are keeping Ireland from becoming a civilized colony of the Crown," the Colonel stated emphatically. "There should be some requirement that they live on their estates a certain number of months a year. Instead, they visit their estates as the mood hits them and leave all their responsibilities in the hands of some ingrate overseer who would sell his mother for a bent farthing. No wonder the Bog Boys are on the rampage again."

"We ought to deal with them the way Ulster treats stubborn Catholic renegades. Hang every one of them."

Sir Wainwright grunted approval. Bryant raised his eyebrows at me as if impatient with the whole subject.

I was glad when the topic of conversation changed to a dissection of French politics.

Bryant leaned closer to me. "You're not drinking your claret, Aileen. Is it not to your taste? I can send someone to the wine cellar for a different vintage."

"Oh, no. This is fine. Delicious," I assured him as I lifted the fragile goblet and sipped the robust, fruity liquid. Not wanting to insult the choice of wine, I made certain that my glass was refilled at least once.

When the last course, a dessert made of cream, brandy and dark chocolate was served, Sir Wainwright gave a smothered belch into his damask napkin and gave the signal to rise.

Dorthea, Claudia, and I returned to the drawing

room while the men disappeared into the library for cigars and brandy. I sat in one of the deep-cushioned chairs placed in front of the fireplace. The wine I had drunk and the huge meal created a lassitude in me that made my attempts at conversation desultory.

Dorthea was unusually subdued and the weight of the conversation fell upon my shoulders. Obviously bored with my attempts at polite chit-chat, Claudia soon made an excuse and left Dorthea and me alone.

"Probably gone back to the stable to tuck her baby in for the night," said Dorthea sarcastically. "I'm sure she must have been a brood mare in another life."

"It must have been lonely for you . . . as a child," I said, touched by the sadness in her face.

She shrugged. "No more than most, I guess. Did you have a happy childhood?"

"Very. My mother gave me all the love any child could want. I guess she was trying to make up for the lack of a father. I wish she'd never married at all."

"You have a stepfather?" she asked in surprise.

"A wastrel of the first order. Gambler and lecher. My mother made me promise I wouldn't stay after her death. She was afraid that . . ."

Her eyes widened. "That he'd come after you? Oh, my heavens! How awful for you, Aileen."

"That's why I can't go back."

"Oh, my goodness." Dorthea leaned forward. Animation was back in her face. Curiosity was like a burning ember that brought warmth and color in her cheeks. "Did he—?"

I shook my head. The wine made me maudlin or I never would have told Dorthea about the night he almost raped me. "My mother was ill in the downstairs bedroom and I heard him come up the steps.

148

He paused at my door and I saw the knob turn. We didn't have locks on the doors and I backed up against the bed board when he came into the room."

Dorthea's eyes widened. "What did you do?"

For a moment I was back in that familiar bedroom, clutching the covers, my heart thumping in my throat. "What do you want?" I had croaked.

He just smiled, a wet, moist smile that made his fat face the epitome of debauchery. "I've come to comfort you. Your mother's dying, you know that. Soon it will be only you and I. A nice, cozy little family. I'll take care of you, honey . . . and you'll be nice to me."

I tried to leap from the bed but he caught me. I started to scream but he put his broad hand over my mouth.

"Quiet!" he ordered. "You don't want your ma distressed, do you? You'll kill her if you don't behave."

He knew I would never do anything to risk shortening my mother's life.

"Good." He took his hand away from my mouth and his thick fingers found my breast. His other hand raised my gown. As he pushed me back on the bed, I raised my legs and with both of my feet kicked him in the stomach as hard as I could.

He gasped for breath and crumbled to his knees. I fled downstairs and slept on a cot near my mother until she died.

During my story, Dorthea had moved to a footstool near my chair and as I talked she held my hand. Tears were in her expressive eyes. "Aileen . . . how dreadful. Why didn't you go to your sweetheart?"

I blinked and then I remembered that she knew someone had kissed me passionately. "He married someone else." The tense was wrong, but the truth was there. Sean was going to marry someone else. I didn't doubt for a moment that he would do whatever was expedient to gain his goals. He'd jump at the opportunity Sir Wainwright was going to lay before him. He'd be a fool not to gratefully accept financial support and a delightful wife as well. His political ambitions would be assured and Dorthea would bring to the marriage the prestige that would benefit a member of Parliament.

"I'm glad you came here," Dorthea said, giving me a loving smile.

A masculine voice joined in. "And so am I," said Bryant, coming into the room. "I was hoping that you two hadn't retired yet. I thought Aileen should see how beautiful the fountains are in the moonlight."

Before I could reply to this invitation, Dorthea said, "I think that's an excellent idea. Aileen needs some cheering up." She bent over my chair and pressed her cheek against mine.

"You're very pensive," Bryant said as we walked through the rose garden.

The night was clear and the stars seemed closer than they did in the heavy moist air of the sea coast. There was silence here, too. No crashing watery fists beating against the shoreline nor winds rising and falling upon the high turrets of the castle. Only a faint rustling through tree branches and a melodic falling of water in nearby fountains.

A breeze ruffled the wisps of hair around my face and I drew in the brisk air gratefully, hoping to clear my head and revive my spirits. The evening had presented such a kaleidoscope of emotions that I couldn't sort them out. In some ways, I wished that Dorthea had not shared her astonishing secret that Sir Wainwright was going to offer her hand to

Sean.

I stumbled and Bryant took my arm. "Careful." His tone was tender.

"Too much dinner wine," I apologized quickly.

He laughed. "You haven't been in Ireland long enough. Drinking is the national pastime here. Even the peasants have their illegal brews. The mountains are full of stills and the poteen they make would knock a sailor's legs out from under him."

I laughed silently and wondered what Bryant would think if I told him I had already experienced that potent whiskey. I must have smiled, for he said, "That's better. Now, no more long thoughts. I don't like pretty ladies to look despondent in my company."

"I doubt that they ever do," I responded honestly. He had the same outgoing enthusiasm as his sister, more refined, more focused, but still open and engaging.

"Shall we sit here?" asked Bryant, indicating a bench near the water's edge. He seated me and then sat close to my side, keeping his arm along the back of the bench. The casual position was practiced and I knew that I wasn't the first girl he had brought to this secluded pond.

"Is this a favorite spot of yours?" I challenged. He would not find me as naive as he hoped. "The bench seems a little worn."

He laughed and for a moment I thought he was going to draw his arm away but he didn't. "I confess to other nights in the moonlight but only because I want you to know that being here with you is very special for me." His hand slipped down upon my shoulder.

The intimate touch did not disturb me nor excite me. I felt comfortable being close to him, somehow protected, and at ease with him. I knew he would be very disappointed at this companionable feeling.

151

"All through dinner tonight, I kept looking at you, grateful that you had found your way into my life. I think you're going to be very important to me."

"We've just met."

"I know that. And I won't rush you. If you'll just give me a chance. You do like me, don't you?"

"Yes."

"And you like being here with me?"

The sprays of water blurred in my vision. Foolish tears brimmed at the corner of my eyes. I longed to turn and find dark, smoldering eyes biting into mine and bold, demanding lips crushing down upon my mouth. Foolish fantasies. Madness I could not afford. There would be nothing for me at Lynhurst after Sean left. I must take care of my own future. I had few choices, but Bryant Wainwright was one of them.

I hated myself when I managed a light, flirtatious laugh. "Yes, I like being here with you." I slipped away from his arm. "And I appreciate the hospitality of your family. Now, I think we should go back."

He chuckled. "As you wish, but be warned, I intend to pursue your company every moment that I can. That sister of mine isn't going to keep you all to herself. And I'm not adverse to being a tagalong, you know."

"She said we were going to church on Sunday. Would you like to join us?" I laughed at the grimace he made.

"That prune-face Whitestead can make breathing a sin. No, thanks, I'll leave the piety to you and my sister. Sometimes I think I'd made a good papist."

"Why?"

He grinned. "You can start each week with a clear conscience. A brief confession and all is forgiven."

"And you have much to confess, I'll wager."

"Not as much as I'd like," he said pointedly.

We were laughing when we came through the drawing room's terrace doors and Dorthea looked relieved that my spirits had revived.

"Let's go into the music room," she suggested. "Bryant loves to sing, don't you, brother dear? I play the pianoforte and we have some wonderful musical soirees, just the two of us. Now that you're here, we can try three parts."

"No," I protested. "Still only two, I'm afraid."

"Nonsense."

Despite my protests, they drew me to an elegant music room which had a beautiful pianoforte on a slightly raised dais. Dorthea's playing was more energetic than skillful but she obviously enjoyed herself as she thumped and laughed and sang with equal enthusiasm. Bryant had a beautiful baritone voice and between the two of them they rattled the gilded mirrors on the wall. My singing voice was pleasant enough but not very forceful, which didn't seem to matter at all. We sang, and laughed, and chided each other's false tones. The evening passed in wonderful companionship. I felt years younger that night when I went to bed than I had that very morning when I left Lynhurst.

The days passed swiftly. True to his word, Bryant spirited me away from his sister whenever he could and when she refused to relinquish her time with me, he very often joined us.

We took evening walks in the garden, spent hours in the library, and had breakfast on the terrace. Always the gentleman, Bryant's attention never exceeded the bounds which I set, although I could sense a growing impatience with my don't-touch manner.

153

"Aileen, I think I'm falling in love with you," he said one evening as we sat in the garden.

Jeweled droplets of water caught the moonlight as a center fountain sent a silver spray into the air. His arm tightened my shoulder and I knew he was going to kiss me.

As if I were watching myself from some detached point, I raised my lips to his. The contact was pleasant and Bryant's embrace was that of a practiced lover. The moonlight, the scent of roses, and a handsome man murmuring declarations of love were meant to stir a woman's desire but I found only faint pleasure in his kisses. I pushed him back gently. "Bryant, it's too soon."

Dorthea and I attended services on Sunday. I readily saw what Bryant meant about the Reverend's dour attitude. His sermon was one of righteous indignation. He pounded the lectern and promised hell's damnation to all who strayed from the true teachings of God. His interpretation of Biblical edicts pictured man as a lost creature sinking in the mires of original sin and wickedness. I felt sorry for the English servants and a few neighboring families who were given a weekly dose of this depressing theology. The sermon was so at odds with Dorthea's personality, I wondered why she went to services at all.

"Because of the singing," she said promptly. "Don't you just feel your soul rising up to heaven when the organ thumps out 'O God, Our Help in Ages Past'?"

"But the sermon was so depressing."

"Oh, I never listen to it," she said practically.

I couldn't help but laugh. What a simple solution. "You're wonderful, Dorthea."

The compliment took her by surprise. For the

first time, she seemed at a loss for words.

"I mean it. You're the most wonderful, vivacious person in the whole world. Don't let anyone ever tell you differently." I was suddenly angry at a father and a stepmother who obviously had ignored Dorthea while she was growing up and even now only seemed to want her as a silent backdrop to their own interests.

She swiped at her eyes as if a tear might be lurking there. Then she gave me a wavering smile. "I've never had a good friend before."

"Neither have I."

We stopped in the lane and hugged each other.

Then she said brightly, "How about a picnic this afternoon? Sunday meals are terribly boring. Claudia and my father usually ride off to visit at one of the other estates and Bryant disappears, so I wander around by myself. But not today! We'll take a basket and walk to a lovely glen and spend the afternoon planning my wedding. You must be my maid of honor. You will, won't you," she said anxiously, sensing my sudden tenseness.

"I don't know, I—"

"Oh, Aileen, please, say yes." Then she clapped a hand to her mouth and laughed. "How stupid, I am. Of course, you won't be able to stand up with me. Here I am, forgetting that I'm not the only one who's making great plans."

I didn't know what she was talking about. "What plans?"

"Don't you see? Oh, it will be wonderful."

As usual, she had left me behind. "What will be wonderful?"

She smiled broadly. "A double wedding at Windbriar, of course."

Chapter Ten

The week before Claudia's birthday party, Bryant devoted his time to entertaining me, and Dorthea planned feminine pursuits which left me little time to myself. Picnics, long walks, stimulating tours through the house and gardens, and hours spent over teas and meals filled the hours of each day and extended into the evening. Song fests in the music room became a favorite after-dinner activity and afterwards we played lively games of whist and chess. I had never played chess before but Bryant was a patient teacher. Since Dorthea couldn't keep her mind on the game long enough to master the moves, she left the two of us to our evening contest. Bryant seemed pleased with my ability to concentrate and I saw admiration in his eyes more than once when I managed some skillful move.

"You're going to be an excellent player," he assured me as he repeatedly took my queen or led me into checkmate.

The lonely days at Lynhurst seemed far away and unreal as my visit extended much longer than I had expected. Dorthea would not hear of my returning to Lynhurst until after Claudia's birthday and I only made a feeble protest about overstaying my welcome.

The two gentlemen who had been house guests left, promising to return with their wives on Saturday. Sir Wainwright and Claudia were busy with their own pursuits and absent from most of the meals. The abundance of food seemed never ending and entrees constantly varied: roast duckling with green peas and stuffing; boiled leg of lamb with parsnips and turnips; smoked bacon with kidney; boiled puddings; berry cakes with clabbered cream; and always bottles of claret for every evening meal and light wine at lunch. I feared that I would soon have to let out my stays.

Preparations for the weekend birthday fete were evident in the scurrying about of housemaids, laying out of rooms, beating of rugs, dusting, and rubbing all the furniture to a high glow with turpentine and beeswax. I tried not to think about the coming weekend when Sean would arrive. The protective cocoon I had wrapped around myself seemed thin and inadequate.

I struggled to keep a pleasing smile on my face when Dorthea chatted ecstatically about her approaching engagement to the man who had held me in his arms and kissed me so possessively. Every time she spoke Sean's name, I relived again those few moments of passion and the fiery desire that had spilled between us. I felt guilty being privy to Dorthea's secret thoughts and I wanted to scream at her to quit talking about her wonderful plans.

"When Sean looks at me with those dark eyes, my knees turn to water," she confessed. "Can you imagine what kind of lover he'll be?" She laughed gaily. "Not that I know exactly what the poets have extolled as the greatest human experience, but I'm going to insist upon a long honeymoon. I don't want to share him with anybody or anything for a long time."

My own future was like a path of nettles and I knew that I must proceed with caution. Dorthea kept winking at me and making comments about her brother's infatuation with me. I wanted to deny that there was anything of a permanent nature between us and yet an instinct for self-preservation would not allow me to deliberately turn away from a chance to secure my future. It was this emotional conflict that made me respond to Bryant's overtures with false pretense. I liked him but I did not return his fevered advances. His touch upon my arm caused no tingling warmth and when he kissed me I felt an impatience that made me withdraw from the embrace as quickly as possible. On the other hand, I enjoyed his friendship and found him to be an affable and entertaining companion.

As the evening walks became a private time between us, Bryant did not propose marriage. In a way I was glad but I began to wonder if his amorous attentions were more of a titillating game than anything else. From what Sean had said about him, I knew that he had engaged in several romantic liaisons. Now that I had allowed him to kiss me, he might want to move into greater intimacy. I made excuses not to be with him alone so much but that only seemed to increase his fervor. Fortunately, Dorthea became more demanding of my time as the weekend approached.

She enlisted my help in choosing the gown she would wear for the important occasion. Although several huge wardrobes were stuffed with gowns, most of the dresses were not harmonious with her sandy hair or blue eyes. A ball gown of white organza with an underlay of blue-green watersilk was my choice out of the piles of clothes she threw on the bed or held up for my approval. I thought the soft pastel color and white would bring out the lovely shade in her eyes and soften her complexion.

She wrinkled up her nose. "That dress was made

for a coming-out affair in London. I hate it. The dressmaker talked me into it. The color is so . . . so ingenue. I much prefer this one."

When she pulled out a velvet trimmed *peau de soie* that was almost tangerine in color, I kept my expression bland. I knew the bright orangish shade would only make her complexion look more ruddy than ever.

For one weak moment, I almost endorsed her choice. Why should I help her look her best? Let Sean see her at her worst. I quickly suppressed the impulse and recognized it for what it was, simmering jealousy. "It's the wrong color for you," I said flatly. "Your bluish gray eyes are your best feature and you should wear gowns that accent them."

"But my coloring is so washed-out! I don't need pastels."

"Yes, you do," I countered. "Bold colors just kill the reddish highlights in your hair and they don't do anything for your skin. You don't need to dress like a tropical parrot in such vivid colors. Your dressmaker was right. The blue-green shade is flattering to your eyes and hair."

"Do you think so?"

"Definitely."

She frowned and then gave a relieved sigh. "I guess you're right. Oh, thank you, Aileen." She gave me an exuberant hug. "I want everything to be perfect. Just perfect. Oh, I'm so scared. Just think, my whole life is about to change. I've got hummingbird wings in my stomach. What if I get sick and disgrace myself? Sometimes I get too excited and end up being embarrassed."

"That's not going to happen," I said firmly. "Don't even think about it."

"You're the best friend a girl ever had. Oh, Aileen, I want you to be as happy as I am. Now,

159

what are you going to wear? Not one of those same three dresses? That will never do. For the most important occasion of my life you must look your best. Take your choice . . . any one of these gowns. We're about the same size, although my waist is not as small as yours. My maid will have time to take in any seams. Now choose. What gown will it be?"

I made a feeble protest but my feminine vanity overruled my pride as she began holding up gowns from the piles on the bed. Ironically, my blond hair and creamy complexion were heightened by the bold colors that she loved so much. She held up each gown to her front and swirled around in great glee. We laughed like two schoolgirls playing dress-up as she showed them off to me. Finally, a garnet silk that would have fought with her sandy hair was my choice.

"Come try it on."

She eyed my modest petticoat, stays, and chemise and insisted that I accept new undergarments from a profuse selection which she said she had bought in Paris. When I protested, she pleaded, "Please, Aileen. Why can't I give gifts to my best friend? You've made me so happy, now it's my turn to do something for you."

I gave in and accepted the beautiful French garments. The luxurious silken fabrics were a sensuous experience against my skin which had only known serviceable cotton and flannel materials.

Folds of the silken gown whispered as it went over my head and fell in full swirls around me. I delighted in the tiny embroidered flowers placed down the front panel of the dress. A tight bodice was cut in a point at my waist and full sleeves fell just below the elbow in gathered cuffs trimmed with the same delicate flowers. The neckline was cut so that my shoulders were almost bare. The display of

160

FREE

BOOK CERTIFICATE

ZEBRA HOME BOOK SUBSCRIPTION SERVICE, INC.

YES! Please start my subscription to Zebra Historical Romances and send me my free Zebra Novel along with my first month's Romances. I understand that I may preview these four new Zebra Historical Romances Free for 10 days. If I'm not satisfied with them I may return the four books within 10 days and owe nothing. Otherwise I will pay just $3.50 each; a total of $14.00 (a $15.80 value—I save $1.80). Then each month I will receive the 4 newest titles as soon as they come off the press for the same 10 day Free preview and low price. I may return any shipment and I may cancel this arrangement at any time. There is no minimum number of books to buy and there are no shipping, handling or postage charges. Regardless of what I do, the FREE book is mine to keep.

Name _____

(Please Print)

Address _____

Apt. # _____

City _____ State _____ Zip _____

Telephone (_____) _____

Signature _____

(if under 18, parent or guardian must sign)

Terms and offer subject to change without notice.

12-89

MAIL IN THE COUPON
BELOW TODAY

GET FREE FREE GIFT

To get your Free ZEBRA HISTORICAL ROMANCE fill out the coupon below and send it in today. As soon as we receive the coupon, we'll send your first month's books to preview Free for 10 days along with your FREE NOVEL.

creamy skin was almost risqué, I thought, and I kept tugging at the cloth to raise it higher on my breasts.

"Nonsense! That's the way the dress was meant to be worn." Dorthea ordered me to parade around the room. "Bryant will love it!" She clapped her hands with delight.

But it was not her brother who was in my thoughts at that moment when I stood in front of the mirror and viewed my startling reflection. *What would Sean think about my appearance?* Then I chided my foolishness. A pretty dress would not change the reality of the situation. Sean Creighton might be attracted to me on some physical level but I knew that his life was ruled by pragmatic and expedient decisions.

I retired to my room when the guests began to arrive on Saturday afternoon. Whether it was the excitement or dread that caused my head to ache, the truth was I wished with all my heart that I could stay hidden in my room while the festivities took place below. I darkened my room by drawing the heavy damask draperies and lay across my bed, clad only in my chemise. I closed my eyes against the throbbing ache across the back of my head.

I wanted to shut out the world but the silence of my room was broken by the sounds of carriage wheels striking against the cobbled stones and voices of people alighting in the courtyard below. Horses' hooves clattered below my windows and I constantly wondered if one of the horsemen might be Sean arriving.

The temptation to slip onto the window seat was strong but I knew such behavior would only inflict more pain. It had been almost two weeks since I'd

161

seen him. My determination to view our brief romantic interlude as unimportant and trivial had been a rational decision, one that had *not* been honored by the feeling part of my mind and body. Even with distance between us, his name could bring a rush of emotion surging through me. How could I endure his presence and Dorthea's joyful, loving eyes upon him?

Dorthea. My wonderful, affectionate friend. I wanted the very best in life for her but I couldn't suppress the despondency that rose in me when I was exposed to the glowing anticipation that radiated from her. Would Dorthea forgive me if I feigned illness and refused to leave my room? This speculation was put at an end when she came bounding into my room, destroying the silence with her cries and wails.

"Aileen!" she sobbed and began talking so fast that I couldn't understand what she was saying. Her face wore a stricken expression and she was wringing her hands.

I sat up and took her by the shoulders as she collapsed on the edge of my bed.

"For heaven's sake, Dorthea, calm yourself. I can't understand a word you're saying." Then alarm leaped through me. "Has something happened to Sean?"

"No, he's here. Just arrived."

Relief was instant. He was all right. At that moment, that was the most important thing. My muscles relaxed. "Then what is it?"

"Oh, Aileen." She covered her face with her hands. "How could Sean do this to me?"

"What has he done? Dorthea! Please, control yourself. Tell me, what happened? What has he done?" I was bewildered by her shattered composure. If Sean had just arrived, there had been no time for her father to talk with him, so he hadn't refused Sir Wainwright's offer of his daughter's hand and a financial backing for his political ambitions. "I don't understand, Dorthea. What is it?"

"He's brought *her*."

"Who?"

"Loretta!"

I blinked. "Was she invited?"

"No, of course not! Why would I want him to bring her? Everything's ruined. Ruined!"

"Calm yourself. It can't be as bad as all that."

"I couldn't believe my eyes," she wailed. "Sean arrived with her in a carriage and when they came in the house, Loretta was clinging possessively to his arm. He was laughing and joking with her and scarcely even looked in my direction. The horrid little vixen! How dare she push herself on us like this! And Claudia made her welcome! Can you believe it? My stepmother greeted her warmly. No consideration for my feelings at all. They all ignored me. Loretta asked Claudia about her blasted horses and you would have thought they were long-lost kin the way my stepmother made over her."

Dorthea sobbed into her hands and I put my arm around her shoulder. I wondered if Loretta had somehow learned about the Wainwright proposal and had come to protect her own interest in Sean. Apparently both Lord Lynhurst and Sir Wainwright saw the value of bringing him into the family as a son-in-law. Quite flattering for a non-titled, non-monied Scotch-Irishman, I thought as I tried to console Dorthea.

"What am I going to do?" She swiped at her eyes.

I doubted that Sir Wainwright was personally interested in Sean's welfare but having a son-in-law in Parliament would bring its own prestige. Apparently

Dorthea's father thought that Sean's standing with the voting Irish, as well as the English aristocracy governing Ireland would ensure his victory at the polls. Securing his daughter's happiness was an additional benefit which Sir Wainwright was not likely to disregard even if a deep paternal affection seemed to be missing between him and his daughter.

"I know why Loretta is hanging on to him," snapped Dorthea with a tone I had never heard before. "She's trying to protect the Lynhurst fortunes. That brother of hers will make them all paupers if he's given full rein of his inheritance."

I had to agree with her that Lord Lynhurst had looked to Sean to keep his estate intact even to the point of encouraging a match with his daughter. My father had specifically educated Sean to handle his affairs and I had witnessed the deep affection Sean had for Loretta and she for him. In spite of Lady Davina's strenuous objections, there would be little she could do if Sean asked for her hand. Lawrence was the man of the house now and he would likely give his blessing, for no other reason than it would ensure more leisure time for himself.

Even though Dorthea had more to offer financially, I knew that my half-sister would not give up her claims on Sean Creighton without a fight. There was little comfort I could offer Dorthea. Loretta was a formidable rival and despite her younger years she had already shown herself to be capable of getting what she wanted. I knew exactly how Dorthea felt. I had run away from Lynhurst because I couldn't endure the sight of them together.

"I can't face him . . . and her!"

I took a deep breath. "Yes, you can." I was determined to give Dorthea as much support as I could. She couldn't run away. She had to face up to the situation and handle it as best she could. "You're going to put on your pretty dress, be your vivacious, sweet self, and play the gracious hostess. This is your home, after all, and you can expect that Sean will pay attention to you out of respect. Show him what kind of a lovely person you are. Don't be intimidated by anything Loretta says and does. She'll show herself to be spoiled and self-centered."

Dorthea raised her tearful eyes. "Do you really think so?"

I nodded, silently fearing that arrangements between Loretta and Sean had already gone too far. I suspected that Dorthea was entering the race years too late. My half-sister already had a protective pattern put in place as far as Sean was concerned. I had seen it the day she had sobbed in his arms and been comforted by him. It would not be easy for anyone to place a wedge between them.

"You'll help me, won't you?" pleaded Dorthea.

My hope of pleading illness fled before her beseeching face. I couldn't send her into the evening's affair alone. How well I knew what it felt like to be the victim of Loretta's cruel barbs. Dorthea's friendship meant a great deal to me. I really had no choice. "Only if you stop making your eyes red with crying. Go bathe your face in cold water. Rest for an hour, and then we'll go downstairs together."

Dorthea hugged me so fiercely that I gasped for breath. "Heaven sent you to me, Aileen. I'll never forget what you've done for me."

"I haven't done anything yet. And if you don't scoot, I'll never be ready in time for dinner."

She bounded to her feet and with her usual energy sailed off to her room, leaving me to wrestle with the knowledge that I must face both Sean and Loretta. Somehow I had become an advocate for Dorthea's interests. The situation was ironic enough to be laughable but as I prepared to face the evening, I wasn't filled with any mirth . . . only dread.

When Dorthea came to my room, dressed in her white and blue-green gown, I thought she looked very feminine and pretty. I could tell that she was uncertain about the pastel color and I tried to reassure her that it was much better than any bright color would have been.

"Now, let's go downstairs and you be your usual, vivacious self."

"Are you sure I look all right?"

"Better than all right. Splendid."

All my reassurances were like shards of pottery broken upon rocks when we came down the staircase and saw Loretta standing in the drawing room. I heard Dorthea's sharp gulp of air.

Loretta was gowned in a vibrant lemon-colored taffeta which set off her black hair and ivory complexion to perfection. Dorthea's favorite color! The gown diminished the appearance of every other woman in the room. She stood out like a brilliant yellow-petaled rose. Dorthea sent an accusing look at me as if I had somehow been traitor to her choice of dress.

I knew then that I had made a terrible mistake. Even though Dorthea could not have competed with Loretta's beauty in such a vivid color, she would have felt good about herself and that confidence would have radiated from the inside out. In that shattering moment, Dorthea's usual vivacious personality shrank and was as subdued as the dress she wore.

As we entered, I saw Loretta's eyes pass over Dorthea's gown with a dismissal and then her gaze fastened on me. An expression of surprise was instantly followed by a curved smile as her eyes

166

traveled over my borrowed gown. She said something to Sean which I'm sure was barbed, probably something about my wearing cast-off clothes. Whatever the remark was, it turned Sean's head in my direction. His eyes met mine — and held. Warmth suffused up into my neck and cheeks. That one moment of contact mocked all my silent lectures about dismissing him from my life. I couldn't tell from his expression whether he was angry, surprised, or indifferent to my appearance or presence.

I broke eye contact with him and smiled at Bryant who was weaving his way through the crowded room toward us.

"You look delightful, Sis," he said to Dorthea, kissing her cheek. Then he took both of my hands. "And you are a vision, dear Aileen; I have never had the pleasure of a lovelier lady's company."

The compliment washed over me without imprint but I managed to murmur a gracious "thank you." My appearance was the least of my concerns at the moment. In fact, my preparations had been quite hasty. While reassuring Dorthea that she could hold her own with Loretta, I had quickly put on the garnet gown and secured my hair in a bun with two curls dangling at the sides of my face. The evening had been ruined before it began and I only wanted to get through it with as much poise as I could.

"They're coming," whispered Dorthea.

I did not need to ask whom she meant. My senses were well aware of Sean's approach. There was no one else in the room for me. Every nerve ending tingled. A frightening expectancy mocked my pretended indifference. I dreaded the moment when he would be close enough to touch. There was no escape. Bryant stood on one side of me and Dorthea the other.

"Good evening, Dorthea," Sean said, making a

polite bow. "May I thank you for the special invitation you sent me for this celebration. I'm honored."

"I'm glad you could come." Dorthea's eyes brightened as she looked at him, and then dimmed as she added, "And you, too, Loretta. How nice of you to surprise us." There was just the right amount of emphasis on "surprise" to indicate a breach of proper manners.

Loretta gave a dismissing wave of her hand. "I knew that the oversight of an invitation was unintentional. And after all, we are old and dear friends, aren't we?" Her laughing eyes belied the truth of her words. "Besides, everyone knows that you and Claudia don't hold with much propriety when it comes to entertaining. I am surprised to see you here, Aileen," she said, as if my presence were a case in point.

"Aileen is my lovely companion for the evening," said Bryant quickly. "We've spent a lovely two weeks with her and I persuaded her to extend her visit to include tonight's festivities."

"Then you'll be ready to return with us on Sunday, Aileen?" asked Sean.

"I haven't made any plans," I answered without looking at him.

"She's welcome to stay here as long as she wants," insisted Dorthea.

Loretta snickered. "The poor, homeless dear needs someone to look after her."

I forgot to keep a tight rein on my temper. "I am very capable of looking after myself and shall return to Lynhurst when I'm ready. Bryant and Dorthea are my friends . . . the only ones I have. They've made me feel very welcome. A new experience for me since I arrived in Ireland."

"I'm sorry you feel that way, Aileen," said Sean, forcing my eyes to his. Was he trying to say something more to me? For a brief moment, I thought he was going to declare he too wanted to make me welcome, but he didn't. "Unfortunately, I must insist that the conditions of your father's will be met. You must reside at Lynhurst and not Windbriar."

"We shall see about that," flared Bryant.

On that pugnacious note we went into dinner. Dorthea sent me a triumphant glance and I saw why. In the seating arrangements, Loretta had been placed at the far end of the table between Sir Wainwright's hunting cronies. Dorthea had arranged to sit on Sean's left and I had been placed on his right, sandwiched between him and Bryant. I despaired to think how I would eat or drink anything.

Sean generously gave his attention to Dorthea and I heard him laughing with her in a relaxed way. Some of her sparkle had returned and I caught Loretta glaring at her from her distant place down the table.

"You seem tense, Aileen," commented Bryant. "Don't you like parties?"

"I'm afraid I haven't been to any birthday fetes as elaborate as this one. It's very nice. Claudia seems to be enjoying herself," I commented in an effort to make polite conversation.

I realized then I had been giving Bryant only superficial attention during the meal while my mind and emotions were captivated by the man sitting at my other side. Our arms were close enough to brush and I wondered if he were deliberately moving so that contact was frequent. Even though we did not look at each other, every breath that Sean drew seemed to be connected in some disturbing way with my own.

The meal dragged on for endless courses and there wasn't a single moment when I wasn't aware of him. When he reached to lift a goblet, I was conscious of his long, dextrous fingers and I remembered poignantly how his fingertips had caressed my cheek. I was forced to meet his eyes when the servants presented steaming dishes between us. His eyebrows raised slightly over the dark depths in his eyes and his lips curved in a polite smile which mocked the sensation of his mouth on mine. His nearness was torture, and when at last he turned to speak with me, I almost fumbled the dessert spoon in my hand.

"I would like to have you return home with me tomorrow, Aileen," he said quietly.

"Home? That's a funny word to use. Lynhurst is not my home."

"It is now . . . unless you are too much of a coward to stay and find your place in the family."

"That's a laugh. No member of the family wants me there."

"Does that matter?"

"Of course, it matters!" I snapped. "What kind of a person wants to live under the same roof with people who show only hate, scorn, and ridicule?"

"You haven't given them a chance."

"You mean they haven't given me one," I countered.

He lowered his voice to a warning whisper. "Don't throw yourself away on Bryant Wainwright. He's just playing with you, the way he plays with all the women who fall under his charming spell."

How dare he! He belittled me and Bryant all in the same breath. "I haven't fallen under anyone's spell," I hissed. "And my relationship with Bryant is none of your business."

Sean started to respond but at the moment an agitated servant rushed into the room, his voice a near shriek.

"Fire! A dozen horsemen. Throwing flaming

torches and running off the stock!"

"My God!"

"The Bog Boys!"

Women screamed and men lurched from their chairs.

"Hand out the guns, Winston!" shouted Claudia, pushing her way out of the room. Her eyes were bright and her voice strong as a rowing captain's. "Saddle up! We'll have ourselves a real shoot."

Sean and Bryant bounded out of the room with the rest of the men. Dorthea and I ran out on the terrace.

Smoke had already sent a pungent dark cloud rolling toward the house from the nearby fields. From our high knoll, we could see tongues of fire licking the night skies and with our eyes follow vanishing torches held by riders setting grain and buildings ablaze.

Amid shouts and confusion, horses were led from the stable and saddled. The mounts whinnied loudly and danced in protest as their nostrils captured smoke-scented air.

With her party gown flowing around her, Claudia mounted a side-saddle, settled a hunting rifle in front of her and kicked her horse into a run. She was one of the first riders to lead a galloping charge away from the house. I lost sight of Sean in the mass of riders who spread in scattered patterns down the sloping terrain toward the fires. We soon heard the sharp report of gunfire.

"They'll be killed," cried Loretta hysterically.

Terror lurched up into my own throat. The scene was a nightmare. Sean! Dear God, no, I prayed. Don't let anything happen to him. Please . . . please.

The rush of armed men away from the stable had left the house and its outbuildings vulnerable.

"Look!"

"There's one of them!"

A rider brandishing a torch broke into the open and raced toward the cluster of outbuildings. Without slowing his steed, he threw a torch upon a tack room jutting out from the stables. Fire instantly began to dance across the roof. The rider gave a triumphant shout, his black steed reared, and then the masked rider rode away into the darkness of the woods.

"Get some buckets," Dorthea screamed at some gawking servants who had run out of the kitchen. "We'll have to form a brigade."

I followed her down the terrace steps.

Horses remaining in the stable filled the air with frenzied cries and tried to beat down the walls of their stalls. Servants from the house began to lead them out, hurrying through the developing smoke from the burning tack room.

Dorthea formed a bucket brigade from a nearby pond to the burning building and I joined the human chain passing the slopping water buckets from one pair of hands to another. My eyes smarted from the acidic smoke and my chest constricted with the intake of foul air. My arms threatened to pull out of their sockets.

If another torch had followed the first one, we would have lost the battle, but the lone rider did not return and no other attackers came close enough to the house to fling a flaming brand upon the stables. A wash of relentless buckets of pond water dashed the burning boards. Orange flames disappeared in hissing smoke before the fire spread from the tack room to the main part of the stables.

"It's out," said Dorthea.

Her dirty face matched her soiled gown and I knew she was as exhausted as I. My hair had fallen from its pins and my silk gown was ruined from water spills.

Wearily, we made our way back to the terrace where Loretta and the other women waited. I think they would have stood there and watched the house burn down without soiling a little finger to save it. They all looked at Dorthea and me as if we were a disgrace to womanhood, indulging in such deplorable physical activity.

"Why don't they come back?" Loretta fretted. "What's happening? I can't stand this waiting." She paced up and down the terrace, peering into the smoky shadows.

We couldn't see anything but clouds of smoke rising darkly against the starry sky. Anxiety built within me as I sat down in a chair and clutched my dirty fists in my wet lap. Either the men had stopped shooting or the gunfire was too far away for us to hear it. Burning haystacks grew smaller and smaller as the dried shucks were consumed.

"Some of the men are coming back!"

We ran to the terrace wall.

Horses' hooves pounded upon the earth and we could see riders coming up the slope toward the house. Like warriors returning from battle, they waved and shouted. "We ran 'em off!"

"Turned tail and ran they did!"

"Damn thieving papists!"

My eyes searched each rider. Sean? Where was he?

Loretta saw him before I did. She shrieked and lunged down the terrace steps and threw herself into his arms.

Thank God, he's safe. I leaned weakly against the stone parapet.

Loretta clung to Sean's arm as they mounted the steps. "Darling! I was so frightened. Thank God, you're safe," she sobbed. "It was just awful! One of them came here! He could have killed us! Set fire to the stable. But we got it out!"

I heard Dorthea spit out an unladylike swear word. She strode forward, pulling me along with her. "What happened, Sean?" she asked anxiously.

Sean looked at Dorthea and then his gaze passed on to me, taking in our disheveled appearance. One eyebrow quirked and I thought a smile quivered at the edges of his mouth. "Members of the fire brigade, I assume?"

I gave him a wan smile. "We had a little excitement of our own."

"What happened, Sean?" Dorthea repeated her question. "Who was it?"

"A raiding party. We didn't get a good look at any of them."

"It was just awful," whimpered Loretta. "I wish we'd never come."

"I told you it wasn't a good idea," countered Sean in a brisk tone.

Dorthea exchanged a joyous look with me. *He didn't want her to come.*

I wondered why. I remembered then that Sean had also warned me about visiting Windbriar. Did he know what was going to happen tonight? The question brought a cold chill. I turned away, not wanting to look at him.

At that moment, Sir Wainwright returned to the house. His bellowing swear words accompanied every step as he raved to Bryant. "Slaughtered my prize bull, the bloody bastards. Ran my cattle into the lough and drowned half of them."

"The same thing has happened all over the county. Ran a bunch of prize cattle off into the sea, they did," a guest complained.

"I'll see the scoundrels hanged, every last one of

them," vowed Sir Wainwright. "They won't perpetrate their evil deeds at Windbriar and get away with it."

"Calm down, father," urged Bryant. "You'll have one of your spells. The damage is done. There's nothing we can do tonight. Let's all go back in the house."

"Bring out the brandy," ordered Sir Wainwright. A murmur of agreement rippled over the male guests.

"And tea for the ladies," added Bryant, taking my arm and leading me inside.

It was several minutes before someone missed Claudia.

"Didn't she come back?"

"I thought she was with you, Father," said Bryant.

"She was," granted Sir Wainwright. "And then she gave a whoop and I saw her ride off into that stretch of woods behind the house. I thought she was heading back toward the stables."

"We'd better get back out there and find her!"

The men mounted their horses again and rode off.

The women waited in the drawing room, twisting their handkerchiefs. A weighted apprehension grew with every passing minute. Even Loretta was mute. Dorthea stood looking out a window and I came over and put my arm around her waist.

I think I knew even before they returned that Claudia Wainwright had gone on her last shoot. Bryant came in the room and walked over to Dorthea. He told her that their stepmother had been found lying on the ground at the edge of the woods.

Claudia's throat had been cut and a black ivy wreath laid upon her chest.

175

Chapter Eleven

I stayed at Windbriar until a few days after the funeral. The same guests who had come to honor Claudia Wainwright on her birthday stood around her grave and listened to Reverend Whitestead drone the words, "Earth to earth, dust to dust." In his eulogy he had expounded on the victim's love of God's creatures, exalted her as a good wife and loving mother to her stepchildren, and a supporter of the true Church of God. He raved about the villainous papist pigs who had done the evil deed, and vowed that the Lord would wreak vengeance upon the heathen perpetrators. There had been whispers of the Watcher's ghost but I knew that whoever had murdered Claudia was only using the myth to his advantage.

Sir Wainwright took Claudia's death hard. He visibly crumpled in stature. Losing inches in rounded shoulders and walking with his head down, he shrunk into an old, small man. His usual verbosity disappeared and he only muttered responses to expressed condolences. He was oblivious to Dorthea's problems as she tried to cope with visitors and expressions of sympathy.

"You poor child. A terrible thing."

"Decent people aren't safe on their own property."

"Cutthroats, every one of them. We'll see them all

176

carted off and hanged."

There was talk of random revenge since the guilty parties could not be identified and I feared that Sir Wainwright's grief would bring unfair reprisals to all those Irish families under his authority. His English overseer was called to the house for long sessions in the library. Letters were dispatched to Dublin and London.

Bryant and Dorthea supported each other as I suspected they had always done in times of crisis and I did my best to help whenever I could. Dorthea's usual vivaciousness disappeared. She carried out her duties with dull eyes and her mouth thin and drawn. Not only had she lost a stepmother in a horrible deed but her wonderful plans had been put aside indefinitely. Sean had come and gone and her father showed little interest in pursuing the course of action he had promised his daughter.

"He just needs time to get over his grief," I assured Dorthea. "I'm certain he will look after your happiness and approach Sean when the time is right."

She shook her head. "It's no use. Loretta has her hooks in him. Sean would never be interested in me, even on a silver platter."

Maybe not silver platter but a political platter is something else. I had seen the fire of ambition in his eyes, the fervent, determined set of his chin, and his resonant voice declaring, "We have to change things at the Parliament level." He would sacrifice his own happiness to carry out his goal. Even Loretta would not have a chance against Dorthea if her father offered the means to put Sean in the House of Commons.

"I don't think you should give up. Wait a while. Let our father deal with his grief and then invite Sean back. Bryant will stand behind you and your

177

father will see to your happiness — and Sean's."

Her eyes brightened. "Do you think so? Oh, Aileen, dare I dream?"

"Of course," I said briskly. "What is life without dreams?" The question was a hollow echo in my own heart.

"Stay here with us," she begged.

"I can't. My father's will ties me to Lynhurst."

"Unless you marry," she said with a gleam in her eye. "If this hadn't happened, Bryant would have proposed, I'm sure of it. Now, we must observe a proper period of mourning."

Bryant said about the same thing on my departure. "My father is so shaken by Claudia's violent death that I must devote my time to him in this crisis."

"I understand. It's time to end my visit in any case."

He kissed me lightly. "But I'll be seeing you," he said. "My father is sending me to Dublin but I'll come to Lynhurst as soon as I can."

"And so will I," promised Dorthea as they helped me into the carriage. Her eyes were moist with tears and so were mine as the carriage pulled away from the house and lumbered down the lane of lime trees.

The return journey was uneventful and when I reached Lynhurst, Dolan came out and ordered a burly servant to take my luggage to my room. I had returned from my visit with an extra small trunk because Dorthea had insisted on giving me several gowns and bonnets.

I followed the servant up the staircase to the third floor. The cold, echoing chambers of the castle were a sharp contrast to the Wainwright's warm English manor house. Since I had not alerted anyone to my return, no fire was lit in the fireplace and the curtains had been drawn against the sun. The hunting tapestry assaulted my nerves like a rasp upon stone and I knew that I could not bear to look at that bleeding deer on my wall morning, noon, and night.

"Take that down," I ordered the manservant when he brought up the last of my things.

He looked at me as if I had taken leave of my senses.

"That tapestry. Take it down. Roll it up and tell Dolan to dispose of it as he wishes."

The iron timbre of my voice did not invite anything but obedience.

"I'll need a ladder, Miss."

"Get one."

He nodded and left. I wondered if I would ever see him again. I was just about to figure out a way to do the job myself when he returned with a young man he called Liam. Between the two of them, they lifted down the large woven picture and left carrying it under their arms.

Callie ran into them just outside my door. She came in with her eyes wide. "Yer back, mum."

Her eyes fled to the blank space on the wall. The outline of the tapestry showed clean against the sooty wall.

"I'm going to be redecorating, Callie," I said with an inspiration born out of quiet desperation. If I had to live in this room, I would make it mine the way Dorthea's Aunt Marta had left her personality on her room at Windbriar.

"And what be that . . . redecorating?" asked Callie, puzzled.

"It means I'm going to paint the walls, change the draperies, look for some different furniture and pictures. And you can help, Callie."

She swallowed hard. "Yes mum." Obviously my

179

authority was in question. "If cook don't mind, mum."

"Don't worry, I'm not going to get you in any trouble. You are going to be assigned to me . . . as my maid," I said with sudden inspiration and slightly drunk with ideas tumbling over themselves. I had no choice at the moment but to live at Lynhurst but I wasn't going to let someone else dictate "how" I lived. I had brought some of the gracious living of Windbriar with me.

Fortified with this new resolve, I changed from my traveling clothes and told Callie to advise me when Mr. Creighton had returned to the castle.

She came to my room about four o'clock. "He's in the library, Miss."

"Thank you, Callie." I smiled at her. "Don't look so worried. I'll have Mr. Creighton speak to cook about changing your duties."

"Yes, mum," she agreed but I could see she didn't quite believe me.

Before I reached the library doors, I began to entertain a few doubts myself. My enthusiastic plans dimmed. How childish they seemed. And yet how terribly important to my sense of belonging. Would Sean just laugh at me? I knew what those intense eyes of his could do to me. Determined that he would not stay me from my new resolve, I swept into the room with an airy "Hello, Sean. I'm back."

He sat his quill pen into the well and stood up. I knew that he was surprised to see me dressed as if for afternoon tea in a soft floral dress which Dorthea had given me. His eyes narrowed as if my appearance didn't quite meet with his approval. Maybe it was the way I held my skirts to manage the slight train in back or the new cap of curls at the side of my face that brought a speculative look at his face. Suddenly I realized that he would never have taken me to his secret place if I had been dressed like this. Still, I felt a new rise of confidence and the smile I sent him was almost a challenge.

"Please sit down," he said almost formally, as if we were new acquaintances. "How is Dorthea?"

"Shattered."

"I'm sorry to hear that. I didn't realize she and Claudia were that close. The poor woman spent her time and energies on horse flesh. Sir Wainwright's second marriage provided him with companionship but Dorthea and Bryant have been on their own."

"They still are—and it's a shame." I scrutinized his expression as I waited for his comment.

"Why are you looking at me like that?" he demanded without speaking further of the family.

"Like what?"

"Like my reply will somehow put me in the dock in front of a judge."

"I'm not judging you."

"Aren't you? Funny, I got that impression." He shrugged. "Well, now that you're back, what are your plans?"

"I'm so glad you asked." I took a deep breath and kept my gaze just below his firm chin while I talked. "I've decided to redecorate and refurbish my room. You know, change the wall color, bring in new drapes and furnishings. I'm certain that there are many lovely things tucked away in various places in the castle that I would enjoy more than the dark, heavy furnishings that are here now. I've already had that horrible tapestry removed. And I've told Callie that I would arrange for her to be my personal maid."

"How long have you been back, Aileen? A few hours? And you're ready to play Lady of the Manor?"

181

I raised my eyes at his derisive tone. "I've decided that if Lynhurst is to be my home, it ought to feel like one—at least in one room of the castle."

"Feminine flipperies aren't going to solve the problems at Lynhurst for you," he said flatly.

"Are you refusing my requests?"

"I'm not sure that I'm the one to grant or deny them."

"You control the purse strings, don't you?" My glare dared him to deny it. "Don't lie to me. Approvals for household expenses pass through your hands."

"True, and it's my responsibility to keep them as low as possible. The tenants cannot bear a new rise in taxes."

"Are you trying to tell me that my request for a decent room will levy new taxes? I don't believe it. Deny Lawrence an extra bottle of port and Lorrie another new dress and there'll be more than enough money to freshen my room. My father would have granted my wishes," I flung at him in a childish taunt.

"Yes, he would have made a spoiled Englishwoman out of you, just the way the Wainwrights apparently have done in two weeks' time. All right, you may have your new furnishings and fresh paint. Take what you want from any of the guest rooms."

"And Callie? You'll assign her to me? She's the closest thing I have to a friend under this roof. No one else will talk with me."

"Then why don't you change that situation?" The challenge was blatant.

"And how do you suggest I do that?"

He came around the desk. "You could start by getting acquainted with Lady Davina. She's a very lonely woman. I think you would win her over if you were willing to expend some time and effort."

"I'm not sure I care to 'win her over' as you put it. All I do is remind her of my mother and I won't listen to her jealous harangues and insults. I don't care how lonely she is!" I glared at him. He didn't seem to care at all about *my* feelings.

I was surprised when he reached out and touched my cheek. "I want you to be happy here, Aileen. Won't you try to make friends with Loretta? Lynhurst castle is your home now."

"It's a horrible place. I hate it. I was much happier at Windbriar. I wish I could stay there and never have to come back here."

He dropped his hand. "Bryant will never marry you."

The flat statement was like a slap to my face. I knew then that I had indeed been considering marriage to Bryant as a way to ensure my future. His amorous attentions had not faltered even through the difficult days following the raid and Claudia's death. He had promised to see me again as soon as he could get away. I knew my eyes had widened at Sean's rude comment. I tried to recover. "Thank you, sir, for that profound announcement. It will be my greatest pleasure to prove you wrong."

"Don't be a child, Aileen!" He seemed ready to grab my shoulders and shake me. "I wasn't handing you any kind of a challenge, you little fool. Bryant isn't the marrying kind. Leave him alone and see that he does the same. He's got a trail of mistresses a mile long. Right now he's bedding one of the daughters from a nearby estate. He'll get her with child, she'll go off to England and have the child, and ruin her life because of the sweet-talking bastard. It's happened before."

"I don't believe a word of it! You just can't stand to see me slipping away from your control. You and my father set it up so I'm nothing more than a chattel to you and this house."

"Believe me, I had no influence upon His Lordship when it came to making his will. The conditions he set up for you were his own idea. I, for one, never thought his daughter would be brave enough to leave England and come here. Why did you, Aileen? Surely, you had other, more reasonable options?"

I wasn't going to tell him the truth. Obviously Sean Creighton had little respect for my judgment. His insufferable attitude indicated to me that he would assume that I had enticed the foul overtures by my stepfather. I felt a sudden fullness in my eyes. "I came because I thought my father would offer me a home."

The simple statement brought a softness to his eyes and lips. "Aileen, you are an exasperating contradiction. Soft and yielding and yet clawed and ready to strike out at everyone around you. You're letting your emotions cloud your judgment."

He reached out a hand to me but I backed away from his touch. I couldn't bear it if he took me in his arms again. Not now.

"I'm not going to hurt you," he said softly.

I wanted to shout at him that he already had. My chin jutted out and I blinked rapidly to clear my vision. "At the moment I must suffer the indignities of living here," I told him, "but I intend to be at dinner every night and come and go as I please. And I shall entertain Bryant Wainwright whenever he calls upon me!" I was rewarded by a dark flash of anger that tightened the smooth sweep of his chin.

"I'm just trying to warn you—"

"Keep your warnings to yourself!"

I swung about, left the library, and made it outside before the tears came so fast that my vision blurred. Anger made my movement rapid and my body stiff as I strode away from the castle. I kicked at a stone and sent it sailing across the stable yard. When the rock hit the wall of the barn, Daddo stuck his head out of a door.

"Sure and I thought 'twas hailin'," he said with a laugh. He took one look at my face and sobered. "Faith, a storm is a brewin' for sure. Well, now, you've come to the right place. I was just a thinkin' the day's gettin' weary and the sunshine's beckonin'. Sure and 'tis time for taking a little stroll. Come on. I'll show ye the prettiest little glen God ever dropped into the Emerald Isle."

With his usual hopping gait, Daddo walked beside me as we headed away from the stables toward a thick stand of trees beyond the castle grounds. I had forgotten my bonnet and gloves but this impropriety didn't seem to matter at the moment. Such social conventions were out of rhyme with the simple joy of walking through the woods with the funny little man who still reminded me of some fey Irish creature.

We made our way along a path, sometimes straight and sometimes crooked, leading into the nearby woods. Daddo hummed, chatted to a blackbird high in an alder tree as if it were an old friend. He spoke gently to a deer that raised its head and watched us go past a pond of clear blue water. In a sunny grove, he bent down to pick several wild blossoms and handed me a sweet-smelling bouquet.

I buried my face in the sweet nectar as we entered a shaded glen. The earth was redolent with tangy scents of evergreen and our feet were cushioned by yellow moss, thick grasses, and crunchy deadfall from the trees. My warring spirits found peace in the dense, green shade and when we came out into the light of a small meadow, I blinked in the sudden brightness. I caught my breath. Splotches of wild colors lay upon the meadow green, yellow gorse and purple stalks of foxglove which waved banners of wine and lavender in thick profusion.

Daddo plopped down under the shade of an alder tree and took a small reed flute from his pocket. I sat down on the ground beside him and he ignored me as if I were no more to him than a nearby thrush who cocked her head and went bobbing through the grass, like a busy mother on her way to market.

I leaned my head back against a tree trunk, closed my eyes, and listened to the sweet notes of Daddo's tune. We must have sat there for nearly a half-hour when the peaceful stillness was disturbed by the sound of laughter and footsteps.

Daddo kept on playing but my eyes darted about to see who was coming. At first I only recognized Shannon, the stableboy, and identification of the two girls at his side came a moment later—Molly's girls, Kerrie and Holly. They came through the woods and Daddo's flute drew the three young people to the place where we sat like the Pied Piper calling the children of Hamelin. The girls were barefooted and wore faded coarse dresses that whipped around their dusty legs. Their hair tumbled freely down their backs and Holly had tucked bright yellow daisies behind both ears.

Shannon and Kerrie had been holding hands but they quickly dropped them when they saw me sitting there with Daddo. Kerrie frowned and said something in a hushed whisper to Shannon.

"Daddo," squealed Holly, rushing ahead and throwing herself on the ground beside him.

He lowered his flute and frowned. "For shame, filling the woods with yer babbling noise, little one."

"I'm sorry, Daddo. I'm just so glad to see you." She hugged the little man with an exuberance that reminded me of Dorthea. "Will ye tell me a story? Patrick is learning to read but he won't share with me. He even has a real book. Father Rooney gave it to him. Patrick let me hold it and turn the pages," she said proudly.

"Sure and he's a smart fellow, that Patrick. A good priest, he'll make," agreed Daddo.

"I wish girls could be priests!" said Holly with a fling of her red curls.

"Don't be a ninny," said her sister, plopping down beside her.

"I'm not a ninny. I just wish I could read like Patrick."

"Girls don't read! They have more important things to do."

Kerrie's tone was so sharp that I couldn't keep silent. "I'm sure you could learn to read if you wanted to, Holly. I'd be glad to teach you."

The young girl's eyes widened as if I'd just said I would tie the moon up with a ribbon and give it to her.

"I don't think Father would like that," retorted Kerrie, glaring at me.

"He wouldn't have to know," said Holly. "I bet Mama would say it's all right."

"Why don't I ask her," I said boldly. The idea appealed to me. Holly was a bright little girl and I saw no reason why she should be denied a chance to learn to read if she wanted to.

"Better that Holly give an ear to the telling of stories," countered Daddo. "Books are not our way. Who can read scribbles on a paper? Don't ye know that it is the *seanachai* who keep the pages of Ireland's glory in their heads . . . not on frail paper and splotted ink? Sure, me grandfather could take

187

two hours to tell a story and nary an eye would blink," Daddo bragged. "Kings, queens, fishermen, warriors and gods, he could tell you about them all and he never read a word in his life. Auch! 'Tis wastin' yer time with all that foolish reading nonsense. Only boys like Patrick who are following in the church need to fill their heads with such book learning."

Shannon was lounging back on one arm, chewing on a long blade of grass. I judged him to be of average intelligence. Was he content with his job as stableboy? "What about you, Shannon? Have you been to school?"

He sat up, putting his arms around his drawn-up legs in a comfortable fashion. "Sure, I attended hedge school for nigh on to four years. That was a rollickin' time, to be sure." He laughed. "We'd sit on a circle of rocks and do our copybooks. When the teacher wasn't looking, we'd have ourselves a time passing a chuck of tobacco about or pitching bits of sheep dung. I learned to write me name and that's about it. All I need, though," he grinned at Kerrie. "I'll take care of meself and me wife with my hands and back. Don't need no learning."

I had heard of hedge schools, outdoor classes held in the shade of a hedgerow. "Doesn't Danareel have a school building?"

Daddo nodded. "We do now. 'Tis a fine one to be proud of. Three years ago we kidnapped our schoolmaster and built him a school."

"Kidnapped him?" I echoed, thinking I must have misunderstood his meaning.

Daddo slapped his leg and Shannon gave a loud guffaw.

" 'Tis right, ye are. The menfolks around here decided it was about time to move the hedge school inside four walls. They put out the word that a schoolmaster was needed but no one came to claim the job. One night, the men of the community formed a posse, they did, and rode into the next county where Mr. Dooley was teaching school. Got him good and drunk, put him in a sack and brought him back to Danareel." Daddo cackled. "Slept the whole way, he did. Some other men brought along Dolly, his wife, and all their belongings. And when Dooley woke up, he was in his own bed in a fine new cottage. They've been here ever since."

"Didn't the other village protest?"

"Protest? Yea, if yer asking if a few heads were cracked and some blood spilled. Them that did the protesting were sent back home and Dooley stayed. He's a fine man who likes his poteen and can spout Latin as good as Father Rooney."

"Latin. What about arithmetic, reading, and writing?" I asked. "Skills that help a man earn a living?"

Shannon grinned at Kerrie. "What good are them things when a man hears wedding bells?" He turned to me. "I'm marrying Kerrie."

"Your father gave his blessing, then?"

Kerrie nodded. "Father Rooney announced the banns last Sunday. Will you play for the wedding dance, Daddo?"

"Sure and 'tis an honor."

"What a celebration it will be. Might even be a good fight or two," grinned Shannon. "You know how it is at weddings and funerals. The poteen runs free."

On this merry note, we walked back to the castle. The young people laughed and sang with Daddo. Holly surprised me by grabbing my hand and whispering. "You won't forget to talk to Ma, will you? About the reading?"

189

I promised I would pay her mother a visit soon.

Her eyes sparkled and she gave my hand a squeeze.

The girls took a path around the castle and Daddo, Shannon, and I walked back to the stables. I idly wondered how it was that Daddo and Shannon were able to saunter away from their jobs in the middle of the day. Then I realized that very little work was going on in the stables, wash shed, or the gardens. There was an ominous quiet in the usually busy grounds. Men lounging about in quiet groups were smoking or spitting tobacco.

Something was brewing. I could feel it. *Oh, no, not Lynhurst!* Was it the Bog Boys' next target? Would there be burning and killing here? My throat was suddenly dry.

"Wait a minute," Daddo said and darted into the stables. When he came back, he surprised me by holding out a small box. "Will ye be taking a package to Lady Davina for me?"

What was this funny little Irishman sending to the lady of the house? I nodded. The box was so light it seemed empty.

"Take care of yerself," he said with a wave of his hand.

A warning or a benign remark?

I entered the castle and had placed my foot on the first step of the main staircase when I heard loud voices coming from the library. The nervousness I had felt outside was instantly magnified. Sean was shouting at someone. Then I recognized the other voice. My half-brother, Lawrence.

Nervous and apprehensive, I moved closer to the half-open doors of the library so I could listen. The impropriety of such eavesdropping didn't even cause the slightest prickle of conscience.

"I'm telling you that you'd better stop your gambling and whoring long enough to do something—now!" swore Sean.

"You talk like an old woman!" snapped Lawrence. "Scared of your own shadow. Just cause some drunken outlaws caused a little trouble at Windbriar . . ."

"I don't call murder 'a little trouble.' And they got away with it. Not a single one of them was caught. Who knows but some of our people were among them? We can't let this thing ferment. It's time to ensure our men's loyalty."

"I'll ensure it with a hanging tree if anybody starts trouble here," bragged my half-brother.

"Not if you're dead, you won't."

There was a silence as if Sean's remark had shaken Lawrence.

"I'll call in the Queen's Dragoons," my half-brother vowed but in a weaker voice.

"They didn't protect your father."

Another silence.

"Why don't *you* do something?" Lawrence raised his voice. "That's what you're paid for! I should fire you!"

I heard Sean laugh. "You can't . . . unless you want to lose some of your inheritance. Your father set his will up so that you couldn't fire me without turning over a nice parcel of your income to me as remuneration. No danger of that, is there?" There was a bitter edge to Sean's voice. "His Lordshisp knew that you loved money more than the responsibility of being a landowner. Quit whining about firing me and do as I tell you."

"All right, blast it all," swore Lawrence. "Why my father trusted you, I'll never know. You're one of them. You'd sell out your Scottish heritage to the papist pigs in a minute. You don't fool me, Sean Creighton. Irish blood runs thick in your veins. I know who's behind the killings and pillage!"

Sean swore. "If you were a man, I'd ram those words down your throat. Now get out and I'll try to save your blasted neck one more time."

I scurried away and bounded up the staircase before Lawrence came stomping out of the library. He crossed the wide hall without seeing me and went into the drawing room. I heard the sound of glasses clinking.

Lawrence's accusation rang in my ears as I mounted the stairs. *I know who's behind the killings and pillage!*

Unbidden speculation rushed over me like a cataract. Sean had warned me not to go to Windbriar. Had he known what was going to happen there? There was so much confusion that night, he could have been the one rider who came back to the house and flung his brand upon the shed . . . and then disappeared into the woods to intercept Claudia and leave her slain with the wreath upon her chest. I knew he could have easily killed Sir Lynhurst on his doorstep. My father obviously trusted him but something could have changed. Sean's guilt in the recent clandestine affairs of the Watcher could have come to my father's ears, but before he could act upon it, he had been murdered. The horrible speculation brought a deep sickness within me. Too many things seemed to fit.

I stopped on the second floor landing and caught my breath. The hard words I had heard between Sean and Lawrence only deepened an uneasiness that seemed to permeate the very walls of the castle. I started to continue my flight up to the third floor when I remembered the small box I had promised to give to Lady Davina.

I turned and went down the hall to her apartment. When I reached her door I was surprised to find it standing open. I stepped inside and saw Rosa straightening up some discarded books and a sewing basket tossed on the floor by the high-backed fireplace chair.

"Yes, ma'am?" She said in a caustic tone when she caught sight of me. Her unfriendly expression and her tone were accusing. Dark, malevolent eyes bore into me and I had to swallow before I spoke.

"I was looking for Lady Davina. I have a package to deliver."

"She's not here. I'll take it."

"No, I want to give it to her myself," I surprised myself by saying. A spurt of stubbornness made me challenge the servant's abrasive manner. I didn't know why this woman hated me so much. I could only assume that she was reflecting her mistress's abhorrence of me. I didn't want to see Lady Davina but I wasn't going to be intimidated by her maid. "I'll return another time."

I had turned on my heel when Rosa muttered to my back. "She's in the tower room."

There was a smirk on her face as if I would now have to ask her for escort. She didn't know that I had been lost so many times along these corridors that I knew very well where the turret rooms were. I had not seen the tower room on this floor but I assumed that Lady Davina would be using the near-est one to her apartment.

"Thank you, Rosa," I said sweetly. "I'll visit her there. Just down the hall and to the right, isn't it?"

She glared. "She don't like to be bothered when she's in the turret room."

"I'll let her decide that. And I'm sorry to have disturbed your duties. I can see that this room needs a lot of straightening before her return." The remark was a cheap barb and I was ashamed that I

193

had let her disrespectful manner get to me.

I quickly walked in the direction of the rounded turret which had rooms on every floor. The door to the one on the second floor was closed and I knocked tentatively.

The box was very light and as I turned it in my hand, I wondered if there was anything in it at all. Had Daddo played some kind of a joke on me? Had the errand been planned to create some embarrassment and add fuel to the bitterness that the lady of the house already held for me? Suddenly, I wanted to turn and flee, but it was too late.

The door opened and Lady Davina stood there. My eyes fled from her hostile expression to the rounded walls behind her. The sight that met my eyes took away my breath. I thought I was hallucinating.

Chapter Twelve

Butterflies! Hundreds of them! Pricked with pins, they were mounted on the walls singularly and in clusters. Identifying names had been carefully printed under each one. Every hue and color, every pattern, and every size of wingspread was represented. As my gaze swung around the curving walls, the room seemed alive with the beautiful insects. Their vibrant colors were a sharp contrast to the squat, dull woman who stood in the doorway.

I brought my astonished eyes back to her face. The weird mound of false hair on top of her head only brought her to my shoulder height. She had been watching me as I viewed the room beyond her and she was prepared to shut the door in my face, but my awed expression must have stayed her hand.

When her gray, sleek dog gave a low, rumbling growl as if ready to leave her side and leap at me, she touched his head. "Easy, Rex." His sharp eyeteeth disappeared under loose skin as he relaxed his mouth but he did not move from his guard position. Every muscle in his body was tense and waiting for her command.

Instinctively I took a step backward.

"What do you want?" she demanded. "How dare you invade my privacy? Isn't it enough that I must endure your presence in every other room in the house?"

"I am truly sorry to bother you," I apologized, holding out the box. "Daddo asked me to bring you this. I assure you that I didn't mean to intrude."

She took the box gently from my hand and I knew what was inside. Butterflies. Daddo must keep her supplied with them. A brightness shone in her eyes and a youthful eagerness crossed her face as she looked at the box in her hands. I was certain that for a moment she completely forgot that I was standing there.

"Forgive me for staring, Lady Davina, but I have never seen such a beautiful butterfly collection."

The softness that had been in her eyes a moment before wavered. She hesitated as if something in my manner kept her from dismissing me.

Her hesitation gave me courage to ask, "Please, may I look at your collection? I promise that I will keep my silence and not disturb you in any way."

"Why would you want to spend your time in such a fashion?" she demanded as if I were lying about my interest and making sport of her in some way.

"Because I am overwhelmed. Truly. I think it's wonderful that you have a collection like this."

"The best in all Ireland," she pronounced with a toss of her head.

"You must be very proud." The sincerity in my voice must have reached her.

"Yes, I am."

Surprisingly enough, she took hold of Rex's collar and ordered him back. The dog turned around reluctantly. Keeping his eyes on me, he lay down on a rug in front of one of the circular windows.

Lady Davina motioned me into the room. "You may come in."

"Thank you."

My astonishment only increased as my gaze swept the walls bathed with light from curved windows. A long table held jars and mounting paraphernalia. Books were stacked upon shelves and several lay open to picture plates of butterflies as if Lady Davina had been categorizing specimens when I disturbed her. A microscope and glass slides stood beside a tray filled with tweezers and mounting pins. All the equipment testified to a dedicated naturalist.

For a moment I could not even look at the butterflies. This astonishing revelation of Lady Davina's personality stunned me. Evidence of this scientific, intellectual pursuit was at odds with the woman I had met several times earlier. I had judged my father's wife to be an embittered, dull woman of narrow interest and inbred nastiness.

I looked at her as if seeing her for the first time, watching the eager expression on her face as she bent her head over the box I had given her. Very carefully she opened it, and then gave a girlish squeal of delight. She held the contents out for me to see. Nestled in some tufts of cottonweed was a purple and red butterfly speckled with spots of orange and yellow. I had never seen anything so colorful. "It's beautiful," I breathed.

"Yes, beautiful! Bless Daddo. He told me he had seen one like this but I didn't believe him. I must take care of this treasure immediately. I've taught Daddo to use a killing jar but sometimes he's slow in getting the specimen to me. Time is important, you see, if I am to achieve the best mounting."

A brightness in her eyes dominated bland features and her face lost its usual dull, homely look. She moved about the small room quickly and purposefully. I kept my promise and remained silent. I knew nothing about the classification of butterflies and their cousin, the moth. Latin names were carefully printed under each specimen and I was astounded at the elaborate phylum.

As if Lady Davina had been deprived of human company for a long time, she broke the silence and began talking about her collection. She assured me that it was far from complete, even though the number of different specimens already mounted seemed infinite. I was fascinated with the metamorphosis that had come over her. Nearly an hour passed before I realized that I should be wary of overstaying my welcome.

"Thank you so much for allowing me to view your marvelous collection. I feel honored and I am grateful to Daddo for asking me to bring you his latest offering." Then a thought hit me. "Do you think he did it on purpose?"

For a moment, neither of us spoke. I was embarrassed and Lady Davina seemed angry that she might have been manipulated.

"Yes, perhaps," she said rather stiffly. "Sometimes he oversteps himself."

"May I come again?"

An inner conflict was evident in her face. The woman was torn between having someone who appreciated her exciting pursuit and keeping me in my proper place. "This is my private retreat. I couldn't have survived all these years without it."

"I'm sorry your life has been so unhappy," I said with a rush. "I truly am. My mother would not have wanted that. She was a very kind person. Whatever unhappiness you have suffered was not of her making."

She sighed, all inner light gone from her face. "No, I suppose not. It's easier to blame the fates or someone else for one's unhappiness. My bleak marriage was of my own making. My father owned a large estate in County Donegal which we only visited a few weeks out of the year. I was foolish enough to accept Lord Lynhurst's proposal during one of those visits. After the wedding, my husband never allowed me to return to England, even for a visit. He knew I would never come back to Ireland if I once returned home. He took control of my inheritance and made certain that I remained as securely pinned to Lynhurst as the butterflies on my wall. I thought things would be different after he died, but even in death he holds me securely in his net."

There was so much hatred in her voice I wondered if she could have slit his throat in a futile attempt to escape. "I'm terribly sorry," was my inane response.

"I don't want your sympathy." She tossed her head proudly. "When I complete my work, I will find the means to publish my studies. Nobody believes in me. Not even my children! My husband took them away from me long ago. You've seen for yourself what selfish creatures they have become. They only laugh at my stupid little pastime."

"I'm not laughing, Lady Davina. I'm envious."

She looked startled. "Envious? Of me?" Her eyes traveled over my fair hair, my slender figure, and came back to my face.

"Yes, envious. Not only of your intelligence but also your strength to find a purpose in life."

She gave an impatient snort. "You will marry. You will have choices."

"At the moment, the only choice I have is to remain here, under your roof, however unpleasant."

She eyed me with a stern, unflinching glare. Rex had risen and stood like a guard dog at her side. They were a formidable and unfriendly pair.

"Please let me come back again," I asked softly. "I won't intrude upon your work but I'll be grateful whenever you feel like talking to me as you did today."

She opened the door and waited until I was in the hall before she said, "You may visit me again."

She closed the door and left me staring at the heavy panels. I returned to my room with a sense of accomplishment. I had faced the lioness in her den and come out unscathed. Her claws were still out, but the time I had spent with her had made them less sharp.

When I went down to dinner, I hoped that she would be there, but only one place was set at the long table. Mine. No one else showed up for dinner and my not-too-subtle questions to a serving maid gleaned me no more information. "Her Ladyship is dining in her room and the others are not here."

I knew it was useless to ask where they had gone. Were Sean and Loretta together? They could have taken one of their rides and chosen not to return for dinner. I thought about Dorthea and wondered if she were right about it being too late to overcome Loretta's claim on Sean. Was he too emotionally involved with my half-sister to give her up for his political ambitions?

The servant left me alone with my food and my thoughts. The angry quarrel I had overheard between Sean and Lawrence lingered with me as I ate in silence. Sean had warned him of trouble brewing. Something had to be done, he had said. I wondered what Sean had in mind. I remembered the quiet, heavy atmosphere around the barn and stables. Suddenly my skin prickled.

I put down my fork. The last morsel of food stuck in my throat. For a moment I just sat there.

The oppressive silence was ominous. The usual sounds of servants moving about their duties were absent. Were they aware that an attack like that made at Windbriar was imminent at Lynhurst? I suddenly pictured the Wainwrights' barn and stable set on fire and the masked rider who had undoubtedly met Lady Claudia in the woods and slit her throat.

I pushed back my chair and hurried up to my room. A feeling of cold panic rose in me. I went out on the balcony and searched the grounds below for any sign of activity. The front courtyard was empty. Moonlight was reflected in the wet surface of the Sea Wall Road far below. No movement was visible on it, nor on the steep road that led up to the castle. The Atlantic's relentless surf was the only sound that filled my ears.

Standing there on the balcony, breathing in the salty air and feeling a teasing breeze against my cheeks, I chided myself for my attack of nerves. I had let my imagination run away with me. Lynhurst Castle was safe enough. I had let the horror of the Watcher's ghost create an oppressive mood. Returning to my room, I closed the door with a definitive bang. So much for my childish apprehension.

The wailing whispers began about midnight. The sudden onslaught of mournful cries jerked me awake. I lit the candles by my bed. It's only the wind, I reminded myself, but as the tumult rose, I was certain that I heard men's voices, low, deep whispers that carried through the very walls of my room. Grabbing my robe, I fled out into the corridor and plunged down the staircase. Spinning around the newel post, I almost lost my balance.

Before I could right myself, someone grabbed me.

I screamed once before my breath was shut off by a broad hand.

"Quiet! Keep still."

I knew immediately who it was as Sean pulled me back against his chest. He turned me around and removed his hand from my mouth. "What's happened? Where are you going?"

"To find someone," I choked. "The night whispers are back. Horrible cries. I couldn't stand to stay in my room and listen to them."

"I told you, it's just the wind in the underground caverns."

"It's different this time. I heard voices . . . men's whispers."

"Nonsense. You're letting your imagination run away with you."

"Come, I'll show you."

Angry that he should dismiss my fright as some female hysteria, I brushed past him and mounted the stairs again. Without thinking about the propriety of such an action, I drew him into my room. Candlelight flickered on the walls. The sounds were still there but only echoes. The male voices had gone, and only a quiet wailing remained.

"It's the wind. Nothing more," he said rather impatiently.

"I heard something different! The voices are gone now . . . but they woke me up! The castle's being invaded, I know it! We'll probably be burned alive in our beds." My lips quivered and I couldn't keep the tears out of my eyes.

He drew me close and patted my head the way I had seen him comfort Loretta. "You're safe. I've posted some extra guards about . . . and I've made certain that all the doors have been locked. That's what I was doing when you came barreling down

202

the stairs like one of the furies."

"How do you know you have not locked in a murderer?" I demanded in a choked voice. "Besides, you can't trust any of the servants. They're all Irish. They hate every drop of English blood."

He set me away. "You've been around Bryant and Sir Wainwright too much!" he snapped.

"It's true, don't you see? First my father, then Claudia. Who knows who will be next? They want us all dead."

"You can't paint a whole population black with one sweep of a brush. That kind of insanity has gone on too long."

"I suppose you're going to change all of that when you get elected to the House of Commons," I chided, letting my fear loose in rising anger.

"What?"

"I know about your political ambitions."

"You should use the past tense. There's little chance of me getting elected to anything now that Sir Lynhurst's backing died with him."

"Oh, I wouldn't be so sure." Then I stopped, aghast at myself. It was not my place to meddle in Dorthea's secret plans. "You'll find a way," I finished lamely. "I suspect you always get pretty much what you want, one way or another."

He pulled me against him. "Do I?"

He lowered his mouth to mine. His kiss was like smoldering coals bursting into flames. His arms held me in a vise that barely allowed me to breathe. The thin cloth of my robe and gown were fragile barriers against the heat of his body.

I arched against him and my arms raised to slip around his neck. I felt a bewildering hunger that coiled deep within me and made me return his kisses with wanton desire. His hands splayed against my back, pressing me closer. His heartbeat was mine, his rising desire mine, and I lost all prudent thought to feeling.

My head reeled with an exquisite dizziness when he raised his head and steadied me against him. "Now, I'm going to show you how much integrity I have, my love," he whispered huskily. "I'm going to leave you before both of us are lost."

Before I could find my voice, he turned and left me standing there in the middle of the room, shaken by his kisses and a silent plea on my lips begging him to remain.

The next morning, I couldn't believe that it had happened. My passionate hunger shocked me. I trembled to think where my rampant desire might have led me. Never one to lie to myself, I knew I had wanted him to stay and if he had not turned away from my clinging embrace, he might have ended up in my bed. The thought brought heat up into my face. For a moment the fantasy of his head pressed upon a pillow next to me set my head reeling. I sat up and covered my face with my hands. Dear God, what was the matter with me?

A quiet knock on the door made me jerk my head up. Was it Sean? Had he come back? I was trembling like a lovesick fool. My breath rose and fell quickly under the folds of my nightdress.

The door opened and Callie entered, bringing my breakfast tray. Sean had kept his word and had the young girl assigned as my personal maid. "What's the matter, mum? Ye look a bit out of sorts this mornin'. Yer color's high."

"The wind was bad last night . . . it disturbed me."

"Have ye heard what's happenin'?"

My heart plunged. "No, what?"

A broad smile matched the sparkle in her eyes. "The master's giving a dance. Dancing, eating, and kegs of poteen to warm the heart. Quite a ta-do, 'tis goin' to be. A barn dance with Daddo wearin' his fiddle out for sure."

"A barn dance?" I echoed. My mind refused to shift harnesses. I had expected the news to be something dire, indeed.

" 'Tis a way of easin' tensions hereabout. Everybody'll come. Whole families. The barn will be full and tables spread from the back door to the stables. Everybody will fill their bellies with food, drink to the saints, and maybe a couple or two will ask Father for banns to be posted." She giggled and put a hand up to her mouth in embarrassment.

"You have someone in mind, Callie?" I teased. "A young man of your own?"

She nodded, looking sheepish. "Liam O'Malley. Sure and he's the best stableboy around. Passes the time-of-day with me every time I take the linen out to the washhouse." She giggled again. "And so handsome, too. He makes me heart jump like a frog over a spill, ye know what I mean?"

I knew very well what she meant.

"You'll be coming, won't ye, ma'am? Yer mother being Paddy and all. Shannon and Daddo are saying you'd be welcome."

"That's very nice. I'd like to come." Would Sean be there? I was certain that he was the one who had planned the affair to settle the brooding unrest. "Yes, of course, I'll come." I laughed and threw back the covers. It was a beautiful, wonderful morning even though the sky was overcast and a soft rain pelted the windows.

After I had eaten and dressed in my serviceable blue serge bodice and skirt, a nervous fluttering in my stomach drove me to action. "Let's take a look through some of the rooms, Callie, and pick out some new curtains. I want to get rid of these dark green ones."

"Yes, mum." She lowered her voice. "Would ye be liking some rose silk? The prettiest window dressings ye'd ever want to see are in a guest room on the second floor. We could nip 'em and bring 'em up here."

We laughed like conspirators. Going up and down the halls, in and out of a myriad of rooms, we spent the morning slipping around the castle, taking down curtains and picking out bed hangings, pictures and rugs. We brought everything up to the third floor and stored our treasures in a room near mine until my walls could be changed to a different color.

"I wish we had some wallpaper."

Callie's eyes widened. "Her Ladyship has some rolls. Ordered them from England she did, about a year ago."

"Maybe she's going to redo her rooms."

Callie shook her head. "Told Rosa to throw 'em out but if I'm remembering rightly Rosa carried them up to the attic. I'll run up and see. Most likely someone tossed 'em out already."

I didn't have much hope that the pattern would be anything I would want but I was pleasantly surprised when Callie brought back a soft blue sprigged print that was very feminine and romantic in design. Too feminine for Lady Davina's tastes, obviously. "Wonderful," I said. "Tell Dolan I want someone to hang it for me as soon as possible."

I was still restless after our morning's activities and decided to walk down to see Molly and ask for her permission to teach Holly to read.

The rain had stopped but mist rode gray whorls

across the water. Wearing my hooded cloak, I left the castle and descended the long staircase to the Sea Wall Road.

At the bottom, I passed heavy doors which had been placed into the side of the rock wall. Sean had said that fishing and boating equipment was stored in the underground chambers. Could I have heard fishermen's voices echoing up into my room last night? I was certain that male whispers had mingled with the wailing wind.

For a moment I was tempted to open one of the doors and see for myself, but I chided myself for such folly. If I were found snooping about, I might very well alienate someone and bring attention upon myself. If some nefarious business was going on, better that I remain ignorant of it. I curbed my curiosity.

Women, children, and men hurried along the road, passing me on foot and in rumbling carts. The women had mantles thrown over their heads, hiding their faces. Some were barefooted but some wore coarse brogues. Not very pretty, I thought, but the flat shoes made of untanned hide with hair left on were more serviceable in the mud than my high-tops.

A scattering of curraghs bobbed in the water some distance from shore and I paused to watch men in these small boats rake in seaweed — new fodder for the boiling iodine pots. A few fishermen were laying nets but apparently no big fishing industries were located on this stretch of coast. Probably because the shoreline was too ragged, I thought as I continued my walk towards the village.

On the outskirts of Danareel, cottages which were scarcely more than weathered shacks were built closely together on each side of mud-churned streets. Black smoke curled out of stovepipes sticking up in the air above thatched roofs. Even though the morning was chilly, several cottage doors stood open. Pigs and chickens came in and out with the same freedom as did barefooted children playing with sticks in the dank ground. Odoriferous refuse from a common dumping ground added a stench to smoke which lay heavy to the ground.

The grimness of the day was not lightened by the poignant scenes of poverty and I was glad when I reached the public-house, Seaward Tavern, and made my way around to the kitchen door. I knew that there was a chance that Mike Ryan would immediately order me off the premises, but I was willing to suffer his crude animosity for the pleasure of seeing Molly again.

"Ye came!" Holly's cheery voice stopped me from knocking on the door.

I turned around. "Hello, there."

The grinning girl stood behind a small fence containing a routing sow and several piglets. An empty bucket in her hand banged against her bare legs as she gave a running leap over the fence and landed in front of me. Her naturally curly hair was like a flaming red bush and she pushed strands out of her eyes and grinned at me. "Kerrie said ye wouldn't come but I knew ye would."

Her beaming young face brought a smile to my own. "Is this a good time for a visit with your mother?"

She nodded and then whispered, "Don't say nothing to Pa about me learning to read and all. He don't take with girls acting like boys. If Ma says yes, I got me a place all picked out to hide my stuff. Patrick gave me a broken pencil. I've been looking at his copybook, wishing I had one, but I cleaned up some paper that came with Pa's last order of tobacco," she told me proudly. "I can write on that."

Her enthusiasm caught at my heart. What if Molly refused? What if my offer only added to Holly's disappointment? Even if she learned to read and write, what kind of unhappiness would such accomplishments bring her? Suddenly I was afraid that I was courting disaster for this bright young girl by opening a world of books to her.

Eagerly, Holly drew me inside that kitchen. "Look who's here, Ma!"

Molly looked up, her hands white with crushed oats. Her eyes widened and then she put a dusty finger up to her mouth. Wiping her hands on her apron, she quickly crossed the kitchen and opened a door that led into their back bedroom. She peered in, nodded in satisfaction, and then closed it again.

When she looked at me again, there was a smile on her round face. "Sure and he's out for the morning. Had some kind of a meeting here last night, drinking a dozen bottles of poteen, they did." She sobered and shook her head. "Sure and 'tis more trouble coming down on us. Won't ye have a seat?" She motioned to the same fireside chair I had sat in the day of my arrival.

"Mama," interrupted Holly impatiently. "She's come to ask ye something."

I would rather have introduced the subject at my own speed but Holly was not about to wait for any polite exchanges that might use up precious time. Molly looked duly puzzled, and a little frightened. She stooped and picked up the whimpering baby. Unlacing her bodice, she sat down on a stool and began to nurse the dark-haired infant. Her questioning eyes met mine. "What is it ye've come to ask?"

"Something for Holly."

Molly's gaze swung to her young daughter. "What's she up to now? Faith, she's gonna be the death of me yet. Between her and Kerrie I don't have a minute's peace. If it isn't that Shannon hanging around planning a wedding, it's Holly up to some shenanigans. What foolishness is bouncing around in her head now?"

"Holly would like to learn to read and write—and I've offered to teach her."

"I can learn it, Ma."

"Read and write?" Molly looked absolutely bewildered. Whatever she had been expecting from her daughter, it wasn't this weird pronouncement. "Whatever for?"

"So I can read Patrick's books!" Holly answered readily.

Molly laughed and shook her head. "Sure and 'tis a priest or a schoolmaster you'll be wanting to be next. That girl! The good Lord mixed up sorely when he sent us a colleen by mistake. Girls don't take to learning like that, child," she gently reprimanded her daughter. "Ain't in the scheme of things. Not in Ireland, anyways."

Holly looked downcast and I argued earnestly that it would do Holly no harm to be able to write her name. "When she marries, it might be an advantage to her husband," I insisted. "She would be able to help him in more ways than just cooking and cleaning for him."

This last statement seemed to get inside Molly's head and rumble around for a few long moments. The baby slurped and gurgled as it kneaded her soft breast and these were the only sounds in the weighted silence. I warned Holly with my eyes to keep still.

Her mother's expression was solemn when she spoke. "A wife should know what's going on. If I did the accounts, there wouldn't be freeloading the way there is now. Mike has no business sense. He'd rather be out getting himself in trouble." She sighed.

I saw that she was weakening and I rushed into the breach. "I could teach Holly up at the castle. There's a nice, quiet vegetable garden where we could spend an hour without disturbing anyone." I thought to myself that Willa would just have to put up with our presence whether she liked it or not.

"Please, Ma, please . . ."

"Schooling takes money. Father Rooney is willing to have free ale in the tavern and a weekly meal in exchange for Patrick's supplies," began Molly. "I don't have an extra farthing for school supplies."

"We won't need anything in the beginning," I assured her, knowing that any kind of a generous offer on my part would be rebuffed as charity. Molly's pride would never allow that.

Without giving an answer, she put the baby in the cradle. "I was planning to visit Addie Harrigan this morning. Her man died with misery in his bones last winter. She's needin' a bit of help. Why don't we take a walk and talk this over? I won't say 'yea' or 'no' right off."

Holly looked disappointed but I gave her an encouraging smile and a wink. Her mother gave her instructions about finishing up the oat cakes and looking after the baby.

"That Kerrie's run off again," Molly told me. "Poor Shannon. He'll never have a hot meal or a fire in his hearth. That girl won't do a lick of work unless you stand over her with a switch." She gathered up some vegetables and cheese into a basket.

Then she took a faded mantle off a hook and threw it over her head. I saw that she was wearing brogues that were too big for her but at least she had something on her feet.

We walked through the village. Nodding to this person and that one, Molly chatted to me about her neighbors. "Addie lives outside the village about a mile," she said. "Her late husband, Tom, made his living cutting turf and selling it in town. Died several months ago, just dropped dead he did. Slumped right over a half-filled turf barrow." She crossed herself. "Bless his soul. Left Addie without a farthing."

"What is she going to do now?" I asked, wondering if the woman had sons to support her.

Molly hesitated as if she were reluctant to answer. "They had six children but didn't raise none of 'em past six years. She be alone, all right, but has a roof over her head as long as she pays the lease-rent."

"How can she do that without someone to support her?"

"There are ways," she said in a tone that put an end to the matter.

The Harrigan cottage was like countless others I'd seen in my travels across Ireland. Made of rock, it had one door in the front and a small window in the back. The woman who answered the door was not much older than Molly, but she wore a perpetual frown that put age lines in her forehead.

"Good day to ye," said Molly brightly. "I've brought you a bit from me garden . . . and some company. Addie, this is my friend from England . . . Aileen O'Connor."

Friend. The word had never sounded lovelier. I could have hugged her.

"I was fixing some tea," the woman said as a

212

greeting.

Molly nodded. "A bit of rain in the air to be sure."

The cramped one-room dwelling offered little choice of seats. To the right of the fireplace was a bed curtained with straw mats. Crude shelves holding wooden vessels and heavy crockery defined the kitchen area. A potato bin, a meal chest and one table and workbench left only room for one small straw chair and two stools in front of the peat fire. Everything was clean and I was relieved not to find the usual menagerie of chickens, geese, and pigs sharing the living quarters even though I realized that the lack of animals was a mark of dire poverty. I wondered how an upright woman like Addie was able to find a way to survive without a man's wages coming into the house.

I sat down on one of the stools, self-conscious about the way Addie was eyeing my plain cloak and modest day dress.

"I spent several years in London before I was married," said my hostess as she tipped a steaming kettle into a chipped teapot.

I'm afraid my expression registered surprise, but as she continued to talk, I realized her English usage was quite correct even though it had overtones of an Irish brogue.

"Yes, it's true. My family owned considerable land in Kearney when I was growing up. From time to time we used to go over for London holidays." The tired lines around her mouth eased a little. "The galleries, the shops, picnics in the park, we did it all. I'll never forget the organ grinders with their funny little monkeys, the smell of roasting chestnuts, and the perfume of elegant ladies as they passed. Strange, isn't it, how smells are the strongest cues to memory."

213

Molly laughed and admitted that a certain kind of tobacco brought back memories of an uncle who had held her on his knee as a child.

Addie Harrigan served us strong tea laced with milk and I wondered if that too was an English habit that had remained with her.

"We lost our land when I was fifteen. My father and brothers were killed trying to keep it. I married Tom Harrigan to keep from starving."

"And a good man, he was," offered Molly.

His widow was pointedly silent.

Suddenly a knock at the door shattered the quiet.

Molly set her cup down so fast that it spilled on the floor. Addie stood up with a gasp and her eyes made a frantic look around as if something might be visible that should have remained hidden.

Sudden tension and anxiety filled the small room like an evil miasma. I didn't know what the matter could be. Why had a knock on the door sent them into such panic?

Addie wiped her hands on her skirt, firmed her shoulders, and walked over to the door. Taking a deep breath she opened it.

Sean Creighton stood there.

Chapter Thirteen

I nearly spilled my tea in my lap. As always, Sean's presence sent my senses reeling. My skin tingled, my breath shortened, and I felt as if I were suddenly pitched on the edge of a great height. I was afraid that my inner confusion showed on my face and in the heat creeping up into my cheeks.

"Come in, Sean," invited Addie in a relieved voice, stepping back to allow him entrance.

His muscular, lithe figure filled the small room and his gaze swept past her and fixed on me in surprise. "What are you doing here, Aileen?" he demanded in an authoritative tone.

His manner made me bristle. Why did he continue to treat me as unwanted baggage wherever I went? Somehow he always seemed to put me in the wrong with a single question. The emotions I felt in his presence swept into anger.

"I'm having a cup of tea with friends. I trust that I'm allowed to enjoy myself in such a fashion."

"What's the matter, Sean?" asked Addie before he could respond to my caustic reply. "Ye have a message?"

He nodded and spoke quickly. "Two excise constables are only about a mile distant."

"Oh dear!" gasped Molly, getting to her feet.

"Can I help?"

"No need," he reassured her. "A wagon will be here in a few minutes. How much stuff do you have, Addie?"

"The shed's half full. The boys were here day before yesterday with a load."

Sean nodded. "I thought as much. Well, we'll have to move it temporarily . . . just in case. They're checking every place along this road. Now sit back down, Addie, act natural if someone comes to the door. I'll take care of everything out back." He sent me an exasperated look. "As soon as I'm finished, Aileen, I'll see you home."

I didn't argue. His urgency had communicated itself to me. I nodded.

"Just go on with your tea party."

"God Bless you, Sean," murmured Addie.

" 'Tis a good son of Ireland, ye be," agreed Molly.

After he had left I asked, "What's going on?"

"It's the excisemen . . . looking for illegal poteen."

"Here?" I gasped.

Addie nodded.

"Your shed is full of whiskey?" I croaked.

Her narrow chin went up. "The men who have stills in the mountain bring it here and I pass it along. The money I make pays my rent and keeps me in food."

"But it's against the law!" I protested. "You could be put in jail."

Her thin mouth tightened. "A widow must survive as best she can."

Molly leaned toward me. " 'Tis common enough for widows to be in the trade, Aileen. Don't ye see, 'tis a way we can take care of the poor dears. Their

216

homes are the middle stop for the poteen when it comes down from the hills."

I couldn't believe what I was hearing—a community welfare plan which made lawbreakers out of destitute women! And Sean was a part of it. He had come to warn Addie and was out back right now, loading illegal whiskey into a wagon. I dared not think what would happen if the government men rode into the yard before he had finished. Why would he take such a chance?

" 'Tis grateful we are for Sean," said Molly as if reading my thoughts. "Many a time he's saved some poor soul from the gallows by warning him in time."

"And protected many a cottier from eviction by using his influence with His Lordship to give the poor man another chance," Addie declared.

"His grandmother would have been proud of him," agreed Molly. "Her blood runs in his veins, to be sure. He looks out for us as much as he can." She sighed. "Och, 'tis a sad thing when I hear some say he's not to be trusted. 'Tis rumored he's on the wrong side in the Tithe War."

"Just because he's Scotch-Irish doesn't mean he'll not fight alongside Irish Catholics," argued Addie.

"Faith, it scares me sometimes to hear my Mike, bragging about how they're going to turn the castle to rubble."

"Surely they wouldn't do such a thing!" I protested.

"When the Bog Boys ride, the devil rides with them. Ye heard what happened at Windbriar, didn't ye?" asked Addie.

"I was there."

Both women gasped. Molly leaned forward. "Did ye see the Watcher?" Her eyes were wide. " 'Tis said the ghost left his wreath upon the poor lady's chest."

"It was no ghost that slit her throat," I said flatly. "The Bog Boys can be credited for murdering an innocent woman."

"Oh, now, ye be wrong," said Molly. " 'Tis the truth that nary a one of them even saw her. Sure and they was surprised as anybody to learn what had happened. And scared, too! 'Twas the Watcher, all right." She crossed herself.

I didn't respond. Her remarks gave every reason to believe her husband was at the center of Bog Boys' activities. Who else would be telling her about the raid? The knowledge sat uneasy with me. I had heard Bryant vow to see the culprits hanged and I couldn't condone what they had done to life and property. Despite Molly's protests, I was sure that one of them, maybe Mike Ryan, had murdered Claudia. I wished Molly had not burdened me with such knowledge. Even though I disliked the man, I didn't want to be the one to turn him over to the law and take a father away from his children.

Molly leaned forward, anxiety creasing her round face. "Ye won't be saying nothin' about Mike, will ye? Me and me mouth running off like rain down a gully 'bout things that are best kept quiet. I know ye like Holly and I'm hopin' ye don't wish me no harm."

"Of course, I don't, Molly." I reached over and touched her arm. "You and Addie can be sure that your secrets are safe with me."

Molly beamed. "I knew ye was one of us the first night I saw ye with Daddo."

Addie twisted her hands nervously. Several times, she got up and peered out the door and then went to the small window and pulled back a faded curtain. "Ach, I wish they'd hurry."

"Sure and 'tis hard waitin'," said Molly.

"I think ye ought to go, Molly." Addie came back and sat down again. "No sense bringing their eyes upon ye. They've been after Mike for years."

Molly laughed. "Sure and begorra, 'tis a hundred times they've searched our place with the stuff about to fall on their heads." She leaned toward me. "Ye'd never be guessin' but nearly a half-dozen rafters are hollow, ye see," she bragged. "The jugs of poteen are hidden in them." She slapped her leg. "Gurrah! They nearly take the walls apart, climb up on the roof, they do, but never eye the rafters."

Addie laughed and then sobered. "Just the same, Molly, I'd feel easier if ye weren't here when they come."

Molly put down her mug reluctantly.

"I think ye should go too, Aileen." Addie turned to me. "The constables get rough sometimes. Traitors, they are, impoverished Irishmen hired by Dublin Castle to enforce unfair laws against other impoverished Irish. If ye have a drop of Paddy in ye, yer fodder for their jails. I don't want yer presence here to bring ye harm, Aileen."

"What about you?" I protested. "Someone should stay with you."

She shook her head. "I know how to handle the varmints. Ye might give way before their harassment."

"Sean told me to stay." Even though I was tempted to leave with Molly, Sean's admonition that he would see me home made me remain. My desire to be with him outweighed my nervousness. I was willing to chance the constables if it meant spending time with Sean. Such was the state of my emotions.

Before Molly left, I pressed a decision from her about teaching Holly to read. She frowned. "What do you think, Addie? Should I be permitting Holly to learn to read and write her name?"

The gaunt woman firmed her chin. "And why not? The good Lord gave woman a mind to think and a belly to make children. I'm believing she should be using both. If Holly wants to learn somethin', I say let her."

Molly sighed. "I don't rightly think any good'll come of it . . . but no harm either. Holly ain't one to stick very long to anything. Guess I could spare her an hour before lunch each day." She laughed. "Her and Kerrie are always up at the stables visiting Shannon and Daddo, anyways. They're all excited about a barn dance come Saturday night." Her mouth spread in a wide smile.

"Goings-on at the castle?" Addie echoed in surprise.

"Sure and I'm looking forward to it meself." Molly's smile faded a little. " 'Tis hopin' I am that Mike'll be behaving himself."

"Land's sake, it's been a long time since the castle put on a feed for us." She visibly brightened. "The new, young lord likes his good times, I hear."

Molly nodded. "Sure and 'tis a good thing to spread some food and drink around. Takes the edge off tempers."

"There's rumbles of trouble," agreed Addie.

With a wave of her hand, Molly went out the door, leaving Addie and me looking at each other. For what seemed like an eternity, we sat in front of the fire and waited for something to happen. Conversation failed us both. We nervously sipped our tea and waited. Both of us jumped when the front door swung open and Sean came in.

"Well, it's done, Addie."

The older woman let out her breath. "I be beholden to ye."

"Nothing's left in the shed," he assured her. "We'll be bringing the stuff back when it's safe."

"The saints be praised. Where'd ye put it?"

"In the schoolmaster's sweathouse." Sean grinned. "It'll be safe enough there unless Mr. Dooley decides to drink it all himself."

They both laughed.

"May God put his blessin' on ye, Sean Creighton." Her wan face softened when she smiled. " 'Tis a good man, ye are. Now, take this pretty colleen and be off with ye before me company arrives. I don't think she'd know how to handle things."

Sean turned to me. "Addie's right. We'd best get moving. I didn't have time to bring another horse. We'll have to ride double on Graymont."

After a quick goodbye to Addie, Sean guided me around the side of the house where his stallion stood waiting.

"Up you go." He lifted me into the saddle.

Since I wasn't a horsewoman, I felt clumsy and awkward. I was glad my full skirts fell over my legs even though I was riding astride.

He swung himself up behind me, and with an arm on each side of me took the reins in his hands. He gave the stallion a sharp kick with his heels and sent Graymont into a quick run away from the small cottage.

I held on with a deathly grip. As a child I had ridden a few times bareback one summer but this prancing steed was nothing like the swaybacked old mare that hung her head and plodded forward at a snail's pace.

Wind swept off my hood and bathed my face. At first, I concentrated so hard on staying with the up and down movement of the horse that I didn't even notice where we were going. Suddenly I realized that we were riding away from the village and the castle. At first I thought it was because Sean wanted to avoid being seen by the excisemen. Then I began to wonder. My escort showed no sign of turning Graymont around even though we hadn't seen a sign of anyone who looked like a constable.

"Where are we going?" I asked. The wind blew the question away.

Sean only shook his head as if he didn't understand what I was saying but there was a smiling glint in his eyes.

What was he up to? Every rise and fall of the horse made our bodies brush together with tantalizing intimacy. With the hood of my cloak hanging down my back, his warm breath bathed my neck. His arms had tightened around my waist to help me keep my balance in the saddle. The stirrups were too long to be of any help.

I knew I should demand that Sean return me to the castle immediately. Instead of making any such protest, I delighted in the exciting sensation of flying over the ground on a racing steed. A foolish abandonment shoved aside any prickling sense of propriety. Riding alone on Graymont I might have been filled with great trepidation, but with Sean guiding the beast, I could only delight in the new experience. In truth, I didn't care where we were going. Just being with Sean on this exhilarating ride diminished any rational thought or protest on my part.

We rode across meadows and fields, along rock

fences and wagon roads. When we entered a thick copse, Sean reined Graymont and allowed him to pick his way over mossy banks and along water flowing into secluded glens. The lush beauty of Ireland engulfed me: gray-green land, granite mountains, rolling moors, a thousand loughs and bogs. Every glen presented a secluded loveliness. We had left the world behind and I expected Sean to rein to a stop at any moment in one of the enchanting spots of grass, moss, trees, and singing waters.

My heart raced with expectation. What would happen then? In my mind's eye, I saw us sitting beside a pond, watching ripples in the water as they made liquid sculptures before our eyes. I remembered the kisses he had given me beside the sea and a deep hunger curled within me.

He must have been reading my thoughts for he pulled me back against him and his cheek rested against my windblown hair.

My puzzlement increased and my disappointment was real when we continued the ride with a purpose I didn't understand.

After we left the woods behind, Sean kicked Graymont into a run and we crossed unfenced, opened fields which lay neglected and fallow. Signs that the property had been abandoned were everywhere. Fences had tumbled to the ground, posts lay decayed and rotted, rock foundations showed where cottages had once stood and now only gaping holes remained. Brackish pools of stagnant water stood clogged and neglected. A long-weathered bridge spanning a sluggish stream seemed precarious but Sean urged the horse across it. I saw then where we were going.

A large early seventeenth-century house stood

immediately in front of us. Its square lines were hidden by rambling vines and overgrown shrubs and trees scraping the stone exterior. The structure gave the impression of a derelict dowager who had lost her beauty to age, but not her pride. The windows were blank, the stable yard empty and all the outbuildings in a state of disrepair.

Sean guided Graymont around the house and reined him to a stop near a back door. He slid to the ground. "Welcome to Rathbridge."

I looked down at him. "I don't understand. Why did we come here?"

"Because I want to show you my home." He took a firm hold on my waist and lifted me down. "Don't you want to see it?"

"Yes, of course. I'm just surprised. I didn't know you were a property owner."

"I'm not. My father gambled Rathbridge away but the property was in my grandmother's family for generations. It's the only real home I've ever known. I come here quite often."

"But aren't we trespassing?"

"Yes." He grinned. "But who's to know?"

His excitement was transmitted to me as he guided me up some uneven steps to a weathered door and took a tarnished key from his pocket.

"Surely, someone is looking out for the property," I protested.

"Does it look as if someone's taking care of it?" he countered as the door swung open on creaking hinges.

"No, but—"

He laughed and motioned me inside. "After you, my lady."

I hesitated. Twice in one day I had found myself in circumstances that could put me at odds with

224

the law. The prospects of being arrested in this strange country were terrifying. "I don't like breaking into someone else's home," I began.

"It isn't anybody's home, as you can see. It used to be mine—and I give you permission to look around. Aren't you the least bit curious to see it?" he teased. "It's a lovely house, even now. Nothing like Lynhurst Castle, I promise you."

He had cleverly baited the hook. I eyed the afternoon sun lowering behind a bank of clouds. "All right, a very quick tour."

"Don't look so apprehensive. I'll take you back right away, if you wish. I suppose it was selfish of me to bring you here. A crazy impulse."

"No, I'm glad. Really. I very much want to see the house where you grew up." Giving him a reassuring smile, I brushed past him.

We entered a large, echoing kitchen which was connected to a series of small pantries which Sean identified as we passed the open doors. Milk and dairy products were handled in one, he told me, garden produce in another, and bakery offerings in another. In the center room, a mammoth kitchen dresser stood against a brick wall opposite a walk-in fireplace. Cooking utensils remained on dusty shelves beside blue and white crockery and wooden glasses. A scattering of chairs, scarred and dirty, circled a large round table.

"The owner took away all the china, silver, and glassware," Sean told me, guiding me out of the kitchen into a center hall that ran to the front door. "Most of the house's furnishings were left because they weren't worth shipping to England to sell."

"Didn't he ever live in the house?"

"No. He lent it out for several years to single

Englishmen who wanted to live in Ireland for brief periods. They treated it like a boardinghouse, ruining the walls and floors, even breaking two of the front Venetian windows. When I returned from college and saw what they had done to it, I wanted to sit down on those steps and cry."

"It must have been very painful for you." I had never seen this sentimental, vulnerable side of Sean before. I could picture him sitting with his head between his hands, mourning over the abuse the house had received. A wash of tenderness swept over me. I slipped my hand in his and we stood in the center of the main hall.

"That's my grandmother's family crest above the mantel." He pointed to a black marble fireplace facing the front door. A shield displaying a stag with huge antlers had been formed in the plaster work. Small crosses adorned the upper corners. "The O'Mallorys date back to the Norman Conquest and this house replaced one that was built in the sixteen hundreds. At that time Celtics lived on this land. Remains of some of their rock edifices still can be found. My grandmother was very proud of her heritage."

"I wonder why she didn't marry an Irish Catholic instead of your Scottish grandfather," I said without thinking.

He didn't take offense at my bluntness. "Love," he answered readily. "She met my grandfather on a trip to Dublin and nothing her family said or did persuaded her to give him up. Their marriage was a happy one. And my grandfather fought for Irish rights along with her family. They thought my father, the only child that lived, would follow the pattern they had laid, but he didn't."

"He's dead?"

He nodded. "Died in London, broke, and owing everyone he ever met. My grandparents made the mistake of sending my father to England to be educated, where his weaknesses were exploited and his ties to Ireland destroyed. I think it was my grandmother's dream that my father would go into politics and fight for the Irish cause."

"And now it's your dream."

"It *was* my dream. Sir Lynhurst's death put an end to that."

Dorthea's secret plans could secure Sean's dream for him. The temptation to say something was so great I had to bite my lower lip to keep the words back. I wondered how deep his commitment to Loretta went. Had my father's will tied him to Lynhurst Castle and Loretta as well?

We walked through arches framed by elaborate woodcarvings, still impressing despite their dull, dry state. Both the drawing room and dining room had been fashioned with molded paneled walls which had probably been a pristine white at one time. Dusty webs trailed across plastered ceilings which displayed floral garlands and intertwining vines. The basic graciousness of the rooms remained despite ugly marks upon the walls, gouges in the floors, and marred woodwork.

The furniture had been covered with gray sheets but dusty family portraits still hung on the walls. Sean identified some of them and reminisced about family celebrations and boyhood memories that were triggered by a painting or a portrait.

"You've talked a lot about your grandmother. What about your mother?"

"She was Scottish. My father met her one summer on an outing in Scotland. I don't know what she was like. I know she was never well and I don't think my grandmother liked her very much." He shook his head. "I suspect that two women under this roof didn't prove very harmonious. Maybe that's why my father spent so much time in London."

A pattering of rain on the front windows brought me back to the present. "It's raining. We'd better get back. I'll see the rest another time."

He nodded. "I guess I've bored you with my family long enough."

"It's not that. It's just that I . . . I think I'd better go."

His eyes locked with mine for a breathless moment. "Yes, I think so, too."

"Thank you for bringing me here."

He slipped his arm around my waist. "I've pictured you here with me," he confessed.

We retraced our steps to the kitchen. As we came through the doorway, a soundless scream lurched into my throat. If Sean hadn't had his arm around me, I might have fainted.

A menacing old man with a gun stood in the middle of the kitchen, his gaze directed away from us into one of the pantries. His dark, swarthy face was in the shadow of his brimmed hat. Every muscle in his thick arms was tensed and his finger poised on the trigger of his rifle. *We were going to be shot without being given a second to explain!*

Sean dropped his arm from my waist and walked straight toward the gunman. "It's only me, Kiley, you old goat."

The man jerked around. "Sean." He swept off his hat and lowered his gun. Gray hair and thick, bushy eyebrows matched the age lines in his weathered face.

"Put down your gun," Sean ordered.

228

"Didn't mean to be startlin' ye none. Was just comin' by and thought I was seein' somethin' move inside."

"We were just doing a little trespassing."

He shook his head. " 'Tain't trespassing to my way of thinkin'. As long as I'm caretaker, you can come and go as you please, Sean."

"And I appreciate the liberty."

I sat down in a chair because fright had made my legs too weak to hold me.

"I think you've given Aileen a bit of fright," said Sean, looking at my ashen face.

"I'm sorry, mum. I didn't mean to scare you."

"It's all right," I said as graciously as I could. I'd have to have a stronger stomach for evading the law if I expected to survive in this country, I thought as my heartbeat began to return to normal.

"Didn't you see Graymont tethered outside, Kiley?" asked Sean.

"No, sir. Ye don't suppose he's run off again? He's got a hankerin' for that mare in the next spread, don't he?" The old man cackled.

Sean swore and looked out a window. "Blasted all! Graymont's slipped his tether, all right."

I looked at the old man and then at Sean. "He's run away?"

"I'm afraid he has."

"But you can catch him?"

Sean swore again. "Graymont is a hot-blooded stallion who has formed an attachment to a mare he services now and again for one of the nearby landowners. He's run off before."

"How long will it take to get him back?"

"Oh, they'll bring him back in the morning," said Sean in a casual tone that infuriated me.

229

In the morning! Suddenly suspicion ran rampant in my mind. There was something contrived about the whole situation. Graymont gone. No way to get back to Lynhurst.

"What about another horse?"

Kiley shook his head. "Don't even have my mule any more. Besides, we're going to have ourselves a gully washer tonight. Startin' already. The river's already running full."

"Must have had a cloudburst upstream," said Sean. "Hope the bridge doesn't wash out."

"Been expectin' her to go nigh on twenty years. Guess she'll last a few more storms. Well now, there's plenty of wood stacked inside, like always," he told Sean.

"Thanks, Kiley."

"Have a nice night." He tipped his hat and disappeared through the back door into the rain.

Sean turned around to me. "I'm sorry."

My hands tightened in my lap. "Quite a surprise, isn't it, Graymont running off like that?" My even tone was at odds with the storm rising within me. He had resorted to a cheap maneuver to keep me here for the night, and I was furious.

"Well, we won't starve. I leave a crock of cheese and a good supply of wine here. We'll build a nice fire . . ."

Hot blood swept up into my face. "I won't stay here! With you—like this!"

"I'm sorry, I really am." He held out his hands in a helpless gesture.

"Don't take me for a fool. I saw the way Kiley was grinning his silly head off. The whole thing is much too obvious."

"What are you saying?"

"I'm saying that this isn't the first time this has

happened. You even admitted that Graymont has run off before."

"But never under these circumstances. I've always been alone."

"I don't believe you."

He shrugged.

"I'm not spending the night with you."

He sat down in a chair next to mine. "Would that be so awful?" he asked softly.

All the disturbing feelings that his nearness engendered within me mingled with my anger. "I don't like being manipulated."

"Nobody is manipulating you, for God's sake. Why are you so blasted pig-headed and obstinate? For once, why can't you accept circumstances as they are?"

"Because you deceived me! I won't stay. If there's no horse, I'll walk."

"You can't. It's too far. You'd never find your way back."

"Then I'll wait the rain out under a haystack. I've done that before."

He started laughing.

"I mean it. I'll sleep in that tumbled-down barn."

"All right. Have it your way." He stood up. "If my company is that distasteful."

I stomped to the door, and flung it open. Pulling my hood over my head, I stood in the doorway looking out. Rain like silvery sheets poured off the roof. One step out into the watery curtain and I would be drenched to the skin. I knew how cold and uncomfortable standing in the rain could be. Clammy clothes clinging like wet plaster to my body, chilling even the marrow of my bones. Memories of downpours on my journey across Ireland taunted me that I would be an utter idiot to venture out in such weather.

I waited for Sean to say something that would give me an excuse to turn back. When he didn't, I slammed the door and turned around, a caustic remark ready on my tongue.

He wasn't in the kitchen. The room was empty.

My footsteps echoed as I walked back to the table and stood there listening.

How dare he walk off like that? *And why not,* some inner voice chided me. If he was innocent, my accusations were insulting and my impassioned vows that I would not remain here with him were childish and rather presumptuous.

I sat down again on a kitchen chair. My hood fell off my head and I rested one cheek in my hand. I wasn't going anywhere. Not in that rain. I really had no choice. Unless I wanted to shiver all night in the old barn, my only recourse was to remain under this roof for the night. Darkness had already fallen. Until someone brought the stallion back, there was no way to get home. No wonder Sean had laughed at me. My haughty ire wasn't going to change the situation.

I thought about the pleasant time we'd enjoyed earlier and slowly my anger dissipated and a new flood of emotions engulfed me. I wanted to be here with him. He had shared an intimate part of his life with me. All my protests had been made in anger and if I were honest, they had been founded in jealousy. I feared that he had brought Loretta here and perpetrated the same ruse on her or another woman. *And what if he did? She is not here now, you are.*

I don't know how long I sat there in the deserted kitchen. Rain beat against the windows and the wind rose and fell in the eaves. The storm outside made the house a haven of comfort. Finally, I took a deep breath and straightened up. I could sit here in the kitchen all night or I could swallow my pride and go find Sean.

I chose the latter course of action.

"Sean?" I called. He wasn't in the drawing or dining room. "Where are you?"

A door to a small study opened. Behind him, a fire leaped with ruddy tongues. A small table had been set with two pewter goblets and two servings of cheese and oat cakes.

"Everything's ready," he said smiling.

"You were pretty sure of yourself," I said, my gaze sweeping the table. "How did you know I wouldn't leave?"

He loosened my cloak and slipped it from my shoulders. "You're not a fool, my love, even though your ready temper makes you talk like one sometimes."

"You can't blame me, in this situation," I flared. "What is everyone going to think when I don't return tonight?"

"Will any one notice . . . or care?" he asked gently.

The simple question drove the truth into my heart. My whereabouts were of little concern to anyone. "You're right. No one cares where I am."

"I care very much where you are." He drew me close. "And that makes you in exactly the right place after all." He tightened his embrace and a tremor went through me.

"Are you chilled?"

I nodded, which wasn't the truth at all. It was another condition entirely that set my body to trembling.

"Come closer to the fire." He led me to a settee,

233

and put a footstool under my feet so they could get warm near the fire. "Now, isn't that better than a wet haystack?" His grin was teasing.

"Much better," I admitted.

"And here's a goblet of wine to warm you." He sat down beside me and clicked my pewter mug. "A toast. To Graymont."

I raised an eyebrow. "Why are we toasting an errant stallion who has left us stranded?"

"Because I never would have had the courage to arrange this myself." He put an arm behind me and his hand curved on my shoulder in a possessive way. "You believe me, don't you?"

I didn't, but it didn't seem to matter any more. He was right; no one cared where I was and I desperately needed to feel that I was important to someone. I settled my head against him and we sat looking into the fire, sipping our wine and munching oat cakes and cheese.

My gaze went lazily around the room. Several candles stood near a stack of books on a table and a small bed had been made up in one corner. Chopped wood was piled on both sides of the fireplace. The tangy smoke of a wood fire was pleasant after the pungent odor of burned turf. "You come here often, don't you?"

He nodded. "This modest room is really my home. Not the large apartment I have at the castle. One day the owner will sell Rathbridge and I won't be able to enjoy it any more, but until then . . ."

"Maybe you'll be able to buy it," I said, thinking about the dowry that Dorthea would bring to the marriage.

He gave a short laugh. "My monthly stipend wouldn't buy even one of the tumbled-down sheds. Many times, I tried to talk His Lordship into buying the property, but he knew how sentimental I was about it and he wouldn't give me a definite 'yes' or 'no.' He was like that, your father, a master of keeping a choice morsel dangling just in front of the lips."

"Like his backing of your bid for a Parliament seat?"

"Yes, but that dream is ashes now."

"Maybe not," I said. "You'd give up anything for that chance, wouldn't you?"

"I suppose so. But let's not talk about me." He took our goblets and set them on the table. "I want to know about you."

"You know everything there is to know about me. You have for a long time, it seems."

"Yes, but just as a name. When I looked into the mirror that first day at the tavern, I didn't think you were real."

"I know. I felt the same way about you. Why did you take an instant dislike to me?"

"It wasn't to you — but the woman I thought had come to Ireland. I took you for a greedy parasite who was going to bleed her father."

"I came because I needed a home."

"I know that now." He tipped my chin and his dark eyes caressed mine. "You demand very little for yourself."

My lips curved in a smile because I realized how wrong he was about me. I was very selfish, especially where he was concerned. I was going to steal this time with him for myself. His future lay with someone else — I knew it, but he didn't. And I wasn't going to tell him. If he were aware that Dorthea was going to offer him his dream, his behavior towards me would be different. No, I would keep Dorthea's secret but I loved the man she was going to marry. Hopelessly and selfishly, I loved Sean Creighton with every fiber of my being. This night was mine, and I was going to claim it.

My hands slid up around his neck and I raised my face to his.

"If I kiss you," he warned, "everything you feared is going to happen."

"I know. Kiss me."

He gave me a slow smile and then pulled back. "Not here."

"Why not?"

"Because I've dreamed of bringing my love home, to this house." He stripped a coverlet from the small bed and handed me a lighted candle. "Shall we retire, my lady?"

His eyes sparkled and I laughed at his obvious play-acting. "Delighted," I replied.

We made our way through the darkened downstairs, bumping into shadowy furniture. "We must reprimand the servants," I giggled. "They've neglected to light the candles."

He put his arm around my waist as we mounted the stairs. In the radius of candlelight, his handsome face brought a wild leaping in my chest and I knew there would never be another man for me. My mother's passionate blood ran in my veins. I knew now how she had felt when she fell in love and why she had never shown any regret for the lover she had taken. The intensity of her love for my father had been enough to last a lifetime—and so it would be with me.

Sean guided our steps to a large chamber at the front of the house. "This will be *our* room." His emphasis on the possessive word was deliberate, shutting out the world, and drawing unto ourselves a private intimacy.

Tossing the coverlet on the bed, he took the candle from me and snuffed it out. There was the sound of rain upon the windows and the rise and fall of our breathing as we stood close together in the darkened room. His hands sought the pins in my hair and the heavy coils fell free down my back. He bent his head and kissed me, his fingers skillfully unfastening the buttons on my bodice.

"You are so lovely," he whispered. His hands molded my breasts and I gave a breathless cry of pleasure. Hardening nipples responded to his touch and desire coiled deep within me.

A surge of shyness mingled with rising passion as he undressed me. The quickening pounding of his heart matched mine as he drew my body against his and then lifted me up and carried me to the bed.

In another moment he was beside me, the coverlet tossed in an abandoned heap over our nakedness. He murmured endearments and his kisses parted my mouth so that his tongue teased my lips and mouth. Time was lost. I was heedless to anything but the need to be held and kissed and smothered by rock-hard muscles quivering upon me. When he swept my legs apart, the first gasp of pain and surprise gave way to a choked, breathless sigh. For the moment he was mine, all mine, and no one could ever take this miraculous joy away from me.

Chapter Fourteen

I awoke the next morning with Sean leaning over me, fully dressed. He was tickling my nose with a piece of tassle grass and I gave an unladylike sneeze. Chuckling, he gave a teasing jerk on the coverlet and I squealed as the cold air hit my torso. This playful lover was a stranger to me. Last night, he had taught my body the wondrous pleasures of love-making. This morning, he laughed as he drew me into his arms. My arms slid around his neck and my bare breasts pressed shamelessly against his chest.

"Good morning." He moved his lips from a light kiss on my eyelids to nibble on my ear. The intense brown of his eyes had lightened and I saw that there was a black feathering around the pupils that gave them their dark color. This morning they were soft and shining. Shocks of ruffled hair drifted down on his forehead and seemed wet with dew.

"You've been outside already?"

"To Kiley's cottage to get our breakfast. He lives a few steps down the lane. I couldn't very well offer you wine and cheese again. The old codger came to my rescue as I knew he would. He offered me wheat cakes, some smoked bacon and black tea. How does that sound to my lady?"

"Marvelous."

"Are you hungry?" His gaze caressed my face and his mouth lowered until it was just a breath apart from mine.

"Yes," I murmured in a husky voice and closed my eyes.

When our lips touched, remembered rapture spiraled through me. I was lost to his deepening kiss, the touch of his hands molding the curves of my back as he held me close to him. My breath quickened. A delicious torment stirred.

He could have made love to me again and I wouldn't have murmured even a weak protest, but for some reason, he curbed his own arousal and drew away. He traced the curve of my cheek and chin with his fingertips. His voice was husky. "You are an enchantress, do you know that?"

I laughed softly. "Only because you think so."

"Believe me, love. You're the kind of woman who can stir a man's blood and dilute his reasoning."

His tone was regretful and I wondered if he were already sorry that he had let me into his life. Then he kissed me lightly and stood up. "Do you need some help dressing?" he asked.

I was tempted to say yes but caution made me shake my head. The night had passed. It was morning and I knew I must let go of him. "Thank you. I think I can manage faster without your help."

He grinned. "No doubt."

I gasped as a sudden thought struck me. "What is Callie going to think when she brings my breakfast and I'm not there?"

"Don't worry about it."

"But what if she alerts everyone? Tells Lady

239

Davina I didn't come home last night and they send out a search party?"

"They won't."

"How can you be so sure?"

"Because Callie's sweetheart, Liam, was one of the fellows who helped me move Addie's whiskey. He knows you're with me."

"You told him you were bringing me here?" I was suddenly cold and it had nothing to do with the brisk air upon my bare shoulders.

Sean nodded.

"And did you also tell him we were going to spend the night?"

"No, of course not, but with the storm, he'll figure it out."

"I'm sure he will," I said frigidly. "And so will everyone else." The incident of the missing Graymont had been contrived, I was certain of it.

He tried to kiss me again but I pushed him back. He looked at me quizzically. "What's the matter?"

"Nothing. I'm hungry. Please leave me and I'll dress." He had told Liam he was bringing me here. I knew how efficient Danareel's gossip was. If one person knew, everyone knew.

"Aileen, don't look at me like that. It's not what you think."

"Isn't it?"

"No. Please trust me, love. There are some weighty problems which I must work out."

His light, bantering tone was gone and so was the teasing sparkle in his eyes. This was the Sean I knew. Purposeful. Dogged and stubborn. I was certain he was a man who would not be swayed from his course by romantic dalliances. So be it. When I had decided to grasp this one night, I had known that there could be nothing permanent between us. He deserved the future that Dorthea could offer him and even if he were prepared to give up his dreams for me, I wouldn't let him.

"It's all right. I understand." Impulsively, I brushed his mouth with a gentle kiss. There wouldn't be another night nor morning like this one and it wouldn't change anything to spoil it by arguing. "Go make the tea," I ordered firmly. "I'll be right down."

He gave me one more lingering kiss before he left. It would be easy to become an emotional beggar, accepting the leftovers of his love and attention. The truth that his life would never be centered on me caused tears to spring hotly into my eyes.

Kiley brought the stallion to the door an hour later and I wondered if Graymont had run off at all. Maybe the caretaker had hidden him in a barn and the whole thing had been a practiced ruse that the two men had arranged more than once. Strangely enough, I didn't care. What little time was left, I wanted to be free of accusations of guilt or blame. What had happened between Sean and me was as much of my making as his.

The morning's haze lifted to reveal a clear blue sky and our ride back to the castle was much too short. I leaned back against Sean, feeling his firm body and welcoming his arms stretching around me to hold the reins. I was tempted to beg him to stop in one of the secluded glens but a quick glance at his face halted my request. The hard set to his mouth and jaw told me his thoughts were weighted. He was almost a stranger again. I had

241

left my tender lover back in the rooms of Rathbridge.

We rode in the clearing behind the castle. When we dismounted at the stables, I felt a dozen pairs of eyes upon us. Hot embarrassment swept up into my cheeks. The servants' grapevine would run rampant with the news that I had been out the whole night and my reputation would be tarnished beyond repair.

"Don't worry," said Sean, as if reading my thoughts. "I'll tell them you spent the night with Addie Harrigan."

"Will they believe you?"

He gave me a slow smile. "And why not?"

How conceited he was!

"Because *I* don't believe anything you say," I said pugnaciously.

"You wound me to the quick." His eyes smiled at me. "They'll believe Addie, in any case."

"How do you know she'll hold to the lie?"

"Because I know Addie. She'll do anything I ask. All we have to do is tell the same story."

"I'm not much of a liar."

"I know."

The way he said it, I knew that my feelings for him were very transparent. If I had told him at Rathbridge that I had no intention of seeing him alone again, he wouldn't have believed me. I really didn't know whether I believed it myself.

Leaving Sean at the stables, I hurried across the courtyard toward the castle. I saw with surprise that Holly was waiting by the garden gate for me. I turned in that direction.

A wide grin creased the freckles on her cheeks. "Morning! Here I be!" She held up a snub of a pencil and some stained wrapping paper.

"Good morning." To tell the truth I had forgotten all about my commitment to her. As much as I wanted to hide myself in the privacy of my room, I knew I could not beg off the lesson I had promised.

"You're ready, then?" I returned her smile. "Well, let's go inside the gate and find a nice soft place to write in the dirt."

"In the dirt?"

I nodded. "We'll find a stick and you can practice your letters without using up your paper. Save it for later when your writing is smaller."

Willa looked up at our entrance and a scowl covered her homely face. I could guess what she was thinking. Not only was my presence unwelcome but now I had brought someone else with me. The kitchen maid's displeasure was obvious but I wanted to conduct Holly's lesson in some place that offered privacy. Except for Willa's hostility, the walled-in vegetable garden was perfect. She'd probably be complaining again to her sister, Rosa, I thought, and I hoped Lady Davina wouldn't put a stop to my coming here.

"Good morning, Willa," I said brightly. "Nice day after the rain."

She didn't return my greeting but turned her broad back on us and went back to pruning some vines.

"Not very friendly, is she?" Holly whispered.

"No. She doesn't like people roaming around in her garden. We'll have to make sure we stay out of her way." I led Holly over to a place in a far corner where the ground had not been prepared for planting. "Go get a hoe from the shed."

The young girl nodded and ran past Willa without even looking at her.

When she brought the hoe back, I said, "Now dig up this spot until it's soft as sand."

Holly attacked the ground with short jabs that easily turned over the soft dirt. I sat down on an overturned bucket and watched. When she had a large square smoothed, I broke off a couple of dry twigs and made the pattern of an "H" for her.

"That's a letter and each letter has a name and a sound. And there are twenty-six letters in the English alphabet."

She looked bewildered and I laughed. "Don't worry, we're not going to learn everything today, Holly. We'll save something for tomorrow's lesson."

She bit nervously on her lower lip. "I ain't too bright."

"That's not true."

Her eyes widened. "Yes, it is. Patrick says girls can't learn."

"Well, Patrick is wrong. Now relax. We'll take it slowly. This letter is called an 'H' and your name begins with it."

"It does? My very own name?"

"Your very own name. Now you try to write that letter just the way I did."

She sat down on a flat rock and began drawing in the soft dirt with her stick. I wasn't at all certain that I had started in the right place in my reading instruction but I reasoned that if Holly could write her name, at least we would have accomplished something.

Very quickly we went on to "O," "L," and finally "Y." I was glad Holly's name was a short one. My pupil worked diligently until the sun was straight overhead.

"That's enough for today," I said, wondering if she would ever get weary and quit. "Now I'll write your name on the paper and you can practice printing your letters at home with a pencil."

She looked at the wrapping paper with her name on it and then gave me a hug that nearly knocked me off my bucket seat. Yes, there was a lot of Dorthea in Holly, I thought with a laugh.

The young girl skipped off happily and my own steps were light as I climbed the stairs to my room.

My door was open and there was a bustle inside which startled me. I stuck my head inside before I entered. The old heavy green drapes and bed hangings were gone. All the furniture had been moved out. Three men were busy hanging the wallpaper.

"Don't stop," I said quickly as the men quit working and turned in my direction. "It's looking very nice."

"We'll be finished before dusk," promised one of the servants. "And we'll be moving ye back in."

I went down the hall to the room where Callie and I had stored my selection of things. The rest of my bedroom furniture was there, including the wardrobe holding my clothes.

I was glad that my room would look brand new when it was finished. It seemed appropriate that I was to have new, softer surroundings. My body had been awakened by a man's touch and all my senses had been heightened. The world had changed because of my new perceptions and at the moment I couldn't sort out my emotions. I still basked in the afterglow of a night of love-making.

Callie found me sorting through the pile of paintings I had scavenged, trying to decide what grouping would replace the horrid hunting tapestry.

"Oh, there ye be, mum."

"Yes, I spent the night with Addie Harrigan and just got back." I didn't dare look at her when I told the lie. Sean was right. I wasn't much of a liar.

"There's visitors asking for ye."

"Visitors?"

"The young Wainwrights, mum. Their carriage just arrived. Their belongings are already taken to the second floor guest rooms."

Bryant and Dorthea? No, it was too soon! I didn't want to give Sean up to her yet. How could I face her when my blood still ran hot from his embrace? Was Dorthea perceptive enough to see the betraying signs of a woman in love? Could I maintain an indifference that would ring true? I doubted it very much but I had no choice.

"Tell them I'll join them for lunch."

"Put the cook in a tizzy, it did, when Dolan told her they'd come."

"What about Lady Davina? Has she seen them?"

"They didn't ask for her, mum. Only you."

I sighed. "All right. I'll be down."

"As soon as the men finish, I'll be moving these things into your room."

"Thank you, Callie. You're an angel."

I left her taking things out of the old wardrobe and putting them in a new cherrywood one that I had chosen. All the way down the stairs I wished that Lady Davina would leave her butterflies and help me entertain the Wainwrights. I knew such hope was folly. She chose to be a recluse and that was that! I was going to have to act as hostess whether I wanted to or not. I wondered how Loretta and Lawrence would contrive to embarrass me during the Wainwrights' visit.

At least, Callie seemed to believe me about last night. Maybe Sean was right and the social scale was such that servants dare not question the morals or behavior of their masters. Apparently, no one was going to question my whereabouts and, thank heavens, I'd made it back before Bryant and Dorthea had arrived.

They were waiting in the drawing room.

"What a nice surprise! I didn't expect to see you so soon," I said, holding out my hands to Dorthea.

Her sparkling eyes lent beauty to her plain face and her smile was as warm as ever. "The place was too lonely without you, Aileen. Bryant and I wandered around like lost souls. Father went to London and we decided to spend a few days with you."

"I hope it will not be inconvenient," said Bryant smoothly, bending to kiss my cheek. "I missed you." His touch on my arm was possessive and lingered in a suggestive squeeze.

More than ever, his amorous overtones made me impatient. I didn't want him to touch me nor fawn over me. Knowing that I mustn't give way to my feelings, I managed to smile and murmur something about missing him, too.

Dorthea's eagle eyes were on the two of us. That secret smile of hers warned me that Bryant might make some kind of a declaration during this visit. What would I say if he asked me to marry him? I felt like turning around and fleeing upstairs. Last night's ecstasy was too fresh for me to contemplate the marriage bed with someone else.

"Shall we go in to lunch?" I said as brightly as my tumbling thoughts would allow. "I'm not certain who will be dining at home today. There

247

doesn't seem to be any regularity about who shows up for meals."

"Where's Sean?" Dorthea asked.

Without meeting her eyes, I responded, "I think he's around somewhere."

"Didn't you see him at breakfast?"

A simple question but, oh, what a devil's whirlwind it raised in me. Yes, I had seen Sean Creighton at breakfast. He had laughingly fed muffin crumbs into my mouth and had taken honey-eyed kisses from my lips. His hand had threaded through my hair which had fallen in flaxen abandonment around my shoulders. How could I keep up a pretense of indifference when such memories were like jolts of lightning surging through me?

"He didn't eat breakfast here," I said. That, at least, was the truth.

We reached the dining room and I didn't know whether I was relieved or sorry to see it empty. If Lady Davina or Sean had made an appearance, the burden of conversation might have fallen on them for brief periods at least.

"You poor darling," gushed Dorthea. "Eating all alone in this horrible, cold place. No wonder you are so miserable here. How could your father do such a thing to you? Make you a veritable *prisoner*. I wish he were alive, I'd tell him a few things. You really should make a fuss, Aileen."

Bryant laughed. "Don't mind my sister, Aileen. She thinks she can straighten out the whole world with that never-stop chatter of hers. I think people give in just to get a little peace," he chided affectionately.

Dorthea laughed back at him and I began to relax. The warm, companionable feeling that I had enjoyed at Windbriar came back as the three of us ate together. They were my only real friends and I was lucky to have someone who liked me enough to care about my situation. We were laughing at a story of Dorthea's when our lunch was interrupted by the arrival of Sean and Loretta.

Laughter froze on my face. Something in the way Sean's glance went from me to Bryant sitting at my side brought warmth to my cheeks.

"We thought we heard strange voices," said Loretta, smiling but without a welcome in her voice. "This seems to be the day for surprises."

She fixed a biting look on me and my stomach gave a sickening plunge. She must have missed Sean last night or this morning . . . or have seen us coming back on Graymont. *She knows!* No simple lie was going to satisfy her. The servants might accept any explanation I chose to give, but Loretta wouldn't be taken in so easily. I knew that the lowering of my eyes was a telltale reflex of guilt. I only hoped Bryant and Dorthea thought my half-sister's glare was due to my entertaining guests without anyone's permission or her usual self-centered manner.

Bryant rose easily to his feet. "Aileen has been inviting us to be her guests," he said, giving his personable smile. He made it sound as if I had been sending invitations by every coach.

"I hope we're welcome," said Dorthea, smiling boldly at Sean.

"But, of course. Delighted to see you, Dorthea."

Sean held out a chair for Loretta and sat down beside her with Dorthea on his other side. The three of them faced Bryant and me across the table. I could see a warm flush mounting in Dorthea's face as she exchanged pleasantries with Sean. On his other side, Loretta's arctic glare chilled me to the marrow.

Servants moved quickly around the table, bringing offerings of whitefish, creamed onions and peas in pastry shells, and spinach greens mixed with tiny bits of honey-soaked raisins. I suspected the cook was serving portions of the evening meal for the unexpected guest luncheon. Five people for the noon meal was most unusual.

I was grateful that Sean took some of the conversational burden off of me. He inquired about Sir Wainwright's health and once again expressed condolences.

"Father has decided to sell part of the stables, now that Claudia's gone," said Dorthea. "There are too many good horses who will never be ridden properly. Neither Bryant nor I are avid equestrians. But you are, Sean. Why don't you come and look over our offerings? I'm sure you might find something that pleases you." She actually looked coy and I wondered if Sean were aware of the double meaning of her words.

Loretta turned to Sean. "It might be nice if you'd pick up some kind of a mount for Aileen," she said in a sweetly acid tone. "Then the two of you wouldn't have to ride double."

Bryant's head swung in my direction. Could he see the hot flush mounting in my neck? I fumbled my fork setting it down.

I felt Dorthea's stunned gaze fixed on me. I knew that Sean's whole future might depend upon the way I handled this moment.

"I didn't think you liked to ride, Aileen," Bryant said.

"I don't," I answered, wrinkling my nose in distaste. "Not even double, but it was too muddy to walk home from Addie Harrigan's and Sean offered to bring me back to the castle. Next time I'll order a coach," I said haughtily and deliberately smiled at Dorthea and Bryant. "Of course, if it had been you, Bryant, my feelings about riding double might have been different."

Dorthea's face relaxed and I deliberately took a sip of wine before letting my gaze slide to Sean's face. What I saw stabbed me with pain. My haughtiness had brought a steel glint to his dark eyes. No softness touched his lips nor the curve of his chin. His hand tightened on his wine goblet as if he wanted to grab me by the shoulders and shake me.

I knew of no other way to protect him. Sir Wainwright would never back him for Parliament if it were known that he had spent the night as my lover. Dorthea would be crushed and hate me forever. The time had come to put a chasm between me and Sean.

Bryant laughed. "You're too much a lady to ride double like a peasant girl."

"I wonder," said Loretta pointedly. "Aileen may surprise us all. Of course, someone with her background can be expected to make a few mistakes."

"As do we all," said Sean smoothly. "But adventure is the result of bad planning, someone said. Do you agree with that, Aileen?"

What could I say but "yes"?

The interminable lunch finally ended. Dorthea suggested a walk along the ocean and looked hopefully at Sean, but he politely declined. Loretta sent a triumphant look in Dorthea's direction but her victory was short-lived. Sean refused Loretta's obvious attempt to claim his attention for herself and took his leave of all of us.

Bryant politely asked Loretta to make our walk a foursome but she only laughed. "Walking is not my sport. Would you care to join me in an exhilarating horseback ride, Bryant? That is, if you feel competent enough for one of our mounts."

"Apparently, you rate your stable quite highly," he responded.

"I think you would find a ride with me challenge enough."

She flung the taunt in such a way that Bryant's affable smile only broadened. "Then I have no choice but to accept."

Loretta sent me a smug smile. Obviously, she felt she had bested me by taking Bryant away. "I hope you don't mind, Aileen?"

Her petty victory was laughable in view of the relief that it brought to me. "Not at all." I was not ready to face Bryant's ardor and I quickly assured him and Loretta that Dorthea and I could amuse ourselves while they were gone.

"See you both for tea, then," said Bryant, allowing Loretta to take his arm as they left the room.

Dorthea just glared at him and muttered under her breath.

"It's all right," I assured her after they'd left.

"No, it isn't!" Dorthea snapped. "She gets her claws into every man around just for the fun of it. Did you see how she tried to keep Sean from even talking to me? Oh, Aileen, I'm so worried that he will make a commitment to her before my father talks to him. If only Claudia hadn't been killed, it would have been settled by now. Do they spend a lot of time together?"

"I'm not sure."

"Do you think they're lovers?"

My mouth was suddenly dry. "I don't know. You must come up and see my room." I slipped my arm through hers and chatted about the redecorating I was doing as we mounted the stairs.

Dorthea's question lingered in a disquieting corner of my mind. Loretta might find out we had been at Rathbridge. I knew she would viciously use the knowledge against me and somehow secure her hold on Sean.

Chapter Fifteen

Dorthea and Bryant stayed for three days but we never recaptured the warmth and companionship we had enjoyed at Windbriar. Bryant only went for that one ride with Loretta and then he turned all his attention to me. Apparently Loretta had proved her point that she could demand his attention whenever she wanted. I suspected he was not enough of a challenge to hold her interest and it was obvious that her sights were set on Sean.

Dorthea was in a constant state of agitation over Sean's sporadic attention to her and I was furious with his indifference.

"He hates me," she wailed.

"Nonsense. He's just busy."

Irritated that I was in a position of having to make excuses for him, I cornered Sean in the library one morning. I went into the room and shut the door behind me. He looked up from his desk and for a moment his expression wavered before it set in rigid lines. He rose and said crisply, "To what do I owe the honor of your presence this morning?"

"There are guests in this house and the least you can do is show some polite interest in Dorthea," I charged angrily.

"So that you can play Lady-of-the-Manor with

Bryant?" he asked coolly. "I'm wondering if my first assessment of you was correct, my dear Aileen. The Wainwright holdings are extensive. Marrying into that family would put a golden cup to anyone's lips."

His words made me sick for I knew, in truth, it was not a golden cup for my lips we were talking about, but one for his. Marriage to Dorthea would make him a member of an affluent English family and all the benefits he was throwing in my face would be his. If he were only aware of the stakes, he would change his attitude, I thought angrily. "I think you would do well to consider what marriage to Dorthea might offer you."

He raised an eyebrow. "Are you here as a marriage broker, my love?"

The endearment only fueled my anger. My heart was breaking and he was mocking me. I firmed my chin. "In a way, I suppose I am."

"How interesting. Why are you trying to marry me off to your friend?"

"She loves you."

His mouth quirked at the corners. "But I don't love her."

"That's beside the point."

"Is it?" He moved so close to me that I could feel his warm breath upon my face. He took my hands. "You can't believe that. I want you and you know it."

Joy caught in my throat but was soon followed by a wash of despair. "That isn't possible. You have too much to lose."

"I agree that there are problems. Your father set his will up so that I forfeit what few assets I have if I abandon my duties at Lynhurst."

He didn't know that Dorthea was going to offer

him a way to break free without any sacrifices. I knew what he had to lose. I couldn't let him do it.

I pulled my hands away from his. "There's no future for us. You have too much at stake."

"Why don't you let me decide that?"

"Because—" I choked off the rest of the words. I could ruin everything for him if I made him choose between me and what Dorthea could offer.

His forehead knitted. "I don't understand you at all. I'm trying to tell you that I love you and ask you to be patient until I can work things out, and you act as if you have something hidden behind your back. What is this all about?"

"I can't tell you."

He pulled me against him and his lips trailed down the curve of my cheek. "Why not?" he murmured.

"Don't."

"Don't what? Kiss you?" His mouth poised a breath away from mine.

"Don't ask me to reveal a confidence," I choked.

"We don't have any secrets between us, love. I know about that delicious small mole in the hollow of your back and—"

"Please . . ." My breath was uneven and my voice husky. I had to stop this madness. If Dorthea found out about our relationship, Sean's chances for Parliament would be gone and he would hate me for destroying his dreams.

His mouth captured mine. I tried to pull away but my emotions were out of control. I responded to his tongue tracing the corners of my opened mouth. A hot sweetness sped through me and only when he drew his mouth from mine did the passion I felt for him turn to bitter sorrow. "You

256

mustn't ever touch me again."

"Because you don't love me?" he taunted softly.

"Because . . . because I'm going to marry Bryant."

A slap on his face wouldn't have brought a more angry flare to his face. "What are you talking about?"

I swallowed hard. "You heard me."

"Has he proposed?"

"No, but he will."

"And you're going to say yes?"

I nodded.

"Why?"

My mouth was dry but I managed to say evenly, "Because it's best."

His lips tightened and he stepped back. The few feet between us formed a chasm. "Yes, of course, that's best. A rich landowner instead of a penniless solicitor. Much better, indeed. I apologize for thinking that love mattered."

"It's not that!"

"Isn't it? Don't take me for a fool, my love. I've watched you play up to Bryant and simper at his dandified attentions. You've just about convinced me that you're the fortune-seeking opportunist I first imagined."

There was no way I could justify my behavior. If Sean thought for a minute I was sacrificing myself for him, he'd throw away the chance he would have with Dorthea. Let him think what he would about me. It would be easier to keep my distance from him if he hated me. I turned away from his caustic remarks and left the room.

The scene in the library with Sean left a numbness within me that I struggled to keep below the surface that afternoon when I walked with Bryant along the coast road. When we passed the place where Sean had taken me down to his cave, pain squeezed my chest. I knew that I would spend the rest of my life reliving those bittersweet memories. I must have inadvertently grimaced.

"You're not happy at Lynhurst, are you, Aileen?" Bryant asked, reading my expression.

I raised my eyes to the huge, stone castle on the hill above us and wondered how I ever thought I would find a home there. "I don't belong," I admitted in a choked voice. "If my father were alive, it might be different, but I came too late."

"I'm sorry things turned out to be such a disappointment for you. Truly, a sad thing to come all this way and find Lord Lynhurst murdered on his doorstep. An ugly way to lose a father."

"His death changed everything."

As we walked, Bryant slipped his arm through mine and expounded on what a fine man my father had been. He made Lord Lynhurst sound generous and sympathetic to the needs of others and I wondered if I could have persuaded my father to finance Sean's political ambitions if he had lived. Our love might have had a chance under those circumstances, I thought with new pain.

"I've been thinking a lot about you, Aileen. After you left Windbriar, my life seemed empty. I know that you have had to make some adjustments and I didn't want to speak until I thought you were ready to hear my offer. Shall we sit here, where we can talk?" He drew me over to some rocks that rimmed the cliff's edge. Far below, white-foamed breakers beat the rocks and then re-

258

ceded, only to come rushing in again with a me-
tered roar.

He's going to propose. The knowledge brought a
tight constriction to my chest. And I was going to
accept. I didn't love Bryant the way I did Sean,
but he would make a good husband and provide
for me. In return, I would be a devoted wife and I
would never betray my vows. Once I set my face
in this direction, I would hold firmly to it. Even
though Sean and I would be thrown together, he
and Dorthea would live in England and if they
returned to Ireland, it would be only for a visit or
for a reelection campaign. If I had had another
choice, I would have taken it. But I didn't.

Bryant sat down on a large rock beside me.
"Would you be amiable to a change in your life,
Aileen?" His arm slipped around my waist.

I nodded and tried to keep my smile firm.

He tightened his embrace. "It would make me
very happy to care for you. There's a small farmhouse not far from Windbriar. You could fix it up
any way you liked. It would be all yours. I'd put it
in your name. You wouldn't want for anything, I
promise you, darling. New clothes, jewelry, a
monthly allowance."

A farmhouse? Clothes? Jewelry?

"Please say yes."

I stiffened. "Say yes to what, Bryant?" The roar
in my ears was as loud as the ocean's.

"You know, a relationship like your mother and
Lord Lynhurst's. The minute I saw you, I knew
why their affair had been so passionate. His Lordship fell madly in love with your mother and my
father says you resemble her. You're everything a
man could desire, my darling Aileen. There's never
been anyone like you in my life. I'm willing to

259

make sacrifices to have you."

I knew then that Bryant Wainwright had never intended to offer me marriage. Hysterical laughter bubbled up in my throat. "I thought you wanted to marry me."

"Aileen, my dearest, you know that's not possible. I have obligations and responsibilities as the only male in our family. I must look to marriage as a safeguard to the Wainwright fortune. If Lord Lynhurst had made you an heir, such a marriage might be possible but as it is . . ." He shrugged.

"Dorthea seemed to think that it was possible," I countered.

"My little sister can escape responsibilities which I, the male heir, must assume. You surely understand my position, darling? Dorthea has her eye on Sean and my father will buy him for her. He will make the arrangements for their betrothal when he returns from England. Having a son-in-law in Parliament appeals to my father."

"But having an illegitimate, penniless daughter-in-law does not." My voice broke, partly in rage and partly in anguish.

"There's no way that I can marry you, my dearest one, but I can offer you an enjoyable life away from Lynhurst. Your own little home, no financial worries. I'll provide for you the way your father provided for you and your mother all through the years."

"Like mother, like daughter? Is that it?"

He smiled. "Something like that. Love fades but a business arrangement does not."

Sean's words came back to me. *Bryant Wainwright is not the marrying kind.*

"What do you say, Aileen, sweetheart? Will you let me make the necessary arrangements?"

I looked into his handsome face and fury washed away the numbness inside. "There is one basic difference between this situation and that of my parents. My mother was deeply in love with my father. She didn't sell herself for money — and neither will I."

"If you care for me —"

"I don't."

"But you were ready to accept a proposal of marriage." He threw the words at me and challenged me to deny them.

I couldn't. I nodded wearily, ashamed of the truth of his words. If he had asked me to be his wife instead of his mistress, I would have accepted. "Thank you for saving us both from a terrible mistake."

When they left that afternoon, Dorthea was subdued and Bryant politely distant.

"Please come and see us," she said as she hugged me.

"Yes, I will." But I knew that I would feel deep shame every time Bryant looked at me, knowing he saw me only as a woman to be bought for his pleasure.

"Sean has promised to come and look over our stable. Father will be back in a few weeks and settle things between us. Won't it be wonderful? You'll be my attendant at the wedding, won't you?"

"If I'm here."

"Where are you going?"

"I don't know."

She looked at her brother who had distanced himself from us. "Did you and Bryant have a lover's tiff?"

"Something like that."

"No matter," she said airily. "You'll make up. Bryant never stays angry with anyone very long. Remember, you'll always be welcome at our house. You're my dear, wonderful friend. Never forget it!"

Tears filled my eyes. "Thank you, Dorthea. I hope you'll always be my friend."

She gave me one last hug and disappeared into the coach.

"Goodbye, Aileen," said Bryant formally. "If you have second thoughts, please let me know."

"I won't."

"Circumstances change," he warned and took his place beside his sister.

I retreated to my newly decorated room and threw myself across the bed. Humiliated by Bryant's invitation to be his mistress, I wanted to crawl into a dark burrow and hide.

When Callie knocked on my door with an evening tray, the room was dark and chilled. My face was tear-stained and my clothes mussed. She quickly lit the candles and coaxed a fire in the grate.

"The dance is tonight, mum," she said, eyeing me as she performed her duties.

"What?"

"The barn dance. Sure and ye'll be coming. Daddo told me to tell ye he'll be fiddling up a special tune for ye."

I'd completely forgotten the Saturday night affair for the Irish peasants. "I'm sorry, but I don't feel like a party."

"All the more reason for ye to be goin'," said Callie in a practical tone. "A few gulps of poteen and a couple of whirls around the floor will put the world to rights, that's for sure. I'll just be laying out yer things—in case ye be changin' yer mind."

I didn't object. My thoughts were too heavy. I had lost my English friends and put a gulf between me and Sean. *I want you,* he had told me that morning in the library. His declaration suddenly bore a different context. Sean hadn't said anything about wanting to marry me! Not once had he mentioned marriage. I gave a bitter laugh. It was very possible I assumed too much, just the way I had with Bryant. Did Sean also see me as a mistress and not a wife? Hot shame rose up into my face. How naive and foolish I'd been. Lawrence had insulted me openly about my parentage. Now, I realized he was the only one being honest with me. Undoubtedly both Bryant and Sean saw me in the same light from the very beginning—the illegitimate daughter of a woman who had been Lord Lynhurst's mistress.

I sat down in a chair and stared at the licking tongues of fire. When I heard sounds of laughter and voices, I walked listlessly over to a window and drew back the silken drapes. The front gate to the castle had been thrown open and a crowd of men, women, and children flowed in a multicolored mass toward the barn and stables. I sat down in the window seat and watched their merry arrival. Rollicking good humor was evident as they shouted and jostled each other. Young and old, their jubilant high spirits mocked my tear-streaked face.

Slowly my self-pity began to dissipate. Some inner voice chided me for forgetting the friendly warmth that Molly and Addie had shown me and the adoration that sparkled in Holly's eyes every time she looked at me. Just because I didn't belong with the Wainwrights and the Lynhursts didn't mean that life was over. I needed to take a lesson from my mother's people. Any one of them suffered more humiliation each day than I could even imagine. Their resiliency mocked my self-indulgence.

I changed into a wine-colored dress that Callie had laid out for me. Impulsively, I combed my hair free and let it hang down my back like an Irish colleen. I flung a yellow shawl over my shoulders and made my way downstairs.

I froze for a moment in the main hall when I heard voices in the drawing room. Lawrence's loud voice indicated that he was already well into his cups. Loretta gave a brittle laugh and I thought I heard Sean respond in softer tones. I hurried down a corridor that led to a rear door of the castle.

"Where are you going?" A demanding voice stopped me.

I turned to face Lady Davina standing in the doorway of the music room. Her eyes swept over my loosened hair and my bright yellow shawl. I could tell that my appearance left her speechless. Her nostrils flared. "What is the meaning of this?"

"Of what?" I countered. I had visited her turret room twice and I had thought we were establishing a relationship that might expand beyond the limited interest of her hobby. I knew that such hopes were ruined by this unexpected encounter.

"Please, explain yourself." Her black eyes flashed. "Your appearance is disgraceful. Only doxies and harlots wear loose hair outside the bedroom."

My smile was tense. "That's not true. Irish girls don't put their hair up until they are married."

"But you are a Lynhurst!"

"Am I?" I gave a bitter laugh. "Everyone has made it very clear that I have no right to claim my father's heritage, so tonight I'm gong to enjoy the festivities as Aileen O'Connor. If you will excuse me, I don't want to be late for the dance."

"You can't go alone—like that!" She looked horrified.

"Would you like to come with me?"

Words failed her. Lady Davina turned back into the room and shut the door in my face.

When I crossed the clearing at the rear of the castle, I threw the shawl over my fair hair and melted into the crowd pouring into the barn.

The building was a large one and as many seats as could be crowded together lined the walls: sacks of corn laid lengthwise, logs of round timber, old creels, iron pots with their bottoms turned up. Children sat on the floor and young men held sweethearts on their laps. In an elevated corner of the room, Daddo sat on a stool, fiddling and exchanging lively banter with older men who sat in front of him. Couples of every description and age crowded the floor, dancing furiously as if Satan's furies were after them. I couldn't tell if they were trying to catch up with Daddo's furious sawing or if he were trying to overtake their flying feet. The floorboards vibrated with the vigorous pounding of dancing couples.

The din of music, dancing, laughter, and loud voices kept me from hearing my name but I saw Holly waving madly at me. She had been faithful to her lessons every day and I was delighted with her progress. Slowly I made my way toward her and saw that Molly was sitting behind her children, laughing and talking with Addie.

"Greetings to ye!" Molly welcomed me with a broad smile. She scooted Patrick off his seat and offered a turned-over iron pot to me. I could see that the young priest-about-to-be was not very happy with this treatment. Flattered and pampered, he was used to being the favored one, accepting preferential treatment over that of his brothers and sisters. His scowl told me my intrusion was not welcome. I wondered if he resented my attentions to his sister. After all, he would not be the only one in the family able to read and write his name.

Holly made up for Patrick's coolness. She grabbed my hand in a squeeze. "I knew ye'd come."

I wondered how she knew it, when I hadn't known it myself. If Bryant had asked me to marry him, I wouldn't be attending a peasants' barn dance tonight, I thought, and suddenly felt free and unfettered.

Kerrie and Shannon were out on the floor and I saw Callie and her young man, Liam, sitting on the sidelines. A variety of dances proceeded in swift order: the reel, jig, fling, cotillion, and a variety of folk dances which I had never seen before. I couldn't understand why some couples were not dancing until I realized that there wasn't room for everyone on the floor at once and a rotation was in progress, starting with those seated next to the door and going clockwise around the barn.

Contests between couples sprang up spontaneously and spectators began to cheer, snap their fingers, and urge their favorites to even more strenuous endeavors. I couldn't believe how agile some of the gray-haired women were and how they flipped their red petticoats and flirted as men danced around them with caps tipped rakishly on one side of their heads.

"Handle yer feet, Maureen, darlin'."

"Off wid the brogues, Paddy, or she'll do ye."

"The blood's in ye, Barney; ye'll win the day!"

The cheering spectators kept the couples dancing until they collapsed amid roars of laughter. Practical jokes ran rampant. Some of the pots were turned upright for unwary young men and their partners to sit on. A black ring like a bull's-eye circled their posteriors when they rose to dance, causing hilarious mirth to circle the crowd.

I don't know how quickly Lawrence's presence was noticed, but the level of the hilarity began to lessen. The dance floor became less crowded and more people stood around the edges of the barn. Finally Daddo's fiddle playing ceased altogether. There was silence and waiting. All eyes were fixed upon the ruddy-faced young man. Lawrence's walk was unsteady as he moved to the center of the floor. His voice was slurred when he said loudly, "Eat, drink, and be merry, for tomorrow you work!" He laughed at his own cleverness.

Where was Sean? This was his idea. He should be here to do the honors and keep Lawrence from making a fool of himself.

Before I knew what was happening, Lawrence had pulled Kerrie out on the floor. He fixed firm hands on her and smirked lewdly at the young girl. Kerrie's expression was a mixture of fright and awe.

Lawrence gave an imperious wave to Daddo. "Play a slow one."

"Oh, dear Mother of God," breathed Molly. "No, not me Kerrie. Sure, he's going to demand the patron's right."

"What are you talking about?"

Molly covered her face with her hands and Addie was the one to answer. "It's the custom. The patron can take the bride unto himself first before her wedding."

"You mean — ?" My eyes widened in horror.

Addie nodded.

"But why doesn't someone protest?"

"And lose their home, land, and the wherewithall to feed their family?" She shook her head. "It's the patron's right, if he wishes to claim it. The old lordship never took a young girl, but this one . . ."

"Mike will kill him," breathed Molly. Her eyes scanned the room for her husband. She crossed herself and her lips moved in a prayer.

"He came with you?" I asked in surprise.

She nodded. "But he's pulling a cork somewhere outside. If someone goes for him . . ." Her frantic eyes fled from the dancing couple to the doorway as if she expected her husband to lurch through it any moment.

Daddo cut the song short and everyone breathed a collective sigh of relief when Lawrence conducted the girl back to Shannon. He made an exaggerated bow to the engaged couple and then walked unsteadily out of the barn.

Maybe that's all there would be to it. I felt Molly relaxing.

The crowd quickly recovered its gaiety and word was passed that tables of food and drink were ready in the courtyard. Geese and fowl of all kinds, legs of mutton, boiled carrots, parsnips, and cabbage provided a feast that filled Irish bellies and was washed down with deep gulps of wine and ale.

Kerrie came over to her mother. She was obviously shaken and frightened. Shannon's face was as rigid as chiseled granite.

"Don't be a worryin'," Molly said with a false smile. "Don't you two be breaking your shins on a stool that may not be in yer way at all," she warned. "And don't be sayin' anything to yer father, Kerrie."

The young girl nodded. Shannon put his arm around her waist and they left together.

I looked away from the dancers and saw Sean standing in the doorway with Loretta. Her arm was looped possessively through his. Sean's gaze circled the room until he found me. Lady Davina must have told him about my disgraceful appearance and behavior, I thought, remembering her horrified expression. If Sean had come to take me back to my room, he'd find out that I didn't give a farthing about his or anybody else's opinion of me.

He said something to Loretta and she flounced away from him. He called to her but she ignored him. Callie and her young man, Liam, were sitting close by. The next minute Loretta was on the dance floor with Liam. The youth was so bewildered that he stumbled over his feet. Loretta laughingly grabbed him in a wild swing and gave him a luminous smile. Hot color washed up into the youth's face. Dark brown curls swung around Loretta's face and the luminous pink gown she wore set off her creamy-white skin. Liam's broad hands engulfed her small waist and he looked as if he held a fairy princess in his arms.

269

I wondered what Callie was thinking but I didn't have time to worry about her. Sean walked across the barn, greeted Molly and Addie, and then his eyes settled on me.

"I'm surprised to see you here, Aileen. When I cam back to the castle this evening, I heard that the Wainwrights had gone." He arched an eyebrow. "Wasn't their departure quite sudden?"

"No."

"Did you settle something definitely with Bryant?"

"I don't think that's any of your concern."

"Would you care to dance?"

"No."

"Would you like some refreshment?"

"No."

"Would you like me to carry you out of here over my shoulder?"

Holly stifled a giggle and Molly laughed outright.

"You wouldn't dare."

He made a movement toward me to prove me wrong.

"All right," I said quickly. "I wouldn't mind some fresh air." I knew he was angry enough to embarrass us both.

"I thought you'd change your mind."

"I'll be back shortly," I told Molly. With as much dignity as I could manage, I pushed through the crowd ahead of Sean, resentful of the firm guiding hand he kept on my elbow. Once outside, I jerked away "Now that you've proven you can manhandle me, what is it that you want to say to me?"

"Let's sit over there."

He nodded to a narrow alley between the barn

270

and stables where some bales of hay provided sitting room and privacy from the people milling around with food and drink in their hands. Whiskey was flowing freely and men's voices were getting louder and louder. I was glad to be in a rather isolated and protected spot.

He sat down on a bale beside me. "You look beautiful tonight, love. I like your hair loose like that, as you know."

The soft, suggestive tone brought back memories of his fingers threading and spreading strands of my hair upon his bare chest. Was he always going to torment me like this? I kept my stiff gaze straight ahead.

"Look at me." He put his hand on my chin and firmly turned my face toward his. Before I could protest, he kissed me, quickly and with possessive firmness. "Now, I want to know—what happened between you and Bryant?"

"I don't think that's any of your business."

He only gave me an infuriating grin. "It didn't go the way you planned. He didn't propose to you, did he?"

The sense of satisfaction in his tone made me bitter. "Oh, he proposed, all right. But not marriage. You were right. Bryant is not the marrying kind."

"I warned you."

"Yes, you did. Now the two of you can get together and have a good laugh about my honorable expectations."

"What do you mean by that?"

"Don't pretend you don't see me as Lord Lynhurst's illegitimate daughter, born to a woman he loved but never married."

He frowned. "Those are the facts, of course."

271

"And isn't it also a fact that you see me as a woman you can enjoy but never marry?"

He never had a chance to answer. A roar like a battle cry turned the congenial merriment in the courtyard into mayhem. The grounds were suddenly filled with men shouting and leaping at each other.

"The blasted fools," swore Sean. "They'll bash in each other's heads."

"What's happening?"

"It's a faction fight. Somebody started it and now they'll all join in and fight each other. That's what fools they are. Always quarreling among themselves." He ducked as a piece of wood came flying through the air.

The hilarity with which the men leaped and capered at each other was at odds with the harsh blows from cudgels of all kinds. The fight was more like a sport than a meeting of adversaries. Any given young man who a moment before had held a sweetheart on his lap now took swings at the same girl's father and brother.

"Whack!"

"Huzza! Huzza!"

"Blood! Blood!"

Rocks flew everywhere.

Men wielded spades, hoes, whips, and churn staffs. They plunged through the crowd cracking heads and limbs.

Sean turned up the bales of hay on which we had been sitting into a barricade and made me crouch down behind them. "Stay here."

"Where are you going?"

"To find Loretta. The little fool will get herself right in the middle of this!"

And you'll be right there to protect her, I

thought with unchristian bitterness. And it would always be like that. I had been a fool to think otherwise.

Sean entered the fray and took a blow on his chin before his fist flashed out to catch the grinning Paddy in the nose. He plunged forward through the fray, fighting his way as men rolled on the ground and fists made contact with anyone who stood up ready to fight.

In the midst of the tumult, I saw Shannon exchange blows with another youth and I winced when a fist landed squarely on one of his eyes. He'd have a black eye for his wedding, that was for sure. I wondered where Kerrie was. I couldn't understand the uncivilized brutality with which these Irishmen fought each other. There was no air of vengeance or even animosity as they spilled blood and knocked each other senseless. A good-natured, rollicking, physical confrontation left noses broken, skulls cracked, and bodies marked with cuts and bruises.

As quickly as it had begun, the fracas settled down. Men slapped each other on the back and went back to eating and drinking. Women and children searched out the men in their family. Bloodied noses were staunched with aprons and torn petticoats. Jugs of whiskey circulated to those in pain until the men who were battered the most wore silly, satisfied smiles upon their faces.

The music started up again and I decided that it was safe for me to leave the narrow alley.

I stood up and took a step away from the barricade when a sharp cry stopped me. At first, I thought it might be the cry of an animal but the terror in it was human.

Several small feed rooms opened onto the nar-

273

row alley between the barn and the stables. I was certain that the loud sobs came from inside one of them.

Walking down the short alley, I listened for the cries and when I heard them coming loudly from behind one of the doors, I flung it open.

The sight that met my eyes was like a swift kick. For a moment I had no breath left in me.

Sprawled on a bed of straw was my half-brother . . . and Kerrie.

I was too late.

Lawrence had already had his way with her.

Chapter Sixteen

Kerrie rushed into my arms, her clothes awry, tears streaming down her cheeks. If I'd had a whip I would have lashed Lawrence, who sprawled obscenely on the hay in a near stupor. I had never felt such rage. To defile this young girl in such a beastly fashion went against every civilized fiber of my being. I knew how beautiful the mating of a man and woman could be. Now Kerrie had been cheated out of that. That wondrous first rapture Kerrie might have had with Shannon had been destroyed and the callous use of her body by my drunken half-brother made my stomach churn with nausea.

I put my arm around her trembling shoulder. "Come on. Let's get out of here."

Shivers wracked Kerrie's body and she sobbed against my chest as we left the shed. Outside I buttoned her bodice and smoothed her skirts. I didn't know what I should do. Where was Shannon? The last time I'd seen him he had been in the middle of the fray. He should have been looking after his betrothed, I thought angrily, instead of showing off his masculine prowess.

I led Kerrie down the short alley and just as we reached the bales of hay where Sean and I had sat, I caught sight of Molly. She was across the crowded clearing, standing at one of the tables, eating a hunk of meat and chatting with another woman.

"Stay here," I ordered Kerrie, easing her down on one of the bales of hay. "I'll get your mother."

I wended my way through the crowd as quickly as I could. The laughing, high-spirited din around me was at odds with the sickening despondency I felt inside.

"Molly! Molly!" I called when I got close enough for her to hear.

She swung around. One look at my face and Molly's smile faded. "What be the matter?"

"You have to come." I took her arm. "It's Kerrie . . ."

"The saints preserve us. What happened?"

"She needs you," was all I said. I pulled Molly through the crowd back to the place where Kerrie waited with her head buried in her hands.

Kerrie threw herself into her mother's arms. Molly looked over Kerrie's head at me.

"His Lordship," I said bitterly in answer to her questioning eyes.

"Did he?"

I nodded. "While the fight was going on." I was too sick to say anything more.

Molly buried her face in her daughter's hair. "Now, now," she murmured. "Don't be takin' on so. Ye be all right. Ye mustn't say anything. 'Twas his right."

I wanted to scream to her that no man had that right! How could she condone the callous rape of a young girl? Fear of repercussions shouldn't allow such a vile custom to exist. Such squire privileges had long ago been abandoned in England.

"I'll be takin' her home," said Molly.

I nodded, watched them leave, and then made my way through the crowd. I heard Daddo's fiddle and the stamp of feet coming from the barn. I wondered where Sean was. Had he found Loretta and had the two of them slipped off together? Was he holding her in his arms? I shoved the painful thought away. He had left me when the fight broke out to take care of Loretta. That was evidence enough of my place in his affections.

Laughter and singing mingled with the loud voices of men joshing each other. The buildup of tension had been eased. They had taken their frustrations out on each other. Was the Watcher here among them? And the Bog Boys? Had they laughed and danced and planned their next attack while eating and drinking with the merry crowd?

I was too heartsick to care. Let them tear the castle down stone by stone. It turned my stomach that Ireland was still tied to such brutal and destructive customs. I didn't belong in this harsh, cruel Irish society nor in my father's class-conscious English world. Maybe that's what "illegitimate" really meant: I didn't belong anywhere.

It was nearly dawn before the last sounds of merriment faded away. Sleep evaded me and I spent most of the night sitting in front of the fire, feeding it chunks of turf and searching my mind for some way to escape from the quagmire of my situation.

Sean had been delighted that Bryant had failed to ask me to marry him. Even though I realized that it would have been a terrible mistake to spend my life in such an unhappy union, I resented Sean's obvious satisfaction. He thought I was se-

277

curely tied to him and Lynhurst. Undoubtedly, he planned to marry Loretta and reduce me to the same status as Bryant had proposed. He had said, "I love you and I want you." He hadn't said, "I love you and I want to *marry* you." Did he have ideas of turning me into his kept woman? I vowed that I would turn myself into a homeless refugee first.

This conviction put some iron back into me and when morning came, my emotions had settled. When Callie brought in my breakfast tray, I was dressed and feeling quite happy.

One look at her ashen face and my appetite faded.

"What happened?"

Her lips quivered. "Liam."

I didn't remember seeing him in the fracas but there were young men who had been hit and knocked to the ground. "Did he get hurt?"

She shook her head and wiped at her eyes with her apron.

"Then what happened?" I demanded impatiently. I should have known what she was going to say but my brain was filled with too many other concerns.

"He went off with her . . . the mistress."

Then I remembered. The last time I'd seen Liam he'd been dancing with Loretta. But Sean had gone to find her during the fight to make certain she was all right. "No, I'm sure you're wrong, Callie. Mr. Creighton was looking after Loretta."

"He couldn't find either of 'em at the dance. Looked all over for her. Raging mad, he was, too."

I remembered the concern in his eyes when he had left me.

278

"I told him that she'd left with Liam." Callie's eyes brimmed with tears. "Her horse was gone. He rode after 'em."

My mouth went dry. Lawrence with Kerrie. Loretta with Liam. My father's children took their pleasure wherever they found it.

"Brought 'em back, too. Fired Liam. Told him to pack up his things and leave."

"I'm sorry, Callie." I was embarrassed and angry.

"He's left for good," she wailed.

"You'll find someone better." But the words echoed hollowly in my own ears. "Why don't you take the day? Go visit your family. Things will look differently tomorrow."

"I love him, mum. Sure and it's like my heart is empty when he's not about."

"Yes," I echoed.

Since it was Sunday, I knew Holly wouldn't be coming for her lesson. If there had been an Anglican church within walking distance, I would have gone to services. Even Reverend Whitestead's dolorous sermons would have been welcome. I heard the Catholic church bells and I wondered if Kerrie would make her confession to the priest.

I wished that I could visit Lady Davina but I knew that I had effectively put an end to any friendship between us. The horror and distaste on her face last night left no doubt as to her low opinion of me. I had verified my low birth and given her the excuse she needed to scorn me. Then I bristled. Who was she to judge my behavior when the conduct of her own two children last night was abominable?

And Sean? He must have been furious to find Loretta dallying with a stableboy. Was she trying to make him jealous? From the crude remarks Lawrence had made about his sister, this kind of thing must have happened before. I wondered if Sean would find out what Lawrence had done. Molly would keep it quiet and in the family. Shannon would have to be told — and Mike? I shuddered to think what the reaction of Kerrie's father would be. An ominous depression settled on me.

The day wore away tediously. I sat in the window seat, mending. When I put down my sewing and looked below, a movement in the trees rimming the edge of the front courtyard caught my eyes. My breathing quickened. Mike Ryan moved furtively toward the castle and it was evident that he didn't want to be seen. Several times the dark Irishman flattened himself behind a tree trunk, waited a few seconds, and then skittered toward the next concealment. His eyes swept over the windows but I didn't think he looked high enough to see the third storey. He held a hook in his hand, the kind that lifted chunks of turf onto a barrow.

He was after Lawrence, I knew it! I held no love for my half-brother but neither did I want to see a hook buried in his chest. I would be content to have Kerrie's father put the fear of God in him, but I must prevent a murder.

I tumbled my mending in a heap on the floor and ran downstairs. Sean! He would know what to do. My running footsteps echoed on the marble floor as I ran to the library. He wasn't there. No one was in the drawing room nor dining room.

"Dolan! Dolan!" I screamed, running toward the kitchen.

"Yes, Miss."

"Is my brother in the house?"

"Don't rightly know, Miss."

"Have someone check his rooms. Tell Lawrence to stay there and lock the door. Right away!"

"But—"

"And put a guard at each door. Don't let Mike Ryan in. He's on the grounds somewhere. I saw him."

Bewildered, Dolan turned to the servants who were clustered in the kitchen doorway and gave instructions to Willa to check on Lawrence. He sent the others to secure the castle doors.

"Where is Mr. Creighton?" I asked Dolan after the servants had scurried away.

"He went for a ride with Miss Loretta after lunch."

"And Lady Davina?"

"I believe I heard Rosa say that she's in the turret room."

Lifting up my skirts, I fled upstairs in an unladylike manner. Someone had to be told about the threat Mike Ryan posed to Lawrence's life. Since no one else was here, Lady Davina would have to take charge of her son. He was her responsibility, after all. For years she had abdicated that responsibility. Now she had no choice. Mike Ryan was going to kill Lawrence. He had made it plain how much he hated the Lynhursts. Now he had a father's revenge to fuel his smoldering hatred. His fury was so intense that he had come alone to seek his personal revenge without the rest of the Bog Boys.

I ran down the corridor to Lady Davina's turret room and knocked loudly on the door. Her dog began barking and lunging at the door.

I heard her say, "Down, Rex. Down."

The animal was still growling when she opened the door. Lady Davina's face registered displeasure at seeing me standing there. "I don't wish to be disturbed," she said in a frigid tone. "Please go away."

I didn't have time for polite apologies. "Lawrence is in danger of his life. I fear Mike Ryan's come to kill him."

Her icy expression did not change but I thought her breath caught for a brief second. "And why would you think such a thing?" she demanded.

I took a deep breath. "Lawrence raped his daughter, Kerrie, last night in the stable."

Her face drained of color. "I don't believe you," she retorted but I knew from her tone that she knew her son.

"It's true. I got there just after it happened. Lawrence was drunk. He danced with Kerrie earlier and knew she was soon going to be married. And he demanded his 'patron' rights."

"No, he wouldn't," she gasped but again her denial lacked conviction.

"We don't have time to argue. Her father has come for his revenge. I saw him sneaking up to the castle — with a turf hook in his hand. He'll kill Lawrence."

"Sean! Tell Sean."

"He's not here. You must talk to your son and take charge of this situation."

"No, I can't." She seemed to shrivel up before my eyes. "You do whatever you think best."

"It's not my place, Lady Davina. Lawrence is your son. His death will be on your conscience."

"He won't listen to me. I've tried and tried. For years, I failed in my efforts to control him. If I go to him, he'll only laugh. He hates me. There's nothing I can do. Nothing."

She made a move to shut the door but I

stopped her with my shoulder. The dog growled and I thought for a moment that she would use him to force me away from the door.

"Please, Lady Davina. Your son needs you. Please come and talk to him. Tell him of the danger. Don't let this lie on your conscience. In spite of everything, you *are* his mother."

She stared at some point beyond me. I wondered if she were remembering the time when she had given him birth and cuddled him in her arms. The starch visibly went out of her. "All right. But it won't do any good. If I tell Lawrence to do one thing, he'll do another."

"Hurry," I urged. "We may not have locked the doors in time."

"Stay here, Rex," she ordered the dog. He made a whining protest but he remained in the open doorway.

"I don't know where Lawrence's rooms are," I said.

"In another wing of the castle . . . on this same floor. Come. We will have a talk with my son about this shameful thing he has done." She elevated her chin and kept erect that foolish-looking pile of hair on top of her head. Despite her protests, I knew that she accepted the truth of my words. I sympathized with the pain she must be feeling.

I wanted to lift up my skirts and run, but Lady Davina walked with a purposeful gait that was unhurried even in these circumstances. She did not invite further comment from me and I expected her to give me a polite but firm dismissal. Maybe she didn't want to face her son alone, or maybe my company, such as it was, was better than none. Whatever the reason, she insisted that I accompany her.

A sense of urgency settled upon me, bringing a tight quivering to the pit of my stomach. We walked through a myriad of passageways and had just started down a long corridor when I saw Willa come out of a room at the end of it. Thank heavens, I breathed. The kitchen maid's robust figure was reassuring.

"Dolan sent Willa ahead to warn Lawrence not to leave his chambers," I told Lady Davina.

When we had almost reached the doorway where the servant stood, she stepped in front of Lady Davina. "I don't think ye should be goin' in," Willa said. Her husky voice was tense as she sent an agitated look from her mistress to me.

"Why? What's the matter, Willa?"

"It's the young master, mum. The warnin' came too late. I found him like that. He's dead, mum."

Lady Davina gave a shriek and pushed into the room. Lawrence lay on his high, elaborately carved baronial bed. Fresh blood had spilled from his throat and shone crimson on the silken pillows and bedcovers.

The floor rose and plunged under my feet.

On Lawrence's chest lay a wreath of black ivy.

Chapter Seventeen

The shock of seeing Lawrence's blood-drenched body brought a numbed detachment which kept the horror from penetrating my mind for a brief moment. My thoughts were slow in handling the situation. Lawrence had been murdered. *Mike Ryan was the Watcher!* The knowledge did not take me by surprise. I had seen the murderous hatred in the man's eyes. I knew Mike Ryan wanted revenge upon the English gentry who had bled the cottiers with taxes. The assault upon his daughter was a bellows fanning another murder. Then a simple question blew away the detached sensation. *Where was the murderer now?*

Terror shattered my numbness. Mike must have entered the castle, learned from some source where Lawrence's rooms were, and made his way here while I was talking to Dolan. *He might still be here!*

My frantic gaze swept the bedchamber. Massive furniture lined the wall, heavy draperies framed the windows, and an open door showed an adjoining room. He could be hiding anywhere in this room or the next. Any moment he might rush us with his bloody hook.

"We have to get out of here. Come on!"

Lady Davina wouldn't respond to my frantic command. She stood staring at her murdered son as if mesmerized by the horror. Deep sobs shook her body.

I turned to Willa standing in the doorway. "Help Her Ladyship." The maid's strong grasp could propel the shocked woman better than I could. "Carry her if you have to. Ryan could still be here. We have to get her safely to her apartment." I feared that Mike Ryan's vendetta might well include Her Ladyship.

Willa nodded and stepped forward. "Come, my lady." She took a firm grasp on Lady Davina's arm.

The raw-boned servant was much taller and heavier than her mistress. Despite Lady Davina's inertia, Willa firmly conducted the weeping woman out of the room and down the corridor.

"We'll take her to her rooms," I said, hurrying along beside them. "And tell Rosa what happened. Then get a search party to Mike Ryan."

The man's name was no more than out of my mouth than it was followed by a scream lurching out of my throat.

Mike Ryan stepped out in front of us! He had been hiding behind a large piece of statuary in the hall.

"So, 'tis my name on yer lips is it?" His dark eyes were frenzied and he waved the vicious hook at us. "Ye'll not be taking me anywheres . . . not till I give the devil his due." He lunged forward.

Willa shoved Lady Davina to one side and leaped straight at Ryan.

They both went down.

Willa's thick arms struck out, landing clenched fists into the man's stomach and knocking the turf

286

hook from his hand. As they wrestled, arms and legs went everywhere.

Mike struck out at Willa but her strength was unbelievable! She took a blow in the face that would have collapsed most adversaries and came right back to land a punch of her own.

I couldn't get by them to run for help. The turf hook flew out of Mike's hand and landed at my feet. I grabbed up the weapon and threw it out of reach. On some detached level, I realized that the edges were bright and that there wasn't any blood on it.

Suddenly Willa overpowered Mike, straddling him in an unladylike position. A knife whipped out of her apron pocket and I saw with horror that the blade was splattered with blood even before Willa plunged it into Mike Ryan's throat. The victim gave a death gurgle as blood spurted like a fountain from the gaping hole across his neck.

Willa stood up and held the knife in a threatening poise at me and Lady Davina. A fuzzy wig had been knocked to one side and her skirt had been lifted in the fight, showing trousers underneath. The hands under the gloves she always wore in the garden were thick and masculine.

The floor dipped crazily under me. I touched the wall for support. *Willa, the garden maid, was not a woman — but a man!*

"Rosa's son, William!" Lady Davina gasped and she stared at him as if she were truly seeing a ghost. "You're dead! You're the one the constables ran into the sea."

"Sure and they thought they did."

"You didn't drown?" Lady Davina repeated in confusion.

"I jumped off the cliff exactly where a ledge

287

below could catch me." His normal voice was deep and husky.

Sean's cave, I thought. That's how he escaped. *Willa was the Watcher! My father's murderer!* He'd been living with us all the time.

"In disguise," I breathed aloud, still bewildered by the revelation.

"Nobody looks closely at a kitchen maid, except you." He glared at me. "Poking around where ye didn't belong." He set the wig straight on his head. "I didn't mean ye ladies harm. Now there's no help for it."

"We won't tell anyone," I bargained in desperation. I wasn't physically strong enough to challenge him and Lady Davina seemed at the point of collapse. "You can get away—"

He shook his head. "There's still much work to be done."

"Please—"

He jerked Lady Davina against his chest and poised his knife at her throat. "If either of ye makes one sound, I'll stick Her Ladyship like a pig. Now, move down that way." He motioned toward a narrow back hall.

I saw a flight of narrow stairs disappearing into shadowy darkness.

"Down there. Move! And no tricks."

"Where are we going?"

"Shut up! Move."

I dared not refuse. Lady Davina's eyes were rounded with fear as William held her. One quick slice of the knife at her throat and she would be as dead as her son and Mike Ryan. I started down the shadowy staircase in front of the killer and Lady Davina. Was there a chance that someone might hear us? I stumbled purposefully, making as

288

much noise as possible.

Lady Davina's whimpering echoed above our footsteps. She was emotionally and physically shattered. I couldn't expect any help from her. My mind raced frantically, trying to think of some way to thwart this living ghost who was a cold-blooded murderer.

How soon would someone miss us? Rosa would most likely be the one to know Lady Davina was gone, but William was her son. She had lied to everyone and claimed that he was her younger sister. No one had suspected the deception, not even Lady Davina. William had been cleverly passed off as Willa, the kitchen maid. No wonder my daily presence in the garden had been resented. Keeping Willa under close observance like that must have made both of them nervous, indeed.

The labyrinth of stairs descended with many endless turns and twists. Down, down, down, until we came to a small landing with a heavy door that seemed familiar. Then I knew why. It was like the thick planked doors which had been built into the sea wall and opened into the caverns under the castle!

"Open it!" William ordered.

I pulled on the tarnished knob and dank, cold air from the subterranean chambers bathed my face with an icy chill. From the opened door, only shadowy light filtered from the staircase into the dark interior. The farther we went down a passageway, the blacker it became. I bit my lips to keep my hysteria from bursting forth in wild cries of protest.

The night whispers I had heard coming from these underground chambers had already laid a pattern of horror and fright within me. All around, like breath on my cold neck, I felt the presence of murdered women and children who had sought refuge from Cromwell's soldiers in these caverns. In my heightened imagination, I felt their blood running slippery under my feet and when I touched dank walls, I recoiled from their clammy feel. I stumbled blindly, held my hands out in front of me, fighting the darkness which seemed alive with horror.

"Please let us go," begged Lady Davina.

William barked, "Turn!" He gave me a shove to the right.

I groped ahead in the blackness. My toe caught on the uneven ground and I pitched forward. My head struck a rock imbedded in the dirt as I fell to the ground. Fiery lights exploded behind my eyes.

A heavy door clanged shut and Lady Davina's weeping rose and fell above the ringing in my ears.

My cheek pressed into the moist ground and my reeling head was too heavy for me to raise. I closed my eyes, bringing the darkness under my lids and then opened them again. There was no change. Never before had I experienced such a complete absence of light. Deep in the earth, where no sunlight lingered to make shadows, it was just as dark with my eyes opened as with them shut. I knew then what blindness was. Blindness! New panic surged through me. Had my fall caused an injury to my eyes? This new horror sent needed strength through my body.

"Lady Davina!" I pushed myself into a half-sitting position. "Can you see anything? Is it dark?" I reached out and felt her arm. "Answer me! Can you see anything?"

Her voice quivered. "No. I can't see anything.

290

It's too dark."

Relief sped through me. I wasn't blind. The real danger was to my life . . . not my eyes. Straining to see something in the pitch-black darkness was more terrifying than keeping my eyes shut, so I closed them tightly. I reached out again and felt the sobbing woman crumpled on the ground beside me. She responded to my touch and moved closer. There was reassurance in sharing the warmth of our bodies.

"We're under the castle," I said. "Sean told me about these corridors and chambers."

"I have never been down here." Lady Davina shivered. "They're filled with bats and horrible things."

"Sean told me they were used for storage." Hope quickened. Maybe we could find something that would serve as a weapon or a tool. Even though I knew the murderer had shut a door upon us, that didn't mean there wasn't some other way out or that we couldn't hide from him. "We have to search this place, whatever it is. And keep moving. If we just sit here and wait, there won't be a chance to save ourselves when he comes back."

"What is he going to do to us?"

"I don't know," I lied. He was going to kill us but I didn't know what scheme he was setting up. How cleverly he had arranged Lawrence's murder! Dolan had sent Willa to warn Lawrence about Mike Ryan, giving the imposter, William, a perfect opportunity. Instead of delivering the message, the servant slit Lawrence's throat, left a wreath of black ivy which could have been hidden in his voluminous pockets, and was just leaving the room when we arrived.

The blame would have fallen perfectly on Mike

Ryan if he hadn't shown himself too soon, and in the struggle the true Watcher's identity was revealed. I knew that whatever plan the Watcher had for us, it would cleverly keep suspicions away from Willa, the kitchen maid.

"We can't just wait. Get up, Lady Davina," I ordered, taking command. "We'll walk around and get our bearings. Try to find something that might serve as a weapon."

"In the dark!"

"Of course, in the dark, unless you happen to have candle and flint in your pockets."

I knew Her Ladyship was used to reaching for a servant's bell for all her needs. A lifetime of comfort and service had not prepared her to be without luxuries ... let alone life-and-death necessities.

"You walk in that direction with your hands out," I ordered. "And I'll go in the opposite. Count your steps and when you touch a wall, tell me."

I waited until she had taken the first step and then I slowly put one foot in front of the other, going in the opposite direction. "Nine ... ten ... eleven ..." I counted under my breath. I was up to sixteen when my fingertips touched a rough dirt wall.

Almost at the same instant, Lady Davina cried out, "I hit a wall. Ten steps." There was such victory in her voice that I smiled. I had never heard such lively satisfaction in her voice.

"Good," I called. "Now turn to your left and feel around the wall until we meet."

The scuffing of our feet mingled with our rapid breathing as we felt our way around the walls. A few steps more and I reached a corner almost

292

immediately. I turned and felt my way along the rough dirt surface until I touched wood. Splinters cut into my fingers as I felt the rough door panels. The next instant I touched Lady Davina's hands coming from the other direction.

"A door," she gasped. "We've found the door."

I had been keeping my eyes shut as I felt my way around the walls. Now, I opened my eyes, expecting to see some faint trace of light around the planks that were just inches away from my nose. Nothing. Utter blackness. The door seemed to be set in the bank of dirt, I decided by touch. "Feel around and see if you can find a latch," I ordered.

We pressed our hands over the heavy planks, splintered and decaying, and found no lock of any kind; but there were a couple of small holes in the wood where a handle might have been. I put one eye against one of those holes. Even though I could see only darkness on the other side, I felt a movement of cool air on my eyeball which told me the small holes went all the way through.

"The door must be bolted on the other side. The handle on this side has fallen off."

"What'll we do now?" asked Lady Davina, waiting for instructions.

"Stay here by the door. We know how wide the chamber is — but not how deep. I'm going to walk straight back to the far wall."

"Do you think there's another exit?" she asked with a new spurt of hope in her voice. Her whimpering had completely disappeared and my fears that I would have a helpless, hysterical woman on my hands had proven unfounded. There was latent courage and strength in the homely little woman.

"There might be another door opposite this one,

293

or a corridor that will lead us out of here."

"I think these underground caves are like rabbit warrens," she said. "They were used as a refuge in war, in early times against Norman pirates and later against Cromwell."

"Sean told me. The people sought safety here and were slaughtered." I heard her intake of breath, and I was sorry the conversation had become macabre. "Don't move. I don't have any idea how far back this enclosure goes."

"Don't leave me, Aileen. I'm so sorry for my nastiness. Please forgive me . . ."

"I'm not going to leave you."

"I will make it up to you, I promise. I have a few jewels . . ."

"Lady Davina! Can't you get it through your head, I don't want anything from you . . . except your friendship. That's all I ever wanted."

"I am ashamed," she said simply and squeezed my hand. "If we don't get out of here alive —"

"Stop talking like that."

"No. I want to say it. I can't go to my Maker without making a confession. My hatred for you and your mother provided me with a defense against the truth that my husband never loved me. The marriage was arranged. I knew that he had not chosen me for my beauty and without my family's background and my dowry, I would have remained unwed. I wasn't under any illusion that His Lordship loved me, but after the children came I thought he would treat me less like one of his possessions." Her tone was bitter. "But I soon found that he had little regard for my feelings. My company seemed distasteful to him; he scorned any ideas or opinions that I had, and we soon had separate rooms in the castle. He hired nannies and tutors for the children and under his direction they were raised as he saw fit. Although my husband didn't seem to be aware of it, he taught them to disregard my feelings."

I had witnessed Lawrence's and Loretta's callous treatment of their mother at dinner that night. What she said must be true. I was glad for the first time that my mother had raised me alone.

"No one enjoys my company," she said wistfully.

"That's not true. You are a very intelligent woman. A scholar. You're far above my mother in intellectual achievements."

It wasn't much, but I had to give this sensitive woman some feeling of worth. I couldn't see Lady Davina's face but I sensed the straightening of her shoulders.

"Thank you, Aileen," she said in a choked voice. "I've made a terrible mistake. You are the daughter I should have welcomed. I promise that if we get safely out of this, I'll never turn away from you again."

She hugged me and I felt wetness streaming down her cheeks.

"It's all right," I assured her, embarrassed by this outburst of affection. "Don't give up. I'm going to see if I can find out how deep this chamber is."

"Do you think he'll slit our throats, too?"

"Not if I can help it. We'll go down fighting."

"Yes," she answered simply.

I stood up in the pitch black darkness. With my hands outstretched, I walked slowly forward into an infinity of darkness. With every step, I feared that an unseen chasm might open up in front of me. Kicking some dirt and small stones ahead of me, I listened for any warning that they had fallen into an abyss.

"Aileen!" Lady Davina called, panic rising in her voice.

"I'm all right," I called to her. Our voices vaulted away above us, hinting at a cavernous ceiling.

"Come back! Please come back." Her voice sounded thin as it rose to an unseen height above us. "Don't leave me."

I stopped, not because of her panicked entreaties, but because my fingertips had touched a wall. Now, I could judge the boundaries of our confinement but the knowledge did little to help us. I let my hands follow the dirt along the back wall, hoping to find another door, but only dank earth embedded with small rocks responded to my touch.

"Aileen!"

"Yes, I'm coming. I'm not going to leave you, Lady Davina. I'm searching for something that might have been left . . . something we could use for a tool or weapon." I crisscrossed the chamber from one end of the wall to the other, hoping my feet would touch some object or that the hands I held out in front might contact something beside dirt wall. Nothing. Absolutely nothing. The dirt chamber was bare.

Suddenly the same horrid moaning and wailing sounds that had tormented me in my room became louder and louder, like a crowd's roaring in my ears. The taunting, screaming noises demoralized me as nothing else had.

Lady Davina called to me again and this time I could hardly hear her. I had been able to accept the darkness on a nonemotional level but the bombardment in my ears was torture. I thought my

296

head would explode. Covering my ears with my hands I returned to Lady Davina and sat hunched on the floor beside her. It seemed an eternity before the inferno of noises began to fade away and we could once more talk to each other without shouting.

"Thank God," I breathed and realized I was shaking in the same manner I had the first night of my arrival. Even though I knew the sounds were a natural phenomenon made by the wind blowing through the passages, the moaning and wailing frayed my nerves like a rasp upon twisted rope.

"How long is he going to leave us here?" choked Lady Davina.

"I don't know."

"Everybody knew William jumped off the sea cliff," she said, still ready to deny the truth.

"He jumped off—but not into the water. There's a place where a ledge extends out at the edge of a small cave. He must have known about it and raced to that spot before he dropped over the side. He said he landed on the ledge. He probably hid inside the cave and no one could see him from above. He could have thrown his hat or something into the water to make it look as if he were being pounded against the rocks."

"When Rosa asked me if her younger sister could come to work at the castle, I never suspected anything at all. I didn't learn until much later that her son had been known as the Watcher. Such happenings were of little interest to me. How soon do you think it will be before somebody misses me?" asked Lady Davina.

"I don't know . . . I'm afraid that you have shut the world out rather effectively. No one feels they can intrude upon your presence without permission." I said with a touch of irony.

"I became a recluse years ago. A means of survival, I guess. Without my butterflies, I would have nothing to keep me from losing my sanity. I kept to my chambers with only Rosa in attendance. I can't believe she'd let her son harm me."

"Maybe she hasn't any choice. He might have threatened her and she fears for her own life. No, I don't think we can expect Rosa to come to our rescue."

"Surely someone will miss *you*," Lady Davina insisted.

"Callie. But she is used to my comings and goings." I thought about the romantic interlude with Sean when I had been gone a whole night. I doubted that anyone would search for me for a day or maybe even more. I sighed. "Neither of us has shown ourselves to be very gregarious."

"Only because there was no one, until you came, who wanted to understand me or my interests," she flared, and I was glad her spirited personality was back.

"In any case, I think William will have plenty of time to set a plan in motion before anyone realizes that we are really gone," I said regretfully. "Is there anyone besides Rosa who would know you're not in your apartment or working in your turret room?"

"No. You're the only one who came to see me . . . and not very often." Her tone chided me for my laxity as if the blame lay with me. "I disliked you intensely in the beginning, but I was starting to think that you might be different and have an intelligence I could admire. But I changed my mind when I saw you the night of the dance. I was sorely disappointed to find you had lowered yourself to drinking and whoring with dirty Irish peasants, Aileen." Her tone was chastising.

"If you had bothered to put your prejudice aside long enough to mix with those 'dirty Irish peasants' you would have discovered that most of them are wonderful, loyal, and friendly people. They have their own customs which are mysterious and full of superstitions, to be sure, but they are poor because of the conditions that you and others have been guilty of imposing upon them. All the years that you've lived in Ireland, you cheated yourself, Lady Davina. You could have had love and admiration from the people you chose to turn your back upon."

"I suppose you approve of Loretta for seeking their company," she scoffed. "Her father and Sean have dismissed Irish stable hands because my daughter encouraged them to be 'friendly.' His Lordship couldn't handle her. Even Sean hasn't been able to settle Loretta down. He promised me to spend as much time as he could with her, trying to protect her until she grows up and starts acting like a proper English lady, but he told me the other day that he won't be responsible for her any more. He's washed his hands of her."

"He said that?" Could it be that my convictions that Sean was interested in marrying Loretta were nothing but jealous suspicions? I felt ashamed. He had been trying to play a father role with her and she was the only one who had been making romantic overtures. What a fool I'd been. Both Dorthea and I had misjudged Sean's interest in the young girl.

"If only Lord Lynhurst had allowed Loretta to go to an English school where she'd meet somebody suitable," her mother lamented.

"You don't view Sean Creighton as suitable?"

Lady Davina was crying softly. "I want my daughter to marry an Englishman and live in England. It's this horrible country that has ruined her." I only half-listened to Lady Davina as she began a rambling reminiscence about her childhood in the south of England.

The time went by. Lady Davina grew silent and my thoughts centered on finding some way to protect ourselves when the Watcher came back. I was disappointed that there had been nothing stored in this chamber. I knew that men came into these underground caverns because I had heard their voices. My head came up.

I stopped Lady Davina in the middle of one of her sentences. "I have an idea."

"What — ?"

"We're going to yell as loudly as we can. The small holes in the door will allow our voices to get out. I know that sounds carry into some of the rooms of the castle. Maybe someone will hear us."

We pressed ourselves against the door and yelled and yelled until our voices were raspy and our throats dry.

Every few minutes we'd try again.

Nothing. Silence. Not even the low murmuring of wind. Dust filled my nostrils and eyes. A sense of being buried alive overcame me. The feeling brought a sob up into my throat. No, we had to get out!

I reached out and touched something hairy. I jerked my hand away and the hairy mass came with me.

"Ouch!" cried Lady Davina. "My hairpiece!"

"I'm sorry," I whispered. An hysterical laugh of

relief rose in my throat. Then my head jerked up. Movement on the other side of the door!

"What's that?" choked Lady Davina.

Someone was outside!

Chapter Eighteen

"He's come," croaked Lady Davina in a whisper.

I pulled her back from the door. What could we do to save ourselves? Hide? Where? My mind whirled in panic as we waited for the sound of the door opening.

"Shhh," I whispered. Somehow I would have to divert the killer and give Lady Davina a chance to escape.

We held our breaths and waited in the dark stillness.

Nothing happened. Then my ears picked up a sound. Scratching on the door. The noise was not identifiable at first and then we heard a low bark.

Lady Davina's dog!

"It's Rex!" she said. "He must have heard our yelling. Rex! Good boy," she called to him.

The dog had found us. Was he alone?

We waited with expected breath, praying and listening.

"He must be alone," I said when nothing more happened. "Will he go get someone?"

"I doubt it but I'll try," said Lady Davina. "Rex, boy, listen!"

The dog barked louder and scratched at the door with renewed vigor. Lady Davina yelled through the small holes of the door. "Go get someone. Rex, bring Dolan to me!"

Rex only barked and scraped the door with his claws.

"Rosa's the only one he really knows," Lady Davina said regretfully. "I can't send him to her . . . not with her son intent on murdering us."

I knew that the command to fetch someone was outside the dog's pattern of behavior. Rex knew his mistress was on the other side of the door and her voice was a cue for him to try and reach her.

"It's no use," Lady Davina said in frustration.

"Wait. I think he's digging under the door," I said with sudden hope. "Call him. Tell him to come. If he can dig his way in, we might have a chance to dig our way out!"

"Good boy, Rex. Come! Come!"

We could hear dirt flying and his claws biting into the old wood. Lady Davina kept encouraging him while I knelt down and felt along the bottom of the door. The dirt began to give way in a small hole as the dog dug from the other side. "He's broken through and the wood is giving way along the bottom!"

I grabbed a splintered piece and pulled on it. I broke it off and reached for another. The dog dug furiously in the dirt, his mistress urging him on, "Good boy, Rex, good boy."

I pulled away the decayed strips of wood along the bottom edge of the door and the hole was soon large enough for him to slip through. He bounded around Lady Davina and she sat on the ground and tearfully hugged him.

"Come, help me dig," I ordered and handed her a piece of splintered wood. The hole was too small for a human body. The moist earth gave way as we used sticks and hands to enlarge the one Rex

303

had made.

"There, that's big enough, I think," I said after what seemed like an eternity.

"My fingers are raw and bleeding," complained Lady Davina. "I won't be able to work with my butterflies until—" Then she broke off as if she realized she'd be lucky to ever see them again.

"I'll try to slip under the door and unlock it." I refused to think what I would do if I got caught halfway under the door.

I lay on my back, stuck my head through the hole and wiggled on my back. Grunting, shoving and pushing, I laboriously maneuvered through the hole. Jagged pieces of wood scratched my face and arms. I sucked in my breath and clawed my way under the splintered door.

At last I was out!

"I made it," I called breathlessly as I wavered to my feet.

The shadowy passageway seemed black after the absolute darkness of the chamber. I threw back the bolt. Lady Davina and Rex bounded out. *We were free!*

The sound of the wind was rising again. I could feel it whipping on my face. Soon the moaning and wailing whispers would fill the underground caverns.

"Hold on to Rex's collar and let him lead us out of here," I told Lady Davina. "Hurry!"

I followed her and the dog along an earthen passageway. Thank God, we had the dog's sense of direction to guide us. In the shadowy darkness, I couldn't make any sense of the twisted corridors.

Suddenly Rex leaped forward, jerking away from Lady Davina's grasp.

"Rex! Come back!" she ordered but the dog

ignored his mistress's command.

In a split second, he was out of sight, leaving us stumbling blindly after him.

"Rex!"

I knew we had taken a wrong turn when we ran into a dirt wall that shut off passage in that direction.

Lady Davina kept calling the dog, putting as much command in her voice as she could. "It's no use! He's run off."

"We'll have to find our way out by ourselves."

"Why would he disobey me like that?" she said, anger mixed with renewed apprehension. "It's not like him."

The darkness lifted enough to hint of light filtering through an unseen opening into the subterranean caverns. "Let's go this way," I said, heading in a direction which seemed to offer a hope of an outside entrance.

Hope had spurted into me because the shadows seemed less dense. When we came around a corner, we stumbled over something lying in the narrow passage.

"Rex!" cried Lady Davina.

The dog was still warm—but quite dead. He lay sprawled at our feet. Blood gushing from his throat made a dark pool under him.

Lady Davina let out a loud wail and I clamped my hand over her mouth.

The Watcher! He was here! Rex must have sensed his approach, run ahead, and been killed before he could give warning. The killer was looking for us in the tunnels! We had to find our way out before he trapped us again.

"Run," I hissed in a whisper.

Was the killer ahead of us or behind us in the

dark passages? I had no idea but an instinctive decision sent us fleeing in the direction that the wind was coming.

Our fleeing steps echoed in the echoing labyrinth of tunnels. But they weren't the only signs of someone running. Above the sounds of our labored breathing and the pounding of our feet upon the dirt and rocks, I heard footsteps coming rapidly behind us.

He'd found us!

"Hurry!" I cried and grabbed Lady Davina's hand, pulling her along as fast as her stocky frame could move. She'd never be able to outrun him. There was more light in the tunnel now, and when we suddenly came upon stored nets, crates, and other fishing equipment, I knew that we were near the outside doors.

I pulled Lady Davina to a stop and thrust her toward a stack of lobster crates. "Hide!"

"Wh—"

"Do as I say!" I gave her a rude shove that nearly sent her to her knees. Then I spurted down the corridor, away from the place where she cowered behind the crates.

Heavy footsteps behind me were loud and very, very near as I reached one of the paneled doors that led to the outside. For a moment, I despaired. Blocked by the closed door and the killer coming up behind me, I entertained a moment of surrender. Only the strong impulse of self-preservation made me give a tremendous lunge at the door—and it creaked open.

I was out!

Escape was only momentary.

Before I had taken two steps outside, rough hands jerked me to a stop. I screamed!

His arms went around me in a deathly vise.

I screamed again and struggled against the vicious hold he had on my chest, but my efforts were futile.

William held me so tightly that all air was squeezed from my lungs.

I gasped for air as he dragged me across the road toward the cliff.

He was going to throw me over the side into the ocean! Cries burst in my burning lungs but refused to find their way out of my mouth.

I thought it was a hallucination when I heard a beloved voice shout, "Let her go!"

The Watcher, dressed as Willa, swung round.

Sean leaped down the stone steps and in the next moment flung himself at my abductor.

The killer loosened his grip on me to protect himself.

I crumpled to the ground, dizzy and weak from the lack of air in my lungs. The sound of blows mingled with a ringing in my ears as I struggled to ward off unconsciousness.

I saw the wig come off in Sean's hand, exposing Willa's deception. Now, Sean knew he was fighting a man and not a kitchen maid. They fought on the edge of the cliff and for a terrifying moment, it seemed as if they were both going over.

"Sean!" I gasped, mesmerized by the horror. One step closer and they both would fall off the precipice. This time there was no ledge to prevent a fall onto the treacherous rocks below.

Sean was going to lose his life to save me!

I wavered to my feet—but it was too late!

A horrible cry rent the air. My eyes would not focus for a moment.

"Sean!"

His arms went around me and I knew that he was not the one who had dropped from sight over the edge of the cliff.

The Watcher had met the very death that he had miraculously escaped once before.

Chapter Nineteen

He cradled my head, stroked my cheeks, and murmured endearments. "Thank God. I was looking for you on the grounds when I heard you scream."

I allowed myself the bliss of his strong arms and loving embrace. The moment was all the more precious because we both had come so close to death. Tears filled my eyes but they were joyful and the sounds issuing from my throat were thankful sobs.

"It's all right, my dearest love, you're safe now."

"Willa . . . she . . . he . . ." I choked.

"I know. William! None of us recognized him. He used to wear a mustache and a beard. We all thought him dead and readily accepted him as Rosa's sister."

My head jerked up. "Lady Davina!"

"Where is she?"

"Hiding!"

With his arm around my waist, we entered the caverns again. I told him how we had been locked in a chamber and how the dog had rescued us and then been killed.

"Where did you leave her?" Sean asked.

"Not far from the door."

"Lady Davina!" called Sean.

No answer.

Had she panicked and lost herself in the underground labyrinth? Was she hurt? Unconscious? She has to be safe, I thought with new panic. I realized then that I truly cared for Lady Davina.

"It's all right. We're safe," I yelled. "Where are you?"

"Aileen?" Her voice echoed in the tunnels.

I cried with relief when we found her crouching behind the crates where I had left her. I put my arms around her shoulders and drew her out of her hiding place. "Don't be frightened. It's all over."

Her eyes were wide with terror and her lips trembled. "Where is he?"

"He fell over the cliff," answered Sean.

"Are you sure?"

I smiled. "We're sure. This time the Watcher will stay dead."

Utter exhaustion and an upheaval of emotions took their toll. I went to see Molly and grieved with her over the loss of her husband. I had not liked Mike Ryan, but no one deserved to end his life in such a horrible fashion.

"Will you be able to keep the tavern?" I asked Molly.

She nodded. "Kerrie and Shannon will be moving in. He's a good lad. Sure and he'll do his best to handle things with my help."

Holly handed me her practice sheets and I knew that she would be the one to help her mother with the accounts. I vowed to get her the books she needed to learn reading, writing, and arithmetic.

All in all, the family might be better off without

Mike, I thought. Molly would raise her children well. Patrick would become a priest and Kerrie would give her grandchildren. In a way, Molly Ryan was a very rich woman.

For several days I stayed in bed, my body fighting a physical and emotional depletion. I heard the mournful roll of drums when Lawrence's body was taken from the castle and laid to rest. The last time I had heard a funeral procession from my room, my father had been in the hearse. A lifetime ago, it seemed. So many things had happened that I didn't even feel like the same person.

New anxieties beset me. Would the provisions of my father's will take away the roof over my head now that Lawrence was dead? If a distant male relative inherited, there would be no place for me here. There had been no opportunity to ask Sean. He had given me into Callie's care upon our return and I had not seen him since.

Rosa had greeted Lady Davina with tearful remorse, confessing that her son had threatened her own life, and that she had lived every day in mortal fear that all of them would be murdered in their beds. Lady Davina allowed the servant to put her strong arms around her shoulders and lead her to her room. Forgiveness might be easier for Her Ladyship from now on, I thought. Facing death had changed her.

My weighted thoughts were disturbed the day after Lawrence's funeral when Dorthea came breezing into my room while I sat listlessly in front of the fire.

"There you are! My poor darling!" She hugged me. "How horrible for you. Can you imagine such a thing! The Watcher masquerading as a woman! And you and Lady Davina nearly killed. It's just too awful! Are you all right?"

"I'm fine. Just tired."

"I told Father I had to come and see you. Besides," her face glowed. "He's come to talk to Sean. Now that Lawrence is dead, Sean won't have to carry out his duties here at Lynhurst. He'll be free to pursue his own career. Oh, Aileen, won't it be wonderful?" She clapped her hands. "My husband, a member of the House of Commons. I know he'll be elected. The Irish peasantry will back him and so will landowners like my father. Do you think September would be a good month for a wedding?"

I tried to keep a fixed smile on my face. My feelings were bittersweet. Deeply glad that Sean was going to have his chance, my personal loss flooded me with rising despair.

"Why are your eyes so sad?" demanded Dorthea. "You don't think Sean's going to say no, do you?"

"He'll accept," I assured her. "Sean's had the dream of fighting for the Irish cause in Parliament for too long. His grandmother instilled it in him when he was just a little boy."

"Oh, I didn't know that. Tell me everything you know about him," she pleaded.

Everything you know about him. The memory of his nakedness pressed against mine made me turn my eyes away.

"What is it, Aileen?"

"Nothing."

Dorthea's expressions of concern were interrupted when Callie knocked on the door.

"Both yer ladies are wanted downstairs . . . in the library," she informed us.

Dorthea gasped. "It's done. My father is going

312

to make the announcement. Come on, Aileen."

My impulse was to cower in my room but I knew that it would be better to have all the emotional pain behind me as soon as possible.

"Go ahead. I'll be down as soon as I change."

Dorthea bounded out of the room.

Callie helped me change into my dark wool dress and brushed my hair into a coil on my neck. My reflection showed violet shadows under my eyes and my coloring was pallid. Sean had accused me of being a terrible liar and I wondered how I could feign happiness when I was dying inside.

With a forced spryness in my steps, I made my way downstairs to the library. I must not let my utter despondency cloud this moment of triumph for Sean and Dorthea. I curved my lips and sailed into the room.

The three occupants sat stiffly in chairs near the fireplace. It was a moment before I realized that my broad smile was utterly out of place.

Dorthea stared at me with a stricken face. Sir Wainwright's expression was fierce, and Sean's bold features were rigid.

"What is it?" My voice was thin.

"Are you a party to this?" Sean demanded, his dark eyes flashing angrily. "This business arrangement? You knew about it, didn't you? That's why you kept pushing me toward Dorthea."

I couldn't deny it. I nodded.

"And you thought I'd accept, didn't you?"

I found my voice. "I thought it best. I knew how much your political dreams meant to you."

"Did you think me a man of so little integrity that I would sell myself to a woman I didn't love?"

Dorthea buried her face in her hands and her

father rose from his chair. "Come, Daughter. I made the proposal as you asked. I should have known better. Sean's refusal is the only one that a gentleman could make under the circumstances." He patted her shoulder. "I've been thinking— would you like to join Aunt Marta in Paris for the fall season?"

Dorthea's head came up. Her eyes were suddenly shining through her tears. "Oh, Father, could I?"

He nodded. "I'm thinking about closing up Windbriar and going back to London. The house is not the same without Claudia."

"You and Bryant could come to Paris, too," said Dorthea, her thoughts spinning away in her usual leaping fashion.

"We'll see. Now, if you will excuse us, we will take our leave." Sir Wainwright nodded to Sean and shook my hand. "And what are your plans, Aileen?"

"I have none."

Dorthea hugged me. "I wish you could come with me. You'd love Aunt Marta."

"I'm afraid that isn't possible."

Dorthea glanced up at Sean, embarrassment coloring her face.

He took her hand. "Thank you, Dorthea, for the honor of wanting me as your husband. I'm extremely flattered. And I hope you find someone who appreciates you."

"Thank you." She leaned up and gave him a kiss on the cheek. "Be happy, Sean," she said and quickly followed her father out of the library.

"I should see them to their carriage," I said.

"No."

For a moment, neither of us said anything. I stood half-turned away from him, my eyes on the floor. Gently he turned me around and tipped my chin. "Did you really think I would marry anyone but you?"

"You deserve to chase your dreams."

"Do you love me?"

"Yes."

"Will you be my wife for ever and ever?"

"I've nothing to offer—"

"Except yourself, which outweighs every other consideration."

"You deserve more than—"

His answer was a kiss that dissolved any rational thought. An acquiescent sigh was my only answer as he explored the clinging sweetness of our embrace. He lifted his mouth from mine and pulled me close so that his cheek rested against mine. "I have nothing to offer you, my love. No home, no security. I'll have to start over somewhere and look for employment. Lawrence's death releases me from my duties here so we can leave. But I have no future—"

A rustling sound of stiff skirts halted his words.

Lady Davina entered the room. It was the first time I had seen her since our ordeal. The mound of false hair was gone and so were her rigid posture and fierce expression. Her facial muscles had softened and her square body seemed to take on curves that had not been there before. Some people took years to make such a dramatic change, but a devastating experience had wrought a metamorphosis in Lady Davina.

"How are you, Aileen?" she asked warmly as I pulled away from Sean, embarrassed that she had found me in such an intimate embrace. "Please sit down." She nodded to a settee. "I have something to say to both of you." Lady Davina took a chair across from us.

"Now then. I heard you say, Sean, that you have no future."

"I do not wish to remain in service at Lynhurst," he said evenly. "I have carried out my duties to your husband and your son to the best of my ability, and I feel that the debt I owed His Lordship for my education has been paid."

"I agree. I don't intend to hold you to any further commitment. All of the Lynhurst estate came to me at my son's death and I am now free to do with the property as I see fit. I will be returning to England myself. I want to put Loretta in a school for proper young ladies."

"I think that would be a good idea. She needs discipline."

"I thank you for your efforts on her behalf. I'm sorry she's such a foolish young lady. In gratitude for your loyalty to our family, I am releasing the assets which were tied to your service to the estate."

Joy rushed into Sean's face. "Thank you, Your Ladyship." His hand squeezed mine. "Your generosity will allow me to purchase Rathbridge. I have asked Aileen to become my wife."

Lady Davina smiled. "You have chosen well, Sean. I owe her my life and meant it when I vowed that I would gladly repay Aileen in any way I could."

Until that moment, I had never thought about claiming such a promise. My heart suddenly started to race. I cleared my voice. "There is one thing, Lady Davina, I would ask of you."

"It is yours, my dear."

"I ask that you financially back Sean's bid for a seat in the House of Commons."

Lady Davina nodded. "If that is your wish, Aileen, I will gladly honor it."

Sean stared at us both, a stunned expression on his face. For once he was at a loss for words and there was suspicious wetness at the corner of his eyes.

Our wedding was two weeks away and Molly and Daddo were busily planning an Irish celebration.

We rode to Rathbridge and left Graymont tethered near the back door.

"Is he secure?" I teased as we walked to the house.

Sean chuckled. "Let him visit his lady love, if he wishes. I'm feeling generous."

With his arm lovingly around my waist, we went through the rooms of our new home. The house was as derelict as before; I didn't see any of the dirt and grime but only the home that I had come to Ireland to find.

"Shall we retire to our chamber, my love?" He lifted me up in his arms and carried me up the stairs.

Postscript

Lady Davina was true to her word; before she moved to England, she gave Sean Creighton the needed financial backing to run for Parliament. Much to the pride of Danareel, Sean was elected by a wide margin and became a member of the House of Commons.

Due to the efforts of Sean and other fighters for the Irish cause, a bill was approved that remitted the much-hated Tithe Tax the following year, in 1838.

THE BEST OF REGENCY ROMANCES

AN IMPROPER COMPANION   (2691, $3.95)
by Karla Hocker
At the closing of Miss Venable's Seminary for Young
Ladies school, mistress Kate Elliott welcomed the invitation to be Liza Ashcroft's chaperone for the Season at
Bath. Little did she know that Miss Ashcroft's father, the
handsome widower Damien Ashcroft would also enter her
life. And not as a passive bystander or dutiful dad.

WAGER ON LOVE   (2693, $2.95)
by Prudence Martin
Only a rogue like Nicholas Ruxart would choose a bride on
the basis of a careless wager. And only a rakehell like Nicholas would then fall in love with his betrothed's grey-eyed
sister! The cynical viscount had always thought one blushing miss would suit as well as another, but the unattainable
Jane Sommers soon proved him wrong.

LOVE AND FOLLY   (2715, $3.95)
by Sheila Simonson
To the dismay of her more sensible twin Margaret, Lady
Jean proceeded to fall hopelessly in love with the silver-
tongued, seditious poet, Owen Davies—and catapult her
entire family into social ruin . . . Margaret was used to
gentlemen falling in love with vivacious Jean rather than
with her—even the handsome Johnny Dyott whom she secretly adored. And when Jean's foolishness led her into the
arms of the notorious Owen Davies, Margaret knew she
could count on Dyott to avert scandal. What she didn't
know, however was that her sweet sensibility was exerting a
charm all its own.

*Available wherever paperbacks are sold, or order direct from the
Publisher. Send cover price plus 50¢ per copy for mailing and
handling to Zebra Books, Dept. 2843, 475 Park Avenue South,
New York, N.Y. 10016. Residents of New York, New Jersey and
Pennsylvania must include sales tax. DO NOT SEND CASH.*

REGENCIES BY JANICE BENNETT

TANGLED WEB   (2281, $3.95)

Miss Celia Marcombe's dark eyes flashed with righteous indignation. She was not a commodity to be traded or bartered to a man
as insufferably arrogant as Trevor Ryde, despite what her high-
handed grandfather decreed! If Lord Ryde thought she would let
herself be married for any reason other than true love, he was
sadly mistaken. He'd never get his hands on her fortune—let
alone her person—no matter how disturbingly handsome he
was . . .

MIDNIGHT MASQUE   (2512, $3.95)

It was nothing unusual for Lady Ashton to transport government
documents to her father from the Home Office. But on this par-
ticular afternoon a gust of wind scattered the papers, and suddenly an important page was lost. A document desperately
wanted by more than one determined gentleman—one of whom
would murder to get his way . . .

AN INTRIGUING DESIRE   (2579, $3.95)

The British secret agent, Charles Marcombe, had done his bit
against that blasted Bonaparte. Now it was time to nurse his
wounds and come to terms with the fact that that part of his life
was over. He certainly did not need the likes of Mademoiselle
Therese de Bourgerre darkening his door, warning of dire emer-
gencies and dread consequences, forcing him to remember things
best forgotten. She was a delightful minx, to be sure, but it would
take more than a pair of pleading emerald eyes and a woebegone
smile to drag him back into the fray!

*Available wherever paperbacks are sold, or order direct from the
Publisher. Send cover price plus 50¢ per copy for mailing and
handling to Zebra Books, Dept. 2843, 475 Park Avenue South,
New York, N.Y. 10016. Residents of New York, New Jersey and
Pennsylvania must include sales tax. DO NOT SEND CASH.*